Moon Over Soho

ALSO BY BEN AARONOVITCH
FROM CLIPPER LARGE PRINT

Rivers of London

Moon Over Soho

Ben Aaronovitch

W F HOWES LTD

This large print edition published in 2015 by
W F Howes Ltd
Unit 4, Rearsby Business Park, Gaddesby Lane,
Rearsby, Leicester LE7 4YH

1 3 5 7 9 10 8 6 4 2

First published in the United Kingdom in 2011
by Gollancz

A CIP catalogue record for this book is available
from the British Library

ISBN 978 1 47129 481 5

Typeset by Palimpsest Book Production Limited,
Falkirk, Stirlingshire

Printed and bound in Great Britain
by TJ International Ltd, Padstow, Cornwall

MIX
Paper from
responsible sources
FSC
www.fsc.org   FSC® C013056

*For Karifa, because every father yearns
to be a hero for his son.*

'Men have died for this music.
You can't get more serious than that'

Dizzy Gillespie

CHAPTER 1

BODY AND SOUL

It's a sad fact of modern life that if you drive long enough, sooner or later you must leave London behind. If you drive north-east up the A12 you eventually come to Colchester, Britain's first Roman capital and the first city to be burned down by that red-headed chavette from Norfolk known as Boudicca. I knew all this because I'd been reading the *Annals* of Tacitus as part of my Latin training. He's surprisingly sympathetic to the revolting Brits, and scathing about the unpreparedness of the Roman generals who *thought more of what was agreeable than expedient*. The classically educated chinless wonders who run the British Army obviously took this admonition to heart because Colchester is now the home of their toughest soldiers, the Parachute Regiment. Having spent many a Saturday night as a probationary PC wrestling squaddies in Leicester Square, I made sure I stayed on the main road and bypassed the city altogether.

Beyond Colchester I turned south and, with the help of the GPS on my phone, got myself onto the B1029 heading down the wedged-shape bit of

1

dry ground jammed between the River Colne and Flag Creek. At the end of the road lay Brightlingsea, lining the coast – so Lesley had always told me – like a collection of rubbish stranded at the high-water mark. Actually, I didn't think it was that bad. It had been raining in London but, after Colchester, I'd driven into clear blue skies and the sun lit up the rows of well-kept Victorian terraces that ran down to the sea.

Chez May was easy to spot: a 1970s brick-built fake-Edwardian cottage that had been carriage-lamped and pebble-dashed to within an inch of its life. The front door was flanked on one side by a hanging basket full of blue flowers, and on the other, the house number inscribed on a ceramic plate in the shape of a sailing yacht. I paused and checked the garden: there were gnomes loitering near the ornamental bird bath. I took a breath and rang the doorbell.

There was an immediate chorus of female yelling from inside. Through the reproduction stained-glass window in the front door, I could just make out blurry figures running back and forth at the far end of the hall. Somebody yelled, 'It's your boyfriend!' which earned a *Shush!* and a sotto voce reprimand from someone else. A white blur marched up the hallway until it filled the view through the window from side to side. I took a step backwards and the door opened. It was Henry May – Lesley's father.

He was a large man, and driving big trucks and

hauling heavy gear had given him broad shoulders and heavyset arms. Too many transport-café breakfasts and standing his round at the pub had put a tyre around his waist. He had a square face, and had dealt with a receding hairline by shaving his hair down to a brown fuzz. His eyes were blue and clever. Lesley had got her eyes from her dad.

Having four daughters meant that he had parental looming down to a fine art, and I fought the urge to ask whether Lesley could come out and play.

'Hello Peter,' he said.

'Mr May,' I said.

He made no effort to unblock the doorway, nor did he invite me in.

'Lesley will be out in a minute,' he said.

'She all right?' I asked. It was a stupid question, and Lesley's dad didn't embarrass either of us by trying to answer it. I heard someone coming down the stairs and braced myself.

There'd been severe damage to the maxilla, nasal spine, ramus and mandible, Dr Walid had said. And although the majority of the underlying muscle and tendons had survived, the surgeons at UCH had been unable to save much of the skin surface. They'd put in a temporary scaffold to allow her to breathe and ingest food, and there was a chance that she might benefit from a partial face transplant – if they could find a suitable donor. Given that what was left of her jaw was currently held together with a filigree of hypoallergenic metal, talking was out of the question. Dr Walid

3

had said that once the bones were sufficiently fused, they might be able to restore enough functionality to the jaw to allow for speech. But it all sounded a bit conditional to me. Whatever you see, he'd said, take as long a look as you need to get used to it, to accept it, and then move on as if nothing has changed.

'Here she is,' said Lesley's dad, and turned sideways to allow a slim figure to squeeze past him. She wore a blue and white striped hoodie with the hood up, the drawstring pulled tight so that it hid her forehead and chin. The lower face was covered by a matching blue and white patterned scarf, and her eyes by a pair of unfashionably large sunglasses that I suspected had been looted from her mum's forgotten clothes drawer. I stared, but there was nothing to see.

'You should have said we were going out robbing,' I said. 'I'd have brought a balaclava.'

She gave me a disgusted look – I recognised it from the tilt of her head and the way she held her shoulders. I felt a stutter in my chest and took a deep breath.

'Fancy a walk, then?' I asked.

She nodded to her dad, took me firmly by the arm and led me away from the house.

I felt her dad's eyes on my back as we walked off.

If you don't count the boat-building and the light engineering, Brightlingsea is not a noisy town, even in the summer. Now, two weeks after the end of the school holidays, it was almost silent, just the occasional car and the sound of the gulls. I stayed quiet until we'd crossed the High Street, where Lesley pulled her police-issue notebook out of her bag, flipped it open to the last page and showed it to me.

What have you been up to? was written in black Biro across the page.

'You don't want to know,' I said.

She made it clear through hand gestures that, yeah, she did want to know.

So I told her about the guy that had had his dick bitten off by a woman with teeth in her vagina, which seemed to amuse Lesley, and about the rumours that DCI Seawoll was being investigated by the IPCC about his conduct during the Covent Garden riots, which did not. I also didn't tell her that Terrence Pottsley, the only other victim to survive the magic that had damaged Lesley's face, had topped himself as soon as his family's backs were turned.

We didn't go straight to the seashore. Instead, Lesley led me the back way down Oyster Tank Road and through a grassy car park where rows of dinghies were parked on their trailers. A brisk wind from the sea moaned through the rigging and clonked the metal fittings together like cow bells. Hand in hand, we picked our way through the boats and out onto the windswept concrete esplanade. On one side, cement steps led down to a beach carved into narrow strips by rotting

5

breakwaters; on the other side stood a line of brightly coloured huts. Most were closed up tight but I did see one family, determined to stretch the summer as far as it would go, the parents drinking tea in the shelter of their doorway while the kids kicked a football on the beach.

Between the end of the beach huts and the open-air swimming pool was a strip of grass and a shelter where we finally got to sit down. Erected in the 1930s, when people had realistic expectations of the British climate, it was brick built and solid enough to serve as a tank trap. We sat down out of the wind on the bench that ran along the back of the alcove. The inside had been decorated with a mural of the seafront: blue sky, white clouds, red sails. Some total wanker had graffiti'd 'BMX' across the sky, and there was a list of names crudely painted down the side wall – Brooke T., Emily B. and Lesley M. They were just in the right location to have been painted by a bored teenager slumped on the corner of the bench. You didn't need to be a copper to see that this was where the yoof of Brightlingsea came to hang out, in that difficult gap between the age of criminal responsibility and the legal drinking age.

Lesley pulled an iPad clone out of her bag and fired it up. Somebody in her family must have been computer-literate. I know it wasn't Lesley, because they'd installed a speech synthesiser. Lesley typed in keyboard mode and the iPad spoke. It was a basic model with an American accent that made her sound like an autistic surfer dude, but at least we could have an almost normal conversation.

She didn't bother with small talk. 'Can magic fix?' she asked.

'I thought Dr Walid had talked to you about that.' I'd been dreading this question.

'Want you say,' she said.

'What?'

Lesley leaned over her pad and stabbed deliberately at the screen with her finger. She typed several separate lines before hitting return. 'I want to hear it from you,' said the iPad.

'Why?'

Return again: 'Because I trust you.'

I took a breath. A pair of OAPs raced past the shelter on mobility scooters. 'As far as I can tell, magic works within the same framework of physical laws as everything else,' I said.

'What magic do,' said the iPad, 'magic can undo.'

'If you burn your hand with fire or electricity it's still a burn – you fix it with bandages and cream and stuff like that. You don't use more electricity or more fire. You . . .'

. . . had the skin and muscles of your face pulled out of shape by a fucking malevolent spirit – your jaw was all smashed up and the whole thing was held together with magic, and when that ran out your face fell off . . . your beautiful face. I was there; I watched it happen. And there was nothing I could do.

'Can't just wish it away,' I said.

7

'Know everything?' asked the iPad.

'No,' I said. 'And I don't think Nightingale does, either.'

She sat silent and unmoving for a long while. I wanted to put my arm around her but I didn't know how she'd react. I was just about to reach out when she nodded to herself and picked up the iPad again.

'Show me,' said the iPad.

'Lesley . . .'

'Show me,' she hit the repeat button several times. 'Show me, show me, show me . . .'

'Wait,' I said, and reached for her iPad, but she pulled it out of my reach.

'I have to take the batteries out,' I said, 'or the magic will blow the chips.'

Lesley flipped the iPad, cracked it open and pulled the battery. After going through five phones in a row I'd retrofitted my latest Samsung with a hardware cutoff which kept it safe but meant that the case was held together with elastic bands. Lesley shuddered when she saw it and made a snorting sound that I suspected was laughter.

I made the shape of the appropriate *forma* in my mind, opened my hand and brought forth a were-light. Not a big one, but enough to cast a pale light that was reflected in Lesley's sunglasses. She stopped laughing. I closed my hand and the light went out.

Lesley stared at my hand for a moment and then made the same gesture, repeating it twice, slowly

8

and methodically. When nothing happened she looked up at me and I knew, underneath the glasses and scarf, that she was frowning.

'It's not that easy,' I said. 'I practised every morning for four hours for a month and half before I could do that, and that's just the first thing you have to learn. Have I told you about the Latin, the Greek . . .?'

We sat in silence for a moment, then she poked me in the arm. I sighed and produced another werelight. I could practically do it in my sleep by this time. She copied the gesture and got nothing. I'm not joking about how long it takes to learn.

The OAPs on mobility scooters returned drag-racing past on the esplanade. I put the light out, but Lesley carried on making the gesture, the movements becoming more impatient with every try. I stood it as long as I could before I took her hand in mine and made her stop.

We walked back to her house soon afterwards. When we reached her porch she patted me on the arm, stepped inside and shut the door in my face. Through the stained glass I watched her blurry shape retreat quickly down the hallway, and then she was gone.

I was about to turn away when the door opened and Lesley's dad stepped out.

'Peter,' he said. Embarrassment doesn't come easily to men like Henry May, so they don't hide it well. 'I thought we might get a cup of tea – there's a café on the High Street.'

9

'Thanks,' I said, 'but I've got to get back to London.'

'Oh,' he said and stepped closer. 'She doesn't want you to see her with the mask off . . .' He waved his hands vaguely in the direction of the house. 'She knows if you come inside she's going to have to take it off, and she doesn't want you to see her. You can understand that, right?'

I nodded.

'She don't want you to see how bad it is,' he said.

'How bad is it?'

'About as bad as it could be,' said Henry.

'I'm sorry,' I said.

Henry shrugged. 'I just wanted you to know that you weren't being sent away,' he said. 'You weren't being punished or something.'

But I was being sent away, so I said goodbye, climbed back in the Jag and drove back to London.

I'd just managed to find my way back onto the A12 when Dr Walid called me and said he had a body he wanted me to look at. I put my foot down. It was work, and I was grateful to get it.

Every hospital I've ever been in has had the same smell – that whiff of disinfectant, vomit and mortality. UCH was brand new, less than ten years old, but the smell was already beginning to creep in at the edges except, ironically, downstairs in the basement where they kept the dead people. Down there the paint on the walls was still crisp and the pale blue lino still squeaky underfoot.

The mortuary entrance was halfway down a long corridor hung with framed pictures of the old Middlesex Hospital, from back in the days when doctors washing their hands between patients was the cutting edge of medical science. It was guarded by a pair of electronically locked fire doors with a sign saying No Unauthorised Access STOP Mortuary Staff Only. Another sign ordered me to press the buzzer on the entryphone, which I did. The speaker gave a squawk, and on the off-chance that this was a question, I told them it was Constable Peter Grant to see Dr Walid. It squawked again, I waited, and then Dr Abdul Haqq Walid, world-renowned gastroenterologist, cryptopathologist and practising Scot, opened the door.

'Peter,' he said. 'How was Lesley?'

'All right, I suppose,' I said.

Inside, the mortuary was much the same as the rest of the hospital, only with fewer people complaining about the state of the NHS. Dr Walid walked me past the security at reception and introduced me to today's dead body.

'Who is he?' I asked.

'Cyrus Wilkinson,' he said. 'He collapsed in a pub in Cambridge Circus day before yesterday, was ambulanced to Casualty, pronounced dead on arrival and sent down here for a routine post-mortem.'

Poor old Cyrus Wilkinson didn't look that bad

apart from, of course, the Y-shaped incision that split him from chest to crotch. Thankfully, Dr Walid had finished rummaging around in his organs and zipped him up before I'd got there. He was a white guy in what looked like his well-preserved mid-forties with a bit of a beer belly but still some definition on his arms and legs. He looked like a jogger to me.

'And he's down here because . . .?'

'Well, there's evidence of gastritis, pancreatitis and cirrhosis of the liver,' said Dr Walid. The last one I recognised.

'He was a drinker?' I asked.

'Amongst other things,' said Dr Walid. 'He was severely anaemic, which might have been related to his liver problems, but it looks more like what I'd associate with a B12 deficiency.'

I glanced down at the body again for a moment. 'He's got good muscle tone,' I said.

'He used to be fit,' said Dr Walid. 'But recently he seems to have let himself go.'

'Drugs?'

'I've done all the quick checks, and nothing,' said Dr Walid. 'It'll be a couple of days before I get the results on the hair samples.'

'What was the cause of death?'

'Heart failure. I found indications of dilated cardiomyopathy,' said Dr Walid. 'That's when the heart becomes enlarged and can't do its job properly. But I think what did for him last night was an acute myocardial infarction.'

Another term I recognised from the 'what to do if your suspect keels over in custody' classes I'd taken at Hendon. In other words, a heart attack.

'Natural causes?' I asked.

'Superficially, yes,' said Dr Walid. 'But he really wasn't sick enough to just drop dead the way he did. Not that people don't just drop dead all the time, of course.'

'So how do you know this is one of ours?'

Dr Walid patted the corpse's shoulder and winked at me. 'You're going to have to get closer to find out.'

I don't really like getting close to corpses, even ones as unassuming as Cyrus Wilkinson, so I asked Dr Walid for a filter mask and some eye protectors. Once there was no chance of me touching the corpse by accident, I cautiously bent down until my face was close to his.

Vestigia is the imprint magic leaves on physical objects. It's a lot like a sense impression, like the memory of a smell or a sound you once heard. You've probably felt it a hundred times a day, but it all gets mixed up with memories, daydreams and even smells you're smelling and sounds you're hearing. Some things, stones, for example, sop up everything that happens around them even when it's barely magical at all – that's what gives an old house its character. Other things, like the human body, are terrible at retaining any *vestigia* at all – it takes the magical equivalent of a grenade going off to imprint anything on a corpse.

13

Which was why I was a little bit surprised to hear the body of Cyrus Wilkinson playing a saxophone solo. The melody floated in from a time when all the radios were made of Bakelite and blown glass, and with it came a builder's-yard smell of cut wood and cement dust. I stayed there long enough to be sure I could identify the tune, and then I stepped away.

'How did you spot this?' I asked.

'I check all the sudden deaths,' said Dr Walid. 'Just on the off-chance. I thought it sounded like jazz.'

'Did you recognise the tune?'

'Not me. I'm strictly prog rock and the nineteenth-century romantics,' said Dr Walid. 'Did you?'

'It's "Body and Soul",' I said. 'It's from the 1930s.'

'Who played it?'

'Just about everybody. It's one of the great jazz classics.'

'You can't die of jazz,' said Dr Walid. 'Can you?'

I thought of Fats Navarro, Billie Holiday and Charlie Parker who, when he died, was mistaken by the coroner for a man twice his actual age.

'You know,' I said, 'I think you'll find you can.'

Jazz had certainly done its best to do for my father.

You don't get *vestigium* on a body like that without some serious magic, which meant that either somebody did something magical to Cyrus Wilkinson,

14

or he was a user himself. Nightingale called civilians that used magic 'practitioners'. According to him, a practitioner, even an amateur one, frequently leaves evidence of their 'practice' at their home, so I headed over the river to the address listed on Mr Wilkinson's driving licence to see whether there was anyone who loved him enough to kill him.

His house was a two-storey Edwardian terrace on the 'right' side of Tooting Bec Road. This was VW Golf country, with a couple of Audis and a BMW to raise the tone a little. I parked on a yellow line and walked up the street. A fluorescent-orange Honda Civic caught my eye – not only did it have the sad little 1.4 VTEC engine, but there was a woman in the driver's seat watching the address. I made a mental note of the car's Index before I opened the cast-iron gate, walked up the short path and rang the doorbell. For a moment I smelled broken wood and cement dust, but then the door opened and I lost interest in anything else.

She was unfashionably curvy, plump and sexy in a baggy sky-blue Shetland jumper. She had a pale, pretty face and a mess of brown hair that would have fallen halfway down her back if it hadn't been tied up in a crude bundle at the back of her head. Her eyes were chocolate-brown and her mouth was big, full-lipped, and turned down at the corners. She asked me who I was and I identified myself.

'And what can I do for you, Constable?' she asked. Her accent was cut-glass almost to the point of parody; when she spoke I expected a Spitfire to go zooming over our heads.

'Is this Cyrus Wilkinson's house?' I asked.

'I'm rather afraid it was, Constable,' she said.

I asked who she was – politely.

'Simone Fitzwilliam,' she said, and stuck out her hand. I took it automatically; her palm was soft, warm. I smelled honeysuckle. I asked if I could come in, and she stood aside to let me enter.

The house had been built for the aspirational lower middle class, so the hallway was narrow but well proportioned. It still had its original black and white tiles, though, and a scruffy but antique oak hall cupboard. Simone led me into the living room. I noticed that she had sturdy but well-shaped legs under the black leggings she wore. The house had undergone the standard gentrification package: front room knocked through into the dining room; original oak floorboards sanded down, varnished and covered in rugs. The furniture looked like John Lewis – expensive, comfortable and unimaginative. The plasma TV was conventionally large and hooked up to Sky and a Blu-ray player; the nearest shelves held DVDs, not books. A reproduction Monet hung over where the fireplace would have been if it hadn't been ripped out at some point in the last hundred years.

'What was your relationship with Mr Wilkinson?' I asked.

'He was my lover,' she said.

The stereo was a boring high-end Hitachi, strictly CD and solid state – no turntable at all. There were a couple of racks of CDs: Wes Montgomery, Dewey Redman, Stan Getz. The rest were a random selection of hits from the 1990s.

'I'm sorry for your loss,' I said. 'I'd like to ask you a few questions, if I can.'

'Is that entirely necessary, Constable?' she asked.

'We often investigate cases where the circumstances surrounding the death are unclear,' I said. Actually we, that is, the police, don't investigate unless foul play is bleeding obvious, or if the Home Office has recently issued a directive insisting we prioritise whatever the crime du jour is for the duration of the current news cycle.

'Are they unclear?' asked Simone. 'I understood poor Cyrus had a heart attack.' She sat down on a pastel-blue sofa and gestured for me to take my place on the matching armchair. 'Isn't that what they call natural causes?' Her eyes glistened, and she rubbed at them with the back of her hand. 'I'm sorry, Constable,' she said.

I told her to call me Peter, which you are just not supposed to do at this stage of an inquiry – I could practically hear Lesley yelling at me all the way from the Essex coast. She still didn't offer me a cup of tea, though – I guess it just wasn't my day.

Simone smiled. 'Thank you, Peter. You can ask your questions.'

'Cyrus was a musician?' I asked.

'He played the alto sax.'

'And he played jazz?'

Another brief smile. 'Is there any other kind of music?'

'Modal, bebop or mainstream?' I asked, showing off.

'West Coast cool,' she said. 'Although he wasn't averse to a bit of hard bop when the occasion called for it.'

'Do you play?'

'Lord, no,' she said. 'I couldn't possibly inflict my ghastly lack of talent upon an audience. One needs to know one's limitations. I am a keen listener, though – Cyrus appreciated that.'

'Were you listening that night?'

'Of course,' she said. 'Front-row seat, although that isn't hard in a tiny little place like The Spice of Life. They were playing "Midnight Sun". Cyrus finished his solo and just sat down on the monitor – I did think he was a bit flushed – and then he fell over on his side, and that's when we all realised that something was wrong.'

She stopped and looked away from me, her hands balling into fists. I waited a bit and asked some dull routine questions to centre her again – did she know what time he'd collapsed? Who'd called the ambulance? Did she stay with him the whole time? I jotted down the answers in my notebook.

'I wanted to go in the ambulance, I really did,

18

but before I knew it they'd whisked him away. Jimmy gave me a lift to the hospital, but by the time I got there it was too late.'

'Jimmy?' I asked.

'Jimmy's the drummer, very nice man. Scottish, I think.'

'Can you give me his full name?' I asked.

'I don't think I can,' said Simone. 'Isn't that awful? I've just always thought of him as Jimmy the drummer.'

I asked who else was in the band, but she could only remember them as Max the bass and Danny the piano.

'You must think I'm an awful person,' she said. 'I'm certain I must know their names, but I just can't seem to recall them. Perhaps it's Cyrus dying like that, perhaps it's like shell shock.'

I asked whether Cyrus had suffered from any recent illnesses or health conditions. Simone said not. Nor did she know the name of his GP, although she assured me that she could dig it out of his papers if it was important. I made a note to ask Dr Walid to track it down for me.

I felt I'd asked enough questions to cover for my real reason for the visit, and then asked, as innocuously as I could, if I might have a quick look around the rest of the house. Normally the mere presence of a policeman is enough to make the most law-abiding citizen feel vaguely guilty and therefore reluctant to let you clomp around their home in your size elevens, so it was a bit of a surprise when Simone just waved at the hallway and told me to help myself.

Upstairs was pretty much what I'd expected – a master bedroom at the front, a second bedroom at the back that was being used, judging from the cleared floor and the music stands lined up against the wall, as a music room. They'd sacrificed the usual half-bedroom to extend the bathroom to allow for a bath, shower, bidet and toilet combo, all tiled with pale-blue ceramics with an embossed fleur-de-lis pattern. The bathroom cupboard was the standard one-quarter male/three-quarters female ratio. He favoured double-bladed dispos-ables and after-shave gel; she did a lot of depilation and shopped at Superdrug. Nothing indicated that either of them was dabbling in the esoteric arts.

In the master bedroom, both fitted wardrobes were wide open and a trail of half-folded clothes led from these to where two suitcases lay open on the bed. Grief, like cancer, hits people at different rates, but even so I thought it was a bit early for her to be packing up her beloved Cyrus's things. Then I spotted a pair of hipsters that no self-respecting jazzman would wear, and I realised that Simone was packing her own things, which I found equally suspicious. I listened, to make sure she wasn't coming up the stairs, and had a poke through the underwear drawers but got nothing except a vague sense of being really unprofessional.

The music room at least had more character;

there were framed posters of Miles Davis and Art Pepper on the walls, and shelves stuffed with sheet music. I'd saved the music room till last because I wanted a sense of what Nightingale called the house's *sensis illic*, and what I called background *vestigium*, before I entered what was clearly Cyrus Wilkinson's inner sanctum. I did get a flash of 'Body and Soul' and, mingled with Simone's honeysuckle perfume, the smell of dust and cut wood again, but it was muted and elusive. Unlike the rest of the house, the music room had bookshelves holding more than photographs and amusingly expensive mementos of foreign holidays. I figured that anyone looking to become a practitioner outside of official channels would have to work their way through a lot of occult rubbish before they stumbled on proper magic – if such a thing was possible. At least some of those books should have been on the shelves, but Cyrus had nothing like that on his, not even Aleister Crowley's *Book of Lies*, which is always good for a laugh, if nothing else. In fact, they looked a lot like my dad's bookshelves: mainly jazz biographies – *Straight Life*, *Bird Lives* – with a few early Dick Francis novels thrown in for variety.

'Have you found something?' Simone was in the doorway.

'Not yet,' I said. I'd been too intent on the room to hear her coming up the stairs. Lesley said that the capacity not to notice a traditional Dutch folk-dancing band walk up behind you was not a survival characteristic in the complex, fast-paced world of the modern policing environment. I'd like to point out that I was trying to give directions to a slightly deaf tourist at the time, and anyway, it was a Swedish dance troupe.

'I don't wish to hurry you,' said Simone, 'only I'd already ordered a taxi before you came, and you know how these chaps hate to be kept waiting.'

'Where are you going?' I asked.

'Just to stay with my sisters,' she said, 'until I find my feet.'

I asked for her address, and wrote it down when she told me. Surprisingly, it was in Soho, on Berwick Street. 'I know,' she said when she saw my expression. 'They're rather Bohemian.'

'Did Cyrus have any other properties, a lock-up, an allotment, maybe?'

'Not that I know of,' she said, and then she laughed. 'Cyrus digging an allotment – what an extraordinary notion.'

I thanked her for her time and she saw me to the door.

'Thank you for everything, Peter,' she said. 'You've been most kind.'

There was enough of a reflection in the side window for me to see that the Honda Civic was still parked opposite the house, and that the woman driver was staring right at us. When I turned away from the door, she jerked her face around and pretended to be reading the stickers on the back of the car in front. She risked another glance, only to find me bearing down on her from across the street. I saw her panic in her embarrassment, and vacillate between starting the engine or getting out. When I knocked on the window, she flinched. I showed her my warrant card and she stared at it in confusion. You get that about half the time, mainly because most members of the public have never seen a warrant card close up and have no idea what the hell it is. Eventually she twigged and buzzed down her window.

'Could you step out of the car please, madam,' I asked.

She nodded and got out. She was short, slender, and well-dressed in an off-the-peg but good-quality turquoise skirt suit. An estate agent, I thought, or something customer-facing like PR or big-ticket retail. When dealing with the police, most people lean against their cars for moral support, but she didn't, although she did fiddle with the ring on her left hand and push her hair back behind her ears.

'I was just waiting in the car,' she said. 'Is there a problem?'

I asked for her driving licence and she surrendered it meekly. If you ask a random member of the public for their name and address, not only do they frequently lie to you, but they don't even have to give it unless you report them for an offence. *And* you have to fill in a receipt to prove that you're not unfairly singling out blonde estate agents. If, however, you make them think it's a traffic stop, then they cheerfully hand over their driving licence which lists their name, including any embarrassing middle names, their address and their date of birth – all of which I noted down. Her name was Melinda Abbot, she was born in 1980 and her address was the one I'd just left.

'Is this your current address?' I asked as I handed back her licence.

'Sort of,' she said. 'It was, and as it happens I'm just waiting to get it back now. Why do you want to know?'

'It's part of an ongoing investigation,' I said. 'Do you happen to know a man called Cyrus Wilkinson?'

'He's my fiancé,' she said, and gave me a hard look. 'Has something happened to Cyrus?'

There are ACPO-approved guidelines for breaking bad news to loved ones, and they don't include blurting it out in the middle of the street. I asked if she'd like to sit in the car with me, but she wasn't having any of it.

'You'd better tell me now,' she said.

'I'm afraid I have some bad news,' I said.

Anybody who's ever watched *The Bill* or *Casualty* knows what *that* means. Melinda started back, then caught herself. She nearly lost it, but then I saw it all being sucked back behind the mask of her face.

'When?' she asked.

'Two nights ago,' I said. 'It was a heart attack.'

She looked at me stupidly. 'A heart attack?'

'I'm afraid so.'

She nodded. 'Why are you here?' she asked.

I was saved from having to lie because a minicab pulled up outside the house and honked its horn. Melinda turned, stared at the front door and was rewarded when Simone emerged, carrying her two suitcases. The driver, showing an uncharacteristic level of chivalry, rushed smartly over to take the cases from her and loaded them into the back of his cab while she locked the front door – both the Yale and the Chubb, I noticed.

'You bitch,' shouted Melinda.

Simone ignored her and headed for the cab, which had exactly the effect on Melinda that I expected it to have. 'Yes, you,' she shouted, 'he's *dead*, you bitch! And you couldn't even be fucking bothered to tell me. That's *my* house, you fat slag.'

Simone looked up at that, and at first I didn't think she'd recognised who Melinda was, but then she nodded to herself and absently threw the house keys in our general direction. They landed at Melinda's feet.

I know ballistic when I see it coming, and so I already had my hand around her upper arm before she could rush across the street and try to kick the shit out of Simone. Maintaining the Queen's Peace – that's what it's all about. For a skinny little thing Melinda wasn't half strong, and I ended up having to use both hands as she screamed abuse over my shoulder, making my ears ring.

'Would you like me to arrest you?' I asked. That's an old police trick. If you just warn people they

25

often simply ignore you, but if you ask them a question then they have to think about it. Once they start to think about the consequences they almost always calm down – unless they're drunk of course, or stoned, or aged between fourteen and twenty-one, or Glaswegian.

Fortunately it had the desired effect on Melinda, who paused in her screaming long enough for the minicab to drive away. Once I was sure she wasn't going to attack me out of frustration – an occupational hazard if you're the police – I bent down, retrieved the keys and put them in her hands.

'Is there someone you can call?' I asked. 'Someone who'll come round and stay with you for a bit?'

She shook her head. 'I'm just going to wait in my car,' she said. 'Thank you.'

Don't thank me, ma'am, I didn't say, I'm just doing . . . Who knew what I was doing? I doubted I could get anything useful from her that evening, so I left well enough alone.

Sometimes, after a hard day of graft, nothing will satisfy but a kebab. I stopped at a random Kurdish place on my way through Vauxhall and pulled up on the Albert Embankment to eat it – no kebab in the Jag, that's the rule. One side of the Embankment had suffered from an outbreak of modernism in the 1960s, but I kept my back to its dull concrete façades and instead watched the sun setting fire to the tops of Millbank Tower and the Palace of Westminster. The evening was still warm enough for shirtsleeves, and the city was clinging to summer like a WAG to a promising centre forward.

Officially I belong to ESC9, which stands for Economic and Specialist Crime Unit 9, otherwise known as 'The Folly', also known as the unit that nice, well-brought-up coppers don't talk about in polite company. There's no point trying to remember 'ESC9', because the Metropolitan Police has a reorganisation once every four years and all the names change. That's why the Commercial Robberies Unit of the Serious and Organised Crime Group has been called 'The Flying Squad' since its introduction in 1920, or 'The Sweeney' if you want to establish your Cockney geezer credentials. That's Sweeney Todd, Cockney rhyming slang for Flying Squad, in case you were wondering.

Unlike the Sweeney, the Folly is easy to overlook, partly because we do stuff nobody likes to talk about. But mostly because we have no discernible budget. No budget means no bureaucratic scrutiny, and therefore no paper trail. It also helps that up until January this year, it had a personnel complement of one: a certain Detective Chief Inspector Thomas Nightingale. Despite doubling the staffing levels when I joined, and catching up on a good ten years of unprocessed paperwork, we maintain a stealthy presence within the bureaucratic hierarchy of the Metropolitan Police. Thus we pass amongst the other coppers in a mysterious way, our duties to perform.

One of our duties is the investigation of unsanctioned wizards and other magical practitioners, but I didn't think that Cyrus Wilkinson had been a practitioner of anything except a superior saxophone. I also doubted he'd killed himself with the traditional jazz cocktail of drugs and drink, but confirmation of this would have to wait for the tox screen. Why would someone use magic to kill a jazz musician in the middle of his set? I mean, I have my problems with the New Thing and the rest of the atonal modernists, but I wouldn't kill someone for playing it – at least, not if I wasn't trapped in the same room.

Across the river, a catamaran pulled away from the Millbank Pier in a roar of diesel. I bundled up the kebab paper and dumped it in a rubbish bin. I climbed back into the Jag, started her up and pulled out into the twilight.

At some point I was going to have to hit the library back at the Folly, and look for historical cases. Polidori was usually good for lurid stuff involving drink and debauchery. Probably from all the time he spent off his head with Byron and the Shelleys by Lake Geneva. If anyone knew about untimely and unnatural deaths it was Polidori, who literally wrote the book on the subject just before drinking cyanide – it's called *An Investigation Into Unnatural Deaths in London in the Years 1768–1810* and it weighs over a kilogram – I just hoped that reading it didn't drive me to suicide too.

It was late evening by the time I reached the

Folly and parked up the Jag in the coach house. Toby started barking as soon as I opened the back door, and he came skittering across the marble floor of the atrium to hurl himself at my shins. Molly glided in from the direction of the kitchens like the winner of the World All-Comers' Creepy Gothic Lolita Contest. I ignored Toby's yapping and asked whether Nightingale was awake. Molly gave me the slight head tilt that meant 'no', and then an inquiring look.

Molly served as the Folly's housekeeper, cook and rodent exterminator. She never speaks, has too many teeth and a taste for raw meat, but I try never to hold that against her or let her get between me and the exit.

'I'm knackered – I'm going straight to bed,' I said.

Molly glanced at Toby and then at me.

'I've been working all day,' I said.

Molly gave me the head tilt that meant, *I don't care, if you don't take the smelly little thing out for his walk you can be the one that cleans up after him.*

Toby paused in his barking long enough to give me a hopeful look.

'Where's his lead?' I asked.

CHAPTER 2

THE SPICE OF LIFE

The general public have a warped view of the speed at which an investigation goes. They like to imagine tense conversations going on behind the Venetian blinds, and unshaven but ruggedly handsome detectives working themselves with single-minded devotion into the bottle and marital breakdown. The truth is that at the end of the day, unless you've generated some sort of urgent lead, you go home and get on with the important things in life – like drinking and sleeping and, if you're lucky, a relationship with someone of the gender and sexual orientation of your choice. And I would have been doing at least one of those things the next morning if I hadn't also been the last bleeding apprentice wizard in England. Which meant I spent my spare time learning theory, studying dead languages and reading books like *Essays on the Metaphysical* by John 'never saw a polysyllabic word he didn't like' Cartwright.

And learning magic, of course – which is what makes the whole thing worthwhile.

This is a spell: *Lux iactus scindere*. Say it quietly,

say it loudly, say it with conviction in the middle of a thunderstorm while striking a dramatic pose – nothing will happen. That's because the words are just labels for the *forma* you make in your mind; *Lux* to make the light and *Scindere* to fix it in place. If you do this particular spell right, it creates a light source in a fixed position. If you do it wrong, it can burn a hole through a lab table.

'You know,' said Nightingale, 'I don't think I've ever seen that happen before.'

I gave the bench a last squirt with the CO_2 extinguisher and bent down to see whether the floor under the table was still intact. There was a burn mark, but luckily no crater.

'It keeps getting away from me,' I said.

Nightingale stood up out of his wheelchair and had a look for himself. He moved carefully and favoured his right side. If he was still wearing bandages on his shoulder, they were hidden under a crisp lilac shirt that had last been fashionable during the Abdication Crisis. Molly was busily feeding him up, but to me he still looked pale and thin. He caught me staring,

'I wish you and Molly would stop watching me like that,' he said. 'I'm well on the road to recovery. I've been shot before, so I know what I'm talking about.'

'Shall I give it another go?'

'No,' said Nightingale. 'The problem is obviously with *Scindere*. I thought you'd progressed through that too swiftly. Tomorrow we're going to start to relearn that *forma*, and then once I'm certain of your mastery we'll return to this spell.'

'Oh joy,' I said.

'This isn't unusual.' Nightingale's voice was low and reassuring. 'You have to get the foundations of the art right or everything you build on top will be crooked, not to mention unstable. There are no short cuts in wizardry, Peter. If there were, everyone would be doing it.'

Probably on *Britain's Got Talent*, I thought, but you don't say these things to Nightingale because he doesn't have a sense of humour about the art, and only uses the telly for watching rugby.

I assumed the attentive look of the dutiful apprentice, but Nightingale wasn't fooled.

'Tell me about your dead musician,' he said.

I laid out the facts, with emphasis on the intensity of the *vestigia* me and Dr Walid had felt around the body.

'Did he feel it as strongly as you did?' asked Nightingale.

I shrugged. 'It's *vestigia*, boss,' I said. 'It was strong enough for both of us to hear a melody. That's got to be suspicious.'

'It's suspicious,' he said, and settled back down in his wheelchair with a frown. 'But is it a crime?'

'The statute only says that you have to unlawfully kill someone under the Queen's Peace with malice aforethought. It doesn't say anything about how you do it.' I'd checked in *Blackstone's Police*

Manual before coming down for breakfast that morning.

'I'll be interested to see the Crown Prosecution Service argue that in front of a jury,' he said. 'In the first instance, you'll need to prove that he was killed by magic and then find out who was capable of doing it and making it look like natural causes.'

'Could you do it?' I asked.

Nightingale had to think about it. 'I think so,' he said. 'I'd have to spend a while in the library first. It would be a very powerful spell, and it's possible that the music you're hearing is a practitioner's *Signare* – his involuntary signature.' Because, just as the old telegraph operators could identify each other from the way each one tapped their key, so every practitioner casts a spell in a style unique to themselves.

'Do I have a signature?' I asked.

'Yes,' said Nightingale. 'When you practise, things have an alarming tendency to catch fire.'

'Seriously, boss.'

'It's too early for you to have a *Signare*, but another practitioner would certainly know that you were my apprentice,' said Nightingale. 'Assuming he'd ever seen my work, of course.'

'Are there other practitioners out there?' I asked.

Nightingale shifted in his wheelchair. 'There are some survivors from the pre-war mob,' he said. 'But apart from them, you and I are the last of the classically trained wizards. Or at least, you will be if you ever concentrate long enough to be trained.'

'Could it have been one of these survivors?'

'Not if jazz was part of the *Signare*.'

And therefore probably not one of their apprentices either – if they had apprentices.

'If it wasn't one of your mob . . .'

'*Our* mob,' said Nightingale. 'You swore an oath, remember. That makes you one of us.'

'If it wasn't one of our mob, who else could do it?'

Nightingale smiled. 'One of your riverine friends would have the power,' he said.

That made me pause. There were two gods of the River Thames, and each of them had their own fractious children, one for each tributary. They certainly had power – I'd personally witnessed Beverley Brook flooding out Covent Garden, incidentally saving my life and that of a family of random German tourists in the process.

'But Father Thames wouldn't operate below Teddington Lock,' said Nightingale. 'And Mama Thames wouldn't risk the agreement with us. If Tyburn wanted you dead she'd do it through the courts. While Fleet would humiliate you to death in the media. And Brent is too young. Finally, leaving aside that Soho is on the wrong side of the river, if Effra was going to kill you with music, it wouldn't be jazz.'

Not when she's practically the patron saint of UK Grime, I thought. 'Are there other people?' I asked. 'Other things?'

'It's possible,' said Nightingale. 'But I'd concentrate

on determining *how* before I worried too much about *whom*.'

'Any advice?'

'You could start,' said Nightingale, 'by visiting the scene of the crime.'

Much to the frustration of the ruling class, who like their cities to be clean, ordered and to have good lines of fire, London has never responded well to grandiose planning projects, not even after it was razed to the ground in 1666. Mind you, this hasn't stopped people from trying, and in the 1880s the Metropolitan Board of Works constructed Charing Cross Road and Shaftesbury Avenue to facilitate better communications both north and south, east and west. That they eliminated the notorious Newport Market slums in the process, and thus reduced the number of unsightly poor people one might espy while perambulating about town was, I'm sure, purely serendipitous. Where the Road and the Avenue crossed became Cambridge Circus, and on the west side today stands the Palace Theatre, in all its late-Victorian gingerbread glory. Next to that, and built in the same style, stands what was once the George and Dragon Public House, but was now named The Spice of Life. According to its own publicity, it was London's premier spot for jazz.

Back when my old man was on the scene, The Spice of Life wasn't a happening place for jazz. It was, according to him, strictly for geezers in roll-neck jumpers and goatees reading poetry and listening to folk music. Bob Dylan played there a couple of times in the 1960s, and so did Mick Jagger. But none of that meant anything to my dad, who always said that rock 'n' roll was all right for those that needed help following a beat.

Up until that lunchtime, I'd never so much as been inside The Spice of Life. Before I was a copper, it wasn't the kind of pub I drank in, and after I was a copper it wasn't the kind of pub I arrested people in.

I'd timed my visit to avoid the lunchtime rush, which meant that the crowds milling around the Circus were mainly tourists. Inside, the pub was pleasantly cool, dim and empty, with just a whiff of cleaning products fighting with years of spilled beer. I wanted to get a feel for the place, and I decided the most natural way to do that was to stand at the bar and have a beer, but because I was on duty I kept it to a half. Unlike a lot of London pubs, The Spice of Life had managed to hang on to its brass and polished wood interior without slipping into kitsch. I stood drinking my half, and as I took my first sip I flashed on horse sweat and the sound of hammers ringing on an anvil, shouting and laughter, a distant woman's scream and the smell of tobacco – pretty standard for a central London pub.

The sons of Musa ibn Shakir were bright and bold, and if they hadn't been Muslims would probably have gone on to be the patron saints of

36

techno-geeks. They're famous for their ninth-century Baghdad bestseller, a compendium of ingenious mechanical devices which they imaginatively titled *Kitab al-Hiyal* or The Book of Ingenious Devices. In it they describe what is possibly the first practical device for measuring differential pressure, and that's where the problem really starts. In 1593, Galileo Galilei took time off from astronomy and promulgating heresy to invent a thermoscope for measuring heat. In 1833, Carl Friedrich Gauss invented a device to measure the strength of a magnetic field, and in 1908 Hans Geiger made a detector for ionising radiation. At this very moment astronomers are detecting planets around distant stars by measuring how much their orbits wibble, and the clever people at CERN are smashing particles together in the hope that Doctor Who will turn up and tell them to stop. The story of how we measure the physical universe *is* the history of science itself.

And what do me and Nightingale have to measure *vestigia* with? Sod all, and it's not even as if we know what we're trying to measure in the first place. No wonder the heirs of Isaac Newton kept magic safely under their periwigs. I had jokingly developed my own scale for *vestigia* based on the amount of noise Toby made when he interacted with any residual magic, and called it a yap, one yap being enough *vestigia* to be apparent even when I wasn't looking for it.

The yap would be an SI unit, of course, and

thus the standard background ambience of a central London pub was 0.2 of a yap (0.2Y) or 200 milliyaps (200mY). Having established that to my satisfaction, I finished the half-pint and headed downstairs to the basement, where they kept the jazz.

A set of creaky stairs led down to the Backstage Bar, which was a roughly octagonal room, low-ceilinged and punctuated with stout cream-coloured columns that had to be load-bearing because they certainly didn't add to the sightlines. As I stood in the doorway and tried to get a feel for any magical ambience, I realised that my own childhood was about to interfere with my investigation.

In 1986, Courtney Pine released *Journey to the Urge Within*, and suddenly jazz was back in fashion and with it came my dad's third and last brush with fame and fortune. I never went to gigs, but during the school holidays he used to take me with him on visits to clubs and recording studios. Some things linger even from before conscious memory – old beer, tobacco smoke, the sound a trumpet makes when its player is just getting it warmed up. You could have 200 kiloyaps of *vestigia* in that basement, and I wouldn't have been able to separate them from my own memories.

I should have brought Toby. He would have been more use. I stepped over to the stage in the hope that proximity might help.

My dad always said that a trumpet player likes

to aim his weapon at the audience, but a sax man likes to cut a good profile and that they always have a favourite side. It being an article of faith with my dad that you don't even pick up a reed instrument unless you're vain about the shape your face makes when you're blowing down it. I stood on the stage and adopted some classic sax-player stances, and as I did, I began to feel something, stage front and right, a little tingle and the melody line of 'Body and Soul' played far away, piercing and bittersweet.

'Got you,' I said.

Since all I had to go on was the magical echo of one particular jazz tune, then I figured it was time to find out precisely which of several hundred cover versions of 'Body and Soul' it was. What I needed was a jazz expert so obsessive that the subject had consumed him to the point where he neglected his health, his marriage and his own children.

It was time to go see my old man.

Much as I love the Jag, it's too conspicuous for everyday police work. So that day I was driving a battered silver ex-Metropolitan Police Ford Asbo that, despite my best efforts, smelled vaguely of old stake-outs and wet dog. I had it stashed up Romilly Street, with my magic police-business talisman in the window to ward off traffic wardens. I'd taken the Asbo to a friend of mine who'd tuned up its Volvo engine and got me a satisfactory bit of zip, which came in handy dodging the bendy buses on Tottenham Court Road as I drove north for Kentish Town.

Every Londoner has their manor – a collection of bits of the city where they feel comfortable. Where you live, or went to college; where you work or your sports club; that particular bit of the West End where you go drinking or, if you're the police, the patrol area around your nick. If you're a native-born Londoner (and, contrary to what you've heard, we are the majority) then the strongest bit of your manor is where you grew up. There's a particular kind of safety that comes from being on the streets where you went to school, had your first snog, or drink, or threw up your first chicken vindaloo. I grew up in Kentish Town, which as an area would count as a leafy suburb if it was leafier and more suburban. And if it had fewer council estates. One such is the Peckwater Estate, my ancestral seat, which had been built just as architects were coming to terms with the idea that proles might enjoy indoor plumbing and the occasional bath, but before they realised that said proles might like to have more than one child per family. Perhaps they thought three bedrooms would only encourage breeding amongst the working class.

One advantage it did have was a courtyard that had been turned over to parking. There I found a clear bay between a Toyota Aygo and a battered secondhand Mercedes with a criminally mismatched side panel. I pulled in, got out, beeped the lock behind me and walked away, secure in the knowledge that because they knew me round here they weren't going to jack my car. That's what being on your manor is all about. Although, to be honest, I suspect the local roughnecks were much more scared of my mum than they were of me – the worst I could do was arrest them.

Strangely, I heard music when I opened the front door to my parent's flat: 'The Way You Look Tonight', played solo on a keyboard, coming from the main bedroom. My mum was lying on the good sofa in the living room. Her eyes were closed and she was still in her work clothes – jeans, grey sweatshirt, Paisley headscarf. I was shocked to see that the stereo was silent and even the TV was switched off. The TV in my parent's house is never switched off – not even for funerals. Especially not for funerals.

'Mum?'

Without opening her eyes, she put her finger to her lips and then pointed towards the bedroom.

'Is that Dad?' I asked.

My mum's lips curved up into a slow, blissful smile that was familiar to me only from old photographs. My dad's third and last revival in the early 1990s had ended when he'd blown out his teeth just before a live appearance on BBC 2, after which I didn't hear Mum speak more than two words to my dad for a year and a half. I think she took it personally. The only time I've seen her more upset was at Princess Diana's funeral, but I think she sort of enjoyed that, in a cathartic way.

The music continued, searching and heartfelt. I remember my mum, inspired by a repeat viewing of *The Buena Vista Social Club*, buying Dad a keyboard, but I didn't remember him learning to play it.

I went into the narrow slot of a kitchen and made us a cup of tea as the tune concluded. I heard my mum shift on the sofa and sigh. I don't actually like jazz that much, but I spent enough of my childhood as my dad's vinyl-wallah, ferrying discs from his collection to his turntable when he wasn't well, to know the good stuff when I hear it. Dad was playing the good stuff, 'All Blues' now but not doing anything too smart-arse with it, just letting the melancholy beauty shine through. I went back through and put my mum's tea down on the simulated-walnut coffee table, then sat down to watch her listen to my dad's playing while it lasted.

It didn't last for ever, or even remotely long enough. How could it? We heard Dad slip off the line and then crash to a halt. Mum sighed and sat up.

'What are you doing here?' she asked.

'I've come to see Dad,' I said.

'Good.' She took a sip of her tea. 'This is cold,' she said, and thrust the mug in my direction. 'Make me another.'

My dad emerged while I was in the kitchen. I

heard him greet Mum, and then a strange sucking sound that I realised with a start was the sound of them kissing. I almost spilled the tea.

'Stop it,' I heard my mum whisper. 'Peter is here.'

My dad stuck his head into the kitchen. 'This can't be good,' he said. 'Any chance of a cuppa too?'

I showed him that I already had another mug out.

'Outstanding,' he said.

When I had them both supplied with tea, Dad asked me why I'd come round. They had reason to be a bit cautious, because the last time I'd turned up unexpectedly I'd just burned down Covent Garden Market – sort of.

'I've got some jazz stuff I need your help with,' I said.

My dad gave me a pleased smile. 'Step into my office,' he said. 'The jazz doctor is in.'

If the living room belonged to my mum and her extended family, then the main bedroom belonged to my dad and his record collection. Family legend said that the walls had once been painted a creamy light brown, but now every centimetre had been colonised by Dad's steel-bracketed, stripped-pine shelves. Every shelf was filled with vinyl records, all carefully stored in vertical ranks out of the sunlight. Since I'd moved out, my mum's sprawling BHS wardrobe had migrated into my old room along with the bulk of her shoe collection. This left just enough room for the queen-sized bed, a full-size electric keyboard and my dad's stereo.

I told him what I was looking for and he started pulling out records. We began, as I knew we would, with Coleman Hawkins's famous 1938 take, on Bluebird. It was a waste of time, of course, because Hawkins barely goes near the actual melody. But I let my dad enjoy it all the way through before I pointed this out.

'It was old-school, Dad. The one I heard. It had a proper melody and everything.'

Dad grunted and dipped into a cardboard box full of 78s to pull out a plain brown cardboard sleeve repaired on three edges with masking tape, containing the Benny Goodman Trio on shellac, with a Victor black and gold label. He has a Garrard turntable which has a 78 setting, but you have to swap out the cartridge first – I laboriously removed the Ortofon and went looking for the Stanton. It was still kept where I remembered it, on the one clear bit of shelf behind the stereo, lying on its back to protect the stylus. While I fiddled with the tiny screwdriver and got the cartridge mounted, Dad carefully slipped the disc out and inspected it with a happy smile. He passed it to me. It had the surprising heft of a 78, much heavier than an LP – anyone weaned exclusively on CDs probably wouldn't have been able to lift it. I took the edges of the heavy black disc between my palms and placed it carefully on the turntable.

It hissed and popped as soon as the needle hit the groove, and through that I heard Goodman make his intro on the clarinet, and then Teddy Wilson soloed on piano, then Benny came in on clarinet again. Luckily, Krupa on drums kept a low profile. This was much closer to the tune poor dead Mr Wilkinson was playing.

'Later than that,' I said.

'That won't be difficult,' said Dad. 'This was only recorded five years after it was written.'

We sampled a couple more on 78, including a 1940 Billie Holiday take that we left on just because 'Lady Day' is one of the few things me and Dad truly have in common. It was beautiful and sad, and that helped me realise what I was missing.

'It's got to be more upbeat,' I said. 'It was a bigger combo, and it had more swing.'

'Swing?' asked my dad. 'This is "Body and Soul" we're talking about, it's never been noted for its swing.'

'Come on, Dad, someone must have done a more swinging version – if only for the white folks,' I said.

'Less of that, you cheeky bastard,' said Dad. 'Still, I think I know what we might be looking for.' He reached into his jacket pocket and pulled out a rectangle of plastic and glass.

'You've got an iPhone,' I said.

'iPod Touch, actually,' he said. 'It's not a bad sound.' This from a man who ran a fifty-year-old Quad amp because it had valves rather than transistors. He passed me the ear-buds and slid his

45

finger around the screen like he'd been using touch controls all his life. 'Listen to this,' he said.

There it was, digitally remastered, but still with enough hiss and pop to keep the purists happy: 'Body and Soul', clear melody and just enough swing to make it danceable. If it wasn't what I'd heard off the body, then it was definitely played by the same band.

'Who is it?' I asked.

'Ken Johnson,' said Dad. 'Old Snakehips himself. This is off *Blitzkrieg Babies and Bands*, some nice transfers from shellac. The liner notes say that it's "Jiver" Hutchinson on trumpet. But it's obviously Dave Wilkins, because the fingering's all different.'

'When was it recorded?'

'The original 78 was cut in 1939 at the Decca studios in West Hampstead,' said Dad. He looked at me keenly. 'Is this part of a case? Only, last time you came over you weren't half going on about some strange stuff.'

I wasn't going down that road. 'What's with the keyboard?'

'I'm revitalising my career,' he said. 'I plan to be the next Oscar Peterson.'

'Really?' That was unexpectedly cocky – even for my dad.

'Really,' he said, and shifted around on the bed until he could reach the keyboard. He played a couple of bars of 'Body and Soul', stating the melody before vamping and then taking the line in a direction that I've never been able to follow

46

or appreciate. He looked disappointed at my reaction – he keeps hoping that I'll grow into it one day. On the other hand, my dad had an iPod, so who knows what might happen.

'What happened to Ken Johnson?'

'He was killed in the Blitz,' said Dad. 'Like Al Bowlly and Lorna Savage. Ted Heath told me that sometimes they thought Göring had it in for the jazzmen. Said he felt safer during the war doing tours in North Africa than he did playing gigs in London.'

I doubted I was searching for the vengeful spirit of Reichsmarschall Hermann Göring, but it wouldn't hurt to check just in case.

Mum turfed us out of the bedroom so she could change. I made more tea, and we sat in the living room.

'Next thing I know,' said Dad, 'I'll be looking for gigs.'

'With you on keyboard?'

'The line is the line,' said Dad. 'The instrument is just the instrument.'

The jazzman lives to play.

My mum came out of the bedroom in a sleeveless yellow sundress and no headscarf. She had her hair quartered and twisted into the big plaits that made my dad grin. When I was a kid, Mum used to relax her hair every six weeks like clockwork. In fact, every weekend saw someone – an aunt, a cousin, a girl from down the road – sitting in the living room and chemically burning her hair straight. If

I hadn't got off with Maggie Porter – whose dad was a dread and whose mum sold car insurance – who wore her hair in locks, at the Year Ten disco, I might have reached adulthood thinking that a black girl's hair naturally smelled of potassium hydroxide. Now personally, I'm like my dad – I fancy it au naturel, or in braids, but the first rule about a black woman's hair is you don't talk about a black woman's hair. And the second rule is you don't *ever* touch a black woman's hair without getting written permission first. And that includes after sex, marriage or death, for that matter. Of course, this courtesy is not reciprocated.

'You need a haircut,' said Mum. And by haircut she meant, of course, shaved short enough for me to get a suntan. I promised her that I'd take care of it, and she stalked into the kitchen to make dinner.

'I was a war baby,' said Dad. 'Your nan was evacuated before she had me, and that's why my birth certificate says Cardiff. Luckily for you she unevacuated us back to Stepney before the end of the war.' Or we might have been Welsh – in my dad's eyes a fate worse than being Scottish.

He said that growing up in London in the late 1940s, it was like the war was still going on in people's heads, what with the bomb sites, the rationing and the patronising voices of the BBC Home Service. 'Minus the high explosives, of course,' said Dad. 'In them days people still talked about Bowlly getting blown up on Jermyn Street, or Glenn Miller's plane going missing in forty-four,' said Dad. 'Did you know he was a proper American Air Force major? To this day he's still listed as Missing in Action.'

But to be young and talented in the 1950s was to live on the cusp of change. 'First time I heard "Body and Soul" was at the Flamingo Club,' Dad said. 'It was being played by Ronnie Scott, just when he was becoming Ronnie Scott.' The Flamingo Club in the late 1950s was a magnet for black airmen down from Lakenheath and the other US bases.

'They wanted our women,' said Dad, 'and we wanted their records. They always had the latest stuff. It was a match made in heaven.'

Mum came in with dinner. We were always a two-pot family, one for Mum and a considerably less spicy pot for Dad. He also likes slices of white bread and marg rather than rice, which would be just asking for heart trouble if he wasn't as skinny as a rake to start with. I was a two-pot child, both rice and white bread, which explains my chiselled good looks and manly physique.

Mum's pot was cassava leaf, while Dad had lamb casserole. I opted for the lamb that evening because I've never liked cassava leaf, especially when Mum drowns it in palm oil. She uses so much pepper that her soup turns red, and I swear it's only a matter of time before one of her dinner guests spontaneously combusts. We ate off the big glass coffee table in the middle of the living room, with a plastic bottle of Highland Spring at its centre. There were pink paper napkins and breadsticks in cellophane wrappers that Mum had swiped from her latest cleaning job. I marged up some bread for Dad.

As we ate, I caught my mum looking at me. 'What?' I asked.

'Why can't you play like your father?' she asked.

'Because I can sing like my mother,' I said. 'But fortunately I cook like Jamie Oliver.'

She gave me a smack on the leg. 'You're not so big I can't beat you,' she said.

'Yeah, but I'm so much faster than I used to be,' I said.

I actually don't remember the last time I sat down with Mum and Dad for a meal, at least not without half a dozen relatives present. I'm not even sure it happened that much when I was a kid. There was always an aunty, an uncle or an evil Lego-stealing younger cousin – not that I'm bitter – in the house.

When I brought this up, Mum pointed out that said Lego-stealing cousin had just commenced an engineering degree at Sussex. Good, I thought, she can jack somebody else's Lego. I pointed out that I was almost officially a full Constable now, and working for a hush-hush branch of the Metropolitan Police.

'What do you do there?' she asked.

'It's secret, Mum,' I said. 'If I tell you, I'll have to kill you.'

'He does magic,' said my dad.

'You shouldn't keep secrets from your mum,' she said.

'You don't believe in magic, do you, Mum?'

'You shouldn't make jokes about these things,' she said. 'Science doesn't have all the answers, you know.'

'It's got all the best questions, though,' I said.

'You are not doing these witchcraft things, are you?' Suddenly she was serious. 'I worry about you enough as it is.'

'I promise I am not consorting with any evil spirits, or any other kind of supernatural entity,' I said. Not least because the supernatural creature I'd have most liked to consort with was currently living in exile up the river at the court of Father Thames. It was one of those tragic relationships: I'm a junior policeman, she's the goddess of a suburban river in south London – it was never going to work out.

Once we were finished, I volunteered for the washing-up. While I was using half a bottle of Sainsbury's own-brand washing-up liquid to scrub off the palm oil, I could hear my parents talking in the next room. The TV was still off, and my mum hadn't spoken to anyone on the phone for over three hours – it was beginning to get a little bit *Fringe*. When I finished, I stepped out to find them sitting side by side on the sofa, holding hands. I asked if they wanted more tea, but they said no, and gave me strange, identical, slightly

51

distant smiles. I realised with a start that were dying for me to leave so that they could go to bed. I quickly grabbed my coat, kissed my mum goodbye and practically ran out of the house. There are some things a young man does not want to think about.

I was in the lift when I got a call from Dr Walid.

'Have you seen my email yet?' he asked.

I told him I'd been at my mum's house.

'I've been collating mortality statistics for jazz musicians in the London area,' he said. 'You'll want to have a look as soon as you can – phone me tomorrow once you've done that.'

'Is there something I should know now?'

The lift doors opened and I stepped out into the tiled lobby. The evening was warm enough to allow a couple of kids to loiter by the main doors. One of them tried to give me the eye, but I gave it right back and he looked away. Like I said, it's my manor. And besides, I used to be that boy.

'From the figures I have, I believe that two to three jazz musicians have died within twenty-four hours of playing a gig in the Greater London Area in the last year.'

'I take it that's statistically significant?'

'It's all in the email,' said Dr Walid.

We hung up just as I reached the Asbo.

To the tech cave, I thought.

The Folly, according to Nightingale, is secured by an interlocking series of magical protections. They were last renewed in 1940, to allow the Post Office to run in a then cutting-edge coaxial telephone cable to the main building, and the installation of a modern switchboard. I'd found that under a dust sheet in an alcove off the main entrance lobby, a beautiful glass and mahogany cabinet with brass fittings kept shiny by Molly's obsessive need to polish.

Nightingale says that these protections are vital, although he won't say why, and that he, acting on his own, is not capable of renewing them. Running a broadband cable into the building was out of the question, and it looked for a while like I was going to be firmly mired in the dark ages.

Fortunately, the Folly had been built in the Regency style, when it had become fashionable to build a separate mews at the back of a grand house, so that the horses and the smellier servants could be housed downwind of their masters. This meant a coach house at the back, now used as a garage, and above that an attic conversion that had once accommodated servants and then served as a party space for the young bucks, back when the Folly had young bucks. Or at least, more than one. The magical 'protections' – Nightingale was not happy when I called them 'forcefields' – used to scare the horses, so they don't extend to the coach house. Which means I get to run in a broadband cable, and at last there is a corner of the Folly that is for ever in the twenty-first century.

The coach-house attic has a studio skylight at

one end, an ottoman couch, a chaise longue, a plasma TV and an Ikea kitchen table that once took me and Molly three bloody hours to assemble. I'd used the Folly's status as an Operational Command Unit to get the Directorate of Information to cough up half a dozen Airwave handsets with charging rack, and a dedicated HOLMES2 terminal. I also had my laptop and my back-up laptop and my PlayStation – which I hadn't had a chance to get out of the box yet. Because of this, there is a big sign on the front door that says NO MAGIC ON PAIN OF PAIN. This is what I call the tech cave.

The first thing I got when I booted up was an email from Lesley with the header *Bored!*, so I sent her Dr Walid's autopsy report to keep her occupied. Then I opened up PNC Xpress and ran a DVLA check on Melinda Abbot's car Index, and found that the listed information matched that on her driving licence. I ran Simone Fitzwilliam as well, but evidently she'd never applied for a licence, or owned a car. Nor had she committed, been the victim of, or reported a crime within the United Kingdom. Or possibly all that information had been lost, inaccurately entered into the databases, or she'd just changed her name recently. Information technology only gets you so far, which is why coppers still go round knocking on doors and writing things down in little black notebooks. I googled them both for good measure. Melinda Abbot had a

Facebook page, as did a couple of people with the same name, but Simone Fitzwilliam had no obvious internet presence at all.

I worked my way through Dr Walid's list of dead jazz musicians – all men, I noticed – in much the same way. They're always doing clever cross-referencing stuff on the TV, and it's all perfectly possible, but what they never show is how sodding long it takes. It was pushing midnight by the time I got to the end of the list, and I still wasn't sure what I was looking at.

I took a Red Stripe from the fridge, opened the can and had a swig.

Definite fact number one: each year for the last five, two or three jazz musicians had died within 24 hours of playing at a gig in the Greater London Area. In each case, the coroner had ruled the deaths either 'accidental' by way of substance abuse, or 'natural causes' – mostly heart attacks, with a couple of aneurysms thrown in for a bit of variety.

Dr Walid had included a supplemental file listing every musician – defined as those who listed their profession as musician – between the ages of eighteen and fifty-four who'd died over the same period. Definite fact number two: while other London musicians dropped dead from 'natural causes' with depressing frequency, they didn't seem to die regularly just after gigs the way the jazzmen did.

Definite fact number three: Cyrus Wilkinson

55

hadn't even listed his occupation as musician, but as an accountant. You never claim to be a freelance or artistic anything, unless you want a personal credit rating lower than an Irish bank's. Which led to definite fact number four: my statistical analysis was pretty much worthless.

And yet, three jazz musicians a year – I didn't believe it was a coincidence.

But Nightingale wasn't going to go for anything that flimsy. And he was still going to expect me to perfect *Scindere*, starting the next morning. I shut everything down and turned it all off at the plugs. That's good for the environment, and, more importantly, stops all my expensive gear getting randomly fried by a surge in magic.

I let myself in through the kitchen. The waning moon lit the atrium through the skylight, so I left the lights off as I climbed the stairs to my floor. On the balcony opposite I glimpsed a pale figure silently gliding amongst the muffled shadows of the west reading room. It was just Molly, restlessly doing whatever it is she restlessly does at night. When I reached my landing, the musty carpet smell told me that Toby had once again fallen asleep against my door. The little dog lay on his back, his thin ribs rising and falling under his fur. He snuffled and kicked in his sleep, hind legs pawing the air, indicating at least 500 milliyaps of background magic. I let myself into my bedroom and carefully closed the door so as not to wake him.

I climbed into bed, and before I turned out the side lamp I texted Lesley – WTF DO NOW?

The next morning I got a text back. It read: GO TLK BAND – IDIOT!

CHAPTER 3

A LONG DRINK OF THE BLUES

The band weren't that hard to find – The Spice of Life had their contact details, and they all agreed to meet me at French House on Dean Street, but it had to be in the evening because they all had day jobs. That suited me because I was still behind on my Latin vocab. I trolled over to Soho just after six, and found them all waiting for me, propping up a wall peppered with pictures of people who had been famous just at the time my dad hadn't.

The Spice of Life playbill listed my lot as the Better Quartet, but they didn't really look much like jazzmen to me. Bassists are famously steady, but Max – really Derek – Harwood was an average-looking white guy in his mid-thirties. He was even wearing a diamond-patterned M&S v-neck sweater under his jacket.

'We already had a Derek in the band before last,' said Max. 'So I went by Max to avoid confusion.' He took a subdued sip from his beer. I'd bought the first round, and was feeling suitably gouged. Max was an integrated systems specialist for London Underground – something to do with signalling systems, apparently.

The pianist, Daniel Hossack, was a classically trained music teacher at Westminster School for the terminally privileged. He had receding blond hair, round Trotsky glasses and the sort of sensible kindness that probably led to him being savagely lampooned by the spotty wits of the lower sixth – that's Year 12 in the new money.

'How did you guys meet?' I asked.

'I don't think we met as such,' said James Lochrane – the drummer. He was short, Scottish, belligerent and taught seventeenth-century French History at Queen Mary's College. 'It would be more accurate to say that we coalesced – about two years ago . . .'

'More like three,' said Max. 'At the Selkirk Pub. They have jazz on Sunday afternoons. Cy lives down there, so it's sort of his local.'

Daniel nervously tapped his fingers on his glass. 'We were all watching this terrible band who were making a fist of—' He stared off in the direction of the last decade. 'I can't remember what it was.'

'"Body and Soul"?' I asked.

'No,' said James. 'It was "Saint Thomas".'

'Which they were murdering,' said Daniel. 'And Cy said, loud enough for everyone, including the band, to hear, "I bet any of us could play better than this."'

'Which is not the done thing,' said Max. All three shared sly smiles at the transgression. 'The next thing I knew we were sharing a table, ordering rounds and talking jazz.'

'As I said,' said James. 'We coalesced.'

'Hence our name,' said Daniel. 'The Better Quartet.'

'Were you better?' I asked.

'Not noticeably,' said Max.

'Worse, in fact,' said Daniel.

'We did get better,' said Max, and laughed. 'We practised at Cy's place.'

'Practised a lot,' said Daniel, and drained his glass. 'Right, who wants what?'

They don't do pints at the French House, so James and Max split a bottle of the house red, I asked for a half a bitter – it had been a long day, and there's nothing like Latin declensions to give a man a thirst.

'Two, maybe three times a week,' said Max.

'So you were ambitious?' I asked.

'None of us was that serious really,' said James. 'It's not like we were kids and desperate to make it big.'

'That's still a lot of practice,' I said.

'Oh, we wanted to be better musicians,' said James.

'We're wannabe jazzmen,' said Max. 'You play the music to play the music, know what I mean?'

I nodded.

'Do you think he's gone across the river for those drinks?' asked James.

We craned our neck and looked over at the bar. Daniel was bobbing amid the crush, his hand raised with an optimistic twenty slipped between his fingers. On Friday night in Soho, going across the river might have been quicker.

'How serious was Cyrus?' I asked.

'He wasn't any more serious than we were,' said James.

'He was good, though,' said Max, and made fingering motions. 'He had that whole sax-player thing going.'

'Hence the women,' said James.

Max sighed.

'Melinda Abbot?' I asked.

'Oh, Melinda,' said Max.

'Melinda was just the one at home,' said James.

'Sally, Viv, Tolene,' said Max.

'Daria,' said James. 'Remember Daria?'

'Like I said,' said Max. 'The whole saxophone vibe.'

I spotted Daniel struggling back with the drinks, and got up to help him ferry them to the table. He gave me an appraising look, and I guessed that he didn't share Max and James's envy for the women. I gave him a politically correct grin and plonked the drinks down on the table. Max and James said cheers, and we all clinked glasses.

They'd obviously forgotten that I was a policeman, which was handy, so I phrased my next question with considerable care. 'So Melinda didn't mind?'

'Oh, Melinda minded, all right,' said James. 'But it didn't help that she never came to any of the gigs.'

'She wasn't a fan,' said Daniel.

'You know how it is with women,' said James. 'They don't like you to be doing anything they can't relate back to themselves.'

'She was into that New Age stuff, crystals and homeopathy,' said Max.

'She was always nice enough to us,' said Daniel. 'Made us coffee when we were rehearsing.'

'And biscuits,' said Max nostalgically.

'None of the others girls were serious,' said James. 'I'm not even sure there was ever any hanky-panky, as such. At least, not until Simone, anyway. Trouble with a capital T.'

Simone had been the first woman to come back to Cyrus's house to watch the rehearsals.

'She was so quiet that after a while you forgot she was there,' said Daniel.

Melinda Abbot didn't forget Simone Fitzwilliam was there, and I didn't blame her. I tried to imagine what would have happened had my dad brought a woman home to watch him rehearse. It wouldn't have ended well, I can tell you that. Tears would have been just the start of it.

Melinda, who obviously subscribed to notions of gentility unknown to my mother, did at least wait until everyone had left the house before meta-phorically rolling up her sleeves and reaching for the rolling pin.

'After that, we were in a lock-up that Max blagged off Transport for London,' said James. 'It was draughty but a lot more relaxed.'

'Though terribly cold,' said Daniel.

'Then suddenly we're all back at Cy's place,' said James. 'Only it's not Melinda serving the coffee and biscuits any more, it's the gorgeous Simone.'

'When did this happen?'

'April, May, around that time,' said Max. 'Spring.'

'How did Melinda take it?' I asked.

'We don't know,' said James. 'We never saw that much of her, even when she was around.'

'I met her a couple of times,' said Daniel.

The others stared at him. 'You never said,' said James.

'She called me, said she wanted to talk – she was upset.'

'What did she say?' asked Max.

'I don't like to say,' said Daniel. 'It was private.'

And so it stayed. I managed to steer the conversation back round to Melinda Abbot's mystical hobbies, but the band hadn't really been paying attention. The French House began to get seriously crowded, and despite the prohibition on piped music I was having to shout to make myself heard. I suggested food.

'Is the Met going to be picking up the bill?' asked James.

'I think we could stretch to some expenses,' I said, 'as long as we don't go mad.'

The band all nodded their heads. Of course they did; when you're a musician, free is a magic number.

We ended up in Wong Kei on Wardour Street, where the food is reliable, the service is brusque and you can get a table at eleven thirty on a Friday night – if you don't mind sharing. I showed five fingers to the guy at the door and he waved us upstairs, where a stern-looking young woman in a red t-shirt directed us to one of the big round tables.

A pair of pale American students, who up till then had had the table to themselves, visibly cowered as we plonked ourselves down.

'Good evening,' said Daniel. 'Don't worry, we're perfectly harmless.'

Both American students were wearing neat red Adidas sweatshirts with MNU PIONEERS embroidered across the chest. They nodded their heads nervously. 'Hi,' one of them said. 'We're from Kansas.'

We waited politely for them to elaborate, but neither said another word to us for the ten minutes it took to finish their food, pay and bolt for the door.

'What's an MNU, anyway?' asked Max.

'Now he asks,' said James.

The waitress arrived and started slapping down the main course. I had shredded duck with fried ho fun, Daniel and Max split egg fried rice, chicken with cashews and sweet and sour pork, James had beef noodles. The band ordered another round of Tsingtao beers, but I stuck to the free green tea which came in a simple white ceramic teapot.

I asked the band whether they played The Spice of Life often, which made them laugh.

'We've played there a couple of times,' said Max. 'Usually the lunch spot on Monday.'

'Get much of a crowd?' I asked.

'We were getting there,' said James. 'We had gigs at the Bull's Head, the National Theatre foyer and Merlin's Cave in Chalfont St Giles.'

'Last Friday was the first evening slot we'd scored,' said Max.

'So what was next?' I asked. 'Record deal?'

'Cyrus would have left,' said Daniel.

Everybody stared at him for a moment.

'Come on guys, you know that's what would have happened,' said Daniel. 'We'd have done a few more gigs, somebody would have spotted him and it would be, "It's been fun, guys, let's not lose touch".'

'Was he that good?' I asked.

James scowled down at his noodles, then stabbed them a few times with his chopsticks in frustration. Then he chuckled. 'He was that good,' he said. 'And getting better.'

James raised his bottle of beer. 'To Cyrus the Sax,' he said. 'Because talent will out.'

We clinked our glasses.

'You know,' said James. 'Once we're done here, let's go find some jazz.'

Soho on a warm summer night is alive with conversation and tobacco smoke. Every pub spills out into the street, every café has its customers outside at tables perched on pavements that were originally built just wide enough to keep pedestrians out of the horse shit. On Old Compton Street, fit young men in tight white t-shirts and sprayed-on jeans admired each other and their reflections in the shop windows. I caught Daniel pinging his radar at a couple of tasty young men checking themselves out outside the Admiral Duncan, but they just ignored him. It was Friday night, and after all that gym time they weren't getting into bed for anything less than a ten.

A tangle of young women with regulation-length hair, desert tans and regional accents slid past – female squaddies heading for Chinatown and the clubs around Leicester Square.

Me and the band didn't so much proceed up Old Compton Street as ricochet from one clique to the next. James nearly tripped over as a pair of white girls ticked past in stilettos and pink knit miniskirt dresses. 'Fuck me,' he said as he recovered.

'Not going to happen,' said one of the girls as they walked away. But there was no malice in it.

James said he knew a place on Bateman Street, a little basement club in the grand tradition of the legendary Flamingo. 'Or Ronnie Scott's,' he said. 'Before it was Ronnie Scott's.'

It wasn't that long since I'd been patrolling these streets in uniform, and I had a horrible feeling I knew where he was going. My dad's been known to wax lyrical about a youth misspent in smoky basement bars full of sweat, music and girls in

66

tight jumpers. He said that in the Flamingo, you basically had to pick a spot you were prepared to spend the night in, because once things kicked off it was impossible to move. The Mysterioso had been designed as a deliberate recreation of those days by a pair of likely lads who would have been the quintessential cheeky Cockney barrow-boy entrepreneurs, if they hadn't both been from Guildford. Their names were Don Blackwood and Stanley Gibbs, but they called themselves The Management. It had been a rare weekend shift when me and Lesley didn't end up on a shout to the street outside.

The trouble was never inside the club, though, because The Management hired the roughest bouncers they could find, strapped them into sharp suits and gave them carte blanche on the door entry policy. They were famously arbitrary in their exercise of power, and even at eleven forty-five there was a queue of hopefuls down the street.

There's always been a tradition of po-faced seriousness about the British jazz scene, and a kind of chin-stroking 'yes, I see' roll-neck-jumperness to the fans – my current company being a case in point. Judging from the punters in the queue, that old tradition was not The Management's target demographic. This was Armani-suit, dress-to-impress, bling-wearing, switchblade-carrying jazz, and I didn't think it likely that me and the band were going to make the cut.

Well, definitely not the band, anyway. And, to

be honest, that suited me because whereas the band had grown on me, a night of semi-professional jazz has never been my idea of a good time. If it had been, my dad would have been a happier man.

Still, James, in the grand tradition of belligerent Scotsmen down the ages, was not prepared to give up without a struggle, so ignoring the queue he went immediately on the offensive.

'We're jazzmen,' he said to the bouncer. 'That's got to count for something.'

The bouncer, a side of meat that I knew for a fact had done time in Wandsworth for various crimes that started with the word 'aggravated', at least gave this some serious consideration. 'I've never heard of you,' he said.

'Maybe, maybe,' said James. 'But we are all part of the same community of spirit – yes? The same brotherhood of music.' Behind his back, Daniel and Max exchanged looks and shuffled back half a metre.

I stepped forward to head off the inevitable violence, and as I did I caught a flash of 'Body and Soul'. The *vestigia* was subtle, but against the Soho ambience it stood out like a cool breeze on a hot night. And it was definitely coming from the club.

'Are you his friend?' asked the bouncer.

I could have shown my warrant card, but once that's out in the open all the useful witnesses have a tendency to melt away into the darkness and develop impressively detailed alibis.

'Go and tell Stan and Don that Lord Grant's son is waiting outside,' I said.

The bouncer scrutinised my face. 'Do I know you?' he asked.

No, I thought, but you might remember me from such Saturday-night hits as 'would you please put that punter down, I'd like to arrest him', and 'you can stop kicking him now, the ambulance has arrived', and the classic 'if you don't back off right now I'm going to nick you as well'.

'Lord Grant's son,' I repeated.

I heard James whisper behind me, 'What the fuck did he say?'

When my dad was twelve, his music teacher gave him a secondhand trumpet and paid, out of his own pocket, for Dad to have lessons. By the time he was fifteen he'd left school, got himself a job as a delivery boy in Soho and was spending his spare time hungrily looking for gigs. When he was eighteen, Ray Charles heard him playing at the Flamingo and said – loud enough for anyone who was important enough to hear – 'Lord, but that boy can play.' Tubby Hayes called my dad Lord Grant as a joke, and the nickname stuck from then on.

The bouncer tapped his Bluetooth and asked to speak to Stan and told him what I'd said. When he got a reply, I was impressed by the way his expression didn't change as he stepped aside and ushered us in.

'You never said your dad was Lord Grant,' said James.

'It's not the sort of thing you just drop into a conversation, is it?'

'I don't know,' said James. 'If my dad was a jazz legend I think I'd at least bring it up just a wee bit.'

'We're not worthy,' said Max as we descended into the club.

'You remember that,' I said.

If The Spice of Life was old wood and polished brass, The Mysterioso was cement floors and the kind of flock wallpaper that curry houses stripped off their walls in the late 1990s. As advertised, it was dark, crowded and surprisingly smoky. In its quest for authenticity, The Management was obviously turning a blind eye to the smoking of tobacco contrary to the provisions of the Health Act (2006). Not just tobacco, either, judging by the fruity tang drifting over the bobbing heads of the punters. My dad would have loved this place, even though the acoustics were rubbish. All it needed was an animatronic Charlie Parker shooting up in the corner, and it would be a perfect theme-park recreation.

James and the boys, in the grand tradition of musicians everywhere, headed straight for the bar. I let them go and moved closer to the band who, according to the front of the bass drum, were called the Funk Mechanics. True to their name, they were playing jazz funk on a stage that was barely raised above the floor. It was two white guys with a black guy on bass and a red-headed drummer with half a kilo of silver attached to various parts of her face. As I worked my way towards the stage, I realised that they were doing a funked-up version of 'Get Out of Town', but they'd given it a completely spurious Latin rhythm that pissed me off. Which struck me as strange, even then.

There were booths, upholstered in tatty red velvet, lining the walls, and people stared out onto the dance floor. Bottles crowded the tables and faces, mostly pale, nodded in time to the Funk Mechanics' butchering of a classic. There was a white couple snogging in a booth at the end. The man's hand was shoved down the front of the woman's dress, the outline of his fingers squeezing obscenely through the material. The sight made me feel sick and outraged, and that's when I realised that these emotions had nothing to do with me.

I've seen much worse in my travels, and I quite like jazz funk. I must have just walked through a *lacuna*, a hotspot of residue magic. I'd been right: something was going down.

Lesley always complained that I was too easily distracted to be a good copper, but then she would have walked right through the *lacuna* without giving it a second thought.

James and the band pushed through the crowd to surprise me with a bottle of beer. I took a swig and it was good. I checked the label and saw it was an expensive bottle of Schneider-Weisse. I looked over at the band, who held up their own bottles.

'It was on the house,' shouted Max, a bit excitedly.

I could feel James wanting to talk about my dad, but fortunately it was too loud and crowded for him to start.

'So this is the modern style,' shouted Daniel.

'So I've heard,' shouted James.

And then I had it, the *vestigia* cool and distant amongst the heat of the dancing bodies. I realised that it was different from the residue of magic that had clung to Cyrus Wilkinson. This was fresher, crisper, and behind the solo there was a woman's voice singing – *My heart is sad and lonely*. Again, the smell of dust and burned and broken wood.

And something else – the *vestigia* that clung to Cyrus had manifested itself like a saxophone, but what I was getting now was definitely a trombone. My dad was always sniffy about the 'bone. He said that it was all right in a brass section, but you could count the number of decent trombone soloists on the fingers of one foot. It's a difficult instrument to take seriously, but even my dad admitted that a man who could solo on a slide trombone had to be something special. Then he'd talk about Kai Winding, or J. J. Johnson. But the guys on stage were trumpet, electric bass and drums – no trombone.

I had a horrible feeling I'd turned up two coupons short of the pop-up toaster.

I let the *vestigia* lead me through the crowd. There was a door to the left of the stage half hidden behind the speaker stacks with STAFF ONLY crookedly stencilled on it, yellow paint on black. It wasn't until I reached the door that I realised that the band had followed me over like lost sheep. I told them to stay outside – so of course, they followed me in.

The door opened straight into the green room/changing room/storage area, a long narrow space that looked to me like a converted coal bunker. The walls were plastered with ancient yellowing posters for bands and gigs. An old-fashioned theatrical dressing table with a horseshoe of bare bulbs was sandwiched between an American-sized fridge and a trestle table covered in a disposable tablecloth in Christmas green and red. A forest of beer bottles covered a coffee table, and a white woman in her early twenties was asleep on one of the two green leather sofas that filled the rest of the room.

'So this is how the other half lives,' said Daniel.

'Makes all those years of rehearsing seem almost worthwhile,' said Max.

The woman on the sofa sat up and stared at us. She was wearing dungarees that were loose to the waist and a yellow t-shirt with I SAID NO SO FUCK OFF printed across the chest.

'Can I help you?' she said. She was wearing dark purple lipstick that had got smeared across one cheek.

'I'm looking for the band,' I said.

73

'Aren't we all,' she said, and held out her hand. 'My name's Peggy.'

'The band?' I asked, ignoring her hand.

Peggy sighed and rolled the kinks out of her shoulders, which pushed out her chest and got everyone's attention – except for Daniel's, of course. 'Aren't they on stage?' she asked.

'The band before them,' I said.

'They've gone,' said Peggy. 'Oh, that bitch, she said she'd wake me up after the set. This really is too much.'

'What's the name of the band?' I asked.

Peggy rolled off the sofa and started looking for her shoes. 'Honestly,' she said. 'I don't remember. They were Cherry's band.'

'Did they have a trombone player?' I asked. 'A good one?'

Max found her shoes behind the other sofa. They were four-inch stilettos, open-toed strap sandals which I didn't really think went with the dungarees. 'I'll say so,' she said. 'That'll be Mickey. He's one in a million.'

'Do you know where they were going after the gig?'

'Sorry,' she said. 'I was just going with the groove.' In her heels she was almost as tall as I was. The dungarees gaped at the sides to reveal a strip of pale skin and a frilly line of scarlet silk knickers. I turned away – I'd lost the *vestigia* when I entered the room, and Peggy wasn't helping my concentration. I got flashes of other stuff, the smell of lavender, of a car bonnet left out in the sun and a ringing sound like the silence that comes after a loud noise.

'Who are you?' asked Peggy.

'We're the jazz police,' said James.

'He's the jazz police,' said Max, meaning me, I suppose. 'We're more like the Old Compton Street irregulars.'

That made me laugh, which shows how drunk I'd got.

'Is Mickey in trouble?' asked Peggy.

'Only if he's been dripping his spit valve on someone's shoulder,' said Max.

I didn't have any more time for banter. There was a second door in the room, marked as a fire exit, so I headed for that. On the other side there was another short, bare grey-brick corridor half blocked with stacked furniture, crates and black plastic bags in spectacular contravention of Health and Safety regulations. Another fire door, this one with push bars, led to a staircase up to street level. The push bars on the door at the top of the stairs were illegally fastened with a bicycle lock.

Nightingale has this spell which can just pop a lock right out of its socket, but apparently I'm at least a year away from learning it. I had to improvise. I stopped a safe distance away and dropped one of my unsuccessful light bombs on the lock. What they lack in finesse they make up for in ferocity. I had to take a step back because of the heat and, squinting, I could see the lock sag within the little rippling globe. When I figured the lock was good and soft, I let go of the spell and the globe popped like a soap bubble. Then I made a nice basic *Impello forma* in my mind. It was the second *forma* I ever learned, so it's something I know I'm good at. *Impello* moves things about, in this case the centre line of the double doors. It smacked the doors open, breaking the lock and slamming them hard enough to knock one off its hinges.

It was impressive stuff, even if I say so myself. And certainly the irregulars, who'd come up the stairs behind me, thought so.

'What the fuck was that?' asked James.

'Thermite chewing gum,' I said hopefully.

The fire alarm in the club went off – it was time to move on. Me and the irregulars did the fifty-metre nonchalant stroll round the corner onto Frith Street in Olympic qualifying time. It was late enough by then for the tourists to have gone back to their hotels, and the streets were noisy with lads and ladettes.

James got in front of me and made me stop walking.

'This has something to do with Cy's death, doesn't it?'

I was too knackered to argue. 'Maybe,' I said. 'I don't know.'

'Did someone do something to Cyrus?' he asked.

'I don't know,' I said. 'If you'd just finished a gig, where would you go?'

James looked confused. 'What?'

'Help me out, James. I'm trying to find this trombone player – where would you go?'

'The Potemkin has a late licence,' said Max.

That made sense. You could get food there, and more importantly alcohol, up until five o'clock in the morning. I headed down Frith Street with the irregulars in tow. They wanted to know what was going on – and so did I. James in particular was proving dangerously canny.

'Are you worried the same thing is going to happen to this trombone player?' he asked.

'Maybe,' I said. 'I don't know.'

We turned into Old Compton Street, and as soon as I saw the flashing blue light on the ambulance I knew I was too late. It was parked outside GAY, the back doors were open and, judging by the leisurely way the paramedics were moving about, either the victim was unharmed or very dead. I wasn't betting on unharmed. A desultory crowd of onlookers had gathered under the wary eye of a couple of PCSOs and a PC I recognised from my time at Charing Cross nick.

'Purdy,' I shouted, and he looked over. 'What's the griff?'

Purdy lumbered over. When you're wearing a stab vest, an equipment belt, extendable baton, nipple-shaped helmet, shoulder harness, Airwave radio, cuffs, pepper spray, notebook and emergency Mars Bar, lumber is what you do. Phillip Purdy had a bit of a reputation as a 'uniform-carrier':

that's a copper who's not good for anything but wearing the uniform. But that was all to the good – I didn't want effective. Effective coppers ask too many questions.

'Ambulance pick-up,' said Purdy. 'Guy just dropped dead in the middle of the street.'

'Let's have a look?' I made it a question. It pays to be polite.

'Are you working?'

'I don't know until I have a look,' I said.

Purdy grunted and let me past.

The paramedics were just lifting the victim onto their trolley. He was younger than me, dark-skinned and African-featured – Nigerian or Ghanaian if I had to guess, or more likely had a parent from one of those places. He was dressed smart: khaki chinos, custom-made suit jacket. The paramedics had ripped open an expensive-looking white cotton shirt in order to use the defibrillator. His eyes were open, dark brown and empty. I didn't need to get any closer. If he'd been playing 'Body and Soul' any louder I could have roped off the street and sold tickets.

I asked the paramedics for a cause of death, but they shrugged and said heart failure.

'Is he dead?' I heard Max say behind me.

'No, he's just having a wee lie down,' said James.

I asked Purdy if he had any identification, and he held up a Ziploc bag with a wallet in it. 'This your shout?' he asked.

I nodded, took the bag and signed the paperwork

carefully to ensure the chain of custody against any future legal proceedings, before stuffing the whole lot in my trouser pocket.

'Was there anyone with him?'

Purdy shook his head. 'Nobody that I saw.'

'Who made the 999 call?'

'Dunno,' said Purdy. 'Mobile, probably.'

It's officers like Purdy that give the Metropolitan Police its sterling reputation for customer service that makes us the envy of the civilised world.

As they loaded the trolley into the ambulance, I heard Max being noisily sick.

Purdy eyed Max with the particular interest of a copper who's facing a long Saturday-night shift, and who could easily make dropping a drunk-and-disorderly off at the cells last at least a couple of hours. Paperwork to be done in the canteen with a cup of tea and a sandwich – curse this bureaucratic red tape that keeps good police officers away from the front lines where the action is! I disappointed Purdy by saying I'd take care of it.

The paramedics said they wanted to be off, but I told them to wait. I didn't want to risk the body going astray before Dr Walid had a chance to look at it, but I needed to know whether this guy had been playing at The Mysterioso. Of the irregulars, Daniel looked the most upright.

'Daniel,' I asked, 'are you sober?'

'Yes,' he said. 'And getting soberer with every passing second.'

'I've got to go with the ambulance. Can you nip

back to the club and get a copy of the playlist?' I gave him my card. 'Call me on the mobile when you've got it.'

'You think the same thing happened to him?' he said. 'As Cyrus, I mean.'

'I don't know,' I said. 'As soon as I know something I'll call you guys.'

The paramedics called over. 'You coming, or what?'

'You all right with this?'

Daniel gave me a grin. 'Jazzman, remember,' he said. I held up my fist, and after a moment of incomprehension, Daniel knocked knuckles with me.

I climbed into the ambulance and the paramedic pulled the door closed behind us.

'Are we going to UCH?' I asked.

'That's the general idea,' he said.

We didn't bother with the blues and twos.

You can't just deposit a body at the morgue. For a start, it has to be certified by a bona fide doctor. It doesn't matter how many bits the body is in; until your actual fully accredited member of the BMA says it's dead, it occupies, bureaucratically speaking, an indeterminate state just like an electron, an atomic cat-in-a-box, and my authority to conduct what was tantamount to a murder investigation on my own recognisance.

Early Sunday morning in Casualty is always a joy, what with the blood and the screaming and the recriminations as the booze wears off and the pain kicks in. Any police officer who's feeling public-spirited enough to show his face can get himself involved in half a dozen exciting altercations, often involving Ken and his best mate Ron, and *it weren't like we were doing anything, officer, honest, it was, like, totally unprovoked.* So I stayed in the treatment cubicle with my nice quiet dead body, thank you very much. I borrowed a pair of surgical gloves from a box in a drawer and went through his wallet.

Mickey the Bone's full name was, according to his driving licence, Michael Adjayi. So a Nigerian family, then, and according to his date of birth, Michael had just turned nineteen.

Your mum's going to be really pissed with you, I thought sadly.

He had a slew of cards: VISA, Mastercard, bank card and one for the Musicians Union. There were a couple of business cards, including one from an agent – I jotted the details down in my notebook. Then I carefully returned everything to the evidence bag.

It wasn't until a quarter to three that a junior doctor turned up and finally pronounced Michael Adjayi definitively dead. It took another two hours, once I'd declared the body a crime scene, to get the doctor's particulars, obtain copies of the relevant documentation, the paramedic's and the doctor's notes, and get the body downstairs and safely into the mortuary, there to await Dr

Walid's tender ministrations. That just left me with the joyous last part, the bit where I contact the victim's loved ones and break the news to them. These days the easiest way to do that is to grab someone's mobile and see what comes up on the call log. Predictably, Mickey had had an iPhone. I found it in his jacket pocket, but the screen was blank and I didn't need to open it up to know that the chip would be trashed. I put it in a second evidence bag, but I didn't bother labelling it – it would be going back to the Folly with me. Once I was sure that nobody was going to interfere with the body, I called Dr Walid. I didn't see any reason to wake him, so I rang his office number and left a message for him to pick up in the morning.

If Mickey really was a second victim, then it meant that the magic jazzman killer – and I was going to have to think of a better name for him than that – had struck less than four days apart.

I wondered if there'd been a similar cluster amongst Dr Walid's lists of deaths. I'd have to check when I got back to the tech cave at the Folly. I was just debating whether to go home or fall asleep in the mortuary staff room, when my phone rang. I didn't recognise the number.

'Hello,' I said.

This is Stephanopoulos,' said Detective Sergeant Stephanopoulos. 'Your particular services are required.'

'Where?'

82

'Dean Street,' she said. Soho again. Of course, why not?

'Can I ask what the case is?'

'Murder most horrid,' she said. 'Bring a spare pair of shoes.'

Past a certain point, black coffee only gets you so far, and if hadn't been for the nasty smell of the air freshener my surly Latvian driver used, I might have fallen asleep in the back of his minicab.

Dean Street was sealed off, from the corner with Old Compton Street to where it met Meard Street. I counted at least two unmarked Sprinter vans and a bevy of silver Vauxhall Astras, which is a sure sign that a Major Investigation Team is on the scene.

A DC I recognised from the Belgravia Murder Team was waiting for me at the tape. A short way up Dean Street a forensics tent had been pitched over the entrance of the Groucho Club – it looked as inviting as something from a biological warfare exercise.

Stephanopoulos was waiting for me inside. She was a short, terrifying woman whose legendary capacity for revenge had earned her the title of the lesbian officer least likely to have a flippant remark made about her sexual orientation. She was stocky, and had a square face that wasn't helped by a Sheena Easton flat-top that you might have called ironic postmodern dyke chic, but only if you really craved suffering.

She was already wearing her blue disposable

forensic overalls, and a facemask hung around her neck. Someone had liberated a pair of folding chairs from somewhere and laid out a forensic suit for me. We call them Noddy suits, and you sweat like anything when you wear them. I noticed there were smears of blood around Stephanopoulos's ankles on the plastic bag thingies that you cover your shoes with.

'How's your governor?' asked DS Stephanopoulos as I sat and started pulling on the suit.

'Fine,' I said. 'Yours?'

'Fine,' she said. 'He's back on duty next month.' Stephanopoulos knew the truth about the Folly. A surprisingly large number of senior police officers did; it just wasn't the sort of thing you talked about in polite conversation.

'Are you SIO on this, ma'am?' I asked. The Senior Investigating Officer on a serious crime was usually at the very least a detective inspector, not a sergeant.

'Of course not,' said Stephanopoulos. 'We have a DCI on loan from Havering CID, but he's adopted a loose collaborative management approach in which experienced officers undertake a lead role in areas where they have the greatest expertise.'

In other words, he'd locked himself in his office and let Stephanopoulos get on with it.

'It's always gratifying to see senior officers adopting a forward-looking posture in their vertical relationships,' I said, and was rewarded by something that was almost a smile.

'You ready?'

I pulled the hood over my head and tightened the drawstring. Stephanopoulos handed me a face-mask, and I followed her into the club. The lobby had a white tile floor that, despite the obvious care taken, had smears of blood on it trailing through a pair of wooden trellis doors.

'The body's downstairs in the gents',' said Stephanopoulos.

The stairs down to the scene were so narrow that we had to wait for a herd of forensics types to come up before we could go down. There's no such thing as a full-service forensics team. It's very expensive, so you order bits of it up from the Home Office, like a Chinese takeaway. Judging by the number of Noddy suits filing past us, Stephanopoulos had gone for the super-deluxe meal for six with extra egg fried rice. I was, I guessed, the fortune cookie.

Like most toilets in the West End of London, the ones in the Groucho were cramped and low-ceilinged from being retrofitted into the basement of a townhouse. The management had lined them with alternating panels of brushed steel and cherry-red Perspex – it was like a particularly creepy level of *System Shock* 2. This was not helped by the bloody footsteps leading out.

'The cleaner found him,' said Stephanopoulos, which explained the footsteps.

On the left were square porcelain wash basins in front of a line of bog-standard urinals, and tucked away on the right, raised up a couple of steps, was the one and only toilet stall. The door was being held open with a couple of strips of masking tape. I didn't need to be told what was inside.

It's funny how the mind processes a crime scene. For the first few seconds your eye just slides away from the horror and fixes on the mundane. He was a middle-aged white guy, and he was sitting on the loo. His shoulders were slumped and his chin was resting on his chest, making it hard to see his face, but he had brown hair and the start of a bald patch at the crown of his head. He was wearing an expensive but worn tweed jacket that had been half pulled down his shoulders to reveal a rather nice blue and white pinstriped shirt. His trousers and pants were around his ankles, his thighs pale and hairy. His hands hung limply between his legs; I guessed he'd been clutching his groin right up until he'd lost consciousness. His palms were sticky with blood, the cuffs of his jacket and shirt soaked in it. I made myself look at the wound.

'Jesus fucking Christ,' I said.

Blood had poured into the toilet bowl, and I really didn't want to be the poor forensics sod who had to go fishing around in it later. Something had excised the man's penis, right at the root just above his bollocks and, unless I was mistaken, left him clutching what was left until he bled out.

It was horrible, but I doubted that Stephanopoulos

86

had dragged me down here for a crash course in scene-of-crime theory. There had to be something more, so I made myself look at the wound again, and this time I saw the connection. I'm no expert, but judging by the ragged edge of the wound, I didn't think it had been done with a knife.

I stood up, and Stephanopoulos gave me an approving look. Presumably because I hadn't immediately clutched my groin and run whimpering from the crime scene.

'Does this look familiar to you?' she asked.

CHAPTER 4

ONE TENTH OF MY ASHES

The Groucho Club – the name intended to reflect his famous quote – was established around the same time I was born, to cater for the kind of artists and media professionals who could afford to buy in their ironic postmodernism. It generally went under the police radar because however trendily antiestablishment its patrons were, they generally didn't get into it on the street come Friday night. Or at least, not unless there was a chance of it making the papers the next day. Enough rehab-worthy celebrities went there to support a niche ecology of paparazzi on the pavement opposite the entrance. That explained why Stephanopoulos had sealed off the street. I imagined the photographers were as vexed as five-year-olds by now.

'You're thinking of St John Giles?' I asked.

'The MO's pretty distinctive,' said Stephanopoulos.

St John Giles was a putative Saturday-night date rapist whose career was, literally, cut short in a club when a woman, or at least something that looked like a woman, bit his penis off – with her vagina. *Vagina dentata*, it's called, and no medically verified cases have ever been recorded. I know because Dr Walid and I trawled all the way back to the seventeenth century looking for one.

'Did you make any progress with the case?' asked Stephanopoulos.

'No,' I said. 'We have his description, his friend's descriptions and some fuzzy CCTV footage, and that's it.'

'At least we can start with a comparative victimology. I want you to call Belgravia, get the case number and port your nominals to our inquiry,' she said.

A 'nominal' is a person who has come to the attention of the investigation and been entered into the HOLMES major inquiry system. Witness statements, forensic evidence, a detective's notes on an interview, even CCTV footage are all grist for the inquiry's computerised mill. The original system was developed as a direct result of the Byford Inquiry into the Yorkshire Ripper case. The Ripper, Peter Sutcliffe, was interviewed several times before he was caught, by accident, by a routine traffic stop. The police can live with looking corrupt, bullying or tyrannical, but looking stupid is intolerable. It has a tendency to undermine people's faith in the forces of law, and is deleterious to public order. Lacking any convenient scapegoats, the police were forced to professionalise a culture which had, up until then, prided itself on being composed of untalented amateurs. HOLMES was part of that process.

In order for the data to be useful, it had to be input in the right format and checked to make sure any relevant details had been highlighted and indexed. Needless to say, I hadn't done any of this on the St John Giles case yet. I was tempted to explain that I worked for a two-man department, one of whom had only just got the hang of cable TV, but of course Stephanopoulos already knew this.

'Yes, boss,' I said. 'What's this victim's name?'

'This is Jason Dunlop. Club member, freelance journalist. He was booked into one of the bedrooms upstairs. Last seen climbing the wooden steps to Bedfordshire just after twelve, and found here just after three by one of the late-night cleaning staff.'

'What was the time of death?' I asked.

'Between a quarter to one and half-two, give or take your usual margin of error.'

Until the pathologist opened him up, the margin of error could be anything up to an hour each way.

'Is there anything *special* about him?' she asked.

I didn't need to ask what she meant by special. I sighed. I wasn't really that keen to get close again, but I squatted down and used it as an opportunity to have a good look at his face. His face was slack, but his mouth was held closed because of the way his chin rested on his chest. There wasn't any facial expression that I recognised, and I wondered how long he'd sat there clutching his groin before he'd died. At first I thought there were no *vestigia* but then, very faintly, in the hundred-milliyap range, I caught the impression of port wine, treacle, the taste of suet and the smell of candles.

'Well?' she asked.

'Not really,' I said. 'If he was attacked by magic it wasn't directly.'

'I wish you wouldn't call it that,' said Stephanopoulos. 'Couldn't we call it "other means"?'

'If you like, boss,' I said. 'It's possible this attack had nothing to do with "other means".'

'No? A woman with teeth in her fanny? I'd have to say that was pretty "other", wouldn't you?'

Me and Nightingale had discussed this after the first attack. 'It's possible she was wearing a prosthetic, you know, like a set of dentures, only inserted . . . vertically. If a woman did that, don't you think she could . . .' I realised that I was making snapping movements with my hand, and stopped it.

'Well, I couldn't do that,' said Stephanopoulos. 'But thank you, Constable, for that fascinating bit of speculation. It's definitely going to keep me awake at night.'

'Not as badly as the men, boss,' I said, and really wished I hadn't.

Stephanopoulos gave me a strange look. 'You're a cheeky bugger, aren't you?' she said.

'Sorry, boss,' I said.

'Do you know what I like, Grant? A good

Friday-night stabbing, some poor sod getting knifed because he looks funny at some other drunk bastard,' she said. 'It's a motive I can relate to.'

We both stood for a moment and contemplated the hazy, far-off days of yesterday evening.

'You're not officially part of this investigation,' said Stephanopoulos. 'Consider yourself as a consultant only. I'm the acting Senior Investigating Officer, and if I think I need you, I'll give you a shout. Understood?'

'Yes, boss,' I said. 'There are some leads I can follow, "other means" of pursuing the investigation.'

'Fair enough,' said Stephanopoulos. 'But any actions that you generate you're to clear through me first. Any normal leads you feed back through HOLMES, and in return I'll make sure any creepy stuff involves you. Is that clear?'

'Yes, guv,' I said.

'Good boy,' she said. I could tell she'd liked the 'guv'. 'Now fuck off and let's hope I don't have to see you again.'

I walked back up to the forensics tent and stripped off my Noddy suit, but carefully, to make sure I didn't get any blood on my clothes.

Stephanopoulos wanted my involvement to be low-profile. Given that the Covent Garden riots had put forty people in hospital, had seen the arrests of two hundred more, including most of the cast of *Billy Budd*, had put a deputy assistant commissioner in hospital and then on disciplinary suspension and Stephanopoulos's own governor on medical leave after I'd stuck him with a syringe full of elephant tranquilliser (in my defence he had been trying to hang me at the time) – and that was before the Royal Opera House was trashed and the market burned down – low-profile was fine with me.

I arrived back at the Folly to find Nightingale in the breakfast room helping himself to kedgeree from one of the silver salvers that Molly insists on laying out on the buffet table every single morning. I lifted the lids on one of the others to reveal Cumberland sausage and poached eggs. Sometimes when you've been up all night you can substitute a good fry-up for sleep. It worked long enough for me to brief Nightingale on the body in the Groucho Club, although I steered clear of the Cumberland sausage, for some reason. Toby sat on his haunches by the table and gave me the alert stare of a dog who was ready for any meaty comestibles that life might throw him.

When the sadly penis-less St John Giles came to our attention, we'd drafted in a forensic dentist to confirm that teeth had done the damage rather than a knife or a miniature bear trap, or something. The dentist had run up a best-guess reconstruction of the configuration of the teeth. It looked remark-ably like a human mouth, only shallower and with a vertical orientation. In his opinion, the canine and incisors were broadly similar to those in the human mouth, but the premolars and molars

93

were unusually thin and sharp. 'More suggestive of a carnivore than an omnivore,' the dentist had said. He was a nice man and very professional, but I got the distinct impression he thought we were having him on.

This had led to a bizarre debate about the process of human digestion, which wasn't settled until I went out and bought some school biology text books and talked Nightingale through the stomach, the intestines, the small intestines and what they were for. When I asked him whether they had covered this at his old school, he said that they might have but that he hadn't been paying attention. When I asked him what had kept his attention, he said rugby and spells.

'Spells?' I asked. 'Are you saying you went to Hogwarts?'

Which led to me having to explain the Harry Potter books, after which he said that yes, he had been to a school for the sons of certain families with strong magical traditions, but it really hadn't been much like the school in the books. Although he did like the idea of Quidditch, they'd mostly played rugby, and using magic on the playing field was strictly outlawed.

'We did play our own version of squash,' he said, 'using the movement forms; that could get a bit lively.'

The school itself had been requisitioned by the military during World War Two, and by the time it was released back to civilian use in the early

1950s there hadn't been enough children to make it worthwhile. 'Or enough teachers,' Nightingale had said, and then fallen silent for a long while. I made a point of not bringing up the subject again.

We did spend quite a lot of time going through the library looking for references to *Vagina dentata*, which led me to Wolfe's *Exotica*. What Polidori was to macabre death, Samuel Erasmus Wolfe was to weird fauna and what Dr Walid calls 'legitimate cryptozoology'. He was a contemporary of Huxley and Wilberforce, and bang up to date with the then latest theories of evolution. In his introduction to *The Role of Magic in Inducing Pseudo-Lamarckian Inheritance*, he argues that exposure to magic could induce changes in an organism which could then be inherited by its offspring. Amongst modern biologists, this sort of thing is known as 'soft inheritance' and, if espoused, causes them to point and laugh. It sounded plausible, but unfortunately before he could complete the part of his book where he proved his theory, Wolfe was killed by a shark while taking the waters off Sidmouth.

I thought that, as a theory, it could explain the 'evolution' of many of the creatures detailed in the *Exotica*. Wolfe had avoided mention in his theory of the *genii locorum*, the local gods, that most definitely existed. But I could see that if a person were to come under the influence of the vast and subtle magic that seemed to permeate

95

certain localities, then perhaps they could be physically shaped by that magic. For example, Father Thames, Mama Thames and even Beverley Brook, who I'd kissed at Seven Dials.

Inherited by the offspring, I thought. Perhaps it was a good thing that Beverley Brook was safely out of temptation's reach.

'Assuming the forensic dentistry confirms that it's the same "creature",' I said, 'can we assume she's not natural? I mean, she's got to be magical in some way – right? Which means she must be leaving a trail of *vestigia* wherever she goes.'

Nightingale poured more tea. 'You haven't picked up anything so far.'

'True,' I said. 'But if she's got a gaff, a nest where she spends most of her time, then the *vestigia* will have had a chance to build up. That should make it easier to spot, and since both attacks were in Soho, the chances are that's where her lair is.'

'That's a bit of a stretch,' he said.

'It's a start,' I said, and flicked a sausage at Toby, who executed a neat standing jump to catch it. 'What we need is something that has a proven track record of hunting supernatural things.'

We both looked at Toby, who swallowed his sausage in a single gulp.

'Not Toby,' I said. 'Someone who owes me a favour.'

When I brokered a peace between the two halves of the River Thames, part of the deal involved

96

an exchange of hostages. All very mediaeval, but the best I could come up with at the time. From the court of Mama Thames, the London contingent, I chose Beverley Brook, she of the dark brown eyes and cheeky face, and in exchange I got Ash, all film-star good looks and the greasy blond charisma of a travelling funfair. After a fairly disastrous stay at Mama Thames's home in Wapping, the eldest daughters had stashed him at the Generator, a student hostel that existed on the boundary where roughneck King's Cross became affluent Bloomsbury. It also put him just a short dash from the Folly, in case of emergencies.

The hostel was based near a courtyard mews off Tavistock Place. On the outside it was strictly English Heritage vanilla Georgian, but inside it was the kind of easy-to-clean primary colours that adorn the set of children's TV shows. The staff were decked out in blue and green t-shirts, baseball caps and mandatory happy smiles, which slipped a bit when they saw me.

'I'm just here to pick him up,' I told them, and their smiles returned to the regulation intensity.

It wasn't lost on me that despite the fact that I'd worked all night, had a kip, a shower and caught up on some paperwork, I still managed to arrive at Ash's room to find him just getting up. He opened the door wrapped in a grubby olive bath towel.

'Petey,' he said. 'Come in.'

The private rooms at the Generator are furnished with bunk beds, in order to retain that crucial youth hostel ambience. Technically, even when you rent a private room, you're required to share it with at least one other guest. Shortly after moving in, Ash, using an oxyacetylene torch liberated from God knows where, had reconfigured his bunk into a double bed. If anyone was going to be sharing a room with him, it was going to be under the same duvet. When the management complained, Mother Thames sent her daughter Tyburn to sort things out. And when Lady Ty puts the fix in, things stay fixed. To be fair to Ash, he rarely spends a night alone. Ty hates him, but since I was top of her shit list before Ash came along, I regarded that as a bonus.

Last night's young woman regarded me cautiously from the safety of the duvet. There wasn't anywhere else to sit but at the end of the bed, so I perched there and gave her a reassuring smile. She looked nervously after Ash as he headed up the corridor towards the communal showers.

'Afternoon,' I said, and she nodded back.

She was pretty in a calculated way: delicate cheekbones, olive skin and curly black hair that fell in ringlets to her shoulders. It wasn't until she'd relaxed enough to sit up and the duvet fell away to reveal a smooth, hairless and totally flat chest, that I twigged that he wasn't a she.

'Are you a guy?' I asked, just to show that the sensitivity training at Hendon hadn't been wasted.

'Only biologically,' he said. 'How about you?'

I was saved from having to answer that by Ash, who swept back into the room and, stark naked, hunted out a pair of faded jeans and a Bra Anancy t-shirt that just had to have come from Effra. Pausing only to French-kiss the young man in the bed, he pulled on a pair of DM boots and out we went.

I waited until we were out of the hostel and heading for the Ford Asbo before asking about the guy in his bed.

Ash shrugged. 'I didn't know he was a guy until we got back to the room,' he said. 'And I was having such a good time I thought, why not?'

For someone who'd never been in a built-up area larger than Cirencester all his life, Ash was turning out to be surprisingly metro.

'Where we going?' asked Ash as we got in the car.

'Your favourite part of town,' I said. 'Soho.'

'You going to buy me breakfast?' he asked.

'Lunch,' I said. 'Late lunch.'

We ended up eating fish and chips al fresco on Berwick Street, which has the offices of TV companies at one end, a street market in the middle and a little furtive knot of sex shops at the other. It also has some world-famous record stores, strictly vinyl only, the sort of places my dad would go to sell his collection – as if that was ever going to happen, this side of him being dead.

I told him what I wanted him to do.

'You want me to hang out in Soho?' he asked.
'Yes,' I said.
'Going to pubs and clubs and meeting new people,' he said.
'Yep,' I said, 'and keeping your eye out for a psychotic, possibly supernatural, killer female.'
'So, go to clubs and look for dangerous women,' he said. 'What does she look like?'
'She looks like Molly, but she may have changed her hair a bit,' I said. 'I'm hoping she'll stand out, you know, to you in particular, in a spiritual way.'
I saw Ash translate that one in his head. 'Oh,' he said. 'Got you. What do I do if I spot her?'
'You call me and you don't get close,' I said. 'This is strictly surveillance, is that clear?'
'Crystal,' said Ash. 'What's in it for me?'
'I bought you chips, didn't I?'
'Tight arse,' he said. 'Beer money?'
'I'll reimburse you,' I said.
'You couldn't front me?'
We found a cashpoint, and I pulled a ton and a half for walking-around money and handed it over. 'I want receipts,' I said. 'Or I'm going to tell Tyburn what really happened that night in Mayfair.'
'It was just a cat,' said Ash.
'There are some things that shouldn't happen to anybody,' I said. 'Not even a cat.'
'It looked good shaved,' said Ash.
'I don't think Tyburn saw it that way,' I said.
'I think I shall start my reconnaissance at Endurance,' said Ash. 'Care to join me?'

'Can't, some of us have got to work for a living,' I said.

'So have I,' said Ash. 'I'm doing your job.'

'Just be careful,' I said.

'As if I were out poaching,' he said. 'On a beautiful moonlit night.'

I watched him pinch an apple off a market stand as he sauntered away.

The thing about Soho is that because it's a bugger to drive through, has no tube station or bus routes through it, you end up walking everywhere. And because you're walking, you run into people you might normally miss. I'd stashed the Asbo on Beak Street, and so turned down Broadwick, but before I could achieve Soho escape velocity I was intercepted on Lexington.

Despite the traffic, I heard the heels before I heard the voice.

'Constable Grant! You lied to me.'

I turned to find Simone Fitzwilliam high-heeling down the pavement towards me. A red cardigan was falling off her shoulders like a stole, over a peach-coloured blouse with its buttons under strain and black leggings to show off all that leg power. As she came close I smelled honeysuckle, rose and lavender, the scents of an English country garden.

'Miss Fitzwilliam,' I said, trying to keep it formal.

'You lied to me,' she said, and her wide red mouth stretched into a smile. 'Your father is Richard "Lord" Grant. I can't believe I didn't see it in your face. No wonder you knew what you were talking about. Does he still play?'

'How are you feeling?' I asked, feeling like a daytime TV presenter.

The smile wavered. 'Some days are better than others,' she said. 'You know what would cheer me up – something scrumptious.'

Scrumptious was not a word that I'd ever heard used by a real person before.

'Where do you want to go?' I asked.

The English have always brought out a strong missionary streak in the rest of the continent, and from time to time hardy individuals have braved the weather, the plumbing and the sarcasm to bring the finer things in life to this poor benighted island. One such pioneer, according to Simone, was Madame Valerie, who founded her patisserie on Frith Street and, after the Germans bombed it there, on Old Compton Street. I'd patrolled past it lots of times, but since it didn't serve alcohol I'd been rarely called to go in.

Simone grabbed my hand and practically dragged me inside, where the display cases glowed in the afternoon light. Ranks of confectionery were arrayed on cream-coloured doilies, pink and yellow, red and chocolate, as gaudy as any model army.

Simone had a favourite table by the stairs, just the other side of the cake displays. From there, she pointed out, you could watch people coming and going *and* keep an eye on the cakes – just in case they tried to make a run for it. She seemed to know what she was doing, so I let her order. Hers was a deceptively compact sandwich of cream, pastry and icing; mine was essentially a chocolate cake with chocolate flourishes and whipped cream sprinkled with chocolate. I wondered if I was being seduced or driven into a diabetic coma.

'You must tell me what you've discovered,' she said. 'I heard you were at The Mysterioso last night with Jimmy and Max. Isn't it a frightfully wicked place? I'm sure you had to positively restrain yourself from arresting miscreants left, right and centre.'

I agreed that I had, indeed, visited the club, and that it was a den of iniquity, but I didn't tell her about Mickey the Bone who, even as we spoke, was waiting for Dr Walid in the mortuary at UCH. Instead I gave her some flannel about ongoing inquiries, and watched her eat her cake. She devoured it like an impatient but obedient child with quick, dainty bites, and still managed to get cream smeared around her lips. I watched as her tongue darted out to lick it off.

'You know who you should talk to,' she said, once all the cream had gone. 'You should talk to the Musicians Union. After all, isn't it their job to look after their members? If anybody should know what's going on, it should be them. Are you going to eat that?'

I offered her the rest of my cake, and she looked

to either side like a guilty schoolgirl before sliding the plate over to her side of the table. 'I've never been very good curbing my appetite,' she said. 'I suppose I'm compensating rather for when I was younger – we were terribly short of all sorts of things back then.'

'Back when?'

'Back when I was young and foolish,' she said. There was a dab of chocolate on her cheek, and without thinking I wiped it off with my thumb. 'Thank you,' she said. 'You can never have enough cake.'

You certainly never have enough time. I paid the bill, and she walked me back to where I'd parked the Asbo. I asked her what she did for a living.

'I'm a journalist,' she said.

'Who with?' I asked.

'Oh, I'm freelance,' she said. 'Everybody is these days, apparently.'

'What do you write about?'

'Jazz, of course,' she said. 'The London scene, music, gossip, most of my work goes overseas. To the Japs mainly, very keen on jazz, the Japs are.' She explained that she suspected some subeditor in Tokyo translated her work into Japanese – her name being one of the things that got lost in translation.

We reached the corner.

'I'm staying just up there on Berwick Street,' she said.

'With your sisters,' I said.

104

'You remembered. Well, of course you did, you're a policeman. No doubt they train you to do such things. So if I tell you my address, you're sure to remember it.'

She told me her address and I pretended to memorise it – again.

'Au revoir,' she said. 'Until we meet again.'

I watched her walk away on her high heels, jaunty hips swaying back and forth.

Lesley was so going to kill me.

Back in the old days, my dad and his mates used to hang out on Archer Street, where the Musicians Union used to be, in the hope of getting work. I'd always imagined it as little knots of musicians dotted along the pavement. Then I saw a photograph which showed the street awash with men in pork-pie hats and Burton suits toting their instruments around like unemployed Mafiosi. It got so crowded and competitive, my dad said, that bands would have secret hand gestures to communicate across the crowd, sliding fist for a trombonist, flat hand, palm down, for a drummer, fluttering fingers for a cornet or a trumpet. That way you could stay friendly with your mates in the crowd even while undercutting them for a gig at the Savoy or the Café de Paris. My dad said you could have walked down Archer Street and assembled two full orchestras, a big band and still have enough bodies left for a couple of quartets and a soloist to tinkle the ivories at Lyon's Corner House.

These days the musicians text each other and arrange their gigs on the internet, and the Musicians Union has crossed the river to set up shop on the Clapham Road. It was a Sunday, but on the basis that music, like crime, never sleeps, I gave them a ring. A guy at the main office, once I'd convinced him this was a police matter, gave me the mobile number for Tista Ghosh, the Jazz Section's welfare officer. I rang her and left a message identifying myself and giving an impression of urgency without actually saying anything concrete. Never record anything you wouldn't want turning up on YouTube, is my motto. Ms Ghosh rang back just as I was reaching my car. She had the kind of precision-tooled middle-class accent that only comes from being taught English as a second language in the cradle. She asked me what I wanted, and I told her that I wanted to talk about unexpected deaths amongst her members.

'Does it have to be this evening?' she asked. Behind her I could hear a band playing 'Red Clay'.

I told her I'd try and keep the interview as short as possible. I love using the word 'interview', because members of the public see it as the first step up the legal staircase that goes from 'helping the police with their inquiries' to spending time at Her Majesty's pleasure locked in a small cell with a large sweaty man who insists on calling you Susan.

I asked her where she was currently.

'At The Hub in Regent's Park,' she said. 'It's the Jazz in the Open Air Festival.'

Actually, according to the poster I saw at the gate later, it was the *Last Chance for Jazz in the Open Air Festival* sponsored by the company formerly known as Cadbury Schweppes.

Five hundred years ago, the notoriously savvy Henry VIII discovered an elegant way to solve both his theological problems and his personal liquidity crisis – he dissolved the monasteries and nicked all their land. Since the principle of any rich person who wants to stay rich is never give anything away unless you absolutely have to, the land has stayed with the crown ever since. Three hundred years later, the Prince Regent hired Nash to build him a big palace on the site with some elegant terraces that could be rented out and thus cover the Prince's heroic attempt to debauch himself to death. The palace was never built, but the terraces and debauchery remained – as did the park, which bears the Prince Regent's title. One end of the park, the Northern Parklands, is given over to playing fields and sports facilities, and at the centre of those sits The Hub, a large artificial hillock with a pavilion and changing rooms built into it. It has three main entrances built in the manner of aircraft dispersal pens that make it look like the ground-floor entrance to the lair of a super-villain. On top is a circular café, whose Perspex walls give a three-sixty panorama of the whole park where customers can sit, drink tea and plot world domination.

It was still sunny, but the air was taking on a warning chill. In August the crowd spread out in front of the temporary stage and, lounging on the concrete apron that surrounded the café, would have been half naked. But by mid-September sweatshirts had been unwrapped from around waists and sleeves pulled down. Still, there was enough golden sunlight to pretend, if only for another day, that London was a city of street cafés and jazz in the park.

The current band were playing something fusiony that even I wouldn't classify as jazz, so I wasn't surprised to find Tista Ghosh nursing a white wine beyond the refreshment tents where the noise would be muffled. I called her mobile and she guided me in.

'I hope you're buying,' she said when I found her. 'I can't make this Aussie fizz last much longer.'

Why not, I thought, I've been getting them in all week. Why stop now?

Ms Ghosh was a slender, light-skinned woman with a sharp nose who favoured long dangly earrings and kept her long black hair tied back in a pony tail. She wore white slacks and a purple blouse, and over that a gentrified biker's leather jacket that was at least five sizes too big for her. Perhaps she'd borrowed it against the chill.

'I know what you're thinking,' she said. 'What's a nice desi girl like me doing in the jazz scene?' Actually I was thinking where the hell had she got that leather jacket from and should she, for religious reasons, be wearing a leather jacket in the first place?

'My parents were deeply into jazz,' she said. 'They were from Calcutta, and there was this famous club called Trinca's on Park Street. You know, I visited there last September – there was a wedding. It's all changed now, but there used to be this great jazz scene, that's where they met. My parents, not the relatives who were getting married.'

The jacket had a line of crudely made badges down the left-hand lapel, the type you could stamp out with a hand press. I surreptitiously read them while Ms Ghosh expounded upon the innovative jazz scene that flourished in India after the war – Rock Against Racism, Anti-Nazi League, Don't Blame Me I Didn't Vote Tory – slogans from the 1980s, most from before I was born.

Ms Ghosh was just telling me about the time Duke Ellington played at the Winter Palace – the hotel in Calcutta, not the birthplace of the Russian revolution – when I decided it was time to put the conversation back on track. I asked whether she was aware of any sudden deaths amongst her members, particularly during or just after a gig.

Ms Ghosh gave me a long, sceptical look.

'Are you having me on?' she asked.

'We're looking into suspicious deaths amongst musicians,' I said. 'This is just a preliminary inquiry. The deaths might have looked like the result of exhaustion, or drug or alcohol abuse. Have you seen anything like that?'

'In jazz musicians,' she said. 'Are you kidding? If they haven't got at least one bad habit, we don't let them in the union.' She laughed, I didn't, she noticed and stopped. 'Are we talking murders here?'

'We don't know at this stage,' I said. 'We're just acting on information received.'

'I can't think of anyone off the top of my head,' she said. 'I can look up my records tomorrow, if you like.'

'That would be really helpful.' I gave her my card. 'Could you do it first thing?'

'Sure,' she said. 'Do you know those guys are staring at you?'

I turned to find The Irregulars watching me from the eaves of the beer tent. Max gave me a wave.

'You don't want to be talking to him, miss,' called James. 'He's the jazz police.'

I said goodbye to Ms Ghosh, and hoped that she still took me seriously enough to look up the information I wanted. To make it up to me, The Irregulars agreed to buy me a drink.

'What are you doing here?' I asked.

'Where the jazzman sups, there sup I,' said James.

'We were supposed to be playing the festival,' said Daniel. 'But without Cyrus . . .' He shrugged.

'You couldn't get anyone else?' I asked.

'Not without lowering our standards,' said James.

110

'Which admittedly were already pretty low,' said Max. 'I don't suppose you play?'

I shook my head.

'Pity,' he said. 'We were going to play the Arches next week.'

'We were actually second from the bottom of the bill,' said Daniel.

I asked Daniel whether he played anything other than piano.

'I do a mean Gibson electric,' he said.

'How would you like to play with a man who is almost a jazz legend?' I asked.

'How can you "almost" be a jazz legend?' asked Max.

'Shut up, Max,' said James. 'The man's talking about his father. You are talking about your father?'

There was a pause – it was common knowledge that my dad had lost his lip. It was Daniel who put it together. 'He's switched instruments, hasn't he?' he asked.

'Fender Rhodes,' I said.

'Is he any good?' asked Max.

'He's going to be better than me,' said Daniel.

'Lord Grant,' said James. 'How cool is that?'

'That's pretty cool,' said Max. 'Do you think he'll agree?'

'I'll find out,' I said. 'I don't see why not.'

'Thank you,' said Daniel

'Don't thank me, man,' I said. 'Just doing my job.'

So, the jazz police to the rescue. If my dad said

yes – which I thought he probably would. The Arches Club was in Camden Lock, which is just down the road from my flat, so logistics would be easy. I decided to let Mum organise the rehearsals – she might enjoy that.

It was only after I'd agreed to see what I could sort out that I realised I'd never heard my father play to an audience before. The Irregulars were so pleased that James had been moved to offer to buy me a pint, several pints in fact, but I was driving so I stuck to just the one. It was just as well, because ten minutes later Stephanopoulos called me.

'We're turning over Jason Dunlop's flat,' she said. 'We've found some things I'd like you to take a look at.' She gave me the address. It was in Islington.

'I'll be there in half an hour,' I said.

Jason Dunlop lived in the half-basement flat of a converted early Victorian terrace on Barnsbury Road. In previous eras, the servants' quarters would be fully underground but the Victorians, being the great social improvers they were, had decided that even the lowly should be able to see the feet of the people walking past the grand houses of their masters – hence the half-basement. That and the increased daylight saved on candles, a penny saved is a penny earned, and all that. The interior walls had been painted estate-agent white and were devoid of decoration: no framed photographs, no reproduction Monets, Klimts or poker-playing dogs. The kitchen units were low-end and brand new. I smelled buy-to-let and recently, too. Judging by the half-emptied packing cases in the living room, I didn't think Jason had lived there long.

'A messy divorce,' said Stephanopoulos as she showed me round.

'Has she got an alibi?'

'So far,' said Stephanopoulos. The joys of dealing with the bereaved when they're both victim and suspect – I was glad I wasn't doing *that* bit of the investigation. The flat only had one bedroom, a pair of masculine suitcases pushed into the corner, a line of packing cases with fingerprint dust smeared on the lids. Stephanopoulos showed me where a pile of books had been carefully arranged on a plastic sheet by the bed.

'Have they been processed?' I asked.

Stephanopoulos said yes, but I put on gloves anyway. It's good practice when handling evidence, and I got a grunt of approval from the sergeant. I picked up the first book. It was old, a pre-war hardback that had been carefully wrapped in white tissue paper. I opened it and read the title: *Philosophiae Naturalis Principia Artes Magicis* by Isaac Newton. I had a copy of the same edition on my desk, with a much bigger Latin dictionary sitting next to it.

'We saw this,' said Stephanopoulos, 'and we thought of you.'

'Are there any more?' I asked.

'We left the box for you,' she said. 'Just in case it was cursed or something.'

I hoped she was being sarcastic.

I inspected the book. Its cover was worn at the edges and warped with age. The edges of the pages had dents and smears from being handled. Whoever had owned this book hadn't left it on a shelf; this had been used. On a hunch I turned to page 27 and saw, just where I'd stuck in a Post-it note with a question mark on it, was the word, written in faded pencil, *quis?*. Somebody else who couldn't work out what the hell Isaac was going on about in the middle part of the introduction.

If someone were really studying the craft, then they'd need Cuthbertson's *A Modern Commentary on the Great Work*. It had been written in 1897 in English, thank God, and no doubt welcomed with open arms by every frustrated student who'd ever tried to light his room with a werelight. I looked in the box and found a copy of Cuthbertson right under a huge modern desk-top Latin dictionary and grammar – it was nice to know I wasn't the only one who needed help. The *Modern Commentary* was, like the *Principia*, old and well-used. I flicked through its pages and came across a faded stamp thirty pages in – an open book surrounded by three crowns and encircled by the words *Bibliotheca Bodleiana*. I checked the *Principia* and found a different stamp, an old-fashioned drawing compass surrounded by the words SCIENTIA

POTESTAS EST QMS. I turned to the frontispiece and found a faint rectangular discoloration. My dad had books with that same pattern, ones that he'd jacked from his school library when he was young. The mark was from the glue that once held a folder into which a library card would have fitted back in the day when dinosaurs roamed the earth and computers were the size of washing machines.

I carefully emptied the packing case. There were six more books, which I recognised as being authentically related to magic, all of them with the *Bibliotheca Bodleiana* library stamp.

I assumed that stamp referred to the Bodleian Library, which I vaguely remembered was in Oxford, but while I didn't recognise the second stamp I recognised the motto. I dialled up the Folly. The phone rang several times before being picked up. 'It's Peter,' I said. There was silence at the other end. 'I need to speak to him right away.' I heard a clunk as the receiver was put down next to the phone. As I waited, I thought it was about time I bought Nightingale a proper phone.

When Nightingale picked up, I explained about the books. He made me list the titles and describe the stamps. Then he asked if Stephanopoulos was available.

I called her and offered her the phone. 'My governor wants a word,' I said.

While they talked I started bagging the books and filling out the evidence tags.

'And you think this makes it more likely?' she

asked. 'Fair enough. I'll send the boy over with the books. I expect you to maintain a chain of custody.' Nightingale must have assured her that we would be as scrupulous as any Home Office lab, because she nodded and handed the phone back to me.

'I think,' said Nightingale, 'that we may be dealing with a black magician here.'

CHAPTER 5

THE NIGHT GATE

Black magic, as defined by Nightingale, was the use of magic in such a way as to cause a breach of the peace. I pointed out that a definition like that was so broad as to essentially include any use of magic outside of that authorised by the Folly. Nightingale indicated that he regarded that as a feature, not a bug.

'Black magic is the use of the art to cause injury to another person,' he'd then said. 'Do you like that definition better?'

'We don't have any evidence that Jason Dunlop ever did any injury to anyone through the use of black magic,' I said. We'd laid out the case files on a table in the breakfast room, along with the books I'd brought back from Dunlop's flat and the remains of Molly's eccentric stab in the direction of Eggs Benedict.

'I'd say we have a fairly clear indication that somebody did him injury,' said Nightingale. 'And strong evidence that he was a practitioner. Given the unusual nature of his assailant, I think it's a safe bet that magic was involved – don't you?'

'In that case, isn't it possible that the Jason

Dunlop murder is related to my dead jazz musicians?'

'It's possible,' said Nightingale. 'But the MOs are very different. I think it's better to keep the two investigations distinct for the moment.' He reached out to where one of the Folly's mono-grammed Sheffield steel forks was jammed upright into a poached egg and flicked it with his finger – it barely moved. 'Are you sure it's not stuck in the muffin?'

'No,' I said. 'It's being held in place by the egg alone.'

'Is that even possible?' asked Nightingale.

'With Molly's cooking, who knows?'

We both looked around to make sure Molly wasn't listening. Up until that morning Molly's repertoire had been strictly British public school: lots of beef, potatoes, treacle and industrial quan-tities of suet. Nightingale had explained once, when we were out having a Chinese, that he thought Molly was drawing her inspiration from the Folly itself. 'A sort of institutional memory,' he'd said. Either my arrival was beginning to change the 'institutional memory', or more likely she'd noticed me and Nightingale sloping off for illicit meals at restaurants.

The Eggs Benedict was her attempt to diversify the menu.

I picked up the fork and the egg, the muffin and what I assumed was the hollandaise sauce, all of which lifted off the plate in one rubbery mass. I offered it to Toby who sniffed it once, whined and then hid under the table.

There was no kedgeree that morning, or sausages, or any poached eggs not smothered in vulcanised hollandaise sauce, not even toast and marmalade. Obviously the culinary experimentation had so exhausted Molly that the rest of breakfast was off the menu. The coffee was still good, though, and when you're going over your case files, that's the important thing.

Murder investigations start with the victim, because usually in the first instance that's all you've got. The study of the victim is called victimology because everything sounds better with an 'ology' tacked on the end. To make sure you make a proper fist of this, the police have developed the world's most useless mnemonic – 5 x WH&H – otherwise known as Who? What? Where? When? Why? and How? Next time you watch a real murder investigation on the TV, and you see a group of serious-looking detectives standing around talking, remember that what they're actually doing is trying to work out what sodding order the mnemonic is supposed to go in. Once they've sorted that out, the exhausted officers will retire to the nearest watering hole for a drink and a bit of a breather.

Fortunately for us, on the first question, *Who is the victim?*, Stephanopoulos and the Murder Team had done most of the heavy lifting. Jason Dunlop had been a successful freelance journalist, hence his membership of the Groucho Club. His late father had been a senior civil servant, and had sent the young Jason to a second-tier independent school in Harrogate. He'd read English at Magdalen College, Oxford, where he was an undistinguished student before graduating with a matching undistinguished second. Despite his unremarkable academic performance, he walked straight into a job at the BBC, where he was first a researcher and then a producer on *Panorama*. After a stint working for, of all things, Westminster Council in the 1980s, he moved back into journalism writing articles for *The Times*, the *Mail* and the *Independent*. I leafed through some of the clippings; lots of articles of the 'you send me on holiday and I'll write you a good review' variety. Family holidays with wife Mariana, a PR executive, and their two golden-haired kids. As Stephanopoulos had told me, the marriage had recently collapsed, lawyers had already been engaged and custody of the children was an issue.

'It would be nice to talk to the wife,' said Nightingale. 'See if she knows anything about his hobbies.'

I checked the transcripts of the interview with the wife, but there was nothing about an unwholesome interest in the occult or supernatural. I made a note to add this to the wife's nominal file on HOLMES, and suggest she be re-interviewed on that subject. I flagged it for Stephanopoulos, but she wasn't going to let us talk to the wife unless we came up with something serious.

'Very well,' said Nightingale, 'we'll leave all the mundane connections in the capable hands of the Detective Sergeant. I think our first move should be to track down the source of the book.'

'I figured Dunlop stole it from the Bodleian Library,' I said.

'That's why you shouldn't make assumptions,' said Nightingale. 'This is an old book. It could have been stolen prior to Dunlop arriving at Oxford and then come into his possession by some other route. Perhaps the person who trained him.'

'Assuming he was a practitioner,' I said.

Nightingale tapped his butter knife on the plastic-wrapped copy of the *Principia Artes Magicis*. 'Nobody carries this book by accident,' he said. 'Besides, I recognise the other library mark. It's from my old school.'

'Hogwarts?' I asked.

'I really wish you wouldn't call it that,' he said. 'We can drive up to Oxford this morning.'

'You're coming with me?' Dr Walid had been very clear about the whole taking-it-easy thing.

'You won't get access to the library without me,' he said. 'And it's time I started introducing you to people connected to the art.'

'I thought you were the last?'

'There's more to life than just London,' said Nightingale.

'People keep saying that,' I said. 'But I've never actually seen any proof.'

121

'We can take the dog,' he said. 'He'll enjoy the fresh air.'

'We won't,' I said, 'not if we take the dog.'

Fortunately, despite the overcast, the day was warm, so we could head up the A40 with the windows down to let out the smell. Truth be told, as a motorway car the Jag isn't that comfortable, but there was no way I was heading into Morse Central in the Ford Asbo – standards have to be maintained, even with Toby in the back seat.

'If Jason Dunlop was trained,' I said as we climbed on to the Great West Road, 'then who was his teacher?'

We'd discussed this before. Nightingale said it was impossible to pick up organised 'Newtonian' magic on your own. Without someone to teach you the difference, *vestigia* are hard to distinguish from the random background noise of your own brain. The same was true of the *forma*; Nightingale always had to demonstrate the form to me before I could learn it. To teach them to yourself you'd have to be the kind of insane monomaniac who'd deform his own eyeball to test his theories on optics – in short, someone like Isaac Newton.

'I don't know,' said Nightingale. 'After the war, there weren't that many of us left.'

'That should narrow down the suspects,' I said.

'Most of the survivors would be very old by now,' said Nightingale.

'What about other countries?' I asked.

'None of the continental powers came out of the war intact,' said Nightingale. 'The Nazis rounded up any practitioners they could find in the occupied countries, and killed any who refused to be coopted. Those who didn't die on their side mostly died fighting against them. The same is true of the French and the Italians. We always believed that there was a Scandinavian tradition, but they kept it very quiet.'

'What about the Americans?'

'There were volunteers right from the start of the war,' said Nightingale. 'The Virtuous Men, they called themselves – out of the University of Pennsylvania.' Others had arrived in the years following Pearl Harbor, and Nightingale had always had the impression that there was some deep animosity at work between them and the Virtuous Men. He thought it was doubtful that any of them could have returned to Britain after the war. 'They blamed us for Ettersberg,' he said. 'And there was an agreement.'

'Well, of course there was,' I said. There was always an agreement.

Nightingale claimed he'd have spotted them if they'd started practising in London. 'They were hardly what you'd call subtle,' he said.

I asked about other countries – China, Russia, India, the Middle East, Africa. I couldn't believe that they hadn't at least some kind of magic. Nightingale admitted that he didn't really know, but had the good grace to sound embarrassed.

123

'The world was different before the war,' he said. 'We didn't have this instantaneous access to information that your generation has. The world was a bigger, more mysterious place – we still dreamed of secret caves in the Mountains of the Moon, and tiger-hunting in the Punjab.'

When all the map was pink, I thought. When every boy expected his own adventure and girls had not yet been invented.

Toby barked as we overtook a juggernaut full of God-knows-what going God-knows-where.

'After the war it was as if I was waking up from a dream,' said Nightingale. 'There were space rockets and computers and jumbo jets, and it seemed like a "natural" thing that the magic would go away.'

'You mean, you didn't bother looking,' I said.

'It was just me,' he said, 'and I was responsible for the whole of London and the South-East. It never occurred to me that the old days might come back. Besides, we have Dunlop's books, so we know his teacher wasn't from some foreign tradition – this is a home-grown black magician.'

'You can't call them black magicians,' I said.

'You realise that we're using "black" in its metaphorical sense here,' said Nightingale.

'It doesn't matter,' I said. 'Words change what they mean, don't they? Some people would call me a black magician.'

'You're not a magician,' he said. 'You're barely even an apprentice.'

'You're changing the subject,' I said.

'What should we call them?' he asked patiently.

'Ethically challenged magical practitioners,' I said.

'Just to satisfy my curiosity, you understand,' said Nightingale, 'given that the only people ever likely to hear us say the words "black magician" are you, me and Dr Walid, why is changing them so important?'

'Because I don't think the old world's coming back any time soon,' I said. 'In fact, I think the new world might be arriving.'

Oxford is a strange place. As you go through the outskirts it could be any city in Britain, the same Edwardian suburban build, fading into Victorian, with the occasional mistake from the 1950s, and then you cross the Magdalen Bridge and suddenly you're in the biggest concentration of late-mediaeval architecture this side of the eighteenth century. Historically it's impressive, but from a traffic-management perspective it meant it took almost as long to thread our way through the narrow streets as it did to drive up from London.

John Radcliffe, Royal physician to William and Mary, was famous in his own time for reading very little and writing almost nothing. So it stands to reason that one of the most famous libraries in Oxford was his creation. The Radcliffe Science Library is housed in a circular domed building that looks like St Paul's with the extraneous religious bits cut off. Inside was a lot of smoothly carved stonework, old books, balconies and the strained hush of young people being unnaturally quiet. Our contact was waiting for us by a notice board just inside the entrance.

Outside the big cities, my very appearance can sometimes be enough to render certain people speechless. So it was with Harold Postmartin, D.Phil, FRS, Curator of Special Collections at the Bodleian Library, who had clearly been expecting Nightingale to introduce someone 'different' as the new apprentice. I could see him trying to parse the phrase *but he's coloured* in a way that wouldn't cause offence, and failing. I put him out of his misery by shaking his hand; my rule of thumb is that if they don't physically flinch from touching you, then eventually they'll make the adjustment.

Postmartin was a stooped, white-haired gentleman who looked much older and frailer than my father but had a surprisingly firm handshake.

'So you're the new apprentice,' he said, and managed to avoid it sounding like an accusation. I knew then we were going to be fine.

Like all modern libraries, the visible bit of the Radcliffe was the tip of an iceberg, while the bulk of the actual collection was submerged under Radcliffe Square in chambers filled with books and the intrusive hum of modern climate control. Postmartin led us down a series of whitewashed brick passages to a no-nonsense metal security door marked NO ADMITTANCE. Postmartin used a swipe card on the security pad and punched in a combination. The door unlocked with a solid clunk, and we trooped in to find a chamber with exactly the same shelves and climate control as the rest of the collection. There was a single institutional desk with a top bare save for what looked like the product of a loveless marriage between an early Mac and an IBM PC.

'It's an Amstrad PCW,' said Postmartin. 'Before your time, I suppose.' He sat down on a purple moulded plastic chair and booted up the antique. 'No hardware connections, no USB ports, three-inch floppy disks that they don't make any more – this is security through obsolescence. Much like the Folly itself. They cannot hack, if I'm using the term correctly, what they cannot access.'

The screen was an alarming green colour, monochrome, I realised, like something from an old film. The three-inch disk actually clunked when the machine started to access it.

'Do you have the copy of the *Principia?*' asked Postmartin.

I handed it over and he started to leaf slowly through the pages. 'Every copy at the library was marked in a unique way,' he said, and stopped at a particular page and showed it to me. 'You see there, that word has been underlined.'

I looked; it was the word *regentis*. 'Is that significant?' I asked.

'We shall see,' he said. 'Perhaps you should write it down.'

I wrote the word in my police notebook, and as I did I noticed Postmartin furtively scribbling something on a pad which he thought was out of my sight. When I was done he flicked through the pages until he found another mark, and again I noted down the word, *pedem* and again I saw him write something else on his pad. We repeated the process three more times, and then Postmartin asked me to read the words back.

'*Regentis, pedem, tolleret, loco, hostium,*' I said.

Postmartin regarded me over the rim of his glasses. 'And what do you think that signifies?' he asked.

'I think it signifies that the page numbers were more significant than the words,' I said.

Postmartin looked crestfallen. 'How did you know?'

'I can read your mind,' I said.

Postmartin looked to Nightingale. 'Can he?'

'No,' said Nightingale. 'He spotted you writing the numbers down.'

'You're a cruel man, Constable Grant,' said Postmartin. 'No doubt you shall go far. The actual words, as you surmised, are irrelevant, but if the page numbers are arranged as a single alphanumeric string they form a unique identification number. Which we can enter into our venerable friend here, and *voilà . . .*'

The PCW's screen displayed a page of ugly green

text: title, author, publisher, shelving notation and a short list of the people who'd borrowed the book. The last person listed was Geoffrey Wheatcroft, who'd signed it out in July 1941 and never returned it.

'Oh,' said Postmartin in surprise. 'Geoffrey Wheatcroft? Hardly what I'd call a nefarious fellow. Not your criminal type at all, is he, Thomas?'

'You know him?'

'I knew him,' said Postmartin. 'He died last year – we were both at the funeral, although Thomas had to come as his own son to allay suspicions.'

'It was two years ago,' said Nightingale.

'Goodness, was it?' asked Postmartin. 'Not a very good turnout, if I remember.'

'Was he an active practitioner?' I asked.

'No,' said Nightingale. 'He got his staff in 1939, wasn't considered a wizard of the first rank, gave it up after the war and took up a position at Magdalen.'

'Teaching theology, of all things,' said Postmartin.

'Magdalen College?' I asked.

'Yes,' said Nightingale suddenly thinking.

I got there first. 'The same college as Jason Dunlop.'

Nightingale wanted to head straight for Magdalen, but Postmartin suggested a spot of lunch at the Eagle and Child. I thought a sit-down was a good idea because Nightingale was favouring his left side again and looking a bit peaky, to be honest.

Nightingale compromised by suggesting we meet at the pub after visiting the college. Postmartin invited me to go with him so that he could fill me in on a few things on the way.

'If you think that's really necessary,' said Nightingale, before I could object.

'I believe it is,' said Postmartin.

'I see,' said Nightingale. 'Well, if you feel that's best . . .'

Postmartin said he thought it was capital, and so we accompanied him back to the car, where I introduced him to Toby who exited the vehicle in a cloud of smell. I suggested that Nightingale take the Jag – that way, we could drive back from the pub and he, at least, wouldn't be walking.

'So this is the famous ghost-hunting dog,' he said.

'I didn't know he was famous,' I said.

Postmartin led me down an alleyway so authentically late mediaeval that it still had a stone culver running down the middle to act as a sewer. 'Not that it's used for its original function,' said Postmartin.

It was busy with students and tourists, each doing their best to ignore the cyclists who tried to mow down both with gay abandon.

I asked Postmartin what role he played in the intricate network of mostly unwritten agreements that constituted English magical law enforcement.

'When you and Nightingale write reports, I'm the one who reads them,' he said. 'At least, those portions that are relevant.'

'So are you Nightingale's governor?' I asked.

Postmartin chuckled. 'No,' he said, 'I'm the archivist. I'm in charge of the great man's papers, and the papers of all lesser beings that have stood on his shoulders since. Even Nightingale and you.'

After all that history it was quite nice to turn onto Broad Street, which at least had a few Victorian terraces and an Oxfam.

'This way,' said Postmartin.

'Newton was a Cambridge man,' I said. 'Why are his papers here?'

'The same reason they didn't want his alchemist works there,' said Postmartin. 'Once he was safely dead, old Isaac became their shining star of science and reason. I doubt they wanted that picture complicated by what was, let's face it, a complicated man at the best of times.'

Oxford continued to be solidly Tudor, with sudden bursts of Georgian exuberance, until we reached the Eagle and Child pub on St Giles.

'Good,' said Postmartin as we sat down in what he called a 'nook'. 'Thomas isn't here yet. One finds it so much easier to have a certain kind of conversation with a sherry in one's hand.'

When you're a boy, your life can be measured out as a series of uncomfortable conversations reluctantly initiated by adults in an effort to tell you things that either you already know or really don't want to know.

He had his sherry, I had a lemonade.

'I take it you understand how unprecedented it

131

was for Thomas to take on an apprentice?' asked Postmartin.

'People have made that pretty clear,' I said.

'I think perhaps he should have taken that step earlier,' said Postmartin. 'Once it was clear that reports of the death of magic had been greatly exaggerated.'

'What gave the magic away?'

'Thomas ageing backwards was a bit of a clue,' said Postmartin. 'I archive Dr Walid's reports, and the bits that I understand are . . . strange.'

'Should I be worried?' I asked. I'd only recently got used to the idea that my governor was born in 1900 and had, according to him, been getting young again since the early 1970s. Nightingale thought it might be linked to the general increase in magical activity since the 1960s, but didn't really want to look a gift horse in the mouth. I didn't blame him.

'I wish I knew,' said Postmartin. He reached into his pocket and handed me a card. It had Postmartin's number, email and, I was surprised to see, Twitter address. 'If you have any concerns, you can contact me.'

'And if I contact you,' I said, 'what will you do?'

'I'll listen to your concerns,' he said. 'And I'll be very sympathetic.'

It was at least another hour before Nightingale joined us, and I then got to watch him sink a pint of bitter while he outlined what he'd discovered. As far as Nightingale could determine, Jason

Dunlop had no contact with Geoffrey Wheatcroft while at university.

Nightingale had thought to pick up a printout of every student and lecturer who'd been at Magdalen at the same time as our man Jason. Plus a list of every student who had ever attended a class by Geoffrey Wheatcroft. It added up to a stack of hard copy of just the right size and thickness for beating a suspect without leaving a bruise – if that's where your idea of law-enforcement took you. If the data was entered into HOLMES, it could be automatically cross-checked against any other names that came up during the mundane phase of the inquiry. The Murder Team under Stephanopoulos had three civilian workers minimum whose only job was to do that sort of tedious, time-consuming but totally vital work. What did the Folly have? You can guess what the Folly had, and he wasn't happy at the prospect.

Postmartin asked what Nightingale planned to do next.

Nightingale grimaced and took another pull on his pint. 'I thought I'd retrieve the remainder of the library cards from Ambrose House. It's time to see where the rest of the books came from.'

Nightingale told me to get off the motorway at Junction Five, and we drove through Stokenchurch, which appeared to me to be a hospital with a rather nice village attached, before turning left onto a B road, which quickly became a narrow lane that ran between the tall green walls of very old-fashioned hedgerows.

'A large part of the estate is rented to local farmers,' said Nightingale. 'The gate is coming up on your left.'

If he hadn't warned me I'd have overshot. The hedgerow abruptly became a high stone wall broken by a wide wrought-iron gate. I stopped the car while Nightingale got out, followed by Toby, and unlocked the gate with a big iron key. He opened the gates with a standard horror-movie creaking noise and waved me through, while Toby made a point of marking the gatepost. I stopped and waited for Nightingale to get back in, but he pointed to where the drive turned suddenly behind a stand of trees.

'Meet me round the corner,' he said. 'It's not far.'

He was right. I turned the corner and there was the main building of the school right in front of me. The Jag crunched to a halt on the gravel drive, and I got out to have a look.

It had been fifty years since it was occupied, you could tell that. The lawn and the formal beds had reverted to bramble, stinging nettles, toadflax and cow parsley – I learned those names later, in case you're wondering – and the house was a weathered grey colour, its large sash windows boarded shut. I'd been expecting something Gothic, but this was more like a Regency terrace that had escaped to the countryside and had shot out in all directions before some cruel architect could round it up and pen it back into its original narrow frontage. It was abandoned but not derelict. I could see the guttering was clear, and patches of roof had been retiled.

Toby came whirring past, yapped a couple of times to get my attention and then headed into a patch of overgrown woods to the left of the school. Clearly he was a country dog at heart. Nightingale arrived soon after.

'I expected it to have been redeveloped,' I said.

'As what?' asked Nightingale.

'I don't know. Country hotel and conference centre, health spa, celebrity rehab clinic?'

'No,' said Nightingale after I'd explained what a celebrity rehab clinic was. 'The Folly still owns the whole estate, and the rents from the farms pay for the maintenance.'

'Why wasn't it sold off?'

'There was a lot of confusion after the war,' said Nightingale. 'By the time it was all sorted out, I was the only person left with any kind of official standing. Selling off the school on my own recognisance seemed . . . presumptuous.'

'You thought the school might reopen?'

Nightingale winced. 'I was trying not to think about the school.'

'The land must be worth a packet now,' I said.

'Do you think it would be improved by becoming a celebrity rehab centre?'

I had to admit this was unlikely. I pointed to the main doors, firmly boarded up and secured with a heavy-duty padlock. 'Do you have keys for that?'

Nightingale grinned. 'This is where you watch and learn.'

We walked to a spot on the left of the stairs up to the main doors where, hidden by the long grass, a narrow flight of steps led down to a thick oak door that was, I noticed, free of any boarding or chains. It also lacked any visible door handles.

'Behold,' said Nightingale, 'the night gate. This was originally built so that the footmen could go straight from their quarters and hop onto the back of their master's carriage before he could get down the stairs.'

'How very eighteenth-century,' I said.

'Quite,' said Nightingale. 'But in my school days we used it for something else.' He placed his palm on the door, about where you'd expect the lock to be, and muttered something Latin under his breath. There was a click, followed by a scraping sound. Nightingale pushed and the door swung inwards.

'There used to be a curfew and we, being the dreadful young men that we were, wanted to go out drinking,' he said. 'It's not easy to beat a curfew when the masters can command the very spirits of the earth and air against you.'

'Really?' I asked. 'The spirits of the earth and air?'

'So they said,' said Nightingale. 'And I for one believed them.'

'So no drinking,' I said.

Nightingale made a werelight and stepped through the door. Not to be outdone, I made my own light and followed him inside. I heard Toby barking from outside, but he seemed reluctant to follow us in. Our werelights illuminated a short corridor of undressed brick that reminded me of the similar service corridors under the Folly.

'Not until you were in the sixth form,' he said. 'Once you were inducted into the common room, the upper sixth would teach you the spell for the night gate and you could go drinking. Unless you were Horace Greenway, who was unpopular with the prefects.'

We reached a T-junction and went right.

'What happened to him?'

'Died during the battle of Crete,' said Nightingale.

'I meant, how did he get to the pub?'

'One of us would open the door for him,' said Nightingale.

'And the teachers never twigged you were sneaking out?' I asked.

We reached a flight of wooden stairs leading up. They creaked alarmingly under our weight.

'The masters knew all about it,' said Nightingale. 'After all, they'd once been sixth-formers themselves.'

As we reached a short wood-panelled landing I caught a flash of *vestigia*, lemon drops and sherbet, wet wool and the sound of running feet. I saw there were brass coat hooks lining both walls, and benches sized for adolescent boys to sit on and change their shoes. I brushed my fingertips on the wood, and felt instead the rough paper of the *Beano* and the *Eagle*.

'Plenty of memories,' said Nightingale when he saw me pause.

Ghosts, I was thinking, memories – I wasn't sure there was a difference.

Nightingale opened a battered wooden door and we stepped out into the huge hall. The suddenly inadequate werelights revealed two massive staircases, and bare stone walls that still showed faded rectangles where framed paintings had once hung. With all the windows covered, we'd have been in pitch darkness if we weren't making our own lights.

'The great hall,' said Nightingale. 'The library's up the sinister staircase.'

I caught myself before I asked him why it was sinister, and then I realised that we were walking up the left-hand staircase. *Sinister* is Latin for 'left', making it the sort of enjoyable schoolboy pun that is such an advert for mixed-gender education. Just imagine if one of their schoolfriends had had the misfortune to be called Dexter, I thought. How they must have laughed. As we ascended, I caught a glimpse of rows of names carved into the far wall but, before I could ask what they were about, Nightingale was on the landing and heading into the cool depths of the school.

The walls were mostly painted brick, with more pale rectangular patches to show where pictures

138

had hung. I'd helped my mum to clean enough to offices to know that whoever Nightingale was contracting to maintain the house was using a big industrial Hoover to do the carpets – you could see the stripes, and judging from the dust it was at least two weeks since they'd been round.

Without books, stacks or furniture, the library looked like just another large room, made cavernous by the shifting illumination of our werelights. I recognised the card-file cabinets by their outline under the dust sheets. The mundane library at the Folly had two just like them. The school library had eight. Fortunately, Nightingale said only one of them had the cards for magical books. Nightingale provided the light while I pulled off the sheet and opened up the drawers. There was no dust, and surprisingly little *vestigia*.

'They were books about magic,' said Nightingale when I mentioned this. 'Not magical books.'

They were standard index cards with the name of the book and library number manually typed on at the top, and a handwritten list of names showing who had borrowed the book and when. We'd popped into Ryman before leaving Oxford and picked up a jumbo-sized pack of rubber bands so I could preserve the order the cards were in. It took me ages to process all the drawers, and I ended up with a black bin bag that wasn't really that much lighter to carry than the cabinet.

'We should have just taken the whole thing with

us,' I said, but Nightingale pointed out that it had been screwed to the floorboards.

I slung the bin bag over my shoulder and, staggering a little, followed Nightingale back to the main hall. I took the opportunity to ask who the names on the wall were.

'Those,' said Nightingale, 'are the honoured dead.' He led me to the dexter staircase and floated his werelight up to show the first names. 'Peninsula Campaign,' he said. There were a handful of names. 'Waterloo Campaign,' just one name. Half-a-dozen for the Crimea, two for the Indian mutiny, maybe twenty more names scattered through a list of the colonial wars of the nineteenth century, more in total than the less than twenty dead in World War One.

'There was an agreement between the Germans and us not to involve magic,' said Nightingale. 'We sat that one out.'

'I bet that made you popular,' I said.

Nightingale floated his werelight along to reveal the honoured dead of World War Two.

'You see, there's Horace,' said Nightingale, illuminating the inscription: Horace Greenway, Kastelli, 21 May 1941. 'And there's Sandy and Champers and Pascal.' The werelight darted across the serried ranks of names, listed as fallen at Tobruk and Arnhem and other places that I dimly remembered from history. But most of them were listed as having died at a place called Ettersberg on 19 January 1945.

I put the bin bag down and made a werelight

bright enough to see the whole of the room – the memorial covered two entire walls from top to bottom. There must have been thousands of names.

'There's Donny Shanks, who made it through the siege of Leningrad without a scratch and then got himself torpedoed, and Smithy at Dieppe and Rupert Dance, Lazy Arse Dance we used to call him,' Nightingale trailed off. I turned to see tears glinting on his cheeks, so I looked away.

'Some days it seems so long ago, and some days . . .' he said.

'How many?' I asked before I could stop myself.

'Two thousand, three hundred and ninety-six,' said Nightingale. 'Three out of five of every British wizard of military age. Many of those who survived were wounded or in such bad shape mentally that they never practised again.' He gestured and his werelight snapped back to hover over his hand. 'I think we've spent enough time in the past.'

I let my light die away, hefted the bin bag over my shoulder and followed. As we were leaving, I asked him who'd carved the names.

'I did it myself,' said Nightingale. 'The hospital encouraged us to take up a hobby. I chose wood-carving. I didn't tell them why.'

'Why not?'

We ducked back into the service corridors. 'The doctors were already worried that I was too morbid.'

'Why did you carve the names?'

'Oh, somebody had to do it, and as far as I could tell I was the only one still active. I also had this ridiculous notion that it might help.'

'Did it?'

'No,' he said, 'not really.'

We stepped out through the night gate and blinked in the evening light. I'd forgotten that it was still daytime outside the school. Nightingale pulled the gate closed behind us and followed me up the steps. Toby had gone to sleep on the sun-warmed bonnet of the Jag. You could see where he'd tracked mud across the paintwork. Nightingale frowned.

'Why do we have this dog?' he asked.

'He keeps Molly amused,' I said, and threw the card files into the back. Toby woke up at the sound of the door and dutifully made his own way to the back seat, where he promptly fell asleep. Me and Nightingale put our seat belts on and I started the car. I had a last look at the blind windows of the old school as I turned the Jag around before I put it behind me and we headed for London.

It was dark by the time we merged with the rush-hour traffic on the M25. Big grey rainclouds were sweeping in from the east, and soon raindrops were splattering on the windscreen. The Jag's old-fashioned handling stayed rock solid, but the wipers were a disgrace.

Nightingale spent the trip back with his face turned away, staring out the window. I didn't try and make conversation.

142

We were just hopping back onto the Westway when my phone rang. I put it on speaker – it was Ash.

'I can see her,' he shouted. Behind him I could hear crowd noises and a thumping beat.

'Where are you?'

'I'm at the Pulsar Club.'

'Are you sure it's her?' I asked.

'Tall, skinny, pale, long black hair. Smells like death,' said Ash. 'Who else could it be?'

I told him not to get any closer, and that I was on my way. Nightingale reached out in the rain and put the spinner on the roof and I started picking up speed.

Every male driver in the world thinks they're an excellent driver. Every copper who's ever had to pick an eyeball out of a puddle knows that most of them are kidding themselves. Driving in traffic is difficult and stressful and really sodding dangerous. Because of this, the Met has a world-famous driving school at Hendon where an integrated series of advanced driving courses is designed to train officers to the point where they can do a ton down a city street and keep the body count in single figures.

As I came off the Westway and into the heavy traffic on the Harrow Road, I really wished I'd been on one of them. Nightingale, as my senior officer, shouldn't have been letting me drive. But then he probably didn't even know there was such a thing as an advanced driving course. Or even, given that they only became compulsory in 1934, a driving test of any kind.

I turned into Edgware Road and found myself doing less then twenty, even with every driver with a guilty conscience scrambling to get out of my way. I took the opportunity to call Ash again. I told him we were less then ten minutes away.

'She's heading for the door,' said Ash.

'Is she with anyone?'

'She's taking some fella out with her,' said Ash.

Shit, shit, shit – so much for keeping it in the family. Nightingale was way ahead of me. He pulled an Airwave set out of the glove box and punched in a number – impressive, given that I'd only taught him how to do that a week ago.

'Follow her,' I said, 'but stay on the phone and don't take any risks.'

I risked waiting until Marble Arch to turn east – Oxford Street is restricted to buses and taxis only, and I was counting on it being quicker to go straight down it rather than ploughing through the weird one-way systems around Bond Street.

'Stephanopoulos is on her way,' said Nightingale.

I asked Ash where he was.

'I'm just coming out of the club,' he said. 'She's fifteen feet in front of me.'

'Heading which way?'

'Towards Piccadilly,' he said.

I worked out the location in my head. 'Sherwood Street,' I told Nightingale, who relayed it to Stephanopoulos. 'Going south.'

'What do I do if she starts in on her boyfriend?' asked Ash.

I swerved around a bus stalled in the road with its emergency lights flashing, my spinner bluing the faces of the downstairs passengers as they watched me slide past.

'Stay away from her,' I said. 'Wait for us.'

'Too late,' said Ash. 'I think she saw me.'

The instructors at the advanced driving school would not have been happy with the way I put the Jag through the lights at Oxford Circus and skidded into a right turn that had me going down Regent Street with blue smoke coming from my wheels.

'Steady on,' said Nightingale.

'The good news,' said Ash, 'is that she's let the poor guy go.'

'They're almost on Denham Street,' said Nightingale, meaning local plod. 'Stephanopoulos is telling them to secure a perimeter.'

I almost screamed when an obviously deaf and blind driver in a Ford Mondeo decided to pull out in front of me. What I shouted at him was fortunately lost in the sound of my siren.

'The bad news,' said Ash, 'is she's coming towards me.'

I told him to run.

'Too late,' he said.

I heard a hiss, a yell and the distinctive noise a mobile phone makes when it's hurled against a hard surface and breaks.

I did half a bootleg turn into Glasshouse Street, which I swear got me applause from the pedestrians and a startled yelp from Toby as he slammed into the passenger door. There was a reason the Jaguar Mk II was the favoured getaway car for blaggers and the Flying Squad, and Nightingale's Jag had definitely been modded for pursuit. Which is why, once her backside had stopped swinging, I could put my foot down and be doing sixty before I was level with the Leicester Arms on the corner.

Then what I thought was the reflection of our spinner turned out to be the emergency lights on an ambulance, and we all learned just how good the upgraded four-wheel disc brakes really were – the answer being good enough. If there'd been one installed, I'd have been eating the airbag. Instead, I had a savage bruise across my chest from the seat belt, but I didn't even notice that until later because I was out the door and running across the junction and up Sherwood Street fast enough to keep pace with the ambulance. It stopped, I didn't.

One side of Sherwood Street has an arcade in the rather sad 1950s ceramic tiled fashion that, having been designed to resemble a public convenience, was perhaps justifiably used by half-cut members of the public who got caught short late at night. As far as the Murder Team could reconstruct it later, it looked as if the penis-eater had been planning to take her latest victim into the shadows for an impromptu snog and vasectomy.

I found Ash prostrate in the centre of a circle of concerned citizens, two of whom were trying to comfort him while he writhed around on the pavement. There was blood on him, on the concerned citizens and on half a metre of iron spike that was stuck through his shoulder.

I got myself some room by shouting 'Police!' at people, and tried to get him into the recovery position.

'Ash,' I said, 'I told you to stay away from her.'

Ash stopped thrashing long enough to get a good look at me.

'Peter,' he said. 'The bitch stuck me with a railing.'

CHAPTER 6

THE EMPRESS OF PLEASURE

The men and women of the London Ambulance Service are not prone to hysterics, given that they spend their days scraping up the victims of fatal car accidents, suicide attempts both successful and botched and members of the public who've 'fallen' in front of a train. Those are called 'one-unders', incidentally. I once asked whether a couple under a train would be a 'two-under', but apparently that's a 'two-one-under'. Anyway, a daily routine consisting of pain and misfortune tends to breed steady and pragmatic personalities. In short, just the kind of person you want manning your ambulance in the middle of the night. The paramedic in the ambulance that picked up Ash was a middle-aged woman with short practical hair and a New Zealand accent. But a couple of minutes into the ride, I could see that her composure was beginning to slip.

'The bitch,' yelled Ash, 'the bitch stabbed me with a railing!'

About half a metre torn from a rather nice bit of Victorian wrought ironwork, judging by the precisely milled orthogonal cross-section. To my untrained eye it looked as if it had gone right through his heart. That hadn't stopped Ash from thrashing around and yelling.

'Hold him down,' shouted the paramedic.

I grabbed Ash's arm and tried to pin it to the trolley. 'Can't you give him something?' I asked.

The paramedic gave me a wild look. 'Give him something?' she said. 'He should be dead.'

Ash tore his arm from my grip and grabbed at the railing.

'Get it out,' screamed Ash, 'it's cold iron, *get it out!*'

'Can we pull it out?' I asked.

That was the last straw for the paramedic. 'Are you fucking crazy?'

'Cold iron,' he said. 'Killing me.'

'We'll take it out at the hospital,' I said.

'No hospital,' said Ash. 'I need the river.'

'Dr Walid will be there,' I said.

Ash stopped thrashing and grabbed my hand. He pulled me closer. 'Please, Peter,' he said, 'the river.'

Polidori talks about cold iron having a *deleterious effect upon the fae and their many cousins*, but I assumed he was making it up or stating the bleeding obvious. Cold iron has a deleterious effect on anyone if you shove it right through their body.

'Please,' said Ash.

'I'm going to pull this out of him,' I said.

The paramedic expressed her opinion that she felt this would be a poor course of action and that,

149

for even contemplating it, I was an anatomically incomplete person of low intelligence and with a penchant for self-abuse.

I got both hands on the railing. It was slippery with blood. Ash saw what I was doing and held himself rigid. It wasn't the ripping sound it made when it came out that bothered me – that was masked by Ash's screaming. It was feeling the vibrations as the bone scraped along the rough edge of the iron that I won't forget.

A jet of blood smacked me in the face. I smelled copper and, weirdly, a mixture of greasepaint and ozone. The paramedic shoved me out of the way and I fell backwards as the ambulance took a corner. She started slapping dressings on entry and exit wounds and taping them in place. The dressings were soaked red before she'd even finished. As she worked, she swore under her breath.

Ash had stopped thrashing and had gone silent. His face was pale and slack. I stumbled forward in the ambulance until I could stick my head into the driver's cab. We were heading up Tottenham Court Road – less than five minutes from the hospital.

The driver was my age, white, skinny and wore a skull-and-crossbones stud in his ear.

I told him to turn around, and he told me to fuck off.

'We can't take him to the hospital,' I said, 'he's booby-trapped.'

'What?' yelled the driver.

'He may be attached to a bomb,' I said.

He hit the brakes and I was thrown headfirst into the cab. I heard the paramedic in the back scream with frustration, and I looked up to find the driver's side door open and the driver legging it down the road.

It was a really good illustration of just why you shouldn't use the first lie that pops into your head. I climbed into his seat, closed the door, put the ambulance into gear and off we went.

The London Ambulance Service uses a fleet of Mercedes Sprinter vans, which are just like your standard Sprinter but with about two metric tons of stuff in the back and the kind of soft suspension designed to avoid killing the patient every time you go over a speed bump.

It's also got a load of extra LCD screens, buttons and switches that I, in the interests of simplicity, just ignored. Which was why we were still doing blues and twos as we sailed past the entrance to the UCH ambulance bay and headed down Gower Street towards the river.

It was about that time, according to the EOC call log, that the paramedic used her Airwave to report that her ambulance had been hijacked by an escaped mental patient masquerading as a police officer.

There's nothing quite like driving an emergency vehicle with a strip of spinners on its roof and a full-sized siren designed to cut through the iPod, car-stereo cocoon that most drivers live in and scare random pedestrians back onto the pavements. Moses parting the Red Sea must have felt like I did as I ploughed across the junction with High Holborn into Endell Street, with a brief moment of déjà vu as I shot down Bow Street and past the scaffolding that marked where they were still repairing the damage done to the Royal Opera House.

It's easy to get messed up trying to go south from Covent Garden. The roads have all been bollarded and blocked to stop them becoming traffic rat runs, but I'd spent two years patrolling out of Charing Cross nick so I knew where they were. I did a sharp right into Exeter Street and a sharp left down Burleigh Street, which caused the paramedic in the back to start screaming at me again. Which was uncalled for, since I felt I was finally getting on top of the ambulance's tricky handling.

'How's he doing?' I yelled over my shoulder.

'He's bleeding to death,' she yelled back.

I merged briefly with the cars on the Strand before cutting across the oncoming traffic and into Savoy Street, a narrow lane that runs straight down to the river just west of Waterloo Bridge. Parking spaces are hard to find in central London, and people tend to pack their cars onto streets with no thought that a vehicle of some width and heft might be driven past by someone with less than full confidence in his control. All told, the actual total damages came in at a tad under twenty thousand – mostly scraped paint, wing-mirrors, side panels and a pair of racing bikes that should never have been left secured to a roof rack in the first place. That's not counting the damage to the ambulance, which I'm sure was entirely superficial.

I bounced off the bottom of the street and out into the Embankment, swerved right and ran the ambulance up onto the pavement in front of the Savoy Pier. I scrambled out of the driver's seat and into the back of the ambulance, where the paramedic stared at me with stunned hatred.

Ash was barely breathing, and the dressing on his chest was completely soaked through with blood. When I asked the paramedic to open the door, I thought for a moment she was going to hit me, but she released the latches and threw them open. She wouldn't help me take Ash out, and I didn't have time to figure out how to work the trolley lift at the back, so I pulled him over my shoulder and staggered out into the drizzle.

I'd actually chosen the Savoy Pier for two reasons. It wasn't in use, so I wouldn't have to clamber over a boat to get to the river, and it had a nice gentle access ramp which would have been perfect to roll the trolley down had I managed to get the damn thing out of the ambulance. Instead, first I had to lumber up the ramp to the gate with Ash in a fireman's lift. He was a big healthy guy, and I suspected I was going to be a couple of centimetres

153

shorter by the time I reached the Thames. There's a thing like an open telephone booth at the top end of the ramp, designed to stop tourists, drunks and the merely criminal from running out onto the pier.

I paused for breath and realised that over the yodel of the ambulance's own siren I could hear other sirens approaching. I looked up and down the Embankment, and saw flashing blue lights coming from both directions. A glance over the parapet revealed that the tide was out, and jumping down there would be a three-metre drop onto stones and mud. I looked at the booth. It had the metal lock I remembered. I had been planning something subtle, but since I didn't have time I blew the whole thing off its hinges.

As I ran down the ramp, I heard the Incident Response Vehicles skidding to a halt behind me and the medley of grunts, shouts and radio chatter that generally announce the Old Bill is here to sort you out. As I ran across the width of the pier something whacked me hard across the thighs. The safety railing, I realised too late, and I went headfirst into the Thames.

The Goddess of the River will proudly tell you that the Thames is officially the cleanest industrial river in Europe, but it is not so clean that you want to drink it. I came up spitting, with a metallic taste in my mouth.

A dark shape bobbed in the water a metre from me – Ash, floating on his back.

I wear a pair of Dr Marten's shoes for general detective work. They're smart, hard-wearing and, crucially, retain some of that horrorshow goodness for kicking that still makes DMs the footwear of choice for all right-thinking skinheads and football hooligans. On the other hand, they're heavy and you do not want to be wearing them while treading water. Once I had them off, I splashed forward to check on Ash – he appeared to be a lot more buoyant than I was. I could hear him breathing, and it sounded stronger than before.

'Ash,' I said, 'you feeling better?'

'Much better,' he said languidly. 'The water's a bit salty, but nice and warm.'

It was bloody freezing for me. I looked back at the pier to see my fellow policemen shining their torches across the water, but it was OK because the tide was still going out and me and Ash were already a couple of hundred metres downstream. Well, OK until we were both swept out into the North Sea, or I died of hypothermia or drowned – or mostly likely an exciting combination of all three.

The current took us under the arches of Waterloo Bridge.

'You never told me she was a pale lady,' said Ash.

'Who's the pale lady?' I asked.

'Lady of death,' he said, and then said something in a language that sounded a bit like Welsh but probably wasn't.

155

'Hey,' said a nearby voice. 'What are you doing in the river?' Young, female, middle-class but with the clipped vowel sounds that come from having parents who believe in education, or else . . . This would be one of Mama Thames's girls.

'That's a difficult question,' I sputtered. 'I was driving home from Oxford, Ash called me and it all went pear-shaped from there,' I said. 'What are you doing in the river?'

'It's our turn on the rota,' said a second voice as we emerged on the other side of the bridge.

Ash was floating happily, and I wondered if I was the only one finding it hard to maintain a conversation while treading water. Something warm brushed against my leg and I twisted in time to see a girl pop her head out of the water. With just the lights from the bank she was hard to see clearly, but I recognised the cat's curve to the corner of her eyes and her mother's strong chin.

'What are you? Lifeguards?' I asked.

'Not exactly,' she said. 'If you make it out of the river under your own steam, fair enough. If you don't, then you belong to Mama.'

The first girl surfaced again and rose out of the water until she was waist-deep and as steady as if she were standing on a box. I noticed she was wearing a black wetsuit with ORCA written across her chest. Enough light caught her face for me to recognise her as Olympia, aka Counter's Creek, one of the younger daughters of Mama Thames, which meant that the other was her twin sister, Chelsea.

'Do you like the suit?' Olympia asked. 'Neoprene. It's the best you can buy.'

'I thought you guys liked to skinny-dip,' I said. Their older sister Beverley had swum naked the last time I'd seen her in the water.

'In your dreams,' said Olympia.

Chelsea surfaced on the far side of Ash. 'I thought I smelled blood,' she said. 'How you doing, Ash?'

'Much better now,' he said drowsily.

'I think we need to get him back to Mama,' she said.

'He told me to get him in the river,' I said. My legs were getting really tired, and I looked around to find the shore a lot further away – I was being dragged out into the central channel.

'What do you want – a medal?' asked Chelsea.

'How about a tow back to shore,' I said.

'Doesn't work like that,' said Olympia.

'But don't worry,' said Chelsea. 'If you go under for the third time, we'll be waiting for you.'

And then, with an unremarkable plopping sound, they all vanished beneath the surface.

I swore at some length at that point, and would have sworn for longer except I was freezing to death. I tried to gauge which bank was closer. It was tricky because the combination of the tide and the current was sweeping me towards Blackfriars Bridge. The same bridge under which

Roberto Calvi, God's own banker, got his neck stretched – not really a promising omen for me. I was freezing, and trying to remember the water survival training I did when I got my swimming certificate at primary school. My legs felt heavy and my arms ached and, as far as I could see, neither bank was closer.

It's remarkably easy to die in the Thames; lots of people manage it every year. I was beginning to worry I was going to be one of them.

I struck out for the south bank, on the basis that the Thames path ran along that side, so it was more likely there'd be members of the public able to render assistance. Plus the Oxo Tower made a convenient landmark. I didn't try to fight the current, and concentrated the last of my strength on getting closer to the bank.

I've never been what you'd call a strong swimmer, but if the alternative is being a statistic it's amazing what you can pull out of the reserves. The world contracted around me until there was nothing but the cold weight of my wet clothes, the pain in my arms and the occasional malicious slap in the face by a wave that would leave me gasping and spitting.

Mama Thames, I prayed, *you owe me: get me to shore.*

I realised suddenly that my arms weren't really working properly, and that it was getting harder just to keep my face above the water.

Mama Thames, I prayed again, *please.*

At some point the tide turned, and I found myself being washed back upstream until a random eddy caught me and gently shoved me onto the dirty mud of the Thames shore. I pulled myself slithering as far up the foreshore as I could manage, before rolling onto my back. I stared up at the rainclouds above, lit a dull sodium-red by the lights of the city, and thought that of the many things I never wanted to do again, this was near the top. I was so cold that my fingers and toes had gone numb, but I was shivering, which I took to be a good sign because I had this vague notion that it's when you stop shivering that you should be really worried. I decided that I could afford to stay where I was and catch my breath, or maybe some sleep – it had been a long day.

Contrary to what you might have been told, it is almost impossible to lie prostrate and groaning in a public place in London without attracting a crowd of putative good Samaritans – even when it's raining.

'Are you all right, mate?'

There were people on the parapet above me. I looked at their quizzical, upside-down faces from where I lay. Helpful people with mobile phones who would hopefully phone the police, who in turn would probably ask me to help them with their inquiries about a certain hijacked ambulance.

Do not meddle in the affairs of wizards, I thought, *for they are soggy and hard to light.*

I considered making a run for it, but the para-

medic and the ambulance driver could both identify me, and in any case, I was just too knackered
to move.

'You just hold on, mate,' said the voice from
above. 'The police are on their way.'

It took the police at least five minutes to get
there, which wasn't bad as response times go. I
was duly wrapped in a blanket and put in the back
of the IRV, where I told them I'd fallen in while
pursuing a suspect and had ended up on the wrong
side of the river. They didn't ask me any of the
usual questions about my imaginary suspect,
which I thought was odd, until the Jag pulled
alongside the IRV and I realised that Nightingale
had already put the fix in.

As we crossed back over Waterloo Bridge, he
asked me whether Ash was all right.

'I think so,' I said. 'Chelsea and Olympia didn't
seem worried.'

Nightingale nodded. 'Good work,' he said.

'I'm not in trouble?' I asked.

'You're in trouble,' he said. 'Just not with me.'

He still made me get up the next morning and
do double practice – the bastard.

After practice, I took the hard copy from Oxford
to the tech cave where I plonked it on the chaise
longue and tried to pretend it didn't exist. Entering
that much data was going to be a pig, and in fact
probably not worth the time it would take me to
do it. When I found Lesley had left me three emails

expressing the unutterable boredom of a small seaside town off season, I had one of those really stupid clever ideas. I emailed her back and asked whether she wanted to do some tedious data entry. She said yes, and I called IPS and arranged to have the copy picked up and biked over. Since you can't ask someone like Lesley, no matter how bored she is, to do something that dull without an explanation, I gave her an outline of who Jason Dunlop was and how we were looking for connections to Geoffrey Wheatcroft.

Lost books of magic, she wrote. *YFKM. Data entry. I'm so sad, me.*

Keep busy, I wrote back. She didn't reply to that one.

Dr Walid had posted me some jpegs of what looked like thin slices of cauliflower but which the accompanying text assured me were thin sections of Michael 'the Bone' Adjayi's brain. When magnified, they displayed the tell-tale neurological damage that was indicative of hyperthaumaturgical degradation – which is what kills you if you do too much magic. And also, as we had learned on our last big case, what happens if some total bastard uses you to do magic by proxy. It's a truism in policing that witnesses and statements are fine, but nothing beats empirical physical evidence. Actually it isn't a truism because most policemen think the word 'empirical' is something to do with Darth Vader, but it damn well should be. To drive the point home, Dr Walid included slices from

Cyrus Wilkinson's brain for comparison – the damage was identical.

This was proof that Mickey the Bone had been done in by the same method as Cyrus Wilkinson. If only I could figure out why.

I packaged up the lists for Lesley and gave them to Molly with strict instructions not to bite the courier when he came to call for them.

Back in the garage, there was a note folded under the Jag's windscreen wiper. It read, in Nightingale's surprisingly inelegant handwriting, *Unsupervised use of the Jaguar is suspended until such time as the appropriate driving certification is presented.* So Nightingale did know about the driving courses, after all.

I took the Asbo – it gets better mileage, anyhow.

Cheam is about as far south-west as you can get in London while officially staying in the capital. It's another typical outer London village which acquired, in short order, a railway station, some posh detached villas in the late Victorian style, and finally a smothering blanket of mock-Tudor semis built in the 1930s. Cheam is what the green belt was established to prevent happening to the rest of South-East England. Pictures of Cheam adorn the walls of planning offices of every Home County to serve as an awful warning. And that was *before* any black people moved into the area.

Chez Adjayi was a big detached Edwardian villa

along a road lined with variations on that theme. Apart from a token oval of greenery, the front garden had been paved with concrete, the better to park a couple of big German cars conveniently in front of the house. I could read the family history in that house. Father and mother had immigrated in the late 1960s, found jobs that they were wildly overqualified for and bought a run-down property in a relatively unfashionable area, and were now living off the fat of the property boom. Father would wear bespoke suits and be the man of the house, Mother would have a bedroom full of shoes and three mobile phones. The kids would be expected to become doctors, lawyers or engineers in descending order of preference.

A young woman around my age opened the door, I guessed she was a sister or close cousin. She had the same big forehead, high cheekbones and flat nose, although her face was plumper and rounder than Michael's and she wore half-moon reading glasses with black enamel frames. She smiled when she saw me, but the smile faded when I told her who I was. She was dressed in sweatshirt and track-suit bottoms. I smelled perspiration and furniture polish. When she let me in, I saw that the Hoover was sitting in the middle of the hallway and that the framed photographs that lined the walls had all been dusted and polished.

I asked her name.

'Martha,' she said, and she must have seen me

wince because she chuckled. 'Yes, I know. I'm in the kitchen,' she said, and led the way. It was a big kitchen with an oak table that was European but held an array of large pots, ladles and plastic washing-up bowls full of cassava and stockfish that was pure West African.

I declined tea and biscuits, and we sat down at the far corner of the table.

'Mum's at the hospital,' said Martha. 'I'm just cleaning up.' She didn't need to explain to me. Enough of my mum's London family had died over the years for me to know the drill. Once word got out that Michael Adjayi was dead, the relatives would start coming around, and God help Martha if the house wasn't immaculate when they got there.

'Was he the eldest son?' I asked.

'Only son,' said Martha bitterly. 'I've got two other sisters. They don't live here any more.'

I nodded to show I understood. Favoured son, the girls work but the boy carries the name. 'How long had he been playing jazz?'

'Mickey? Since forever,' said Martha.

'Did you think he was good?'

'He was brilliant,' she said.

I asked if her parents minded that he was going to be a musician, but she said that Mickey had it covered. 'He had a place at Queen Mary's, reading law,' she said. 'He figured that would give him at least four years to become famous.'

And once he was famous, Mother and Father

wouldn't care – as long as he was rich as well. Martha obviously thought it was a workable plan. I asked about his love life, and apparently that wasn't a problem either – at least, not as much of a problem as it might have been.

'White girl?' I asked.

'Yeah,' she said, 'but Cherie was really nice and a bit posh so, you know, that softened the blow for Mum and Dad.'

Martha didn't know the girlfriend's details, but she promised to ask her parents when they got back. She couldn't think of anybody who had it in for Mickey, or anything suspicious at all. 'He just went out one afternoon,' she said, 'and came back dead.'

On my way back from Cheam I got a call from Ms Ghosh at the Musicians Union. She wanted to tell me about the new wave of Anglo-Indian jazz that was coming out of Mumbai these days. I let her go on – it was better than the radio.

'Anyway,' she said eventually, 'there was one case. A member called Henry Bellrush, died suddenly just after a gig. The reason I remember is because I'd met him a couple of times and he always seemed so fit and healthy. London Marathon and all that . . . sort of thing.'

She gave me the address. It was in Wimbledon, and since I was still south of the river I headed over. Plus, I was pretty certain that sooner or later the whole hijacking-an-ambulance thing was going

165

to land on my head. I wasn't in a hurry to rush back for that.

'I'm not sure,' said Mrs Bellrush as she offered me a cup of tea, 'that I quite understand what you're doing here.'

I took the cup and saucer – the visitors' china, I noticed – and cradled it in my lap. I didn't dare put it down on the immaculate mahogany coffee table, and resting it precariously on the arm of the sofa was out of the question.

'We periodically review non-hospital fatalities,' I said.

'Whatever for?' asked Mrs Bellrush, and seated herself opposite me, neatly tucking her legs to the left. Anita Bellrush, widow of Henry 'the Lips' Bellrush, was in her mid-fifties, dressed in mauve slacks and a carefully ironed white silk blouse. She had sandy-blond hair and narrow blue eyes. She lived in the kind of 1930s brick-built detached house with bay windows that you can find in the suburbs all over Britain, but in this case it was located in Wimbledon. It contained a lot of good solid oak furniture overlaid with a layer of doilies, flowery chair covers and Dresden pottery. It was chintz, but not the cat-lady chintz I was used to. Perhaps it was Mrs Bellrush's manner, or her steely blue eyes, but I got the distinct impression that this was aggressive chintz, warrior chintz, the kind of chintz that had gone out to conquer an Empire and still had the good taste to dress for dinner. Any Ikea flat-pack that showed its face round here was going to be kindling.

'Because of Harold Shipman,' I said. 'You remember him?'

'The doctor who killed his patients,' she said. 'Ah, I see. You do random checks of routine deaths in order to ensure that the reporting is accurate. Presumably you also apply pattern-recognition systems to see if you can spot any anomalous trends?'

It sounded like a great idea, but I suspected we didn't because one of the first rules of police work is that trouble will always come looking for you, so there's no point looking for it.

'I just do the leg-work,' I said.

'Somebody always has to do the leg-work,' she said. 'Biscuit?'

They were expensive ones, with the dark chocolate covering with the greater than five per cent cocoa solids.

Henry Bellrush had learned to play the cornet in the Army. He'd enlisted in the Corps of Royal Engineers, and had risen through the ranks to Major before taking early retirement at the turn of the century.

'We met in the Army,' said Mrs Bellrush. 'He was a dashing captain and so was I; it was very romantic. In those days, once you were married you were out, so I moved into Civvie Street.' And ironically found herself in the same line of work as she had been in the Army. 'Only much better paid, of course,' she said.

I asked what kind of work, but Mrs Bellrush said she couldn't tell me. 'All very hush-hush I'm afraid,' she said. 'Official Secrets Act and all that jazz.' She looked at me over the rim of her tea cup. 'Now what is it you want to know about my husband's death?'

If ever a man had enjoyed his retirement it had been Henry Bellrush, what with the garden, the grandchildren, the holidays abroad and, of course, his music. He and some friends used to play at the local pub – strictly for their own enjoyment.

'But he joined the Musicians Union,' I said.

'That was Henry,' said Mrs Bellrush. 'He came up from the ranks – never lost that sense of solidarity with the common man.'

'You didn't notice anything unusual in his behaviour?' It was a standard question.

'Such as what?' she asked, just a tad too defensively.

'Staying out late, unexplained absences, forgetfulness,' I said, all of which got nothing. 'Changes in spending habits, unusual receipts, credit-card bills.' That got a reaction.

Her eyes met mine and then she looked away.

'He'd been making regular purchases from a shop in Soho,' she said. 'He didn't try to hide it from me, and it was all there on his credit-card statement. After he died I found some receipts still in his wallet.'

I asked where they were from.

'A Glimpse of Stocking,' she said.

'The lingerie shop?'

'You know it?'

'I've walked past it,' I said. Actually I'd once spent about ten minutes looking in the window, but to be fair I was on patrol, it was three in the morning, and I was very bored. 'Are you sure he wasn't buying a present for you?'

'I'm sure I never received anything quite as daring as a scarlet Alloetta corset in raw silk with matching satin knickers,' she said. 'Not that I would have been averse. Shocked, perhaps, but not averse.'

People don't like to speak ill of the dead even when they're monsters, let alone when they're loved ones. People like to forget any bad things that someone did, and why should they remember? It's not like they're going to do it again. So I kept the next question as emotionally neutral as I could.

'Do you think he might have been having an affair?'

She stood and walked over to an antique folding desk and retrieved an envelope.

'Given the nature of the purchases,' she said, handing me the envelope, 'I can't think of an alternative explanation – can you?'

Inside the envelope were a sheaf of receipts, most of them of the kind printed out by a modern till, but a couple handwritten in what I suspected was a deliberately archaic fashion – these had *A Glimpse of Stocking* printed at the top.

He might have been a transvestite, I thought, but I kept that to myself.

Giacomo Casanova, the original Italian stallion, arrived in London to find one of his ex-lovers and babymothers holed up in Carlisle House, the former residence of the Earl of Salisbury, which faced onto Soho Square. Her name was Theresa Cornelys and, for her services to dissipation, debauchery and the home-furnishing industry, she was once declared the Empress of Pleasure.

Carlisle House became London's first members-only club. For a modest subscription one could enjoy an evening of opera, good food and, it was rumoured, convivial intimate company. It was Theresa who established the time-honoured Soho tradition of packing them in, getting them drunk and fleecing them till they squeaked. Alas, she was a better hostess than a bookkeeper and eventually, after two decades, several bankruptcies and a comeback tour, she died alone and penniless in a debtors' prison.

The rise and fall of Theresa Cornelys proves three things: that the wages of sin are high, that you should 'just say no' to opera, and that it's always wise to diversify your investment portfolio. This was the advice followed by Gabriella Rossi, also Italian, who arrived in London as a child refugee in 1948. After a career in the rag trade, she opened her first branch of A Glimpse of Stocking in 1986, where she profited from the wages of sin, albeit tastefully, said no to opera, and made sure that her portfolio was suitably robust. When she died in 2003 it was as Dame Rossi, knighted for her services to naughtiness and leaving behind a small chain of lingerie shops.

The Soho branch was managed by a skinny blonde woman dressed in a no-nonsense trouser suit, but with no blouse and worryingly thin wrists. She seemed genuinely amused when I showed her my warrant card, and although she had no recollection of Henry Bellrush, she laughed out loud when I suggested that he might have been buying for himself.

'I doubt that,' she said. 'This particular type of corset has a "vintage" waist. It's designed to be ten inches smaller than the hips – I doubt a man could wear that.'

The shop was artfully cluttered with antique display racks and cabinets to give it a pleasantly retro feel, so that even the English could enjoy frilly underwear safe in the knowledge that it came wrapped up with an ironic, postmodern bow. On one wall there were framed photographs of women, all either monochrome or in the faded tones of 1960s colour photography. The women were mostly half-naked or dressed in corsets and the kind of frilly knickers that probably got my father in a twist. One was the famous Morley portrait of Christine Keeler sitting backwards on a rather uncomfortable-looking Scandinavian chair. Several had been autographed, and I recognised one of the names – Rusty Gaynor, the legendary queen of Soho strippers in the 1960s.

The manageress checked carefully through the receipts.

'Definitely not a man,' she said. 'Not in these sizes. Although judging from the rest of the items, we're talking about a big, healthy girl here. If I had to make a guess, I would say these were bought for a stage act.'

'What kind of act?'

'A burlesque dancer,' she said, 'without a doubt. Probably one of Alex's girls. Alexander Smith. Puts on shows down at the Purple Pussycat. Very tasteful.'

'A stripper, you mean?' I asked.

'Oh dear,' said the manageress, 'you mustn't call them that.'

The difference between stripping and burlesque, as far as I could tell, was class.

'We don't have poles on stage,' said Alexander Smith, burlesque impresario. He was a thin, fox-faced man in a fawn-coloured suit with 1970s lapels but not – because there are limits to decency – a kipper tie. Instead he wore a plum-coloured ascot with matching pocket handkerchief and, probably, silk socks. He was so completely camp that it didn't really come as too much of a surprise that he was married with grandchildren. No gay man would have to work that hard. Smith cheerfully showed me the photographs of 'her indoors'

172

– his wife, and little Penelope and Esmeralda, and explained why poles were the work of the devil.

'Inventions of Beelzebub himself,' he said. 'Stripping is about getting your kit off in time to the music. There's no real eroticism to it; the punters want to see her minge and she wants to get paid. Wham, bam, no thank you ma'am.'

Over his shoulder I watched as a fit-looking white woman on the club's small stage rotated her hips to Lounge Against the Machine's cover of 'Baby's Got Back'. She was wearing a dancer's leotard and a baggy pink sweat top and I had to admit that, despite the lack of minge, I was suitably entranced. Smith turned to see what I was watching.

'It's about glamour,' he said, 'and the art of sensuality. The sort of show you could bring your mother to.'

Not *my* mother, I thought. She doesn't do ironic postmodernism.

I showed Smith the picture of Henry Bellrush I'd got from his wife. 'That's Henry,' said Smith. 'Has something happened to him?'

'Was he a regular?' I asked, to move us on.

'He's an artiste,' said Smith. 'A musician. Beautiful, beautiful cornet player. He does this act with this lovely girl called Peggy. Very classy, just him on the cornet and her moving as he played. She could hold an audience transfixed just by taking her glove off. They used to sigh when she went topless 'cause they knew it was almost over.'

173

'And their relationship was strictly business?' I asked.

'You keep using the past tense,' said Smith. 'Something *has* happened, hasn't it?'

I explained that Henry Bellrush was dead and that I was conducting routine inquiries.

'Well, that's a shame,' said Smith. 'I wondered why they hadn't turned up for a while. In answer to your question, those two were strictly professional: he liked playing and she liked dancing. I think that's as far as it went.'

He also liked buying her the costumes, too; or perhaps he saw it as an investment. I wondered whether I should tell his wife.

I asked if he had any publicity pictures of the mysterious Peggy, but although he was sure they existed, he didn't have any at the club.

I asked when their last gig was and he gave a date back at the start of the month, less than a day before Bellrush died. 'Was it here?' I asked. Fourteen days was a long time for transient *vestigia* to be retained, but it was worth a try.

'No,' said Smith. 'Much more classy than this – it was part of our Summer Burlesque Festival at the Café de Paris. We hold one every year to raise awareness of burlesque amongst the public.'

I emerged blinking into weak afternoon sunlight, and before I could get my bearings I was ambushed by Simone Fitzwilliam.

'Constable,' she said brightly, and slipped her

174

arm through mine, 'what brings you to my neighbourhood again?' Her arm was warm and soft against my side, and I smelled honeysuckle and caramel.

I told her I was still investigating some suspicious deaths.

'Including poor Cyrus?' she asked.

'I'm afraid so.'

'Well, I'm determined to put that behind me,' she said. 'Cyrus wouldn't have wanted me to mope. He believed in living in the moment and double-entry bookkeeping. But then, if we were all the same, where would be the fun in that? So where next will our sleuthing take us?'

'I need to check out the Café de Paris,' I said.

'Oh,' she said, 'I haven't been there for such a long time. You must take me, I could be your plucky sidekick.'

How could I argue with that?

I lied my way into the Café de Paris by claiming I was following up a spot check by Clubs and Vice and that I could be in and out in five minutes. The day manager either bought it or wasn't being paid enough money to care either way.

The interior was a riot of gold leaf, red velvet and royal-blue curtains. The main room was oval with a split staircase at one end and small stage at the other. A balcony swept around the circumference and it reminded me uneasily of the Royal Opera House.

'You can just feel the history,' said Simone,

clutching my arm. 'The Prince of Wales used to come here regularly.'

'I hope the food is macrobiotic then,' I said.

'What in the world is macrobiotic?' asked Simone.

'You know, beans and rice,' I said, and stopped when I realised I didn't know what macrobiotic was either. 'Healthy food,' I said.

'That doesn't sound like the Prince,' she said. She skipped around to face me. 'We have to dance.'

'There's no music,' I said.

'We can hum,' she said. 'You do know how to hum, don't you?'

'I need to check the stage,' I said, trying to convince myself at the same time.

She pretended to pout, but the corner of her scarlet lips twitched and gave her away. 'When constabulary duty's to be done,' she said, 'a police-man's lot is not a happy one.'

The small stage had enough room for its in situ baby grand and maybe a trio, if the singers were thin. I couldn't see the buxom Peggy strutting her stuff, however tastefully, without falling off the edge. I said as much.

'Ahem,' said Simone. 'I think you'll find the stage can be extended forward to create more space. I believe theatrical people call it an "extendable stage". Mind you, I'm certain I remember the band being at the other end.'

I could feel them, layers of *vestigia* etched into the walls of the Café de Paris, flashes of laughter, the smell of tea, snatches of music, a sudden sharp

176

taste of blood on my tongue. It was like an old church far too entangled in too many lives and events to be able to pick out any one thread. Certainly nothing recent. A *vestigium* isn't laid down like a groove in a record; it's not like a tape recording. It's more like the memory of a dream, and the harder you grasp at it the faster it melts away.

Another flash – brick dust and a ringing silence. I remembered; the Café de Paris had been hit during the Blitz, killing most of the musicians including the legendary bandleader Ken Johnson. That might explain the silence. Polidori once described a plague pit he investigated as being *an abyss of solitude* – cheerful bugger that he was.

'You promised me a dance,' said Simone.

Actually I hadn't, but I took her in my arms and she pressed in closer. She started to hum as we artlessly swayed in a small circle. I didn't recognise the tune. Her grip on my waist tightened and I grew hard against her. 'You can do better than that,' she said.

I put some grind into the sway and for a moment I was back at the Brixton Academy with Lisa Pascal, who lived on the Stockwell Park Estate and seemed determined to be my first ever, although actually she ended up being violently sick on Astoria Park Walk and I slept on the sofa in her mum's front room.

Then I heard it: Johnny Green's opening bars but with a swing beat and a voice singing far away

. . . My heart is sad and lonely/For you I sigh, for you, dear, only. Simone was short enough to rest her cheek against my chest, and it was only when I noticed that she was copying me that I realised I was humming the tune. Her perfume mingled with the *vestigia* of dust and silence, and the words were clear enough for me to sing them softly. *Why haven't you seen it?/I'm all for you, body and soul.*

I felt Simone shudder and put her arm around my neck and pull me down until she could whisper in my ear. 'Take me home.'

We were practically running by the time we got to Berwick Street, and Simone had her keys out and ready for a front door that opened straight onto a steep staircase with dirty communal carpeting, forty-watt bulbs and those pop-out timer switches that never last long enough for you to get all the way to the top. Simone led me up a third flight of stairs that dog-legged around some bizarre retrofit put in back in the 1950s, when this was a flat for French Maids and 'Ring top bell for models'. It was a steep climb and I was beginning to flag, but the sway of her hips dragged me up the fourth and final flight and we burst out onto the roof. I managed to get brief impressions of iron railings, bushy green pot plants, a bar table with a furled white and blue sunshade and then we were kissing, her hands pushing down the back of my jeans, yanking me forward. And we went down onto a mattress.

Let's be honest here, there's no way to get out of a pair of tight jeans with any dignity, especially if a beautiful woman has one hand in your boxers and an arm wrapped around your waist. You always end up frantically kicking your legs in an effort to get the damned things past your ankles. I was a gentleman, though, and helped her off with her leggings – everything else we were wearing had to wait because Simone wasn't looking for a slow build-up. She pulled me between her thighs and having lined me up to her satisfaction, pulled me the rest of the way in. We went at it for ages, but finally I looked up to find her rearing above me with the waning moon watching us over her shoulder, her waist bucking under my palms. She threw her head back and bellowed and with that, we both came together.

She flopped down on top of me, her skin feverish and sweaty, her face buried in my shoulder.

'Fuck me,' I said.

'What, again?' she asked. 'There's no stopping you, is there?'

I was instantly hard again, because nothing gets a man going like a bit of flattery. Yes, when it comes to sex, we really are that shallow. It was chilly, and I shivered as I rolled her over onto her back. She opened her arms wide but I ignored them and let my lips trace a line down to her belly button. Her hands grabbed my head – urging me lower, but I stretched it out. Treat 'em mean, keep 'em keen, that's my motto. I put my mouth where the money was and I didn't let up until her legs were pointing straight up in the air and her knees were locked. Then I climbed my slippery way back up and introduced myself once more. Simone's ankles locked behind my backside and her arms snaked round my shoulders and for quite a long period, coherent thought was something that happened to other people.

We came apart with a sticky pop, and for a moment we just lay there and steamed in the night air. Simone kissed me open-mouthed, hungry, for a long moment, and then levered herself off the mattress.

'I'll be back in a minute,' she said.

I watched the heavy sway of her pale buttocks as she padded across the roof and slipped in through the door. There was still enough moon and street light to see that the top of the terrace had been converted into a roof garden, and a good professional conversion it was too, with solid flags underfoot and waist-high iron railings. Wooden tubs stood at the four corners, each planted with something that was either a really big plant or a very small tree. The mattress I was lying on was actually a proper outdoor seating cushion with a water-resistant PVC covering. It was cooling off under my naked buttocks, and so was I.

From below came the muttering, shouting party noise of another Soho evening. I became very conscious of the fact that I was lying stark-bollock-naked on top of a roof in central London. I really hoped the guys at Air Support weren't called into patrol, otherwise I could end up on YouTube as that naked dickhead on the roof ROFL.

I was seriously considering looking for my clothes when Simone arrived back with a duvet and an old-fashioned picnic hamper with F&M stencilled on the side. She dropped the basket by the mattress and flung herself and the duvet around me.

'You're freezing,' she said.

'You left me on the roof,' I said. 'I nearly froze to death. They were scrambling the air-sea rescue helicopters and everything.'

She warmed me up for a bit, and then we investigated the hamper. It was a real Fortnum and Mason picnic hamper complete with stainless-steel flask of hot chocolate, a bottle of Hine cognac and a whole Battenberg cake wrapped in greaseproof paper. No wonder it took her so long to come back.

'You just had this lying about?' I asked.

'I like to be prepared,' she said.

'Did you know Casanova used to live around here when he was in London?' I said. 'When he went out for an assignation he used to carry a little valise with eggs, plates and a spirit stove in it.' I slipped my hand around the warm, heavy curve of her breast. 'That way, wherever he ended up he could still have a fried egg for breakfast.' I kissed her – she tasted of chocolate.

'I never knew Casanova was a Boy Scout,' she said.

181

We sat under the duvet and watched the moon setting behind the roofs of Soho. We ate Battenberg cake and listened to the police sirens whoop up and down Charing Cross Road and Oxford Street. When we were suitably refreshed, we had mad sex until what passes for the dawn chorus in Soho was welcoming the first blush of the new day.

I like to think old Giacomo would have approved.

CHAPTER 7

ALMOST LIKE BEING IN LOVE

Sir Robert Mark was commissioner of the Metropolitan Police from 1972 to 1977, and is famous for two things – the Goodyear tyre adverts where he said the words, 'I believe this to be a major contribution to road safety', and Operation Countryman, an investigation into corruption within his own force. Back in what the *Daily Mail* calls the good old days, a conscientious copper could triple his income just by sticking his hand out at the right moment, and an armed blagger could walk away from a collar for just a modest consideration. Though to be fair, they always tried to make sure that someone was charged with the offence so at least justice was seen to be done, and that's the main thing. Commissioner Mark, who took a dim view of this, initiated the most sweeping anti-corruption drive the Met had ever seen, which is why he's the figure that police parents use to keep their little baby police officers in line. Behave, or nasty Sir Robert Mark will come round and boot you off the force. This is probably why the current commissioner had a portrait of Mark hanging in the atrium of his office, strategically placed so that he faced the row of uncomfortable green faux-leather seats that me and Nightingale were forced to wait on.

When you're a lowly constable, nothing good can come of getting this close to the big man himself. Last time I'd been there I'd been sworn in as an apprentice wizard. This time, I suspected it was going to be mostly swearing. Next to me Nightingale seemed relaxed enough, reading the *Telegraph* in a tan lightweight Davies & Son suit that was either brand new or, more likely, coming back into style from some earlier epoch. I was in my uniform because when confronted with authority a uniform is a constable's friend, especially when it has been ironed to razor sharpness by Molly, who seemed to regard a trouser crease as a conveniently located offensive weapon.

A secretary opened the door for us. 'The Commissioner will see you now,' she said, and we stood up and trooped off to face the music.

The Commissioner's office is not that impressive, and while the carpet wasn't too budget-conscious, no amount of wood panelling could disguise the dull grey mid-1960s concrete bones of the New Scotland Yard building. But the Metropolitan Police has over 50,000 personnel and a working budget of four and a half billion quid, and is responsible for everything from antisocial behaviour in Kingston to anti-terrorism in Whitehall, so the Commissioner's office doesn't really need to try that hard.

The Commissioner sat waiting for us. He was wearing his uniform cap, and that was when I truly knew we were in deep shit. We stopped in front of the desk and Nightingale actually twitched, as if suppressing the impulse to salute. The Commissioner stayed in his chair. No handshakes were offered, and we were not invited to sit.

'Chief Inspector Nightingale,' he said, 'I trust you've had a chance to acquaint yourself with the reports pertaining to the events of last Tuesday night.'

'Yes, sir,' said Nightingale.

'You are aware of the accusations levelled by members of the London Ambulance Service and the preliminary report by the DPS?'

'Yes, sir,' said Nightingale.

I flinched. The DPS is the Directorate of Professional Standards, fiends in human form that walk amongst us to keep the rank and file in fear and despondency. Should you feel the cold damp breath of the DPS on your collar, as I did then, the next thing you need to know is which bit is doing the breathing. I didn't think it would be the ACC, the Anti-Corruption Command or the IIC, the Internal Investigations Command, because hijacking an ambulance would best be categorised as criminally stupid rather than stupidly criminal. Or at least, I was hoping that's the way they would see it, and that I'd be done by the MCAV, the Misconduct Civil Actions and Vetting command, whose job it was to deal with those officers who

185

have laid the Met open to being sued in the courts – by traumatised paramedics, for example.

'Do you stand by your assessment of Constable Grant's actions that night?'

'Yes sir,' said Nightingale. 'I believe that Constable Grant, faced with difficult circumstances, evaluated the situation correctly and took swift and decisive action to prevent the death of the individual known as Ash Thames. Had he not removed the cold iron from the wound or, having removed it, had not transported Ash to the river, I have no doubt that the victim would have died – from loss of blood at the very least.'

The Commissioner looked directly at me, and I actually found myself holding my breath until he looked back at Nightingale.

'You were left in a supervisory position despite your medical condition because I was assured that you remain the only officer qualified to handle "special" cases,' he said. 'Was this a mistake on my part?'

'No, sir,' said Nightingale. 'Until such time as Constable Grant is fully trained I remain the only suitably qualified officer currently serving in the Metropolitan Police. Believe me, sir, I am as alarmed at this prospect as you are.'

The Commissioner nodded. 'Since it appears that Grant had no choice but to act as he did, I am willing to chalk this up to a failure of supervision on your part. This will be considered a verbal reprimand, and a note will be entered into your record.' He turned to me and I kept my eye on a nice safe patch of the wall a couple centimetres to the left of his head.

'While I accept that you are inexperienced and being forced to use your own judgement in circumstances that lie . . .' the Commissioner paused to choose his words '. . . outside of conventional police work, I would like to remind you that you swore an oath both as a constable and as an apprentice. And you were warned when you did so that extraordinary things were expected of you. At this point, no disciplinary action will be taken and no note will be appended to your record. However, in future I wish to see you exercise more tact, more discretion and to try and keep the property damage to a bare minimum. Do you understand?'

'Yes sir,' I said.

'The property damage,' said the Commissioner, turning back to Nightingale, 'including that to the ambulance, will be paid for out of the Folly's budget, not the Met's general contingency fund. As will any legal costs and damages that arise out of civil litigation taken against the Metropolitan Police. Is that understood?'

'Yes, sir,' we both said.

I was sweating with relief. The only reason that I wasn't facing a serious disciplinary hearing was because the Commissioner probably didn't want to explain to the Metropolitan Police Authority why a lowly Constable was currently de facto head

187

of an Operational Command Unit. Any advocate I called in from the Police Federation would have had a field day with my lack of effective supervision by a senior officer – Nightingale being on sick leave, remember. Not to mention the health and safety implications of being forced to jump into the Thames in the middle of the night.

I thought it was all over, but it wasn't. The Commissioner touched his intercom. 'You can send them in now, please.'

I recognised the guests; the first was a short, rangy middle-aged white man looking surprisingly dapper in an M&S ready-to-wear blue pinstriped suit. No tie, I noticed, and his hair was as resolutely comb-resistant as a hedgerow. Oxley Thames, wisest of the sons of Father Thames, his chief councillor, media guru and hatchet man. He gave me a wry look as he took the seat offered by the Commissioner to the right of his desk. The second was a handsome fair-skinned woman with a sharp nose and slanted eyes. She wore a black Chanel skirt suit that, had it been a car, would have done nought to sixty in less than 3.8 seconds. Lady Ty, Mama Thames's favourite daughter, Oxford graduate and ambitious fixer, she seemed pleased to see me, which didn't bode well. As she joined Oxley I realised that the bollocking wasn't over, and this was to be *The Bollocking 2: This Time It's Personal.*

'I believe you know Oxley and Lady Tyburn,' said the Commissioner. 'They've been asked by their "principals" to clarify their position with regard to Ash Thames.' He turned to Oxley and Ty and asked who wanted to go first.

Ty turned to the Commissioner. 'I have a question for Constable Grant. If I may?' she asked.

The Commissioner made a gesture that suggested I was all hers.

'At any point,' she said, 'did it cross your mind what would have happened to my sister had Ash been killed?'

'No, ma'am,' I said. It was the truth. It hadn't crossed my mind at all, and when it did, just then, it wasn't a comfortable feeling at all.

'Which is an interesting admission, given that you helped negotiate that agreement,' she said. 'Were you unaware of the exact nature of an exchange of hostages, perhaps? Or did you just forget that should death befall Ash while he was in our care, my sister's life would have been forfeit? You do know what the word "forfeit" means?'

I went cold, because I hadn't given it a thought, not when recruiting Ash for the surveillance job, or even when I was sailing down the Thames with him. If he'd been killed then Beverley Brook, Lady Ty's sister, would have faced the ultimate forfeit. Which meant I'd nearly killed two people that night.

I glanced at Nightingale, who frowned and nodded for me to reply.

'I do know what the word forfeit means,' I said. 'And in my defence, I'd like to say that I never

189

expected Ash to put himself in harm's way. I considered him a sober and reliable figure, like all his brothers.'

Oxley snorted, which earned him a glare from Lady Ty.

'I hadn't counted on him being quite so brave or quick-witted,' I said, and got a look from Oxley that conveyed the notion that there's such a thing as laying the blarney on too thick. It didn't matter, because the reason you don't fight with Lady Ty is she just waits for you to finish dancing about and then gives you a smack.

'While I'm of course aware of the role played by Inspector Nightingale and Constable Grant in facilitating a conciliation framework,' said Lady Ty, 'I think it would be better, in light of recent events, if they took a less proactive stance with regards to matters relating to riverine diplomacy.'

I was moved almost to applause. The Commissioner nodded, which just proved that the fix was in – probably with the Greater London Police Authority and the Mayor's Office. He probably felt he had enough on his plate without us dishing out any more. He turned to Oxley and asked whether he had anything to add.

'Ash is a young man,' said Oxley, 'and it's well known that boys will be boys. Still, I don't think it would hurt if Constable Grant was to exercise a hair more responsibility when dealing with him.'

We waited a moment for more, but Oxley just looked blank. Lady Ty didn't look happy, so maybe the fix wasn't as firmly in place as she would like.

I gave her my secretive little-boy smirk, the one that I've been using to drive my mum berserk since I was eight. Her lips thinned, but she was obviously made of sterner stuff than my mum.

'That seems reasonable,' said Nightingale. 'As long as all parties stay within the agreement and the law, I'm sure we can give assent to a hands-off approach.'

'Good,' said the Commissioner. 'And while I'm always glad to have these little chats, let's try and keep them out of my office in future.'

With that, we were dismissed.

'That could have been worse,' I said as we walked past the eternal flame of remembrance that burns in the New Scotland Yard foyer. It's there to remember those brave men and women who have fallen while doing their duty and to remind us, the living, to be bloody careful.

'Tyburn's dangerous,' said Nightingale as we headed for the underground car park. 'She thinks she can define her role in the city through bureaucratic manoeuvring and office politics. Sooner or later she'll come into conflict with her own mother.'

'And if that happens?'

'The consequences could well be mythic,' said Nightingale. 'I think it would be in your interests not to be standing between them when that occurs.' He looked at me thoughtfully. 'Or anywhere within the Thames Valley, for that matter.'

Nightingale was due a check-up at UCH, so he dropped me off in Leicester Square and I called Simone.

'Give me an hour to clean up,' she said. 'And then come over.'

I was still in my uniform, which would have made drinking in a pub a bit of a problem, so I grabbed a coffee at the Italian place on Frith Street before proceeding at a leisurely pace up Old Compton Street. I was just thinking of picking up some cakes from Patisserie Valerie when my highly tuned copper's senses were irresistibly drawn, like those of a big-game hunter, by the subtle clues that something was amiss in Dean Street.

Plus the police tape, the forensics tent and the uniformed bodies who'd been given the exciting task of guarding the crime scene. My professional curiosity got the better of me, so I sidled up to have a look.

I spotted Stephanopoulos talking to a couple of other DSs from the Murder Team. You don't just step into someone else's crime scene without permission, so I paused at the tape and waited until I could catch Stephanopoulos's eye. She stamped over a minute later and clocked the uniform.

'Back on patrol with us mere mortals, are you?' she said. 'I think you got off lightly. The even money in the incident room was that you were going to be suspended with extreme prejudice.'

'Verbal warning,' I said.

Stephanopoulos looked incredulous. 'For hijacking an ambulance?' she said. 'You get a verbal warning? You're not making any friends amongst the rank and file, you know.'

'I know,' I said. 'Who's dead?'

'Nothing to do with you,' said Stephanopoulos. 'Construction foreman from Crossrail. Found this morning in one of his access shafts.' Although the bulk of new Crossrail stations were finished, the contractors still seemed intent on digging up the streets. 'Might just be an accident, anyway; health and safety on these sites is almost as bad as it is in the Met.'

Health and safety was the current obsession of the Police Federation. Last year it had been stab vests, but lately they felt that police officers were taking unnecessary safety risks while pursuing suspects. They wanted better H&S guidelines to prevent injury and, presumably, remote-controlled drones to do the actual chases.

'Did it happen in the dark?'

'No, at eight o'clock this morning in full daylight,' said Stephanopoulos. 'Which means he was probably pushed, but – and this is the important bit as far as you're concerned – there is definitely nothing remotely supernatural about the scene, thank God. So you can just bugger off.'

'Thanks, Sarge,' I said. 'I shall do that.'

'Wait,' said Stephanopoulos. 'I want you to check the follow-up interviews with Colin Sandbrow – they should be on the system by now.'

'Who's Colin Sandbrow?'

'The man who would have been the next victim if your weirdo friend hadn't got in the way,' she said. 'If you think you can do that without generating more property damage.'

I laughed to show that I was a good sport, but cop humour being what it is I knew I'd be carrying that ambulance around for the rest of my career. I left Stephanopoulos to impose her will on the crime scene, and slipped through St Anne's Court and D'Arblay Street to Berwick Street. Since I hadn't been paying attention the night before, I had to stop and get my bearings before I spotted the door – sandwiched between a chemist's and a record shop that specialised in vintage vinyl. The black paint was peeling and the little cards on the entryphone were either smudged or missing entirely. It didn't matter. I knew she was on the top floor.

'You wretch,' spluttered the entryphone. 'I'm not ready.'

'I can go round the block again,' I said.

The lock buzzed and I pushed the door open. The stairs didn't look any better in the daylight; the carpet was pale blue and worn through in places, and the walls showed stains from where people had put their hands out to balance themselves. On each floor there were blind doors which, in Soho, could lead anywhere from strict discipline at reasonable rates to a television production company. I paced myself so I wasn't panting when I reached the top floor, and knocked on the door.

When Simone opened it and saw me in my uniform, she skipped back a step and clapped her hands. 'Look at this,' she said. 'It's a strippergram.'

She'd been cleaning in a pair of grey tracksuit bottoms and a navy-blue sweatshirt that looked as if it had been cropped with a pair of nail scissors. Her hair was wrapped in a scarf in an English way that I'd only ever seen on *Coronation Street*. I stepped forward and grabbed her. She smelled of sweat and Domestos. It would have been straight onto the floor right then if she hadn't gasped out that the door was still open. We broke long enough to close the door and stumble to the bed. Only one bed, I noticed, but it was king-sized and we did our best to use every bit. At some point my uniform came off and we never did find out what happened to her sweatshirt – she left the scarf on, though, because something about it turned me on.

An hour and a bit later, I had a chance to look around the flat. The bed took up one whole corner of the main room and was, apart from one over-stuffed leather armchair, the only thing to sit on. The only other furniture was a mismatched trio of wardrobes lining one wall and a solid oak chest of drawers that was so big the only way to get it into the room must have been to winch it in through the window. There was no TV that I could see, or a stereo, although a suitably small MP3 player might have vanished amongst the drifts of cloth that had colonised the room. I'm an only child, so I've only ever had to live with one woman at a time and so wasn't prepared for the sheer volume of clothes that could be generated by three sisters sharing one flat. The shoes were particularly pervasive; serried ranks of, to me, almost identical open-toed slingback stilettos. Tangles of sandals had been stuffed into random nooks, while boxes of court shoes filled the gaps between the wardrobes. Pairs of boots, from calf-length to thigh-high, hung from nails on the wall like rows of swords in a castle.

Simone saw me eyeing a pair of fetish boots with six-centimetre spike heels and started to wriggle out of my arms. 'Want me to try them on?' she said.

I pulled her back against my chest and kissed her neck – I didn't want her going anywhere. She twisted in my arms and we kissed until she said she had to pee. Once your lover's gone you might as well get up, and so I folded myself into the bathroom, a tiny cubbyhole with just enough room for a surprisingly modern power shower, toilet and the kind of small, odd-shaped sink designed to fit into the space of last resort. While I was in there, my copper's instincts got the better of me and I rummaged through their medicine cabinet. Simone and her sisters were clearly in favour of the long-term storage of dangerous chemicals because there were strips of paracetamol and prescription sleeping tablets that dated back ten years.

'Are you going through my things?' asked Simone from the kitchen.

I asked how her and her sisters managed to get along with such a small bathroom.

'We all went to boarding school, darling,' said Simone. 'Survive that, and you can handle anything.'

When I came out she asked me if I wanted tea. I said why not, and we had a full English tea – on a tray with blue and gold Wedgwood crockery, blackberry jam and heavily buttered crumpets.

I liked looking at her naked, reclining on the bed like something out of the National Gallery with a cup of tea in one hand and a crumpet in the other. Given that we'd just had quite a good summer her skin was very pale, translucent almost. When I lifted my hand from her thigh a pink outline remained.

'Yes,' she said. 'Some of us don't tan very well – thank you for reminding me.'

I kissed the spot better by way of apology, and then the curve of her belly by way of invitation. She giggled and pushed me away.

'I'm ticklish,' she said. 'Finish your tea first, you savage. Have you no manners?'

I took up the willow-pattern tea cup and sipped the tea. It tasted different, exotic. A posh blend, I suspected, from another Fortnum and Mason hamper. She fed me some crumpet and I asked her why she didn't have a TV.

'We didn't have television when we were growing up,' she said. 'So we never got into the habit of watching. There's a radio somewhere for listening to *The Archers*. We never miss an episode of *The Archers*. Although I must admit, I can't always keep all the characters straight; they do seem to be always getting married, having secret love affairs and as soon as I've grown familiar with them they die or leave Ambridge.' She looked at me over the rim of her teacup. 'Not a follower of *The Archers*, are you?'

'Not really,' I said.

'We must seem like such Bohemians to you,' she said, finishing her tea. 'Living all higgledy-piggledy in one room, no television, in amongst the flesh-pots of Soho.' She placed tea cup and tray on the floor by the bed before reaching out to pluck the empty cup from my fingers.

'I think you worry too much about what I think,' I said.

Simone removed the tea cup safely from the bed and kissed me on the knee.

'Do I?' she asked, and grabbed me with her hand.

'Definitely,' I said, trying not to squeak as she kissed her way up my thigh.

Two hours later she threw me out of bed, but in the nicest possible way.

'My sisters will be back soon,' she said. 'We have rules. No men in the bed past ten o'clock.'

'There have been other men?' I said, while looking for my boxers.

'Of course not,' she said. 'You're my first.'

Simone was pulling on random items that she'd found on the floor, including a pair of satin knickers that fit her like a second skin. Watching them go on was almost as sexy as watching them come off would be. She caught me panting, and wagged her finger at me.

'No,' she said. 'If we start again we'll never stop.'

I could have lived with that, but a gentleman knows when to give in gracefully and depart the scene. Not without some serious snogging in the doorway first, though.

I walked back through Soho with the scent of honeysuckle in my nostrils and, according to subsequent records, helped officers from Charing Cross and West End Central break up two fights, a domestic and a hen party that had ended with an attempted sexual assault on a male stripper. But I don't remember any of that.

You practise *Scindere* by levitating an apple with *Impello* and then fixing it in place while your teacher tries to dislodge it with a cricket bat. The next morning I put up three in a row and they didn't so much as wobble when Nightingale smacked them. He hit them hard enough to pulp them, of course, but the bits just hung about like a food accident on a space station.

The first time Nightingale demonstrated the *forma*, I'd asked how long the apples would stay fixed in place. He'd said that it depended on how much magic the apple had been imbued with. For most apprentices that meant anything up to half an hour. Such vagueness neatly summed up Nightingale's attitude to empiricism. I, on the other hand, was prepared this time. I'd brought a stopwatch, an antique clockwork one with a face as big as my palm, my notebook and the transcript of Colin Sandbrow's interview from the *Vagina dentata* case notes. While Nightingale headed back upstairs, I sat down at a work desk and started in on the file.

Colin Sandbrow, jammy bastard, aged twenty-one, in from Ilford for a night on the tiles. Met what he thought was a Goth who didn't talk much but seemed amenable to a bit of outdoor knee-trembling action. Looks-wise Sandbrow was at least young and fit, but his face had a sort of routine sandy plainness – as if his creator had been working on him at the end of the day and was looking to make up a quota. This probably explained why he had been just as keen to leave the club.

'Didn't you think it was a little suspicious that she was so enthusiastic?' Stephanopoulos had asked.

Sandbrow indicated that he hadn't been inclined to look a gift horse in the mouth, although in future he would take a more cautious approach when dealing with members of the opposite sex.

It started raining apple pulp sixteen minutes and thirty-four seconds after I'd done the spell. I put aside the interview and made a note of the time. I'd taken the opportunity to put plastic bags underneath, so I didn't have to do much cleaning up. Both my textbooks and Nightingale were a bit vague about where the power that was holding the apple was coming from. If the magic was still being sucked out of my head, how many could I put up simultaneously before my brain shrivelled? And if it wasn't coming from me, where was the power coming from? I'm an old-fashioned copper – I don't believe in breaking the laws of thermodynamics.

I finished my notes and headed up and out to the coach house and the rudiments of twenty-first-century comfort – wide-screen TV, broadband and HOLMES. Which is how I came to catch Nightingale making himself comfortable on the sofa with a can of Nigerian Star Beer in one hand and the rugby on the TV. He had the grace to look embarrassed.

'I didn't think you'd mind,' he said. 'There're two more crates of this stuff in the corner.'

'Overspill,' I said. 'From when I propitiated Mama Thames with an artic full of booze.'

'That clarifies a great deal,' he said, and waved his can. 'Don't tell Molly about the beer. She's become a tad overprotective.'

I told him that his secret was safe with me. 'Who's playing?' I asked.

'Harlequins and Wasps,' he said.

I let him get on with it. I like a bit of football and a legitimate boxing match but, unlike my mum, who will watch anything involving a ball, even golf, I've never been that into rugby. So I sat down at my desk and fired up my second-best laptop which I use as a HOLMES terminal, and got stuck back into the case.

Stephanopoulos's people were very thorough. They'd spoken to all Sandbrow's friends and any random customers they could track down. The club bouncers were adamant that they hadn't seen the suspect enter, despite the fact that the CCTV footage clearly showed her walking right past them. The whole attack reminded me much more of the incident with St John Giles back in the summer than it did of the murder of Jason Dunlop – I was about to put a note pointing that out on the file when I noticed that Stephanopoulos had already spotted it.

I wondered how Lesley was doing. She hadn't answered any of my texts or emails, so I called her house and got one of her sisters.

'She's in London,' she said. 'Had an appointment with her specialist.'

'She never said.'

'Well she wouldn't, would she,' said her sister.

'Can you tell me what hospital?'

'Nope,' she said. 'If she wanted you to know she was in town, she'd have told you.'

I couldn't argue with that.

Nightingale's rugby finished and he thanked me for the beer and left. I switched over to the news to see whether a certain hijacked ambulance was still rotating around the twenty-four-hour news cycle but it had been knocked off by some serious flooding around Marlow. Lots of nice pictures of cars aquaplaning down rural roads, and pensioners being ferried about by the Fire Brigade. For a moment I had a horrible suspicion that the floods might have been a reaction by Father Thames to Ash being injured, but when I googled the details, I found that it had all kicked off during the following night when I'd been cavorting on the roof with Simone.

That was a relief. I was in enough trouble already, without inadvertently flooding part of the Thames Valley.

A woman from the Environment Agency was asked why they hadn't issued a flood warning, and she explained the Thames had a complex watershed made even more complicated by the interaction of human development.

'Sometimes the river can just surprise you,' she said. There'd been a second unexpected surge late the night before, and she was refusing to rule out a repeat later that day. Like most Londoners, my attitude was that only rich people could afford to live next to a river, so I could withstand their discomfort with fortitude.

I finished up on HOLMES and shut everything down. Stephanopoulos had found no connections between our two and a half victims. Worse, St John Giles and Sandbrow had visited on impulse the clubs where they met our mysterious killer. In her notes attached to the nominal reports Stephanopoulos argued, and I agreed, that two young men had been targeted at random, but that the attack on Jason Dunlop felt more like a hit. If only because the Pale Lady, as I now thought of her, had made contact with her victim in a public place and in front of potential witnesses. Maybe it was a work-life balance thing. Maybe the two nightclub boys were recreational and Jason Dunlop was work.

Mum phoned me, and reminded me that I was supposed to be introducing Dad to The Irregulars that afternoon. I pointed out that this was her third phone call to remind me, but, as is usual with my mum, she didn't take a blind bit of notice. I assured her I would be there. I considered calling Simone and inviting her along, but I decided that I was on to far too much of a good thing to want to risk having her meet the family – especially my mum.

I called her anyway, and she assured me she was languishing without me. I heard female laughter in the background, and some comments pitched too low for me to hear. Her sisters, I suspected.

'Definitely languishing,' she said. 'I don't suppose you could pop round later and ravish me at your convenience?'

'What happened to no men in the bed past ten?' I asked.

'I don't suppose you have a bed,' more laughter in the background, 'that you don't have to share?'

I wondered if I could sneak her into the Folly. Nightingale had never actually forbidden overnight visitors, but I wasn't sure how I'd bring it up in the conversation. I'd slept in the coach house myself, but the sofa would be cramped for two. Worth thinking about, though.

'I'll call you later,' I said, and idly looked up hotel prices in central London – but even with my healthy finances, it just wasn't going to happen.

It was only then that it occurred to me that less than two weeks ago she'd been the grieving lover of Cyrus Wilkinson, late of the very band my dad was rehearsing with that afternoon. All the more reason, I thought, for not inviting her along.

Just about every council estate I know has a set of communal rooms. There's something about stacking people up in egg boxes that makes architects and town planners believe that having a set of communal rooms will compensate for not having a garden or, in some of the flats, enough room to swing a cat. Perhaps they fondly imagine that the denizens of the estate will spontaneously gather for colourful proletarian festivals and cat-swinging contests. In truth, the rooms generally get used for two things – children's parties and tenants' meetings, but that afternoon we were going to shake things up and have a jazz rehearsal instead.

Since James was the drummer he was the one with a van, a suitably decrepit Transit that we could have left unlocked, with the keys in the ignition and a sign on the front windscreen saying 'Take me,

I'm yours' and have no fears about it still being there when we came back out again. As I helped him carry his drum kit from the van to rehearsal room, he told me that it was totally deliberate.

'I'm from Glasgow,' he said, 'so there's bugger all London's got to teach me about personal safety.'

We had to do three more trips for the amps and the speakers, and it being school home time, we soon collected an audience of wannabe street urchins. Presumably the street urchins in Glasgow are bigger and tougher than the ones in London, because James paid them no mind. But I could see Daniel and Max were uncomfortable. Nobody does hostile curiosity like a bunch of thirteen-year-olds who are putting off doing their homework. One skinny mixed-race girl cocked her head and asked whether we were in a band.

'What's it look like?' I asked

'What kind of music do you play?' she asked. She had an entourage of little friends who giggled on cue. I'd gone to school with their elder brothers and sisters. They knew me, but I was still fair game.

'Jazz,' I said. 'You wouldn't like it.'

'Yeah,' she said. 'Swing, Latin or fusion?'

The entourage duly laughed and pointed. I gave her the eye, but she ignored me.

'We did jazz last term in music,' she said.

'I bet your mum's looking for you,' I said.

'No,' she said. 'Can we come and watch?'

'No,' I said.

'We'll be quiet,' she said.

'No, you won't.'

'How do you know?'

'I can see into the future,' I said.

'No you can't,' she said.

'Why not?'

''Cause that would be a violation of causticity,' she said.

'I blame *Doctor Who*,' said James.

'Causality,' I said.

'Whatever,' she said. 'Can we watch?'

So I let them watch and they lasted two minutes into 'Airegin', which was longer than I'd expected them to.

'That's your dad, innit,' she said helpfully when my dad put in an appearance. 'I didn't know he could play.'

It was weird, watching my dad sit down and play keyboard with a bunch of musicians. I'd never seen him play live, but my memories are full of black and white photographs and in those he always had his trumpet in his hand. Trying to hold it in the same way Miles Davis had, like a weapon, like a rifle at parade rest. He could play the keyboard, though. Even I could tell that. But it still felt like the wrong instrument to me.

It bothered me for the rest of the session, but I couldn't figure out why.

After the rehearsal I'd expected us to troop up Leverton Street for a pint at the Pineapple, but my mum invited everyone back to the flat. As we headed up the stairs, the mouthy girl from the rehearsal stopped me in the stairwell. This time without her posse.

'I heard you can do magic,' she said.

'Where did you hear that?'

'I got my sources,' she said. 'Is it true?'

'Yeah,' I said, because sometimes the truth shuts up kids faster than a clip round the ear, and has the added advantage of not being an assault on a minor in the eyes of the law. 'I can do magic. What about it?'

'Real magic,' she said. 'Not like tricks and stuff.'

'Real magic,' I said.

'Teach me,' she said.

'I'll tell you what,' I said. 'You get a GCSE in Latin and I'll teach you magic.'

'Deal,' she said, and stuck out her hand.

I shook. Her palm was small and dry in mine.

'You promise on your mum's life,' she said.

I hesitated, and she squeezed my hand as hard as she could.

'On your mum's life,' she said.

'I don't swear on my mum's life,' I said.

'OK,' she said. 'But a deal's a deal – right?'

'Right,' I said. But I was suspicious by that point. 'Who are you?'

'I'm Abigail,' she said. 'I live up the road.'

'You really going to learn Latin?'

'Am now,' she said. 'Laters.' And she went skipping up the road.

I counted my fingers to make sure they were all there, and I didn't need Nightingale to tell me that I'd handled that one wrong. One thing was for certain, Abigail who lived up the road was going on my watch list. In fact, I was going to create a watch list just so I could put Abigail at the top of it.

By the time I got upstairs to the flat, the musicians had gravitated into the bedroom where they were cooing over my dad's record collection. My mum had obviously hit the snack freezer at Iceland pretty hard, and there were plates of mini-sausage rolls, mini-pizzas and bowls of hula hoops on the coffee table. Coke, tea, coffee and orange juice were available on demand. My mum was looking very pleased with herself.

'Do you know Abigail?' I asked.

'Of course,' she said. 'Her father is Adam Kamara.'

I vaguely recognised the name as being one of several dozen relations loosely defined as cousins – a relationship that could range from being the offspring of one of my uncles to the white guy from the Peace Corps who wandered into my grandad's compound in 1977 and never left.

'Did you tell her I could do magic?'

She shrugged. 'She was here with her father, she may have heard things.'

'So you talk about me when I'm not here?'

'You'd be surprised,' she said.

Yes I would, I thought, and helped myself to a handful of hula hoops.

At my mother's command, I stuck my head around the bedroom door to ask The Irregulars whether they wanted any snacks. My dad said they'd be out in a minute, no snacks allowed near the collection, obviously, and continued his discussion with Daniel and Max about the transition from Stan Kenton to the Third Stream. James was sitting on the bed with an LP in his hands, and he was caught in the terrible dilemma of the serious vinyl aficionado – he wanted to borrow it, but he knew that if it was his he'd never let it out of the house. He really was close to tears.

'I know it's unfashionable,' said James, after going on about Don Cherry for a while. 'But I've always had a soft spot for the cornet.' Which was when, had I been a cartoon character, a little light bulb would have gone 'ding' over my head.

I borrowed my dad's iPod and thumbed through his selections, looking for the track I wanted. I took it through to the kitchen and out onto the balcony with its unparalleled vista of the flats opposite. I found it – 'Body and Soul', off *Blitzkrieg Babies and Bands* – Snakehips Johnson giving the tune such a danceable swing that Coleman Hawkins had to invent an entire new branch of jazz just to get it out of his head. It was also the version I'd heard in the Café de Paris while dancing with Simone.

The *vestigia* left on the body of Mickey the Bone had sounded like a trombone. At Cyrus Wilkinson's demise it had been an alto sax – the instruments

210

the musicians had played in life. Henry Bellrush had played the cornet, but I hadn't sensed a cornet at the Café de Paris.

I'd sensed Ken 'Snakehips' Johnson and his West Indian Orchestra, who had all died there, at the Café de Paris, more than seventy years ago.

That couldn't be a coincidence.

The next morning I talked myself out of practice and headed for Clerkenwell and the Metropolitan Archive. The Corporation of London, the organisation dedicated to ensuring that the City, the financial bit of London, is untainted by all this newfangled democracy that's been rearing its ugly head in the last two hundred years or so. If an oligarchy was good enough for Dick Whittington, they argue, then it's good enough for the heart of twenty-first-century London. After all, they say, it works in China.

They are also in charge of the archives of the London County Council, which are kept in a workmanlike but still elegant art deco building with white walls and grey carpet. I flashed my warrant card at one of the librarians, and she quickly pulled up a list of documents and showed me how to order.

She also suggested that she check the digital archive, to see if there were any images available. 'Is this a cold case?' she asked.

'A very cold case,' I said.

First up from the store room was LCC/CE/4/7,

a cardboard box full of manila folders tied up with dirty white ribbons. I was looking for item No. 39, reports from 8 March 1941. The identification was handwritten in black ink, and I untied the folder to find the report printed in purple type on pale yellow paper, a sure-fire sign, said the librarian, that they'd been duplicated with a mimeograph. It was marked SECRET and dated 9 March 1941. Its title was SITUATION REPORT AS AT 0600 HOURS and it listed, in order of importance, damage to factories, railways, telecommunications, electricity supply, docks, roads, hospitals and public buildings. St Thomas's Babies' Hostel in Lambeth had been hit and, I was relieved to read, no casualties taken. I was oddly relieved, given that it had all happened half a century before I was born. I found what I was looking for halfway down the third page.

2140: HE Café de Paris, Coventry Street Casualties – 34 killed, approximately 80 seriously injured

While I was waiting for the other files to be brought up, the librarian called me over to the information point to show me some of the pictures she'd found in the digital archive. Most of them came from the *Daily Mail*, which must have had a photographer on the scene almost as soon as the bombs fell. In monochrome everything looked curiously bloodless. It wasn't until you realised that the light grey tube poking out from under a table was a woman's forearm and that you were looking at a charnel house. There were six more pictures of the interior of the nightclub, and several of casualties arriving at Charing Cross Hospital, pale faces and stunned expressions amongst the blankets and primitive equipment of a wartime hospital.

I almost missed it, but some flicker of recognition made me click back one and check.

The picture was confused, and I couldn't identify where it was taken, possibly the ambulance loading bay. A group of women were being led past the camera, all but one of them hunched over with blankets round their shoulders. One face was staring at the camera, the expression erased by shock into a smooth pale oval. A face that I recognised, and which I'd last seen in the green room at The Mysterioso the night Mickey the Bone had died.

She'd called herself Peggy – I wondered if that was her real name.

CHAPTER 8

SMOKE GETS IN YOUR EYES

The Café de Paris had been built twenty feet below ground level, and was considered safe by management and customers alike. Unless you took cover in the Underground system, no civilian shelter in London was built nearly as deep. Later, it was determined that two bombs penetrated the building above the nightclub – one failed to detonate, while the other dropped down an airshaft and exploded right in front of the band, killing the musicians and most of the dancers. Ken Johnson had his head blown clear off his shoulders, and there were reports of customers killed where they sat, remaining upright at their tables. Eyewitnesses remembered that there had been a great many Canadian nurses and servicemen in the club that night, but despite going down to the storage area with the librarian, I couldn't find anything that remotely resembled a casualty list. I found duplicates typed on paper as thin as tissue, concerning an exchange of correspondence dealing with complaints that ambulances hadn't arrived quickly enough to deal with the casualties, and a report on the shocking boldness of the looters who had steamed through the site nicking valuables.

There was nothing more on the mysterious Peggy who, if it were the same person, would have to be pushing ninety, if not more. A year ago I would have considered that unlikely, but these days I was working with a guy who was born in 1900, and he wasn't even the oldest person I'd met. Oxley had been a mediaeval monk, and his 'father' dated back to the foundation of the City in the first century AD.

Blackstone's Police Operational Handbook recommends the ABC of serious investigation: Assume nothing, Believe nothing and Check everything. But you've got to start somewhere, and I was going to start with Peggy.

The archive has a whitewashed room with lockers, two coffee makers and one of those machines that dispenses chocolate bars and stale snacks. I got a coffee and a Mars Bar and called in a PNC check on Peggy, female, IC1, eighteen to twenty-five. The civilian operator laughed at me down the line, and said she wasn't even going to tell me how big the set of nominals was that had been returned. I asked her to limit the area to Soho and go back as far as 1941. To her credit, she didn't ask me why.

'Not everything from that far back is on the system,' the operator said. She had a Scouse accent, so she managed to make it sound as if this was personally my fault. She hummed something from the late 1990s chart under her breath while she checked. 'I've got a load of nominals that fit those parameters,' she said. 'Mostly prostitution and drug arrests.' But nothing that stood out. I asked her to forward the nominal list to the HOLMES case file I'd been building. She was impressed – most coppers don't even know you can do that.

Peggy had been at The Mysterioso the night Mickey the Bone had died. She'd mentioned Cherry, who was probably Cherie, Mickey's bit of posh that his sister had talked about. In the old days I would have had to schlep back down to Cheam to show a picture to the sister, but all I had to do now was call her on her mobile and text it to her instead. I cropped the 1941 image until it was just the face, and sent that.

'She looks kind of familiar,' said Mickey's sister. In the background I could hear voices and music muffled by a firmly closed door – the wake for her brother was continuing.

'Do you have an address for Cherie?' I asked.

'She lived up in town,' said Mickey's sister. 'I don't know where.'

I asked if she had any pictures of Cherie; she said she thought she might, and promised to text them over if she found any. I thanked her, and asked how she was coping.

'OK I guess,' she said.

I told her to hang in there – what else could I say?

Thanks to the magic of science, I copied the rest of the pictures onto a flash drive which, thanks to the science of magic, I'd tested and found they didn't get messed up every time I did a spell. As far as I could determine, nearby use of magic only degraded chips that had power running through them at the time, but it frustrated me that I didn't even have a theory as to how magic actually worked. A little analytical voice in my head pointed out that any working hypothesis was probably going to involve quantum theory at some point – the part of physics that made my brain trickle out of my ears.

I arranged for the bombing reports and the other documents to be copied, and made sure to thank the librarian properly before heading to where I'd parked the Asbo that morning.

When I got back to the Folly, I found Dr Walid in the atrium talking to Molly.

'Ah, good, Peter,' he said. 'I'm glad you came back. Let's have some tea, shall we?'

Molly shot me a reproachful look and went gliding off towards the kitchen. Dr Walid led me over to a collection of overstuffed red armchairs and mahogany occasional tables that nestled under the overhang of the eastern balcony. I noticed he had his medical bag with him, a modern ballistic plastic case covered in burgundy leather whose one concession to tradition was the stethoscope wound round the handle.

'I'm concerned,' he said, 'that Thomas has been pushing himself too hard.'

'Is he all right?'

'He's picked up an infection and he's running a fever,' said Dr Walid.

'He was okay at breakfast,' I said.

'Man could be dead on his feet before he'd admit to it,' said Dr Walid. 'I don't want him disturbed for the next couple of days. He was shot through the chest, Peter, there's tissue damage there that will never fully heal and it will make him prone to chest infections like the one he's got now. I've put him on a course of antibiotics, which I expect Molly to make sure he completes.'

Molly arrived with the good Wedgwood tea set on a lacquered wooden tray. She poured for Dr Walid with quick dainty movements, and pointedly left without pouring mine. Obviously she blamed me for Nightingale's relapse – perhaps she knew about the beer.

Dr Walid poured my tea and helped himself to a Hobnob.

'I heard Lesley is in town for an operation,' I said.

'She's going to be fine,' said Dr Walid. 'You just need to make sure that when she asks for your help, you're ready to give it. How do you feel about her injuries?'

'It didn't happen to me,' I said. 'It happened to Lesley and Dr Framline, and that poor Hare Krishna sod and the others.'

'Do you feel guilty?'

'No,' I said. 'I didn't do it to them, and I did

my best to stop it happening. But I feel guilty that I don't feel guilty, if that helps.'

'Not all my patients start off dead,' said Dr Walid, 'not in my medical practice, anyway. Sometimes, no matter what you do, the outcomes can be less than optimal. It's not whether you feel responsible, it's whether you don't shy away when she needs you.'

'The thought of her face scares me to death,' I said, before I could stop myself.

'Not as much as it scares her,' he said, and patted my arm. 'Not as much as the thought that you might reject her scares her. Make sure you are there when she needs you – that's your responsibility in this – your part of the job, if you like.'

We were way over our daily quota of emo, so I changed the subject.

'Do you know about the nest of vampires in Purley?' I asked.

'That was a nasty business.'

'Nightingale called what I felt there the *tactus disvitae*, anti-life,' I said. 'He implied that the vampires sucked "life" from their environment.'

'As I understand it,' he said.

'Have you ever had a chance to section the brain of one of their victims?'

'Usually they're in an advanced state of desiccation when we get them,' said Dr Walid. 'But one or two of them have been fresh enough to get some useful results. I think I know where you're going with this.'

'Did the brain sections show signs of hyper-thaumic degradation?'

'It's hyperthaumaturgical degradation,' said Dr Walid. 'And yes, they showed terminal levels of HTD, damage to at least ninety per cent of the brain.'

'Is it possible that "life" energy and magic are essentially the same thing?' I asked.

'That wouldn't contradict anything I've observed,' he said.

I told him about the experiments I'd run with pocket calculators, and about how the damage done to their microprocessors had resembled the damage done to the human brain by HTD.

'That would mean magic was affecting biolog-ical and non-biological constructions,' said Dr Walid. 'Which means it might be possible to develop some form of non-subjective instrumen-tality.' Dr Walid was just as frustrated as I was with the Toby the Dog method of magic detection. 'We have to replicate your experiments. This has to be documented.'

'We can do that later,' I said, 'but what I need to know now is about the effect this might have on life extension.'

Dr Walid gave me a sharp look. 'You're talking about Thomas,' he said.

'I'm talking about the vampires,' I said. 'I checked in Wolfe, and he lists at least three cases where it was confirmed that the vampires were at least two hundred years old.'

Dr Walid was too good a scientist to just accept the word of a natural philosopher from the early nineteenth century, but he conceded the evidence indicated that it was a possibility. Really, you'd expect a cryptopathologist to be a bit more credulous. Still, I wasn't going to let a little bit of scepticism get in the way of a perfectly good theory.

'Let's say for the moment that I'm right,' I said. 'Is it possible that all the creatures with extended lives, the *genii locorum* – Nightingale, Molly, the vampires – isn't it possible that they're all drawing magic from the environment to keep themselves from ageing?'

'Life protects itself,' said Dr Walid. 'As far as we know, vampires are the only creatures that can take life, magic, whatever – directly from people.'

'Exactly,' I said. 'Let's forget about the gods, Molly and the other weirdoes for a moment and concentrate on the vampires. Would it be possible for there to be a vampire-like creature that fed off musicians – that the act of making music made them uniquely vulnerable?'

'You think there are vampires that feed off jazz?' he asked.

'Why not?'

'Jazz vampires?'

'If it walks like a duck and quacks like a duck . . .' I said.

'Why jazz?'

'I don't know,' I said. My dad would've had an answer. He would have said it had to be jazz because that was the only proper music there was. 'I suppose we could line up different kind of musicians, expose them to our vampire and see which ones suffer brain damage.'

'I'm not sure that would meet the BMA's ethical guidelines on human experimentation,' he said, 'not to mention the difficulty of finding volunteers to be guinea pigs.'

'I don't know,' I said, 'musicians? If you offered them money. Free beer, even.'

'So this is your hypothesis for what happened to Cyrus Wilkinson?'

'It's more than that,' I said. 'I think I may have stumbled upon a sort of trigger event.' I explained about Peggy and Snakehips Johnson and the Café de Paris, and it all sounded thinner and thinner even as I was laying it out.

Dr Walid finished his tea as I wound down.

'We need to find this Peggy,' I said.

'That much is certain,' said Dr Walid.

I didn't feel like doing data entry, and I still couldn't get Lesley on the phone. So I cropped a high-resolution image of Peggy in 1941 and printed out a dozen copies on the laser printer. Armed with those, I headed into Soho to see if I could find anyone who remembered her, starting with Alexander Smith. After all, Peggy and Henry Bellrush were one of his top acts.

When he wasn't paying women to take off their clothes in an ironic, postmodern way, Alexander

Smith operated out of a small office on the first floor above a former sex shop turned coffee bar on Greek Street. I buzzed the intercom and a voice asked who I was.

'PC Grant to see Alexander Smith,' I said.

'Who did you say you were?' asked the voice.

'PC Grant,' I said.

'What?'

'Police,' I said. 'Open the sodding door.'

The door buzzed and I stepped into another narrow communal Soho staircase with worn nylon carpet and handprints on the walls. A man was waiting for me on the landing at the top of the stairs. He seemed quite ordinary when I was at the bottom, but like one of those weird corridor illusions he got bigger and bigger the further up I got. By the time I reached the top he was ten centimetres taller than me, and appeared to fill the landing from one side to the other. He was wearing a navy-blue High and Mighty suit jacket over a black Led Zeppelin t-shirt. He also had no visible neck and probably a blackjack concealed up his sleeve. Staring up his hairy nostrils made me quite nostalgic. You don't get old-fashioned muscle like that in London any more. These days it was all whippet-thin white guys with mad eyes and hoodies. This was a villain my dad would have recognised, and I wanted to embrace him and kiss him firmly on both cheeks.

'What the fuck do you want?' he asked.

Or maybe not.

'I just want a word with Alexander,' I said.

'Busy,' said No-Neck.

There are a number of police options at this point. My training at Hendon Police College emphasised polite firmness – 'I'm afraid, sir, that I must ask you to stand aside' – while my street experience suggested that the best option would be to call in a van full of Tactical Support Group and have *them* deal with the problem, using a taser if necessary. On top of that, generations of Cockney geezers on my dad's side were yelling at me that this was a diabolical liberty and he deserved a good kicking.

'Look, I'm the police,' I said. 'And we could, you know, do the whole thing, but you'd get arrested and blah, blah, blah and stuff, whereas I just want a chat. So what's the point of all . . . this?'

No-Neck thought about this for a moment, before grunting and shifting enough to let me squeeze past. That's how real men settle their differences, through reasoned discussion and a dispassionate analysis. He farted as I reached the inner door, a sign, I decided, of his respect.

Alexander Smith's office was surprisingly neat. A pair of self-assembly desks, two walls lined with bracket shelves covered with magazines, books, papers, overstuffed box files and DVDs. The windows had dusty cream blinds, one of which had got stuck halfway up some time around the turn of the century and hadn't been touched since.

Smith had been working on a Power Book but closed it ostentatiously when I walked in. He was still a dandy in a lemon-yellow blazer and crimson ascot, but outside of the club he seemed smaller and meaner.

'Hello, Alexander,' I said, and threw myself into his visitor's chair. 'How's tricks?'

'Constable Grant,' he said, and I noticed that he'd picked up an involuntary leg tremor. He noticed me noticing and put his hand on his knee to stop it. 'What can I do you for?'

Definitely nervous about something. And even though it probably had nothing to do with my case, a little extra leverage never hurts.

'Have you got something you need to be doing?'

'Just the usual,' he said.

I asked him if his girls were all right, and he visibly relaxed. This was not the source of his nerves.

Bollocks, I thought. Now he knows I don't know.

To prove it, he offered me a cup of instant coffee, which I declined.

'Are you expecting company?' I asked.

'Eh?'

'What's with the gorilla on the door?'

'Oh,' said Smith, 'that's Tony. I inherited him from my brother. I mean, I couldn't get rid of him. He's practically a family retainer.'

'Isn't he expensive to feed?'

'The girls like to have him around,' said Smith. 'Is there anything particular that I can do for you?'

I pulled out one of my 1941 prints and handed it to Smith. 'Is that Peggy?'

'Looks like her,' he said. 'What about it?'

'Have you seen her recently?'

'Not since the gig at the Café de Paris,' he said. 'Which was spectacular. Did I tell you that? Fucking spectacular.'

And weirdly coincidental, but I wasn't going to tell Smith that.

'Do you have a home address?' I asked.

'No,' said Smith. 'This is a bit of a cash-only business. What the Revenue don't see, the Revenue don't worry about.'

'I wouldn't know,' I said. 'I'm PAYE myself.'

'That could change,' said Smith. 'Anything else you're interested in? Only some of us don't get paid by the hour.'

'You go back, don't you?' I asked.

'We all go back,' he said. 'Some of us go back further than others.'

'Was she around then?'

'Who?'

'Peggy,' I said. 'Was she dancing back in the nineties?'

'I generally get nervous when they're still at infant school,' he said.

'How about in the nineteen-eighties?'

'Now I know you're mucking me about,' he said, but he hesitated just a little bit too long.

'Maybe not her, then,' I said. 'Maybe it was her mum – same sort of look.'

'Sorry. I was abroad for most of the seventies and eighties,' he said. 'Although there was one bird used to do one of them fan dances at the Windmill Theatre, but that was 1962 – that would be a bit far back even for Peggy's mum.'

'Why'd you have to leave the country?'

'I didn't have to,' he said. 'But this place was a shit-hole, so I got out.'

'You came back, though.'

'I missed the jellied eels,' he said. But I didn't believe him.

I wasn't going to get anything else useful, but I made a note to look up Smith on the PNC once I'd got back to the tech cave. I gave No-Neck Tony a friendly pat on the shoulder as I squeezed past.

'You're a living treasure, my son,' I said.

He grunted and I was satisfied, as I went down the stairs, that we'd made a connection.

Anyway, confirmation – either Peggy's grandmother bore an uncanny resemblance to her granddaughter, or Peggy had been around since 1941 feeding on jazz musicians. So far, all my confirmed sightings of Peggy and all the recent deaths had taken place around Soho. So that seemed the place to start. It would also be useful to pin down some 'known associates', particularly Cherry or Cherie – Mickey the Bone's girlfriend. This is the point when somebody working on a proper investigation asks his governor for some bodies to do a door-to-door canvass, but there was only me. So I started at one end of Old Compton Street and worked my way down.

They didn't know her in The Spice of Life or Ed's Diner, or the other food places at the east end of the street. One of the ticket staff at GAY said she looked familiar, but that was it. A woman working in a corner newsagent-cum-mini-supermarket said that she thought she'd seen Peggy come in and buy cigarettes. I didn't get anything at the Admiral Duncan except a couple of offers to take me out to dinner. They knew her in Trashy Lingerie as 'that posh bird who comes in every so often and turns her nose up at our stock'. I was thinking it might be worth heading up to A Glimpse of Stocking, when a madwoman ran out of Patisserie Valerie calling my name.

It was Simone, high heels skidding on the pavement as she swerved to avoid a startled pedestrian. She was wearing a pair of faded stretch jeans and a burgundy cardigan that gaped open to reveal nothing but a crimson lace bra underneath – front catch, I noticed. She was waving and yelling, and I saw there was a smear of cream on her cheek.

Once she saw that I'd spotted her, she stopped shouting and self-consciously pulled the cardigan closed across her chest.

'Hello, Peter,' she said as I walked over. 'Fancy running into you like this.' She touched her face, found the cream, grimaced and tried to rub it off with her sleeve. Then she wrapped her arms around my neck and pulled my face down for a kiss.

'You must think me perfectly demented,' she said as we broke.

'Pretty demented,' I said.

She pulled my head down again and asked me in a whisper whether I was free that afternoon. 'You left me alone all yesterday,' she said. 'I think you owe me an afternoon of carnal pursuits at the very least.'

Given it was that, or several hours of door-to-door canvassing, I didn't really have to work that hard. Simone laughed, slipped her arm through mine and led me up the street. I waved a hand at the Patisserie Valerie. 'What about your bill?' I asked.

'You mustn't worry about the patisserie,' she said. 'I have an account.'

It started raining some time after lunch. I woke up in Simone's big bed to find the room filled with grey light and rain drumming against the window. Simone was pressed warmly up against me, her cheek against my shoulder, one arm flung possessively across my chest. After some manoeuvring, I managed to check my watch and found that it was past two o'clock. Simone's arm tightened around me, her eyes opened and she gave me a sly look before kissing the hollow of my neck. I decided that it was too wet for doing door-to-door anyway, and that I would compensate by doing all that boring data entry as soon as I got back to the Folly. My schedule suitably modified, I rolled Simone over on her back and set to seeing how worked up I could get her without using my hands. She sighed as my lips found her nipple, which wasn't the effect I was going for, and gently stroked my head.

'Come up here,' she said, and tugged at my shoulders, pulling me up and between her legs so that I slipped in without even trying and then, when she had me arranged to her satisfaction, she held me there, a look of contentment on her face.

My hips twitched.

'Wait,' she said.

'I can't help it,' I said.

'If you could just restrain yourself a moment,' she said, 'I'll make it worth your while.'

We stayed locked together. I felt a strange vibration in my chest and belly which I realised was Simone humming deep in her diaphragm, or whatever it is singers use. I couldn't quite make out the tune, but it made me think of smoky cafés and women in padded jackets and pillbox hats.

'Nobody makes me feel like you,' she said.

'I thought I was the first,' I said.

'Hypothetically,' she said. 'If there had been others, none of them would have made me feel the way you do.'

I twitched again, but this time she lifted her hips to meet me.

Afterwards we dozed again, sweaty and content

and lying in each other's arms. I would have stayed there for ever if I hadn't been driven out of bed by my bladder, and a guilty sense that there were things that I needed to be getting on with – important things.

Simone lay sprawled naked and inviting across the bed and watched me getting dressed under deliberately heavy-lidded eyes.

'Come back to bed,' she said, and let her fingers drift idly around one erect nipple, then the other.

'I'm afraid the mighty army of justice that is the Metropolitan Police never sleeps,' I said.

'I don't want the mighty army of justice to sleep,' she said. 'On the contrary, I expect it to be most diligent in its dealings with me. I'm a bad girl, and I need to be held accountable for my actions.'

'Sorry,' I said.

'At least take me to your father's concert,' she said.

I'd told her about Dad's upcoming gig, but I hadn't told her that Cyrus Wilkinson's old band would be playing with him.

'I want to meet your mum and your dad and your friends,' she said. 'I'll be good.'

I knelt down by the bed and kissed her. She clutched at my arms and I thought, sod it – they're going to find out sooner or later. I told her she could come.

She finished our kiss and threw herself back on the bed.

'That is all I wanted,' she said, and waved her

hand in a regal fashion. 'You may go about your duties, Constable, and I shall languish here until we meet again.'

The rain had slackened off to a light drizzle that, if you're a Londoner, barely counts as rain at all. Even so, I splashed out on a black cab to take me back to the Folly, where Molly served up steak and kidney pudding with roast potatoes, peas and carrots.

'She always does this when I'm ill,' said Nightingale. 'It'll be black pudding for breakfast tomorrow. Thickens the blood.'

We were eating dinner in the so-called Private Dining Room, which adjoined the English library on the first floor. Since the main dining room could sit sixty, we never used it in case Molly got it into her head to lay all the tables. Nonetheless me and Nightingale had dressed for dinner – we both have standards, and one of us had been exerting himself that afternoon.

I knew from experience that you didn't dive into one of Molly's steak and kidney puddings until some of the superheated steam had had a chance to dissipate, and the interior had ceased to be hot enough to fire pottery.

Nightingale swallowed a couple of pills with some water and asked about the case.

'Which one?' I asked.

'The jazz musicians first,' he said.

I filled him in on the Café de Paris bombing, and my search for Peggy and possibly Cherie.

'You think there's more than one,' he paused. 'What are you calling them?'

'Jazz vampires,' I said. 'But I don't think they're feeding on the music. I think that's just a side-effect, like the sound a generator makes when it's turned on.'

'*Tactus disvitae*,' said Nightingale. 'Another species of vampire – Wolfe would be pleased.'

The pudding was cool enough for me to dig in. An afternoon with Simone had left me starving and, according to Nightingale, Molly made her puddings with ox liver, which he said was the proper old-fashioned recipe.

'Why doesn't Molly go out to buy stuff?' I asked.

'Why do you ask?'

'Because she's different,' I said, 'like the jazz vampire and the Pale Lady. But, unlike them, we've had a chance to learn what makes her tick.'

Nightingale finished a mouthful and wiped his lips on his napkin.

'The Pale Lady?'

'That's what Ash called her,' I said.

'Interesting name,' said Nightingale. 'As to the food, as far as I know she has everything delivered.'

'She shops on the internet?'

'Good God no,' said Nightingale. 'There are still some establishments that do things the old-fashioned way, whose staff are still capable of reading a handwritten note.'

'Could she leave if she wanted to?' I asked.

'She's not a prisoner,' said Nightingale. 'Or a slave, if that's what you're alluding to.'

'So she could just walk out the door tomorrow?'

'If she so desired,' said Nightingale.

'What's stopping her?'

'Fear,' said Nightingale. 'I believe she's frightened of what's out there.'

'What is out there?' I asked.

'I'm not sure,' said Nightingale. 'She won't say.'

'You must have a theory,' I said.

Nightingale shrugged. 'Other creatures like Molly,' he said.

'Creatures?'

'People, if you prefer,' said Nightingale. 'People who, like Molly, are not the same as you or I or even the *genii locorum*. They were changed by magic, or they were born into lineages that have been changed. And as far as I know, this leaves them – incomplete.'

Nightingale, despite literally being a relic of a bygone age, had learned to modify his language around me because when I'd looked into the literature, the most common terms started with 'un-' – unfit, unsuited, undesirable – and behind them came the terms starting with 'sub-'. However, with a bit of running translation, it was clear that 'incomplete' people like Molly were vulnerable to abuse and exploitation by their more powerful supernatural brethren, and by practitioners with no moral scruples. Magicians, according to Nightingale, of the blackest hue.

'Sorry. Ethically challenged practitioners,' said Nightingale. 'My first "governor", Inspector Murville, had handled a notorious case in Limehouse in 1911. It involved a famous stage magician working under the name of Manchu the Magnificent, who had collected some very strange "people" and was using them to carry out his nefarious plans.'

'And his nefarious plans were what, exactly?' I asked.

Nothing less than the overthrow of the British Empire itself. Apparently Inspector Murville, as he set off on his crusade, had it on good authority that Manchu the Magnificent operated an opium den on the Limehouse Causeway. There, the yellow devil sat like a fat spider at the centre of a web of plots, white slavery being merely the start of it.

'What's white slavery when it's at home?' I asked.

Nightingale had to think about it for a bit, but apparently when he was young white slavery mostly referred to the trafficking of white women and children for the purposes of prostitution. The inscrutable Chinese were supposedly behind this dastardly trade in lily-white female flesh. I wondered if part of the outrage came from a guilty conscience. I said as much.

'There were established cases, Peter,' said Nightingale sharply. 'Women and children were bought and sold in beastly circumstances and suffered real hardship. I doubt they found the historical irony much of a comfort.'

Inspector Murville, convinced of the seriousness of the threat, organised a raid with half the available wizards in London and a mob of constables loaned to him by the Commissioner. Cue a great deal of banging down of doors and shouting of 'Hold still, you oriental devil' and then a certain amount of stunned silence.

'The great Manchu the Magnificent,' said Nightingale, 'was revealed to be a Canadian by the name of Henry Speltz, although he was married to a Chinese woman with whom he had five daughters, all of whom had acted as his beautiful assistant "Li Ping" at one time or another.'

Nothing was found at the house except for a strange young European girl who lived in the household and worked as a maid. Under caution, Speltz told Inspector Murville that the girl, whom nobody in the household had thought to name, had been found cowering in one of his disappearing cabinets at the end of a matinée performance at the Hackney Empire.

I mopped up the last of the onion gravy with the last bit of bread in the basket. Nightingale had left half his pudding untouched. 'Are you going to finish that?' I asked.

'Help yourself,' said Nightingale, and I did while he finished the story.

Some things never change, and a senior police officer doesn't organise a costly raid and admit to failure, or violating the Magna Carta, until he's done his best to convict someone of something.

Had Speltz actually been Chinese, things might have gone very hard for him. But in the end he was formally charged with disturbing the peace and let go with a police caution.

'The girl was taken into protective custody,' said Nightingale. 'Even old Murville could sense there was something not quite right about her.' He looked quickly towards the doors. 'Have you finished?' he asked.

I said I had, and Nightingale grabbed the now empty plate and put it back in front of himself just in time for Molly to come drifting into the dining room pushing the sweet trolley. As she cleared the plates, she gave Nightingale a distinctly suspicious look. But she couldn't prove anything.

She scowled at us, and we smiled back.

'Very nice,' I said.

Molly laid out a custard tart and, with one last suspicious look aimed at me, silently left the dining room.

'What happened to the girl?' I asked as I served up the tart.

'She was brought here and examined,' said Nightingale. 'And found to be too abnormal to be fostered . . .'

'Or put into a workhouse,' I said. Under a thick layer of nutmeg, the custard was just as good as that of the Patisserie Valerie. I wondered if I could smuggle some out for Simone. Or, better yet, smuggle her in for dinner.

'It may put your mind at rest to know that we

had an agreement with Corum's Foundling Hospital,' said Nightingale. 'She would have been placed there but for the unfortunate fact that once allowed into the Folly, she would not allow herself to be taken out.'

From under the table I could hear Toby looking for the last of the leftovers.

'This is Molly we're talking about,' I said.

'So she slept in the scullery and was raised by the staff,' he said.

I helped myself to another piece of tart.

'Postmartin was right,' said Nightingale. 'I let myself get too comfortable. And while I lived here with Molly, the world continued on without me.'

I was stuffed, but I forced myself over to the coach house to do some data entry. Once there, I was irresistibly drawn to the sofa and Arsenal v Tottenham. It was going badly for Spurs when my phone rang and a strange voice said, 'Hello, Peter.'

I checked the caller ID. 'Is that you, Lesley?'

I heard a rasping, breathy sound. 'No,' said Lesley, 'it's Darth Vader.'

I laughed. I didn't mean to, but I couldn't help myself.

'It's better than Stephen Hawking,' she said. It sounded like she was trying to talk with a plastic bottle in her mouth, and I got the strong impression that it was painful to do.

'You were in London for an operation,' I said. 'You could have told me.'

'They didn't know if it would work,' she said.

'Did it?'

'I'm talking, aren't I?' said Lesley. 'It bloody hurts, though.'

'Want to go back to text?'

'No,' she said. 'Sick of typing. Have you checked your cases on HOLMES yet?'

'Not yet,' I said. 'I've been doing door-to-door.'

'I went through the records you sent over, and Professor Geoffrey Wheatcroft didn't ever formally teach Jason Dunlop, but Dunlop did dedicate his first novel "For Master Geoffrey, from whom I gained my true education". Isn't that what you trainee wizards call your teachers?'

Not this apprentice. But 'Master' doesn't mean the same thing to white boys at Oxford. Given the books in Dunlop's flat, it had to mean, barring a really bizarre set of coincidences, that Geoffrey Wheatcroft had taught Dunlop formal Newtonian magic.

I said as much to Lesley.

'Thought so,' she said. 'Question is, was he the only one? And if he wasn't, how do we find out?'

'We need to check the Murder Team's files and see if known associates or nominals track back to Magdalen College around the time he was there.'

'I love it when you talk dirty,' she said. 'It makes you sound like a real copper.'

'Do you think you can do that?' I asked.

'Why not?' she said. 'It's not as if I have anything better to do. When are you coming up to see me?'

239

'Soon as I get a chance,' I said, lying.

'I've got to go,' she said. 'I'm not supposed to talk too much.'

'You take care,' I said.

'You too,' she said, and hung up.

How many apprentices could one master teach? You needed a trained wizard to act as what Nightingale called an 'exemplar', to demonstrate the form. But I didn't see why you couldn't do that with more than one person at a time. It would depend on how motivated your students were. At somewhere like Nightingale's old school you'd be dealing with your usual range of talent and enthusiasm. But university students learning magic for fun? Nightingale said it took ten years to be a proper wizard, but I'd managed to do quite a lot of damage within three months of starting training – I didn't think Jason Dunlop, or any fellow students, would be any different.

I fired up the HOLMES terminal and started looking for connections to Oxford University that had lasted beyond his time there. That got me a list of twenty-plus names, mostly former students, whose paths had crossed professionally or, as far as the Murder Team could tell, socially with Jason Dunlop.

In a major inquiry, a person who comes to the attention of the police as part of that inquiry is listed on HOLMES as a *nominal*. Any task that an investigating officer decides needs doing is called an *action*. Actions are prioritised and put on a list, and officers are assigned to carry them out. Actions lead to more nominals and more actions, and the whole investigation quickly becomes a whirling vortex of information from which there seems no escape. HOLMES lets you do word searches and comparison tests, but half the time that just leads to more actions and more nominals and more items of information. Deal with this for any length of time, and you start to get nostalgic for the good old days when you just found a suspect you thought looked a bit tasty and beat a confession out of them with a phone book.

Background checks on the Oxford University names had a low priority, so I started with the PNC to see if any of them at least had criminal records, and to nab likenesses from their driving licences. This was not a quick process, but at least it meant I was still awake and dressed when Stephanopoulos called me at one in the morning.

'Grab your overnight bag,' she said. 'I'll be picking you up in ten minutes.'

I didn't have an overnight bag, so I grabbed my gym bag and hoped that nobody asked me to a formal dinner while I was away. I bunged a spare Airwave in with my back-up laptop just to be on the safe side. To save time, I went out the side door and walked up Bedford Place to Russell Square. It was drizzling, and the moisture put yellow halos around the street lamps.

Stephanopoulos wouldn't have called me out of

hours for anything less than another murder, and the overnight bag said it was out of London.

I heard it coming before I saw it, a black Jaguar XJ with twenty-inch wheels and, unmistakably from the sound, a supercharged V8 engine. From the way it pulled up, it was obvious that the driver had been on all the courses I hadn't been on and was authorised to drive insanely fast.

The back passenger door opened and I slipped into the smell of newly liveried leather seats to find Stephanopoulos waiting for me. The car took off as soon as the door closed, and I found myself slipping around on the back seat until I managed to wrestle my seat belt into place.

'Where are we going?' I asked.

'Norwich,' said Stephanopoulos. 'Our friend's been grazing again.'

'Dead?'

'Oh, yes,' said the man in the front passenger seat. 'Quite dead.' Stephanopoulos introduced him as Detective Chief Inspector Zachary Thompson.

'People call me Zack,' he said as he shook my hand.

And I shall call you Chief Inspector, is what I didn't say. Thompson was a tall man with a narrow face and an enormous beak-like nose. He had to be tougher than he sounded to get through life with a nose like that.

'Zack,' said Stephanopoulos, 'is the SIO on this case.'

'I'm her beard,' he said cheerfully.

242

Now, I'm not part of the Met's famous canteen culture. I do not mourn the good old days when coppers were real coppers, not least because that spares me from what would have been almost continuous racist abuse. But even I get nervous when senior officers tell me to call them by their first name – no good can come of that sort of thing.

'Is there anything unusual about this one?' I asked. 'I mean, more unusual than usual?'

'He's ex-job,' said Stephanopoulos. 'Detective Chief Inspector Jerry Johnson, retired from the Met in 1979.'

'Is there a connection to Jason Dunlop?'

'There's a notation in Dunlop's diary from March,' said DCI Thompson. '"Meet J. J. Norwich."' His credit-card trace shows that he bought a return ticket from Liverpool Street to Norwich on that day. We think Johnson might have been a source for a story Dunlop was working on.'

'If it's the same J. J.,' I said.

'You let us worry about that,' said Stephanopoulos. 'You're there to check for signs of black magic.'

To my amazement, we fell in behind a pair of motorcycle outriders, and by the time we hit the M11 we were doing over 120mph.

CHAPTER 9

THE FORCING HOUSE

My dad says that being a Londoner has nothing to do with where you're born. He says that there are people who get off a jumbo jet at Heathrow, go through immigration waving any kind of passport, hop on the tube and by the time the train's pulled into Piccadilly Circus they've become a Londoner. He said there were others, some of whom were born within the sound of the Bow Bells, who spend their whole life dreaming of an escape. When they do go, they almost always head for Norfolk, where the skies are big, the land is flat and the demographics are full of creamy white goodness. It is, says my dad, the poor man's alternative to Australia, now that South Africa has gone all multicultural.

Jerry Johnson was one of the latter type of non-Londoner, born in Finchley in 1940 by the grace of God and died in a bungalow on the outskirts of Norwich with his penis bitten off. That last detail explaining why me and the scariest police officer in the Met, her beard and two motorcycle outriders were doing a steady ton plus change up the M11. It was two in the morning as we came

244

off the motorway, so we filtered onto the A-road almost without slowing down. We reached the crime scene in under ninety minutes, which was impressive, only to find the Norfolk Constabulary had already taken the body away, which was not. Stephanopoulos stamped off with DCI Thompson to bite chunks out of the local plod, which left me to sidle up to the crime scene on my own.

'No sign of forced entry,' said DC Trollope.

Contrary to my dad's prejudices, the local plod were neither stupid nor noticeably inbred. If the kissing cousins of Norwich were getting it on, then at least their offspring weren't joining the police. Instead, DC David Trollope was the kind of sober, fit young man that would warm the heart of any back-seat home secretary in the land.

'Do you think he let his assailant in?' I asked.

'It seems that way,' he said. 'What do you think?' Police officers, like African matrons at a wedding, are acutely aware of the subtle and all but invisible gradations in status. We were the same rank and about the same age, but the disadvantage I suffered from being on his patch had to be balanced against the fact that I'd arrived in a Jaguar XJ V8 that had been borrowed from Diplomatic Protection. We settled for a kind of uneasy bonhomie and, like the African matrons, providing nobody had spiked the punch bowl, we'd probably get through the encounter without an embarrassing incident.

'Did he have an alarm system?' I asked.

'Yeah,' said Trollope. 'A good one.'

245

The bungalow was a hideous red-brick structure built, if I had to guess, in the early 1980s by some hack architect who'd been aiming at art deco and hit Tracy Emin instead. The interior was as characterless as the exterior: World of Leather sofa, generic flat-pack furniture, fitted kitchen. There were three separate bedrooms, which surprised me.

'Did he have a family?' I asked.

Trollope checked his notes. 'Ex-wife, daughter, grandchildren – all living in Melbourne, Australia.'

The two spare bedrooms looked as if they were last furnished in the 1980s and were neat, tidy and unlived-in. Trollope said that Johnson had a Polish woman who 'did' for him twice a week. 'It was her that found the body,' he said.

In the master bedroom, which was still off limits to people not wearing Noddy suits. I stood in the doorway and examined the bed as best as I could. The forensics team had removed the sheets and pillows, but the mattress was still in place with a reddish brown stain a third of the way up from the footboard. Too much blood had soaked in for it to dry out since the body had been removed, so I could still smell it as I walked away to check the other rooms. I'd brought my own gloves with me, but I asked Trollope if he had a spare pair to give him something to feel superior about.

If Johnson had died in his bedroom, then he'd spent most of his life in the living room. LCD wide-screen TV, DVD with the remotes still on the coffee table by a copy of the *Radio Times*. There was an antique fold-down writing desk that Trollope said hadn't been dusted yet, so we left it well alone. A couple of glass-fronted bookcases filled with paperbacks. Penguins, Corgis and Panthers from the 1960s and 1970s – Len Deighton, Ian Fleming and Clive Cussler. It looked like the fiction section of a charity shop. The bookshelves were the type that came in two parts, the bottom section acting as a pedestal for the top and being slightly deeper, and having opaque doors. Carefully, because they hadn't been dusted either, I opened the bottom sections to find them both empty except for a couple of scraps of paper – I left those for forensics as well.

There were a couple of surprisingly good hunting prints on the wall, as well as a framed photograph of his graduating class at Hendon. I couldn't work out which shiny young uniform he was. Beside it was a photo of him being handed a commendation by a senior officer who I later learned was Sir John Waldron, Commissioner of the Metropolitan Police from 1968 to 1972, no less. There were family photographs on the mantelpiece, a wedding complete with unfortunate sideburns and flares, a pair of children, a boy and a girl, at various ages, toddler, infant school, on a pale yellow beach by a green ocean somewhere foreign. There were a couple taken outside the bungalow where the kids looked to be nine or ten – nothing after that. I did a quick mental calculation and guessed that the latest picture had been taken in the early 1980s. More than thirty years ago.

'The family in Australia are still alive, aren't they?' I asked. 'They weren't all tragically killed in a car crash, or something like that?'

'I'll have to find out,' said Trollope. 'Why?'

'Thirty years is a long time to go without any new photographs,' I said.

The last couple of pictures were in the second rank, half hidden by the wife and kids. More men in kipper ties, sideburns and embarrassingly wide lapels, photographed in a bar that looked familiar and which I suddenly recognised as the French House in Soho. I also realised I was looking at the young Alexander Smith, the night-club owner, looking like a dandy even back then in a crushed-velvet smoking jacket and ruffled shirt.

'You didn't happen to get any details about his career, did you?' I asked.

Trollope checked his notebook again, but I knew even before he said it that the bulk of DCSI Johnson's career had been spent in and around Soho.

'He was CID at West End Central, and before that he was in something called the OPS,' he said. I asked the dates, and he said 1967 to 1975.

The OPS was the Obscene Publications Squad, the single most corrupt specialist unit of the most corrupt division of the Metropolitan Police. And Johnson had been a member during the most corrupt decade since London thief takers stopped being paid by the collar.

No wonder Alexander Smith was in the photograph. The OPS had run a protection racket for porno shops and strip clubs. You paid them so much cash a day and they made sure you didn't get raided. Or if you did, they made sure you'd get lots of warning, so you had a comfortable and civilised interval in which to move all the hardcore stuff somewhere else. As an added bonus, you could bung the boys in blue a 'drink' and they'd go round and raid your competitors, and then sell their confiscated stock to you out of the back of the evidence room at Holborn nick. It also explained how Johnson could afford to take early retirement, and probably why he'd had to take it.

Which made me look at the three remote controls casually left on the coffee table.

I squatted down by the TV stand. It was your typical grey laminated chipboard cheap piece of rubbish and quite difficult, because of the tangle of wires at the back, to clean the dust off effectively.

'Give me a hand over here, would you?' I asked Trollope, and explained what I wanted him to do. Carefully, so as not to disrupt any forensic evidence, we both took a side of the DVD player and lifted it up. Underneath there was a clear rectangle of light grey where something had protected the laminated surface from years of dust, something with a smaller footprint than the DVD player. I nodded and we gingerly put the player back down.

'What?' asked Trollope.

'He had a VHS player,' I said, and pointed at the remotes on the coffee table. One for the TV, one for the DVD and . . .

'Bugger,' said Trollope.

'You need to tell your scene-of-crime guys that somebody's stripped this house of VHS tapes,' I said.

'Why did he still have VHS?' asked Trollope. 'Do you know anyone who still has a VHS?'

'It has to be something he couldn't risk getting digitised,' I said.

'These days?' said Trollope. 'It would have to be something really disgusting or illegal. Child porn, or snuff movies or, I don't know, kitten-strangling.'

'The wife will have to interviewed,' I said. 'Maybe she knows something.'

'Maybe that's why she left,' said Trollope. 'Reckon there's a trip to Australia in it?'

'Not for us,' I said. 'They never send DCs abroad. It's always "experienced officers" who get the free trips.' We shared a moment of gloomy solidarity. 'If you had a bunch of stuff that you were desperate to keep hidden,' I said, 'where would you stash it?'

'Garden shed,' said Trollope.

'Really?'

'That's where my dad kept his grass,' said Trollope.

'Really?'

'Grow your own is a long tradition in these parts.'

'You ever been tempted to bust him for possession?'

'Only at Christmas,' he said.

Ideally we would have trooped out and had a look in the shed ourselves, but you don't do that on a modern crime scene without checking with forensics first, and they said we couldn't go out until they'd checked the lawn for footprints. And they couldn't do that until morning. Fair enough. So we went and reported unto Stephanopoulos, who was mightily pleased with both of us and bestowed her munificence in the form of sandwiches and coffee. Which we had to go and eat out in the road, so as not to get crumbs on the crime scene. It was surprisingly cold, but the Norfolk Constabulary had parked a couple of Transit vans outside so we sheltered in one of them. Even this close to Norwich, the sky was amazingly wide and full of stars. Stephanopoulos noticed me noticing. 'City boy,' she said.

I suggested that Johnson's ex-wife be interviewed in Australia and she agreed, although she felt the Victoria Police were more than capable of handling that without the need to send a British officer over, senior or otherwise. Trollope snorted.

'Something funny, Constable?' asked Stephanopoulos.

'No, ma'am,' he said.

The sandwiches were the kind that get stocked by the twenty-four-hour shops attached to petrol stations, and which managed the trick of being

251

both soggy and stale. I think mine was ham salad, but I barely tasted it. Stephanopoulos put hers down after the first bite.

'We need to know what it was Johnson told Dunlop,' she said.

'I'll bet it had to do with the Obscene Publication Squad,' I said. 'What else would he have to talk about?'

'There's more to people than the job,' said Stephanopoulos.

'Not this man,' I said. 'If he had any special interests they were on the stolen tapes. I think he may have been killed, in part, in order to recover them.'

'I see it,' said Stephanopoulos. 'OPS plus videotapes, plus story to a journalist, some juicy scandal from the 1960s? Maybe somebody wanted to shut him up. If we find out what the story was, we'll find out who has a motive.'

I told her about Alexander Smith's presence in one of the photos on the mantelpiece.

'Who's he when he's at home?' she asked.

'Nightclub impresario,' I said. 'Goes all the way back to the sixties, had an extended vacation on the Costa del Sol in the seventies and eighties.'

'Is he a gangster?' asked Trollope.

'He's dodgy, is what he is,' I said.

'How did he come to your attention?' asked Stephanopoulos.

'During the course of another inquiry,' I said, and glanced at Trollope. I wasn't sure how much

Stephanopoulos would want me to say outside of the Met.

'Do you think they're related?' she asked.

'I don't know,' I said. 'But it's definitely a place to start.'

Stephanopoulos nodded and pointed at me. 'You get some kip. I want you nice and fresh tomorrow,' she said, and then looked at Trollope. 'You – your boss has given you to me as my plaything, so I need you to run some errands for me – all right?'

'Yes ma'am,' said Trollope.

'What are we doing tomorrow?' I asked.

'We're going to have a nice long chat with one Alexander Smith,' she said.

I found it surprisingly easy to sleep across the back seat of the Transit, but I woke up to a clear and freezing morning and was really glad when DC Trollope turned up in an unmarked Mondeo to ferry me and Stephanopoulos to the train station. I swapped mobile numbers with Trollope because it never hurts to network, and headed inside in search of coffee. Norwich station was your standard late-Victorian brick, cast-iron and glass shed retro-fitted with the bright moulded plastic of various fast-food franchises. I gratefully staggered in the direction of Upper Crust and considered asking if I could stick my head under their coffee spigot, but settled for a couple of double espressos and a chicken tikka masala baguette instead. Stephanopoulos didn't approve.

'The chicken in that is embalmed, dried and pressed very flat, and then sprinkled with extra chemicals,' she said.

'Too hungry to care,' I said.

We caught the express to Liverpool Street and Stephanopoulos got us a warrant-card upgrade to first class which, on a short route like that, meant slightly bigger seats and slightly fewer plebs. This suited Stephanopoulos because she was asleep before the train left the station.

There was no wifi on the train, so I booted up a PDF of *Latin for Dummies* on my laptop and spent an hour and a half getting to grips with third-declension adjectives. We were twenty minutes out of Liverpool Street and the suburbs were a comforting rainy smear when Trollope called me.

'They let me into the shed,' he said. 'I was right. The door was forced.' The entry method had everyone puzzled because the lock and a small circle of the surrounding wood had been popped right out. 'Nobody can work out how it was done,' he said.

I knew. It was a spell. In fact, it was one I'd seen Nightingale use on the garden gate in Purley when we were dealing with the vampire nest. Either our black magician was getting careless, didn't know that there was anyone capable of hunting him, or just didn't care that we might be alerted to his presence.

According to Trollope, the shed had been the usual mess, gardening tools, flower pots, hose and bits of bicycle.

'I don't think we're ever going to find out if something was nicked or not,' he said. Forensics were dusting for fingerprints all the same. The details of that and the lock, along with the report on the two possible footprints found in the lawn, were being attached to the relevant nominal on HOLMES. I thanked Trollope and promised to let him know if anything exciting happened.

Stephanopoulos woke up with a snort just as we were pulling into the station, and gave me the briefest look of confusion before she got orientated. I filled her in on the lock in the shed and she nodded.

'Should we get your governor in?' she asked.

Dr Walid had been firm. 'Not yet,' I said. 'Let's see if I can't get confirmation from Alexander Smith first, before we get him out of bed.'

'Oh yes, Smith,' said Stephanopoulos as the train came to a stop. 'A villain of the old school. This should be a treat.'

Stephanopoulos decided to use West End Central for the interview. Built in the 1930s on Savile Row, it's a big square office block that's been clad in expensive Portland Stone in the hope that it will disguise its essential dullness. Just across Regent Street from Soho proper, it's the main base of operations for Clubs and Vice, and Stephanopoulos persuaded an old friend of hers who worked there to pick up Alexander Smith for us. The idea was to promote in his head that he was just small fry caught in a great big impersonal grinding machine.

We were aiming for a cross between Kafka and Orwell, which just goes to show how dangerous it can be when your police officers are better read than you are. We let him marinate in the interview room for an hour and a bit while me and Stephanopoulos sat in the canteen drinking the bloody awful coffee, and sketching out our strategy for the coming interrogation. Well, actually, Stephanopoulos did the sketching while I sat there and filed it all away under best practice.

Alexander Smith had been abroad in the 1970s and 1980s all right – living near Marbella in southern Spain on the notorious Costa del Crime along with a lot of tough middle-aged men who sounded like Ray Winstone and had all the moral fibre of damp tissue paper. He was a villain of the old school, but a smart one because he never got caught or prosecuted. He'd owned a club but his main income had been from acting as a middleman between bent coppers and the porn barons of Soho. He literally knew where the bodies were buried, and would be expecting us to want to focus on that.

'But he's scared,' said Stephanopoulos. 'He hasn't asked for a brief or even a phone call – he actually *wants* to be banged up.'

'Why not just ask for protection?'

'Villains like that don't ask for protection,' said Stephanopoulos. 'They don't talk to the police at all unless they're looking to buy you. But he's scared of something, and we need to find out what it is. When we do, we jam in the knife, give it a twist and he'll open up like a winkle.'

'Not an oyster, then?' I asked.

'You follow my lead,' said Stephanopoulos.

'What if we start getting into my area of expertise?' I asked.

Stephanopoulos snorted. 'In the event of us charting that small corner of a foreign field, you get to ask the questions you need to ask,' she said. 'But be sensible and be careful because I don't like to kick people under the table – it's unprofessional.'

We finished off our awful coffee and had a brief discussion about stack size. It's not unknown for police officers going into an interview to pad out their files with a few reams of fake paperwork, the better to convey the notion that we, the police, know everything already, so you might as well just save time and tell us what *you* know. But Stephanopoulos felt that an old lag like Smith wasn't going to fall for that. And besides, we wanted to convey the idea that we weren't that bothered.

'He wants something from us,' said Stephanopoulos. 'He wants to be talked into giving it up. The more he thinks we don't care, the keener he'll be to talk.'

Smith was back in his blue blazer, but the carefully matching button-down shirt was open at the collar and his face was grey and unshaven. We made a big production of putting the tapes in the

257

machine, introducing ourselves and advising him of his rights.

'You understand that you're not under arrest, and that you may terminate this interview at any point you wish.'

'No, really?' asked Smith.

'You're also entitled to a lawyer or some other representative of your choice.'

'Yeah, yeah,' said Smith. 'Can we just get on with it?'

'So you don't want a brief?' I asked.

'No, I do not want a sodding brief,' said Smith.

'You seem in a hurry. You've got somewhere to go?' asked Stephanopoulos. 'Somebody waiting for you, perhaps?'

'What is it you want?' asked Smith.

'The thing is, we want to clarify your involvement in a number of crimes,' said Stephanopoulos.

'What crimes?' asked Smith. 'I was a respectable businessman back then, I owned a club, that was it.'

'Back when?' I asked.

'The old days,' said Smith. 'Isn't that what you're asking about? Because I was a respectable businessman.'

'But Smithy,' said Stephanopoulos, 'I don't believe in respectable businessmen. I've been a copper for more than five minutes. And the constable here doesn't think you're respectable either, because it happens that he is a card-carrying member of the Workers Revolutionary Party and so regards all forms of property to be a crime against the proletariat.'

That one caught me by surprise, and the best I could manage was, 'Power to the people.'

Smith was staring at us as if we were both mad.

'So,' I said. 'You were involved in a lot of crime back then, Smithy?'

'I wasn't an angel,' he said. 'And I'll put my hand up to having to deal with some less than salubrious elements in my day. That's one of the reasons I moved abroad, to get away from all that.'

'Why did you come back?' I asked.

'I got a yen for dear old Blighty,' he said.

'Really?' I said. 'You told me that England was a shit-hole.'

'Well, at least it's an English-speaking shit-hole,' said Smith.

'He ran out of money,' said Stephanopoulos. 'Didn't you, Smithy?'

'Do me a favour,' he said. 'I could buy you and all the senior officers in this station and still have enough left over for a flat in Mayfair.'

'Make me an offer,' said Stephanopoulos. 'I could get a new chicken run. And her indoors is always asking for an extension to the conservatory.'

Smith, who wasn't about to say anything that could be misconstrued or digitally edited into an admission of guilt, gave us a suitably ironic smile.

'If it wasn't the money,' I said, 'why'd you come back?'

'I went to Marbella because I'd made my wedge,' he said. 'I'd retired. Got myself a nice villa for me and the wife, and I ain't going to kid you, life was sweet, away from the rain and all the shit. Everything was good until the fucking eighties, when the Russians started turning up. Once their snouts were in the trough, there was shootings and kneecappings and a man wasn't safe in his own home. I thought, if I'm going to put up with this bollocks I might as well do it back in London.'

'Marbella's loss is London's gain,' said Stephanopoulos. 'Isn't that so, Constable?'

'Definitely,' I said. 'You bring much-needed folkloric colour to the historic byways of London.'

We knew from reports that Stephanopoulos had wrangled out of the Serious and Organised Crime Agency that what had really brought Smith back to London was a series of drug deals that had gone bad. His product had been regularly confiscated in Spain and Amsterdam, and when he finally got on the plane to Gatwick all he left behind was debts and his wife, who'd subsequently moved in with a Brazilian dentist. That must have hurt.

'Where you from?' he asked me.

'Where do you think?' I said, because the cardinal unbreakable law of the police interview is never give information away – especially about yourself.

'I don't know,' he said. 'But I don't seem to know shit any more.'

260

'Do you know Jerry Johnson?' asked Stephanopoulos.

'Who the fuck's that?' he asked, but he'd flinched and he knew we'd seen it.

'Detective Chief Inspector Johnson,' I said, and pushed the photograph from Johnson's house in front of Smith. He looked surprised to see it.

'This is about Greasy Johnson?' asked Smith. 'That prick?'

'So you did know him?' I asked.

'He used to wander around Soho with his hand out,' said Smith. 'Just like the rest of the filth. Just like they do now, in fact. How is old Greasy? I heard he got the boot.'

I had a nice crime-scene photograph of Jerry Johnson lying naked on his bed minus his wedding tackle all ready to slide under Smith's nose, but Stephanopoulos tapped her finger once on the table, which meant *hold back*. I looked closely at Smith, and saw that his leg had picked up the same tremor I'd seen in his office. We wanted him scared, but we didn't want him so scared that he clammed up or tried to do a runner.

'He was murdered yesterday,' said Stephan-opoulos. 'At his home in Norfolk.'

Smith's shoulders relaxed. Relief, defeat, despair? I couldn't tell.

'You knew about it in advance,' I said, 'didn't you?'

'Don't know what you're talking about.'

'Yesterday,' I said, 'when I came calling – that's

why you had No-Neck on the door, that's why you were sweating.'

'I'd heard some whispers,' said Smith.

'What kind of whispers?' asked Stephanopoulos.

'That somebody I thought was dead might not be,' he said.

'This dead bloke got a name?' asked Stephanopoulos.

'Johnson was in with this strange bloke – like a magician, he was,' said Smith.

'Did card tricks, did he?' asked Stephanopoulos.

'Not that kind of magician,' said Smith. 'This was like real voodoo magic, only it was a white geezer.'

'You said it was like voodoo?' I asked. 'Did the man call on loas to possess him? Did he carry out rituals and sacrifices?'

'I don't know,' said Smith. 'I steered well clear.'

'But you thought he could do real magic?' I asked.

'I don't think,' he said. 'I saw it.'

'Saw what?'

'At least, I think I saw it,' said Smith, and he seemed to shrink down into the collar of his shirt. 'You're not going to believe me.'

'I'm not going to believe you,' said Stephanopoulos. 'But Constable Grant here is actually paid to believe in this stuff. He also has to believe in faeries and wizards and hobgoblins.'

'And hobbitses,' I said.

Smith bristled. 'You think this is funny. Larry

262

Piercingham, who they used to call Larry the Lark because he liked to do his rounds early. Remember him?'

'I'm not as old as I look,' said Stephanopoulos as I noted the name.

'I don't know the details, but he got on the wrong side of the magician . . .'

'Did he have a name?' asked Stephanopoulos.

'Who?'

'This magician, what was his name?'

'I don't know,' said Smith. 'When we talked about him he was just the Magician and mostly, all things being equal, we didn't talk about him at all.'

'So what happened to Larry the Lark?' I asked.

'Larry was in with a hard mob from Somers Town, blaggers and handle men and the like. The sort of people that used to do proper scores back in the old days. These were not people that you disrespected – you understand?' asked Smith.

We did. Somers Town used to be a concentrated block of villainy sandwiched between Euston and St Pancras stations. In the days before Rottweilers, it was the sort of place where people kept a sawn-off shotgun by the front door – in case of unwelcome guests or social workers.

Larry who, when he wasn't robbing security vans, worked as casual muscle for various porn-brokers, pimps and whatever, just went missing one day. His missus wandered around for a bit asking everyone whether they'd seen him, but nobody had.

'Not that anyone was actually looking for him,' said Smith.

A month later, there's a big sit-down celebration at the Acropolis on Frith Street. All the Somers Town gang are there, plus selected guests from the cream of the Soho underworld.

'What was it in aid of?' asked Stephanopoulos.

'I don't fucking remember,' said Smith. 'I don't think anyone there remembers what it was in aid of originally.'

It was a Greek Cypriot place, lots of grilled meat and fish and olives.

'Proper Greek nosh,' said Smith. 'None of that Kurdish stuff.'

'If this was proper villains,' said Stephanopoulos, 'why were you there?'

'I had an interest in some of their enterprises,' said Smith. 'But mainly I was there because they invited me, and when people like that invited you somewhere, you went.'

Smith didn't notice anything unusual until about two hours in, when most of the food was gone, and a pair of waiters came in with a large covered salver, cleared a space and plonked it down in the middle of the table.

'What's this, then?' asked Michael 'the Mick' McCullough who was, if not the undisputed governor of the mob, currently the least dead or banged-up. 'It's not my birthday.'

Somebody suggested that it might be the stripper.

'Bit of a midget stripper,' said McCullough, and

reached out and pulled the lid off. Underneath was the head of Larry the Lark, as fresh-looking as the day it was cut off. Garnished with holly and mistletoe, no less. I made a note of that in case it was important.

The Somers Town mob were, by definition, hard men, and not averse to spilling a bit of claret themselves. They knew how to put the frighteners on people, and they weren't about to let themselves get discombobulated by something as routine as a head on a plate.

'That,' said McCullough, 'has got to be the ugliest stripper I've ever seen.'

That got a laugh from the mob, right up to the point where the head spoke.

'Help me,' it said.

The voice, according to Alexander Smith, sounded a bit like Larry the Lark's, but had a whistling quality as if his breath was being forced through a pipe. Well, this did put the frighteners on the Somers Town mob, who knocked over their chairs getting away from the table except for Michael McCullough, who wasn't a superstitious man.

'It's a trick, you stupid pillocks,' he'd shouted and, reaching out, flipped the salver over.

'I think he expected to find a hole in the table,' said Smith. 'To be honest, so did I, with Larry the Lark crouched down there having us on – having a laugh. Only there was no hole, no Larry. At least, no Larry's body.'

The head went bouncing across the table and onto the floor with all the hard men, all the blaggers and enforcers squealing like little girls and scrambling to get out of the way. Not McCullough, though, because one thing you could say about McCullough was that he was without fear. He stalks round the table and picks up the head by its hair and waves it at the rest of the guests.

'It's a fucking trick,' he shouted. 'I don't believe it – what a bunch of pansies.'

'Mickey,' said the head of Larry the Lark. 'For Christ's sake, help me.'

'What did McCullough say?' asked Stephanopoulos.

Smith's heel rat-tatted on the tiled floor of the interview room

'I don't know,' he said. 'Because like everyone else, I got the fuck out of there. After that, nobody talked about that night, nobody talked about Larry the Lark, and the restaurant closed. I kept my head down, made my money and left the country.'

'What did the Magician want from Detective Chief Inspector Johnson?' asked Stephanopoulos.

'The usual,' said Smith. 'He wanted to be protected from any undue interference by the forces of law and order.'

I asked what it was that needed protecting.

'A club,' he said. 'On Brewer Street.'

'There's no club on Brewer Street,' I said.

'It was very exclusive,' said Smith.

'What did Johnson get from the Magician?' asked Stephanopoulos.

'Greasy Johnson had needs,' said Smith. 'He was a very needy boy, he had special needs.'

'Like what?' asked Stephanopoulos. 'Drugs, gambling, booze, girls – what?'

'Sex,' said Smith.

'What kind of sex?' I asked. 'Boys, girls, short socks, sheep?'

'The last one,' said Smith.

'Sheep,' said Stephanopoulos. 'You're bloody kidding me.'

'I don't know if it was sheep exactly,' said Smith. 'But definitely animal-related. Do you know what a cat girl is?'

'From manga,' I said. 'Girls with cat ears and tails. They're called Neko-chan, I think.'

'Thank God for the Japanese, eh?' said Smith. 'Otherwise we wouldn't have names for all this stuff. That's what Greasy Johnson liked. Cat girls.'

'You mean, girls dressed up as cats,' said Stephanopoulos.

'Look,' said Smith, 'I didn't know about these things, and I made a point of not ever finding out about them but dressed up as cats? That's not what I heard. Freaks of nature, that's what I heard.'

'Was he still around?' asked Stephanopoulos.

'Who?' asked Smith.

'The Magician,' said Stephanopoulos. 'Was he still here when you got homesick and came home?'

'No, he wasn't,' said Smith. 'I made a special point of asking around – if he'd been here I'd have gone to Manchester instead.'

'Manchester,' I said. 'Really?'

'Blackpool, if Manchester wasn't far enough.'

'But he was gone?' I asked.

'Not a sniff,' he said.

Stephanopoulos took her cue. 'So who killed Jerry Johnson, then?'

'I don't know,' he said. The leg tremor was back with a vengeance.

'Was it the Magician?' she asked.

'I don't know.'

'Was it the fucking Magician?'

Smith's head twitched from side to side. 'You don't know what you're asking,' he said.

'We can protect you,' she said.

'What do you think you know about it, eh?' asked Smith. 'You don't know nothing.'

'Show him, Constable,' said Stephanopoulos.

I opened my hand and conjured up a werelight. I put a lot of red into it and some blur and flicker to make it look impressive.

Smith stared at it with a gratifying expression of stupefied surprise.

'We know what we're talking about,' I said. I'd been practising this variation as a low-energy demonstration piece in the hope that it would be less likely to blow out any local electronics.

Even so, I gave the tape recorder a worried glance and shut it down quickly just to be on the safe side.

Smith stared at me. 'What's this?' he asked. 'We've got magic coppers now? Since when?'

'Since Bow Street,' I said.

'Yeah,' said Smith. 'Where was you lot when Larry the Lark got himself topped?'

That was a good question, and one I planned to ask Nightingale when I had a moment.

'That was the seventies,' I said. 'This is now.'

'Or you could always go back to Marbella,' added Stephanopoulos helpfully.

'Or Manchester,' I said.

'Or Blackpool,' said Stephanopoulos.

'Burlesque amongst the illuminations,' I said.

'There's another bloke,' said Smith suddenly. 'Another fucking magician, I don't know where he came from. One minute he wasn't there, and the next minute he was.'

'When did he appear?' I asked.

'In the summer,' said Smith. 'A couple of weeks after that fire at Covent Garden.'

'Did you see him?' I asked.

Smith shook his head. 'I never saw nothing,' he said. 'And nobody said nothing, neither.'

'Then how did you know he was there?' asked Stephanopoulos.

'You modern coppers think you've got it all sussed,' said Smith. 'This is Soho, this is my manor, this is my patch. I'm like a tiger. I know when something's changed in my patch. Fuck, I can tell when someone's opened a new Chinese takeaway, so yeah, so when something that evil creeps back in – I felt it.' He gave us a pitying look. 'An old-style copper would have felt it too, even a tosser like Johnson would have known something was up.'

'And gone round looking for a bung,' said Stephanopoulos.

Smith shrugged his shoulders. 'What else are they for?' he asked.

'So why didn't you scarper?' I asked.

'I don't dabble in anything I'm not supposed to these days, and I cater to a whole different set of punters now – I'm kosher,' he said. 'So why worry? Besides, everything I've got is invested in my business.'

'So what changed?' I asked.

'I reckon it was you,' he said. 'That first time, you were barely out the door when he comes waltzing in and sits down in the same chair.'

'Who did?' asked Stephanopoulos.

'That's just it,' said Smith. 'I don't know. I can remember his voice, what he said, but I can't remember his face.'

'How can you not remember his face?'

'You ever forget where you put your bleeding keys?' asked Smith. 'It's just like that, I know he was there, I know he sat in front me but, fuck me, I cannot remember what he looked like.'

'How do you know he was this new magician then?' asked Stephanopoulos.

'Are you deaf?' asked Smith. 'Do you think I'm demented, that I've got mad cow's disease? I don't remember the man's face – does that sound like a natural phenomenon to you?'

Stephanopoulos glanced at me but I could only shrug – magically speaking, this was getting way above my pay grade. I was also getting a cold feeling in my stomach about the way my two cases were beginning to merge.

'What did Mr Forgettable want?' I asked.

'He was asking after the same bird you were,' he said.

'Peggy?' I said.

He nodded. 'What did I know about her, what did I know about you, and hadn't I been one of the people at Larry the Lark's debut? That's what he called it – his debut.'

Stephanopoulos tensed. She wanted to know who Peggy was, but the second cardinal rule of an interview is that the police must maintain a united front at all times. You certainly don't ask each other questions in front of a suspect. Technically that's actually a breach of rule one; never give away information, but we're the police so we like to keep things simple.

'You're sure this was not the same man as the old Magician?' asked Stephanopoulos.

'What can I say?' said Smith. 'He was young and he was posh – that's all I know.'

'Where was the old Magician's club?' I asked.

'You really don't want to know,' said Smith.

271

'Yeah, Smithy,' I said. 'As it happens, I absolutely do want to know.'

Unless the wheels have come off big time, you don't just stroll round to a location and kick in the door. Apart from anything else, it's not that easy to kick in a door, and the last time I tried to do it I broke a toe. Commercial premises are usually harder to get into than private homes, so we first made sure that a specialist entry team was available and then booked them for later that afternoon. That left us enough time to apply for a search warrant under Section Eight of the Police and Criminal Evidence Act 1984, using carefully selected highlights from Alexander Smith's interview. I say 'us', but one of the advantages of working with a full Murder Team is that Stephanopoulos had lots of minions to do the paperwork for her. Meanwhile, me and her retired to the Burlington Arms for a stiff drink – we reckoned we'd earned it.

In the indifferent old days, a proper coppers' bar would have had a lino-covered floor, nicotine-stained wood panelling and brass furnishings that were antique only by virtue of the fact that nobody could be bothered to replace them. But times had changed, because now you could get a passable Cumberland sausage in onion gravy with chunky chips upstairs in the dining room, very nice with a Scrumpy Jack cider and just the thing after a hard morning's interrogation. Stephanopoulos had the leek soup with a side order of rocket and a single malt. I noticed a karaoke machine in the corner, and asked whether it got a lot of use.

'You should be here for competition nights,' said Stephanopoulos. 'Clubs and Vice versus Arts and Antiques gets very heated – they had to ban "I Will Survive" after there was a fight. Tell me about your investigation.'

So I told her about the dead jazzmen, and my efforts to track the person or persons unknown who seemed to be feeding off them.

'Jazz vampires,' said Stephanopoulos.

'I wish I hadn't started calling them that,' I said.

'What do you think the magician wants with them?' she asked.

'I don't know,' I said. 'To study enslavement, we need to know more.'

That was the cue for a minion, in the form of a rather sour-faced DC, to enter with the search warrant and present it to his boss. Stephanopoulos was careful to wait for him to leave before asking me how I thought we should handle the raid.

Unless you're going to knock and ask nicely, there are basically two ways to execute the search warrant. The first is the traditional rush, smash in the door and run in screaming 'police' and 'clear', giving a swift kicking to anyone who doesn't lie down on their face as soon as you tell them. The second likewise has no formal name, but involves sidling up to the front door in plain clothes, knocking it in and diving in like a posse of really persistent door-to-door salesmen. I suggested the latter, considering that we didn't know what we were blundering into.

'Keep some people on standby,' I said. 'Just in case.'

'Easy for you to say,' she said. 'It's not your overtime budget.' She finished her scotch. 'Who goes in first?'

'I do,' I said.

'Not going to happen.'

In the end, we compromised and both went first.

In the 1950s and 1960s property in Soho was cheap. After all, who wanted to live in the middle of smoky old London? The middle classes were all heading for the leafy suburbs, and the working class were being packed off to brand-new towns built in the wilds of Essex and Hertfordshire. They were called New Towns only because the term 'bantustan' hadn't been invented yet. The Regency terraces that made up the bulk of the surviving housing stock were subdivided into flats and shop fronts; basements were expanded to form clubs and bars. As property prices started rising, developers snatched up bombsites and derelict buildings and erected the shapeless concrete lumps that have made the 1970s the shining beacon of architectural splendour that it is. Unfortunately for the proponents of futurism, Soho was not to be overwhelmed so easily. A tangle of ownership, good old-fashioned stubbornness and outright corruption held development at bay until the strange urge to turn the historic centre of British cities into gigantic outdoor toilets had ebbed. Still, developers are a wily bunch and one scam, if you can afford it, is to leave the property vacant until it falls derelict and thus has to be demolished.

That's what our target looked like. Sandwiched between a Food City mini-market and a sex shop on Brewer Street, it was down and neglected compared to its neighbours. Dirty windows, blackened walls and peeling paint on the door frame. As part of the process of getting a search warrant, one of Stephanopoulos's minions had done a property search that uncovered a typical company shell game with regards to ownership – we couldn't wait for them to unpick it, so we got a warrant for the whole building.

We sat in an unmarked silver Astra and watched the place for an hour before going in, just to be on the safe side. Nobody went in or out, so after checking that all the teams were in position, Stephanopoulos gave the 'go' order.

We all piled out of the cars and did the hundred-metre sidle to the side door, where one of the entry team whipped out twenty kilograms of CQB ram and smacked it open with one practised swing. His mate went in first, holding a rectangular plastic shield ahead of him while a third entry-team guy stepped up behind him with a shotgun at the ready. The shotgun was in case the owner of the property had a dog, but we don't like to talk about that because it upsets people.

Me and Stephanopoulos went in behind them, which counts as going in first if you're not on the entry team, in case you were wondering, wearing our stab vests under our jackets and extendable batons on our belts. Beyond the door was a windowless hallway with a closed internal door on the left and a double stairway going down on the right. When I tried the light switch, we were rewarded with a dim light from an unshaded forty-watt bulb. Ancient flock wallpaper in gold and red covered the walls, peeling where it met the ceiling.

Stephanopoulos tapped one of the entry specialists on the shoulder and pointed at the door. The CQB swung again and the shield and shotgun team went up the stairs, followed by a mixed half-dozen from the Murder Team and the local Tactical Support Group. Their job would be to clear the top floors of the building while me and Stephanopoulos went downstairs.

I shone my torch down the shadowed depths of the staircase. They were carpeted with the kind of hard-wearing, short-haired nylon carpet that you find in cinemas and primary schools. It was red and gold, to match the flock wallpaper. I got a strong sense of foreboding, which could have been *vestigia* or just a sensible reluctance to go down the creepy dark staircase.

We could hear the team working their way up through the building like a herd of baby elephants in a builders' merchant's. Stephanopoulos looked at me, I nodded and we started down the stairs. We'd borrowed a pair of heavy-duty torches from the TSG and their light illuminated a ticket office on the first landing. Beside it was an alcove with a counter, and behind that was a yawning darkness that I hoped was just the cloakroom.

I went down cautiously, hugging the wall so I could get the earliest view around the corner – I seriously didn't want anything springing out. The stairs doubled back, descending into more darkness and a door in the far side of the landing marked STAFF ONLY. I smelled mildew and rotting carpet, which was reassuring. I leaned over the cloakroom counter and shone my torch around the interior to reveal a shallow L-shaped room lined with rails and empty clothes hangers. I climbed over and checked inside. There were no coats or long-forgotten bags, but there were bits of paper on the floor – I picked one up. It was a ticket stub. I walked around to the staff door and opened it to find Stephanopoulos staring warily down the stairs.

'Anything?' she asked. I shook my head.

She clicked her fingers and a couple of Murder Team detectives came padding down the stairs with gloves and evidence bags. Stephanopoulos pointed at the staff door and they dutifully trooped past me to do a more thorough search of the cloakroom. One of them was a young Somali woman in a leather biker jacket and an expensive black silk hijab. She caught me looking and smiled.

'Muslim ninja,' she whispered.

Normally the police like to make a lot of noise going into a building because, unless you're dealing with a psycho, it's better to give any potential arrests a chance to carefully think through their options before they do something stupid. We were being quiet in this case – not something that came naturally – so that I could feel for any *vestigia* as we went down the stairs. I'd tried explaining *vestigia* to Stephanopoulos, but I don't think she really got it, although she seemed keen enough to let me go first.

I saw the base of the cabinet first, mahogany and brass caught in the beam of my torch, more coming into view as I descended the steps. There was a double reflection from the front and back of a glass case, and I realised I was looking at a fortune-telling machine parked incongruously in the centre of the entrance to the club proper. I flashed my torch around the room behind and caught glimpses of a bar, chairs stacked on tables the dark rectangles of doorways further in.

The *vestigia* gave it away: a vivid flash of sunlight and cigarette smoke, petrol and expensive cologne, new leather seats and the Rolling Stones singing 'I Can't Get No Satisfaction'. I took a couple of quick steps back and shone my torch at the cabinet.

The manikin in the fortune-telling machine wasn't the usual head-and-shoulders model. Instead, the head rested directly on a pole of clear glass reinforced with bands of brass. Protruding from the truncated neck were two leathery bladders looking unpleasantly like lungs. The head itself was wearing the obligatory pantomime turban, but lacked the standard-issue spade-shaped beard and pencil moustache. The skin was waxy and the whole thing looked disturbingly real – because of course it was.

'Larry the Lark, I presume,' I said.

Stephanopoulos joined me. 'Oh, my God,' she said. She pulled a mug shot out of her pocket, an artefact, I assumed, from Larry the Lark's criminal career, and held it up for comparison.

'He looked better when he was alive,' I said.

I felt it just before it happened. It was weirdly like the sensation I got when Nightingale was demonstrating a *forma* or a spell. The same catching at the corner of my mind. But this was different. It whirred and clanked as if made of clockwork.

And the real clockwork started as, with a dusty wheezing sound the bladders below Larry's neck inflated and his mouth opened to reveal disconcertingly white teeth. I saw the muscles in his throat ripple, and then he spoke.

'Welcome one and all,' he said, 'to the garden of unearthly delights. Where the weary pilgrim may cast off the cloak of puritanical reserve, unlace the corset of bourgeois morality and gorge himself on all that life may offer.'

The mouth remained open, as hidden machinery

clanked and whirred to fill the bladders with air once more.

'Please, for Christ's sake kill me,' said Larry. 'Please, kill me.'

CHAPTER 10

FUNLAND

Stephanopoulos put her hand on my shoulder and pulled me back to the base of the stairs. 'Call your boss,' she said.

Larry's bladders had inflated for a third time, but whether it was to plead for death or to remind us that delicious snacks were available at the concession stand, we never found out – as soon as we were more than a metre away his mouth closed and the bladders deflated with an unpleasant whistling sound.

'Peter,' said Stephanopoulos. 'Call your boss.'

I tried my Airwave – amazingly, it got a signal – and called the Folly. Nightingale picked up, and I described what I was looking at.

'I'm on my way,' he said. 'Don't go any further in – don't let anything out.'

I told him I understood, and he hung up.

'You all right down there, guv?' called a voice from upstairs. It was the constable with the head-scarf – Somali Ninja Girl.

'I'm going to sort things out upstairs,' said Stephanopoulos. 'Will you be okay down here?'

'Yes,' I said. 'I'll be as happy as Larry.'

'Good man,' she said. She patted me on the shoulder and up she went.

'Try and get some lights down here,' I called after her.

'As soon as I can,' she called back.

I kept my torch on and angled slightly downward, to give me a reassuring wash of light as far as Larry's cabinet. Larry's face, thank God, was reduced to shadow. There was a glint of light from the darkness beyond. I shone my torch and caught a line of bottles along the back of the bar. I thought I heard breathing, but when I turned the torch back on Larry both he and his bladders were still.

Nightingale had said not to let anything out. I really wished he hadn't said that, or at least, that he had said what it was he thought might be in there.

I wondered how long magic could preserve dead flesh. Or had Larry's head been pickled and stuffed like a hunting trophy? Was there a brain inside? And if there was, how was it being supplied with nutrients? Dr Walid had once taken cell swabs and blood samples from Nightingale, but they had grown in culture exactly as you'd expect cells from a forty-year-old man to grow. When I asked whether he'd got cultures from any of the river gods, he laughed and told me that I was welcome to try and obtain some whenever I wanted. Neither of us even considered getting Molly to donate. Dr Walid's theory was that, however it worked, it worked at the level of the whole body. So once cells became physically detached from the body, they no longer retained whatever quality it was that was keeping them young.

'Or reducing replication errors,' Dr Walid had said. 'Or reversing entropy, for all I know. It's frustrating.'

Ash had been nearly dead when he'd gone into the Thames, and now I was reliably informed he was strolling around Chelsea and cutting a swathe through the green-welly brigade. Something had repaired the gross tissue damage in his chest, and if that was possible for him, then why not Lesley's face? Maybe she had been right – what magic had done, magic could undo.

I heard a noise from the darkness behind Larry's cabinet – a scrabbling sound that seemed too regular to be rats. I shone my torch in that direction, but all I caught was a tangle of shadows amongst the table legs. Larry's eyes glistened at me – they didn't look like glass.

I heard the scrabbling again.

I tried my Airwave, and asked Stephanopoulos whether she had an ETA on Nightingale or even the portable lights. As it's a digital system, you don't get the weird atmospherics of an analogue walkie-talkie. Instead, the person you're talking to drops out at random intervals. I think Stephanopoulos told me that 'something' was going to be ten minutes, and I was to stay where I was.

More scrabbling.

I took the batteries out of the Airwave, turned off my phone and conjured a nice bright werelight which I floated off into the foyer beyond Larry's cabinet. Once you've mastered the *Impello* form, you learn to guide whatever it is you're moving about, but it's tricky. A bit like operating a remote-controlled plane with your toes. As the werelight curved around the cabinet, I noticed that Larry's eyes actually moved to follow the light. I tried to bring it around in a circle to check, but all I managed was to slow it down and make it wobble. I actually had to close my eyes and concentrate to get the thing to stay. But when I opened them, I had my first good look at the foyer.

More of the ubiquitous red and gold flock wallpaper, and heavy red velvet curtains framing archways further into the club. Dully gleaming stained-pine doors with brass plates marked GENTLEMEN and LADIES on the right. The bar had a mirrored back wall, which meant that I could see in the reflection that there was nothing lurking beneath the bar.

My dad had played in clubs that looked like this. I'd been clubbing in clubs like this – which made me realise how suspiciously unrotten the curtains were – despite the smell of mildew. Then I saw, hanging from a light fitting, the familiar folded-up neon shape of a compact fluorescent low-energy light bulb – definitely not commercially available in the 1970s. Somebody had been down here

284

recently, and often enough to think it worth shelling out for some new bulbs.

This time, when the scrabbling came I saw movement at the far end of the foyer, where the curtains half hid the archway to the rest of the club. There was a strange kicking motion in the curtains. I managed to bob my werelight in the right general direction and saw two human legs, probably female, protruding from below them. They were dressed in stockings – the same rich red colour as the wallpaper. And one of the feet was still shod in a matching scarlet pointy-toe stiletto. As my light wobbled closer the legs began to kick, a spastic mechanical movement that reminded me horribly of early biological experiments with frogs. There were no human sounds apart from the heels drumming against the carpet. The curtains hid anything above the thighs – assuming there was anything above the thighs.

It was possible a human being was in distress, and I had a duty to check it out – if only I could make my feet take a step forward. The legs began to kick more violently, and I noticed that my werelight was beginning to dim and take on a redder hue. I was well practised at werelights by this point, and they never normally changed colour without me changing the *forma*. I'd seen this before when I'd 'fed' the ghost of Captain de Veil, and my best guess was that as the magic was drained off, the short-wavelength, higher-energy light dropped away first. Although saying it like that

285

really doesn't convey how sodding sinister the effect was in real life.

The legs kicked faster, the remaining shoe coming loose and spinning off into the shadows. The light grew dimmer, and still I couldn't make myself go forward.

'Shut it down, Peter,' said Nightingale from behind me. I popped the werelight and immediately the legs stopped kicking. He'd arrived with a bunch of serious-looking forensics people in Noddy suits carrying their evidence collection kits in camera cases. At the back, a couple of Murder Team guys, including Somali Ninja Girl, were wrestling some portable floodlights down the last flight of stairs. Nightingale himself was in a Noddy suit, which despite being the most modern item of clothing I'd ever seen him wear still made him look like the lead from a 1950s black and white sci-fi classic. He had one of his silver-topped canes in his right hand and a coil of nylon rope slung over his shoulder.

'Do not feed the animals,' he said.

'You think there might be something alive in there?' I asked.

'That's something we're going to have to discover for ourselves,' he said.

As the forensics people helped set up the lights, Nightingale stepped into a climber's harness, attached one end of the rope and handed the coil to me. He beckoned me closer and spoke quietly so the others wouldn't hear.

'There's a possibility there may be booby traps,' he said. 'If the rope goes slack, then you use it to haul me out. But under no circumstances are you to follow me in. Anything that is too much for me to handle will utterly destroy you – is that clear?'

'Crystal,' I said.

'There's also a small chance that something other than myself might try to escape out through here,' he said. 'It may look somewhat like me, it may even be wearing my body but I'm counting on you to know the difference. Understand?'

'And if that happens?'

'I'm trusting you to hold it back long enough for the others—' he nodded his head at the forensics team and other officers '—to escape. Hit it with everything you've got, but your best hope will probably be to try and bring the ceiling down on top of it.'

'Down on you, you mean.'

'It won't be me,' said Nightingale, 'so you needn't worry about hurting my feelings.'

'That's reassuring,' I said. 'Assuming I survive my heroic rearguard action, what then?'

Nightingale gave me a delighted grin. 'Remember the vampire nest in Purley?'

Where we'd bunged a couple of white phosphorus grenades into the basement where the vampires had been living, or undeading, or whatever it was they did. 'How could I forget?'

'A similar procedure to that,' said Nightingale. 'Only on a larger scale.'

'And after that?'

'That really won't be my problem,' he said cheerfully. 'Though you should go and see Postmartin as soon as you can.'

'Are you sure you're up to this?' I asked. 'If you have a relapse, Dr Walid will kill me.'

Just then, the portable floods kicked in and filled the foyer with a harsh white light. Larry the Lark's face was bleached as white as bone and the red stockings on the woman's legs became the colour of blood. Nightingale took a deep breath.

I turned to the people waiting by the floods. 'Ladies and gentlemen, I strongly advise that you shut down any laptops, iPads, iPhones, Airwave handsets – in fact anything you have that has a microprocessor in. Shut it down and take the battery out.'

The forensics techs looked at me blankly. One of them asked why. It was a good question, and I really didn't have time to answer it. 'We think there may be an experimental EMP device rigged further in,' I said. 'So just to be on the safe side . . .'

They weren't really convinced, but there were probably enough weird rumours about Nightingale to make them all comply.

'What's an EMP?' asked Nightingale.

'It's complicated, sir,' I said.

'Tell me later then,' he said. 'Everybody ready?'

Everybody was. Or at least, they said they were.

'Remember,' said Nightingale, 'you'll hardly be in a position to haul me to safety if you allow yourself to be caught by whatever caught me.' He turned, hefted his cane in his right hand and stepped forward. I paid out the rope as he gave the Cabinet of Larry a wide berth and headed for the curtained archway.

Somali Ninja Girl sidled over. 'What's going on?' she asked.

'Want to help?' I asked.

'Yeah,' she said.

'You can take notes,' I said.

She pulled a face.

'I'm serious,' I said.

'Oh,' she said, and pulled out her notebook and pen.

Through a gap in the curtains I saw Nightingale stop and kneel down by the women's legs. 'I've got a female cadaver here,' he called back, and Somali Ninja Girl started writing. 'Naked, mid-twenties, Caucasian, no visible injuries or rigor. What looks like a silver pin has been pushed into her right temple, the skin seems to have healed around the wound so I'm guessing this is either a decorative piercing or possibly a thaumatological device.'

Somali Ninja Girl paused in her writing and looked at me.

'Put magical,' I whispered. 'Magical device.'

Nightingale stood up and moved forward. Judging from the rope passing through my hands he went another three metres before stopping.

'This area has been extensively modified quite

recently,' said Nightingale, his voice surprisingly clear. 'Metal cages have been fitted into what I can only assume were seating alcoves. Four on the left-hand side and four on my right. First cage on the left is empty, second contains the cadaver of . . . a monkey of some description, or ape, or possibly an adult male. The third cage contains what looks like the remains of a big cat, black fur, a panther or leopard at a guess. The last cage on the left is empty. I'm going to look at the right-hand cages now.'

I shifted position to the left, so as to keep the rope in a straight line while Nightingale moved to the right.

'First cage on the right contains the cadaver of a Caucasian female with some degree of hybrid-isation or surgical modification. The body is clothed in a tiger-striped leotard that has been altered to allow room for a tail – I can't tell whether it's prosthetic or natural.'

Cat girls, I thought queasily. Real cat girls.

'Cages two and three are empty,' said Nightingale. 'Thank God.'

He moved again, and another couple of metres of rope played out through my hands.

'I've found a booby trap.' This time Nightingale had to raise his voice for it to reach us. 'It looks like an improvised demon trap.'

I glanced at Somali Ninja Girl, who paused before writing the words 'demon trap'.

'It's of a German type,' shouted Nightingale.

'But judging from the components, it was manufactured quite recently. I'm going to attempt to disarm it, so Peter, I'd like you to stand by just in case.'

I shouted that I was ready.

The *vestigia* that came before the blast was exactly like the sensation you get when cresting the highest rise on a roller coaster, the moment of terror and excitement before the plunge. And then a confused jumble of sensations, the feel of velvet on my cheek, the stink of formaldehyde and a sudden panting surge of sexual desire.

Then the physical blast wave hit us, a rolling wall of overpressure that was like having someone slap me in the ears from behind, and made me and everyone stagger backwards. I heard Somali Ninja Girl say something short and Coptic, and someone else behind me wanted to know what the fuck that was.

'Demon trap,' I said, trying to sound knowledgeable, and just in time for all the floodlights to blow simultaneously. Suddenly in the dark Larry the Lark's cabinet lit up with a gay sparkle of small coloured bulbs, the bladders filled with air and he opened his mouth and shouted 'At last!' With a choking rattle, the bladders of air emptied themselves for the last time. Then silence, and a clunk as Larry's jaw fell off his face and hit the base of the cabinet.

I fumbled in the dark for my torch, turned it on and quickly got it trained on the foyer. Other beams of light stabbed out of the darkness. Everyone else was as keen as I was to make sure that whatever came back through the foyer was somebody we knew.

The rope was slack in my hands.

'Inspector,' I called. 'Are you okay?'

Suddenly the rope went taut and I had to brace myself in order not to be pulled over.

'I'm quite all right,' said Nightingale. 'Thank you for asking.'

I coiled up the rope as he returned. His face was pale in the torchlight. I asked him again if he was all right, but he just gave me a strange grimace as if remembering some serious pain. Then he unclipped the rope and went over to talk to the head forensics guy. Whatever he said, the forensics guy wasn't happy. When Nightingale had finished, the man called over two of the younger-looking techs and told them something in a low voice.

One of the techs, a young man with Trotsky specs and an emo fringe, protested, but his boss shut him down and sent him and his mate packing up the stairs.

Nightingale came over and asked Somali Ninja Girl to run upstairs and tell Stephanopoulos that the building was secure, but that we hadn't found any suspects.

'A demon trap?' I asked.

'That's just a nickname,' said Nightingale. 'It's a booby trap; I suppose you could call it a magical land mine. I haven't seen one of those since 1946.'

'Shouldn't I know about these things?' I said.

'The list of things you need to know about, Peter, is extraordinarily long,' said Nightingale. 'And I have no doubt that you will eventually cover them all. But there's no point learning about demon traps until you've studied basic enchantment.' He held up his cane to show that the silver top was blackened and melted in places. Enchantment, I knew from my reading, was the process by which inanimate objects are imbued with magical qualities.

Nightingale examined the cane ruefully. 'Although I may be demonstrating how it's done in the next couple of months,' he said. 'That being the case, we may as well provide you with a training staff while we're at it.'

'The demon trap,' I said. 'Did you recognise the signature?'

'The *Signare*?' he asked. 'Not the individual, but I think I know who trained the vicious little so-and-so.'

'Geoffrey Wheatcroft?' I asked.

'The very same.'

'Could he have been the original magician?'

'That's something we're going to have to look into,' said Nightingale.

'He'd have to have schlepped back and forth between here and Oxford,' I said. 'If he was doing that, then he must have had an assistant.'

'One of his pupils?'

'Who might have gone on to be our new magician,' I said.

'This is all terribly speculative,' he said. 'We need to find the assistant.'

'We should start interviewing all the people who had contact with Geoffrey Wheatcroft or Jason Dunlop.'

There was an ironic cheer as one of the portable floodlights was restarted.

'That's an ambitious list of suspects,' said Nightingale.

'Then we start with the ones who knew both of them,' I said. 'We can do it under the pretext of investigating Jason Dunlop's murder.'

'First,' said Nightingale. 'I want you to go and secure Smith's office.'

'You don't need me here, then?' I asked.

'I'd rather you didn't see what's in there,' said Nightingale.

For a moment I thought I'd misheard him. 'What *is* in there?' I asked.

'Some very beastly things,' said Nightingale. 'Dr Walid has people coming in who've handled this sort of situation before.'

'What sort of situation?' I said. 'What sort of people?'

'Forensic pathologists,' he said. 'People who've worked in Bosnia, Rwanda – that sort of situation.'

'Are we talking mass graves here?'

'Amongst other things,' he said.

'Shouldn't I—'

'No,' said Nightingale. 'There's nothing in there

that it would profit you to see. Trust me in this, Peter, as master to apprentice, as a man who's sworn to protect and nurture you. I don't want you going in there.'

And I thought, do I really want to go in there?

'I can see whether No-Neck Tony knows anything while I'm at it,' I said.

Nightingale looked relieved. 'That is an excellent idea.'

Stephanopoulos lent me Somali Ninja Girl, who's name was Sahra Guleed and who turned out to be from Gospel Oak, which is just up the road from where I grew up – different school, though. When two ethnic officers meet for the first time, the first question you ask can be about anything but the second question is always, 'Why did you join?'

'Are you kidding?' said Guleed. 'You get to legally rough people up.'

The answer is nearly always a lie – I knew an idealist when I saw one. Despite the drizzle, the Saturday-night crowds were thick on Old Compton Street, and we had to dodge our fair share of drunks. I spotted my old mate PC Purdy loading a dazed-looking middle-aged man into the back of an IRV. The man was dressed in a pink tutu, and I was sure I knew him from somewhere. Purdy spotted me and gave me a cheery wave as he climbed into the front of the car – that was him out of the rain for the next couple of hours.

Since, with a bit of persuasion earlier, Alexander

Smith had given permission for us to search his office, I had his keys. But when we got to the door on Greek Street, it was ajar. I looked at Guleed, who flicked out her extendable baton and gestured for me to take the lead.

'Ladies first,' I said.

'Age before beauty,' she said.

'I thought you liked roughing people up?'

'This is your case,' she said.

I extended my own baton and went up the stairs first. Guleed waited, and then came padding up a couple of metres behind me. When there's just two of you, it's always wise to maintain a decent interval. That way, should anything happen to the copper in front, the copper behind has time to react in a calm and rational manner. Or, more likely, run for help. When I got to the first landing, I found the interior door to Smith's office was open and the cheap plywood around the lock was splintered. I waited until Guleed had caught up, and then gently pushed the door open with my left hand.

The office had been ransacked. Every drawer had been pulled out, every box file emptied. The framed posters had been yanked off the walls and the backs slashed open. It looked messy, but very thorough and systematic. This being Soho, it's possible to make a lot of noise before somebody dials 999, but I did wonder where No-Neck had been while the office was getting trashed. I found out when I stepped on his leg. Stepping on some poor bastard has got to be about the worst way to discover a body. I backed off.

No-Neck had been half buried under a pile of papers and glossy magazines. All I could see was the leg I'd stepped on, and enough of his face to make the identification.

'Oh dear,' said Guleed when she saw the body. 'Is he dead?'

Carefully, so as not to disturb the crime scene, I squatted down and felt for a pulse where, on somebody normal-shaped, there'd be a neck – there was nothing. While Guleed called Stephanopoulos, I pulled on my gloves and checked to see if there was an obvious cause of death. There was. Two entry wounds on his chest, hard to spot because of the black t-shirt: they'd gone in just after the Z and the second P in *Zeppelin*. The wounds showed what might have been powder burns from a close-range discharge. But since this was my first possible gunshot victim, what did I know?

According to Guleed, the first thing we needed to do was get out of the office and stop contaminating the crime scene. Since she was a fully paid-up member of a Murder Team, I did what she said.

'We have to check upstairs,' she said. 'In case any suspects are still in the building.'

'Just the two of us?' I asked.

Guleed bit her lip. 'Good point,' she said. 'Let's stay where we are. That way we stop anyone trying to leave or get into the crime scene.'

'What if there's a fire escape at the back?'

'You just had to say that, didn't you?' She tapped her baton against her thigh and gave me a disgusted look. 'OK,' she said. 'You go and secure the fire escape, and I'll stay here and guard the scene.'

'On my own?' I asked. 'What if there isn't a fire escape?'

'You're taking the piss, aren't you?'

'Yes,' I said. 'Yes, I am.'

Her Airwave squelched. It was Stephanopoulos. 'Yes boss,' said Guleed.

'I'm coming up Greek Street,' said Stephanopoulos. 'Just the one body, then?'

'So far,' I said.

'So far,' said Guleed into the Airwave.

'Tell Grant that I'm going to ban him from Westminster,' said Stephanopoulos. 'I really don't need the overtime this badly. Whereabouts in the building are you?'

'We're on the first-floor landing.'

'Why isn't one of you covering the fire escape?' asked Stephanopoulos. 'If there is a fire escape.'

Me and Guleed engaged in one of those silent, pointing arguments that you have when you're trying to sort something out without alerting someone on the other end of the phone. I'd just emphatically mouthed *I'll* go at Guleed, when we heard the front door being pushed open.

'Don't bother,' said Stephanopoulos. 'I'm already here.'

She stamped up the steps, pushed past us and had a look round from the doorway.

'What's his name?' asked Stephanopoulos.

I had to admit that all I knew was that his first name was Tony and that he worked for Alexander Smith as muscle and that he had no neck. Subtle clues in her manner told me that Stephanopoulos was less than impressed with my police work.

'You idiot, Peter,' she said. 'How could you not get his name? Everything, Peter, you have to nail down everything.'

I could hear Guleed not sniggering behind me – so could Stephanopoulos.

'I want you,' Stephanopoulos jabbed a finger at me, 'to go back to West End Central and re-interview Smith about who this guy is and what he knows about him.'

'Shall I tell him he's dead?'

'Do me a favour,' said Stephanopoulos wearily. 'Once he finds out about this he's going to shut the fuck right up, and I don't blame him.'

'Yes, guv,' I said.

Guleed asked if Stephanopoulos wanted her to go with me.

'Christ no,' she said. 'I don't want you picking up any more bad habits from him.' She looked at me again. 'Are you still here?'

It's a truism that in a secure building like a police station, once you're past the perimeter security you walk around unchallenged by adopting a purposeful stride and holding a clipboard. I don't recommend testing this, for two reasons: one, there's nothing worth nicking from a police station that you can't get easier from somewhere else, usually by bribing a police officer. Two, it's full of police officers, who are often suspicious to the point of clinical paranoia. Even an acclaimed uniform-carrier and all-round waste of space like PC John Purdy. This evening, he made a spectacular bid to get his name inscribed in the police Book of Remembrance. As events were reconstructed later, Purdy, having successfully navigated his tutu-wearing prisoner into the custody suite, was on his way to the canteen to do his 'paperwork' when he spotted an IC1 female walking up a side staircase in the direction of the CID interview rooms. On the CCTV footage from the stairwell, he's clearly seen calling after her and, when she fails to respond, he follows her up the stairs.

At just that moment, at least according to the time code from the CCTV camera in the foyer, yours truly was flashing his warrant card and getting buzzed into the building. I then head, with my Costa Coffee double macchiato in one hand and a cinnamon swirl in the other, for the central staircase and make my way up towards the same interview room – at this stage I'm one floor down.

Interview rooms used to be just ordinary offices fitted out with a table, a couple of chairs, good soundproofing and a place to leave the telephone books when you were finished. These days, a modern interview room has two camera positions, a tape recorder, a one-way mirror and a separate recording suite, from which an enterprising Senior Investigating Officer can monitor several interviews at once or have a bit of a kip. Since at West End Central all of this has to be shoehorned into the space designed in the 1930s as a modest open-plan office, it meant that the access corridor outside the interview rooms was a bit narrow. The single CCTV camera that covered the corridor began to malfunction at about the time I started up the steps, and none of the recording equipment in the interview rooms was turned on. This was all to the good for me, because it meant that when I came around the corner and found myself face to face with the Pale Lady, my thirty seconds of stunned indecision were not recorded for posterity.

Apart from her hair, which had been shorn off into a ragged pageboy, she looked exactly like the witness descriptions: white face, big eyes, disturbing mouth. She was dressed in grey joggers and a salmon-pink hoodie, and she didn't see me at first because she was attempting to shake PC John Purdy off her leg. He was stretched out on the floor with his left arm, broken in two places I learned later, dragging beside him and his right hand locked around the Pale Lady's surprisingly slender ankle. One of his eyes was beginning to swell shut and there was blood pouring from his nose.

I don't know if it was shock or the fact that I

had a mouthful of cinnamon swirl, or just because I'd already had a day of weird shit and was getting a bit punch-drunk, but I just couldn't make myself move.

Purdy saw me, though. 'Help,' he croaked.

The Pale Lady looked at me and cocked her head to one side.

'Help,' said Purdy again.

I tried to tell him to let go and move away, but it came out muffled by a shower of cinnamon crumbs.

Without taking her eyes off me, the Pale Lady elegantly lifted one hand and then slammed it down on Purdy's wrist. I heard bones break, and Purdy whimpered and let go. She smiled, revealing far too many teeth – I'd faced a smile like that before. I knew what was coming next. She tensed, so did I, then she surged towards me with a terrifying burst of speed, head thrust forward, mouth open, teeth bared. As she sprang at me I threw my coffee in her face. I'd just bought it. It was very hot.

She screamed and I flung myself out of her way. But because the corridor was narrow, her shoulder slammed into mine, and the impact spun me around and dumped me on the floor. It was like being hit by a fast-moving cyclist. I rolled to avoid any follow-up and staggered to my feet, only to find that the Pale Lady was long gone. Each interview room has an alarm button by the door, and I slapped my palm on one as I stepped over Purdy and slammed into the room where we'd stashed Alexander Smith.

He was slumped back in his chair, head thrown back, mouth open, and what looked like a bullet hole in his chest with the same charring around the cloth of his shirt that I'd seen on No-Neck earlier.

A uniformed PC cautiously stuck her head round the door and pointed a taser at me. 'Who are you?' she asked.

'DC Grant,' I said. 'Suspect is an IC1 female, grey tracksuit bottoms, pink hoodie.' If I left it there some idiot was going to get himself gutted trying to tackle her. 'Psychiatric patient, very dangerous, possibly armed. Probably still in the building.'

The PC looked at me in astonishment. 'Yeah, right,' she said.

'Have you done the first aid course?' I asked.

'Last month,' she said.

'OK, give me the taser and you see to Purdy,' I said.

She handed me the taser. It was heavy, plastic and looked like something from *Doctor Who*. Even in her state of shock she could tell that Smith was dead, so she went off to get the first aid kit for Purdy.

I stepped back over Purdy and took a moment to check he was still alive. 'Help's on its way,' I told him. 'What the hell were you doing here?'

His face was white and sweaty with pain but he

actually laughed – sort of. 'It's got a better canteen,' he said.

I told him to take it easy and headed for the stairs.

The thing about policing is that it's something you do out on the streets rather than inside the police station. During a normal working day, the civilian staff will outnumber your actual constables by a ratio of three to one. Which means that when there's a crisis at the local nick, everybody has to rush back to deal with it, and that takes time. Feral the Pale Lady might have been, but I didn't think she was stupid. Which meant she was going to go out by the fastest possible route, before all the police officers came rushing back in.

Since the IRA bombing campaigns started in the 1970s, police stations in London have developed a very clear idea of what constitutes inside and outside, and have placed a great deal of re-inforced laminated Perspex between the two. West End Central was no exception. But the entrance also featured a marble-faced external staircase that had definitely been built with no concern for the needs of wheelchair-users, and so there's a second door, at pavement level and just to the left of the main entrance, knocked into the façade – conveniently located at the base of the stairwell so that you can wheel yourself straight into the lift. The designers weren't stupid, though. It was a very thick door, and alarmed in such a way that the desk sergeant in reception could check you over on CCTV before he buzzed you out. It would have been totally secure if a young Detective Constable hadn't been returning to the station with an arm full of Chinese takeaways and decided that it would serve as a useful short cut to the CID offices.

The Pale Lady hit him when he was halfway through the door. I came down the stairs just in time to see him go down in a spray of what turned out to be sweet and sour sauce.

'Call it in,' I yelled as I jumped over him and into the pouring rain.

I'd seen her veer right down Savile Row and charge down the middle of the road. A silver Mercedes S1500 swerved to avoid her and piled into the side of a parked Porsche Carrera, setting off car alarms along the whole street. I stayed in the road behind and concentrated on trying to close the distance – as far as I knew, I was the only officer with a visual on the suspect. It was Saturday night in the West End, and despite the weather the crowds were out. If I lost contact, she'd vanish without a trace.

I stuffed the taser into my jacket pocket and fumbled for my Airwave. I tried it a few times until I remembered that I'd neglected to put the batteries back in. The Pale Lady was running out of road as Savile Row made a T-junction with Vigo Street. She went left, towards Regent Street and Soho. I lost hold of the Airwave as I followed her around the corner, and it went spinning under a parked car.

Vigo Street was little more than an alleyway with pretensions, a narrow little road lined with coffee shops and sandwich bars that linked Savile Row with Regent Street. It was late enough for them to be closing, and the Pale Lady was having to dodge around pedestrians, presumably because running over them might slow her down even more. I managed to get my phone out of my pocket. Like every police officer under the age of forty I have the bypass number for Metcall on speed dial – that's a number that routes you directly through to a CAD operator without all that 'Which service do you require?' stuff.

When you're sprinting after a suspect through a narrow street in heavy rain, it's almost impossible to hear someone talking to you on your phone, so I waited a suitable interval and started breathlessly identifying myself and the suspect I was chasing. It's hard to talk and stay with a fleeing suspect, especially one that runs across a major thorough-fare without waiting for the lights to change.

Regent Street was a slow-moving river of wet metal, but I thought she might even make it until White Van Man came to my rescue and she went spinning off the front of a Ford Transit. She rico-cheted off the back of a Citroën with a thin scream of rage and went staggering for the entrance to Glasshouse Street.

Fortunately for me, the river of metal ran itself

aground on the rocks of potential insurance claims, and so the traffic had stopped moving by the time I followed her across. I was now less than five metres behind the Pale Lady, so I pulled out the taser and tried to remember what its effective range was. I also realised where she was heading – twenty metres further on Glasshouse Street branches left into Brewer Street. She was heading back to the club.

Then she just accelerated away. I'm a young man, I'm fit and I used to sprint at school. But she just left me standing like a fat kid on sports day. I came to a stop at the corner of Brewer and Glasshouse, put my hands on my knees and tried to catch my breath. The diehard smokers outside the Glassblower pub on the corner gave me an ironic cheer.

You bastards, I thought, I'd like to see *you* run her down.

I heard a siren in the distance and looked up to see her running back towards me. Behind her I saw the flashing lightbars of at least two IRVs. When she saw me waiting for her, she gave me a look not of hatred or fear but a sort of weary disgust. As if I were a particularly persistent unwanted smell. I was somewhat insulted, so I shot her in the chest with my taser.

The Metropolitan Police uses an X26-model taser manufactured by the imaginatively titled Taser International Company. It uses a compressed nitrogen charge to fire two metal prongs into the suspect and then zap them with 50,000 volts. Which causes neuromuscular incapacitation, which causes them to fall over. Which was why I was a tad disappointed when the Pale Lady just grunted, blinked and then tore the prongs out of her chest. She glared at me, I took an involuntary step backwards and she spun on her heel and shot off down Glasshouse Street, bowling over diehard smokers as she went.

I dropped the taser and rocked forward for a good start. Even though my shoes slipped on the wet road, I like to think I trimmed a bit of time off my start. If I could get close enough to give her a heel tap, I could bring her down long enough for me and half a van of TSG to land on top of her.

She tore down Glasshouse Street with what I realised were bare feet slapping on the road surface. I came after her, sweating and blowing. But, weirdly, either she was slowing down or I was warming up, because I was gaining. But where was she going? At the far end of Glasshouse Street was Piccadilly Circus, lots of traffic, lots of tourists to get lost in and a tube station. The tube. There were steps down to Piccadilly Circus station right where Glasshouse met the Circus.

I was right. As she reached the ugly pink facade of the doughnut shop, she started angling right for the station entrance. I dug for it, but I didn't have enough left to get me closer than two metres. Then she suddenly veered left again and started curving round past the big Boots and heading for Shaftesbury Avenue. I couldn't figure it out until I saw a pair of PCSOs idling in front of the steps down to the station – the Pale Lady must have thought they were after her.

She went across the traffic island, bounced off a hatchback and ran right over the bonnet of a Ford Mondeo before sprinting past the Rainforest Café, bowling tourists aside as she went. I went round the cars to a chorus of hooting and headed after her, but I groaned out loud when she did a sharp turn into the Trocadero Centre. The only way in was a set of escalators going up a floor. Chasing someone up stairs or escalators is always a nightmare because there's a chance they'll be waiting in the blind spot at the top to kick you back down again. But I couldn't risk losing the Pale Lady, so I ran up the down escalators on the assumption that if she were waiting for me it would be on the wrong side. It was a good theory, and had she been waiting for me I'd have been well pleased with myself.

The Trocadero was a five-storey bastard child of a building built in the baroque style in 1896, and sorely used over the centuries as everything from a music hall to a restaurant and a waxworks. In the mid-1980s the interior was completely gutted and replaced with the sets from *Logan's Run* – or that might just be the way I remember it. It's got a cinema and a multi-level amusement arcade that I remember well, because my mum used to clean it. And one of my uncles knew a trick to blag free goes on *Street Fighter II*.

I caught a flash of salmon pink as I crested the escalator and saw the Pale Lady jump the short flight of steps that led down to the mezzanine level. A bunch of plump white girls in black hoodies scattered as she landed amongst them. As I chased her I was praying, 'Please God don't go into the cinema', because short of a minefield, a multiplex is the last place you want to chase a suspect. She skidded on the waxed floor and went left.

I yelled 'Police!' at the plump white girls who scattered again.

One of them yelled 'Wanker' as I jumped the stairs and followed the Pale Lady along the mezzanine. She went past a café with a drift of aluminium chairs and tables half blocking the way. Some poor sod stood up at the wrong moment and got the Pale Lady's forearm smashed into his head. He went down hard, upending a table and sending a tray spinning over the railings and down into the atrium three storeys below.

'Police,' I yelled again, which just got me bewildered looks from the bystanders. I really don't know why we don't just save our breath. Which I needed to save at that point, I can tell you.

The Pale Lady ran up another short flight of stairs and into a dark noisy cavern full of flashing lights. An electric-blue neon sign over the entrance said, *Welcome to Funland.*

It was packed, mostly teenagers and young men who were killing time before the clubs opened. They were playing slot machines and old-fashioned racing games that I remembered from ten years ago. If the Pale Lady had gone to ground amongst all those bodies I might have lost her, but either she was on a timetable or she was smart enough to know that the wrath of the Metropolitan Police was about to fall on her from a great height. Nobody kills a suspect in a police station and gets away with it – at least nobody without a warrant card.

Amongst the games and slot machines, two escalators led upward to the next floor. When I saw a teenaged boy pointing and his mate pulling his phone to film something out of my sight, I knew the Pale Lady was going up that way. I'd already spotted that if I jumped onto the skittles machine I could jump again, high enough to grab the escalator rail and vault onto the steps. I landed just short of the Pale Lady riding up, lying flat on her back to stay hidden. She hissed and lashed her foot out at my face, but I got out of the way in time to hear her heel go past my ear with a sound like ripping silk. I reared back and tried to stamp on her other knee, but she scrambled back and tried to kick me in the bollocks. I twisted and her kick grazed off my thigh, but hard enough to stagger me. She was just about to kick me again when we reached the top of the escalator.

She screamed and I realised that her hair, as

311

short as it was, had caught in the metal teeth at the top of the escalator. She thrashed, did a sort of roll and then a desperate headstand to pull it clear. I grabbed my baton, extended it and lashed down as hard as I could. I didn't think I'd get a second chance like this.

They train us to use our batons, you know. They don't just issue them to us and say *Try not to kill anyone*. There are light taps for warnings, a full arm swing that's deliberately slow to make your suspect flinch back, the sneaky slap to the thigh that isn't easy to see on the news footage. But the basic principle is always that the amount of force is always controlled and appropriate. This is why I lunged forward while she was upside down and hit the Pale Lady in the hip with everything I had. Something crunched under the baton and she howled loud enough to cut through all the music and sound effects. Then she kicked me in the cheek.

It wasn't her best effort, but it was hard enough to snap my head back so that I didn't see the end of the escalator and stumbled off while she flipped herself backwards, twisted and tried to crawl away. I wasn't having that, so I threw myself on her back. I fell heavy, to try and drive the air out of her. But in an astonishingly fluid motion she arched her back and flung me into the side of a Spinna Winna machine. My elbow smashed into the glass, and I felt a sensation that told me I was on the numb-now, pain-later plan. I straightened up just in time to see her fist coming for my face. She must have been slowing down, because this time I got safely out of the way and her hand splintered into the glass and through. I whirled round and brought my baton down on her wrist just as hard as I could. Again a crack, and a spray of blood as the glass cut her skin. She let out a wet gasp and turned her head to stare at me.

'Give it up,' I said.

There was pain in her face and anger, and the sort of self-pity you see on the face of thwarted bullies. She bared her teeth in a snarl of defiance and wrenched her hand out of the Spinna Winna machine, a curl of blood splattering my face. I lunged forward with my head down and got my shoulder jammed into her chest. She hammered at my shoulders while I drove her back towards the balcony railing. She was unnaturally strong, but I was still bigger and heavier than her. And if I could stay inside her reach, I might be able to pin her down long enough for back-up to arrive.

Surely back-up should be arriving soon.

Her back hit the barrier and we came to a shuddering halt. I made a grab for her knee to see if I could trip her up, but she caught me a stunning blow on the side of the head and then threw me hard enough that I fetched up on my side three metres away. I shook my head and looked up to see the Pale Lady charging towards me with blood staining her clothes and murder in her eyes. She could have at least tried to make her escape – I wasn't going to follow her any more. But I think she knew she was going down and was planning to make somebody pay before she went. That somebody being me.

I didn't have time to shout a warning, I just made the correct shape in my head and shouted, louder than I had intended, '*Impello*.'

The spell picked her up and slammed her back against the railing and then, horrifyingly, she toppled backwards and was gone.

CHAPTER 11

THESE FOOLISH THINGS

The central atrium at the Trocadero Centre is four storeys high, with an open basement that added another storey to the fall. The space is criss-crossed at random intervals by escalators, presumably because the architects felt that disorientation and an inability to find the toilets were an integral part of the shopping experience. I was told much later that the Pale Lady had bounced off the side of one of the escalators on her way down, that she may even have been angling to try and land on it but couldn't quite make the distance. That impact broke her back in two places, but she was still alive when she hit the basement floor head first.

Instantaneous, said Dr Walid.

A thirty-metre drop at 9.8 metres per second per second – I make that about two and a half seconds to watch the ground coming up to meet you. That's not what I call instantaneous.

Back-up was less than a minute away. They saw her fall. They were on hand to seal off the floor and take witness statements. I gave a brief statement to Stephanopoulos, before Nightingale insisted that we go to Casualty. The next thing I knew, we were in the Casualty unit at UCH, and Dr Walid was hovering in the background and making the F2 junior doctor who was treating me nervous. Then Dr Walid noticed that Nightingale was a bit pale and unsteady, and forced him to lie down in an adjacent treatment cubicle. The junior doctor visibly relaxed and started chatting to me as he checked my various scrapes and bruises, but I don't remember what he was talking about. Then he bustled off to arrange some X-rays and left me with a redheaded Australian nurse who I recognised from the Punchinello case. She winked at me as she cleaned the blood off my face and glued a cut on my cheek that I wasn't even aware I had.

'May the blessings of the river be upon you,' said the nurse as they wheeled me off to X-ray and zapped me a couple of times, before wheeling me back to my cubicle to lounge around in a draughty hospital gown for an hour or so. It may have been longer because I think I dozed off. Being Saturday night, there was a lot of drunken shouting and moaning and the sound of my fellow members of the constabulary telling people to 'calm down' or asking them what had happened. Dr Walid popped his head in to say that he was keeping Nightingale in overnight. I asked for some water, he felt my forehead and then vanished.

Somebody with a Scouse accent a couple of cubicles down said that he just wanted to go home. The doctor told him that they had to reset his leg first. The Scouser insisted he felt fine, and the doctor explained that they had to wait for the drink to wear off so they could anaesthetise him.

'I want to go home,' said the Scouser.

'As soon as you're fixed up,' said the doctor.

'Not home *here*,' said the Scouser mournfully. 'I want to go back to Liverpool.'

I wanted the fluorescent lights to stop giving me a headache.

Dr Walid came back with water and a couple of Nurofen tablets. He couldn't stay because he had a brand-new body to look at. After some more time, the junior doctor came back.

'You can go home now,' he said. 'Nothing is broken.'

I think I walked back to the Folly – it's not that far.

I woke up the next morning to find that breakfast hadn't been served. When I went down to the kitchen to find out why, I discovered Molly sitting on the table with her back to the door. Toby was sitting beside her, but at least he looked up when I came in.

'Is something wrong?' I asked.

She didn't move. Toby whined.

'I'll just go and have breakfast out,' I said. 'In the park.'

That seemed fine with Molly.

Toby jumped up and followed me out.

'You are so mercenary,' I told him.

He yapped. I guess from Toby's point of view a sausage is a sausage.

The Folly sits on the south side of Russell Square, the centre of which is occupied by a park with fixed gravel paths, big trees which I didn't know the names of, a fountain that was specifically designed to get children and small dogs soaking wet and on the north side, a café which does a decent double sausage, bacon, black pudding, egg and chips. It was actually quite sunny, so I sat on the terrace outside the café and mechanically shovelled the food into my face. It really didn't taste of anything, and in the end I put my plate on the floor and let Toby finish it off.

I walked back to the Folly and in through the main door, where there was a drift of junk mail. I scooped it up. It was mostly flyers for local pizza joints and kebab houses, although there was one crudely designed leaflet from a Ghanaian fortune-teller who felt we could only benefit from his insight into future events. I dropped the lot into the magazine rack that Molly leaves in the atrium for that purpose.

I felt a bit queasy, so I went into the toilet and threw up my breakfast and then climbed back into my bed and went to sleep.

I woke up again in the late afternoon, sticky and with the discombobulated feeling you get when you sleep through the day for no good reason. I went down the corridor and ran a bath in the claw-footed enamel monstrosity that we have instead of a proper shower. I got it as scalding as I could take, yelped when it lapped against the bruises on my thigh and stayed in there until my muscles had relaxed and I'd got bored of impersonating Louis Armstrong singing 'Ain't Misbehaving'. I couldn't shave because of the cut on my cheek, so I left my chin with manly stubble and went to look for some clean clothes.

When I was growing up, the only way to keep my mum out of my room would have been to install steel security doors, and probably not even that would have helped. It did mean that I've never been precious about people coming into my bedroom, especially if all they're going to do is clean it and do the laundry. I put on khaki chinos, the quality button-down shirt and my good shoes. I looked in the mirror – Miles Davis would have been proud of me – all I needed was a trumpet. There's only one thing you can do when you look that good, so I picked up my mobile and called Simone.

It didn't work – I'd blown the chip when I used magic on the Pale Lady.

I took one of my back-up phones from the drawer in my desk, a crappy two-year-old Nokia with a pay-as-you-go SIM card. It already had my standard numbers saved, so I added Simone's and called her.

'Hi baby,' I said. 'Want to go out?'

When she stopped laughing, she said that she'd be delighted to.

Only students and people from Basildon go clubbing on a Sunday, so we went to the Renoir to see *Spirit of the Escalator, un film de Dominique Baudis* which turned out, despite the subtitles, to be a romantic comedy. The Renoir is an art cinema that sits underneath the Brunswick Centre, a cream-coloured shopping centre and housing development that reminded me of an Aztec pyramid turned inside out. It's less than two minutes' walk from the Folly, so it was convenient. It's also still got the old-fashioned seats where you can snuggle up to your girlfriend without injuring yourself on a cup holder. She asked me about the cut on my cheek, and I told her I'd been in a scuffle.

Afterwards we had supper at YO! Sushi, which Simone had never eaten at before, despite there being a branch practically outside her front door.

'I'm terribly loyal to the Patisserie Valerie,' she said by way of explanation.

She loved the little coloured bowls trundling around the conveyor belt, and was soon piling empty ones up by her plate like so many mounds of skulls. She was actually quite a dainty eater, but steady and determined. I picked at a bowl of spicy salmon rice. My stomach still wasn't really settled, but it was a pleasure to watch the obvious delight she got from each dish. Fortunately YO! Sushi closed before she exceeded my credit-card limit, and we tumbled out of the Brunswick Centre and walked back along Bernard Street towards Russell Square tube station. It had rained while we were in the cinema, and the streets were slick and fresh. Simone stopped walking and dragged my head down so she could kiss me. She tasted of soy sauce.

'I don't want to go home,' she said.

'How about my place?' I said.

'Your place?'

'Sort of,' I said.

The coach house is not the perfect crash pad, but I certainly didn't want Simone meeting Molly when she was in one of her moods. Simone blew right past my two grand's worth of consumer electronics and went straight to the studio under the skylight.

'Who's this?' she asked. She'd found the portrait of Molly reclining nude while eating cherries.

'Somebody who used to work here years ago,' I said.

She gave me a sly look. 'Turn around,' she said. 'And close your eyes.'

I did as I was told. Behind me I heard the stealthy rustle of clothes, a suppressed curse followed by a zip unfastening, the thump of her boots hitting the floor, the whisper of silk as it slipped over her skin. There was a long pause, and then I heard the creak of antique furniture as she made herself comfortable.

She made me wait a little bit longer.

'You can turn around now,' she said.

She was reclining, nude and beautiful, on the chaise longue. She didn't have a bowl of cherries,

321

so she'd let her fingers drift down to twist in the brown curls of her hair. She was so delicious I didn't know where to start.

Then I saw it, a blotch like a port-wine birthmark in the corner of her mouth. I thought it was a smear of something she'd been eating, but then it ripped while I was staring at it. With a hideous crunch her jaw splintered as a crude triangle of skin peeled back from her face. I saw muscle, tendon and bone stretch and pop, and her jaw hung slack like that of a cut puppet.

'What's wrong?' asked Simone.

Nothing. Her face was back as it had been, wide, beautiful, the arc of her smile fading as I staggered backwards.

'Peter?'

'Sorry,' I said. 'I don't know what happened there.' I knelt down by the chaise longue and cupped her cheek in my hand – the bones beneath her skin were reassuringly solid. I kissed her but, after a moment, she pushed my face away.

'Has something happened?'

'I was involved in an incident,' I said. 'Somebody died.'

'Oh,' she said and put her arms around me. 'What happened?'

'I'm not really supposed to talk about it,' I said, and slipped my hand down her hip in the hope that it would distract her.

'But if you could talk about it,' she said, 'you'd talk about it with me?'

'Sure,' I said. But I was lying.

'Poor thing,' she said, and kissed me.

I found that if I held her close, I didn't have any more nightmares. At one point in the proceedings the chaise longue shifted alarmingly and I heard the crack of splintering wood. We hurriedly separated just long enough for me to put a few cushions on the floor and throw a blanket over them. She pushed me onto my back, straddled me and it all got wonderfully strenuous and sweaty until finally she flopped down on me as boneless and as slippery as a fish.

'It's peculiar,' she said after she'd caught her breath. 'I used to always want to go out. But with you I just want to stay in all the time.'

She rolled off and slid her hand down my stomach to cup my balls. 'Do you know what I'd really like now?' she asked.

'There's cakes in the fridge,' I said.

I was hard again, and slipped her hand up to grab hold.

'You're a terrible man,' she said. She gave me a quick shake as if judging my readiness and then, pausing briefly to kiss it on the head, got up and made her way to the fridge. 'That Jap food's all very well,' she said. 'But I don't think they know how to make decent patisserie.'

Later, exhausted but unable to sleep, I lay with her under the skylight and watched the rain rippling down the panes. Again Simone slept with her head on my shoulder, a leg slung possessively across my thighs and her arm draped around my waist – as if making sure I couldn't slink away in the middle of the night.

I'm not a player, but I'd never had a girlfriend who'd lasted more than three months. Lesley said that my exes knew that past a certain point I'd lost interest, and that's why they always packed me in first. That's not the way I remember it, but Lesley swore she could have constructed a calendar based on my love life. A cyclical one, she said, like the Maya – counting down to disaster. Lesley could be surprisingly erudite sometimes.

On the other hand, I thought as Simone snuggled up against me, even in the worst-case scenario there's at least another two months left to run. Then, of course, that corner of my brain that is for ever a policeman wanted to know whether I was sure Simone wasn't involved in the case of the dying jazzmen. After all, she'd been living with Cyrus Wilkinson. But then Henry Bellrush was still living with his wife when he died. More tellingly, if Simone was really a creature of the night who seduced and then sucked the life out of jazz musicians, why was she sleeping with me – who had utterly failed to inherit his father's talent or even his taste for music? Nor had her face appeared in any of the pictures from 1941.

You actually get a lecture on this during training, which I admit most of us snoozed through because it wasn't associated with any tests or essay-writing. I did remember the lecturer warning that a copper's natural instincts could quickly spill over into unwarranted paranoia. Life is unbelievably messy, the lecturer said, and coincidences happen all the time. If you're still suspicious in the morning, I told myself, you can check her alibi against suspicious deaths last year, because nothing builds a healthy relationship like the third degree over the breakfast table.

Having thought that just before I drifted off, I hoped it wasn't a bad omen when I woke to find that Simone had slipped out at the crack of dawn and left me sleeping.

I was summoned that morning to the John Peel Centre in Hendon, where I was 'debriefed' by a couple of officers from the Directorate of Professional Standards. This took place in a conference room with tea, coffee, Sainsbury's Value digestive biscuits and was all very civilised. After establishing that I had a legitimate reason to be on that floor of West End Central, they asked me about the chase to the Trocadero Centre and the consequent death of the suspect in a fall from the upper balcony. Apparently the CCTV footage was very clear – I was nowhere near the suspect when she went over the railing, therefore I could not have pushed her, nor could I reasonably have been expected to reach her in time to stop the fall. They seemed satisfied that I should return to duty, although they warned me that this was just the start of their investigation.

'We may have more questions for you later,' they said.

I'm fairly certain they were supposed to offer me psychological counselling at that point, but they didn't. Which was a pity, because I would have rather liked it. Sadly, the rules are very clear. As a red-blooded police officer, you can only accept counselling when it is foisted on you by *Guardian*-reading social-worker types. I don't need it, you protest to your mates, but you know these touchy-feely jobsworth types. Then you down your pint and soldier on, dignity intact.

As well as the statement to the DPS, I had to generate my own report for the files, which I did from the safety of the coach house, sending them off to be vetted by Lesley before I submitted them. She suggested I make a couple of deliberate mistakes because nothing says 'cover-up' like perfectly consistent statements, so I pretended that I was a member of the public and misremembered some stuff. She also made it clear that rushing into the Trocadero Centre without back-up had been foolish and, worse, unprofessional. She was sorry to say that I was clearly deteriorating badly without her there to curb my bad habits. I let her go on at me for some time, not least because she seemed to enjoy it so.

I promised to be more careful in future.

Dr Walid released Nightingale from hospital that afternoon, and he returned to the Folly long enough to change his clothes before heading back to supervise the forensic work at the club. I asked if he needed me, but he said no and gave me a reading list, one of which was a gloss by Bartholomew that was in Latin. I think he was hoping I'd spend all day with the text in one hand and a dictionary in the other, but I just typed the relevant sections into an online Latin translator and then tried to interpret the gibberish that came out the other end.

I think Bartholomew was conjecturing that it might be possible to use magic to combine the characteristics of two creatures in *violation of the great chain of being*, that great hierarchy of creatures, slime at the bottom and angels at the top, ordained by God. Somebody had annotated my copy by writing in the margin in very small capitals something in Latin that my web translator rendered as: *People are made nature and vice-versa.*

Real cat girls, I thought. The Strip Club of Doctor Moreau. I wondered what it would be like to sleep with something as sleek and furry as a tiger. Whoever was running the club would have a made a fortune. The old ethically challenged magical practitioner had Chief Inspector Johnson to help keep it quiet but the new guy, his possible apprentice, the Faceless One, how had he planned to keep it secret?

The next morning, Nightingale took me for a tour of the Strip Club of Dr Moreau. The landing and cloakroom area had been turned, appropriately enough, into a changing room for personnel to get in and out of their Noddy suits. Dr Walid was waiting for us and warned us to watch our feet. Lengths of cable had been run down the stairs and neatly secured against the walls with gaffer tape.

'We wanted to avoid activating any electric circuits in the club itself,' said Dr Walid. 'Just in case.'

He led me down to the foyer, where I noticed that the Cabinet of Larry had been removed completely, as had the kicking legs. 'I've had to lease extra space at UCH,' said Dr Walid. 'I've never had this much material before.'

The curtains in the foyer had been taken down, and we stepped through into the next room which proved to be the club proper, where the dance floor and stage would have been if cages hadn't been bolted to the floor. They looked brand new, and similar to the cages that labs keep their animals in.

'Exactly the same,' said Dr Walid when I pointed this out. 'Bollingtek Animal Containment Systems – we use them at the hospital. They were installed some time this year.'

'Stephanopoulos has her people tracing the serial numbers,' said Nightingale.

The cages were empty, but I could smell the bitter tang of animal shit. I saw fingerprint powder dusted around the locks and any other surface that a keeper might have put their hand on while looking after the inmates.

'How many were there?' I asked.

'Five in the cages,' said Dr Walid. 'I'm still doing tests, but they all seem to be chimeras.'

That was a term I'd had to look up the night before when translating Bartholomew. It means a creature that has some cells with one set of DNA and other cells with another set of DNA. It's vanishingly rare in mammals, and usually happens when two eggs are fertilised by different sperm and then merge before going on to grow into a foetus. Not that Bartholomew knew what tetragametic chimerism was – the fathers of genetics, Crick and Watson, weren't even a gleam in their grandfathers' eyes when he'd been writing. Bartholomew had described chimeras as the degenerate product of unnatural unions created through the foulest and blackest magic. But I had a horrible feeling that both definitions might fit.

'Were any of them alive?' I asked.

Dr Walid looked uncomfortably at Nightingale, who shook his head.

'One of them was still alive,' said Nightingale. 'But it died after we moved it.'

'Did it say anything?' I asked.

'It never regained consciousness,' said Dr Walid.

We agreed that, given the newness of the cages, they must have been the work of the New Magician rather than the Old. 'Do we think Geoffrey Wheatcroft is the Old Magician?' I asked.

'We don't have any link between him and this place,' said Nightingale. 'In addition, I find it somewhat unlikely that he could pursue an academic career and maintain a double life as a nightclub impresario.'

'But he definitely trained the New Magician?' I asked. 'The Faceless One?'

'Oh, without doubt,' said Nightingale. 'I'm quite certain of that.'

'I like "Faceless One",' said Dr Walid. 'Did you come up with that?'

'He could have had accomplices,' I said. 'Another practitioner who handled the London end. That's possible, isn't it?'

'Quite possible,' said Nightingale. 'Good thinking.'

'Or more than one partner. There could be – what do you call a group of magicians?' I asked. 'A gang, a coven?'

'An argument,' said Dr Walid. 'It's an argument of wizards.'

We both looked at Dr Walid, who shrugged.

'You both need to read more widely,' he said. This from a man who did peer review for the *European Journal of Gastroenterology and Hepatology*.

'A cabal,' said Nightingale. 'It's called a cabal of magicians.'

'Operating under our noses since the sixties,' said Dr Walid.

'Just to add salt to the wound,' said Nightingale.

'I should start running down the names that we got from Oxford and cross-referencing them with known associates of the Soho gangs,' I said.

'Not before I show you something else,' he said.

I actually went cold when he said that – I'd been very happy to find that everything had been cleaned out, and I really wasn't that keen to see anything else. Nightingale led me further into the club. Beyond the cages, there was another STAFF ONLY door that took us to a short corridor and a suite of rooms that might once have been offices or storage. They were all largely the same, grubby mattresses on the floor, a loose collection of clothes and shoes stuffed into cardboard boxes, a DVD player and an old-fashioned electron-gun TV, a few pathetic attempts to brighten up the walls, a picture of kittens and a Justin Timberlake poster. It was depressingly familiar to anyone who has ever helped raid a safe house used by human traffickers.

'How many?' I asked.

'We found plenty of DNA evidence,' said Dr Walid. 'Blood, semen, hair follicles. So far we've identified eight individuals – all chimerae.'

'Oh, God,' I said.

'He must have another safe house,' said Nightingale. 'But it could be anywhere.'

It wasn't all bad news. Lesley called later with a whole new way for me to dig myself into a hole. She'd discovered it while trawling through the records from Oxford University. She hadn't found any obvious connections between Wheatcroft and Alexander, but . . .

'Guess whose name I did come across?' she asked.

'Prince Harry?'

'Don't be silly,' said Lesley. 'Harry went to Sandhurst. No, a certain other undergraduate going by the name of Cecelia Tyburn Thames.'

'Lady Ty knew Wheatcroft?' I asked.

'No, you idiot,' said Lesley. 'But—' She broke off to cough some more. She moved the phone away from her mouth, but I could hear her coughing and swearing. Then a pause as she drank some water.

I asked if she was okay, and she said she was. There was going to be a second operation some time towards the end of the year to see if they could restore greater functionality to her voice box.

'But,' she said, 'the point is that Tyburn was at Oxford at roughly the same time as Jason Dunlop, and you once told me that one of her sisters could smell the magic on you.'

'That was Brent,' I said. 'She's four years old.'

'That just means a natural ability,' said Lesley.

I said it was unlikely that Tyburn, even if she had spotted any magic at Oxford, was going to tell me.

'You just don't want to see Tyburn again,' said Lesley.

Damn right I didn't want to see Tyburn again. I'd humiliated her in front of her mother, which meant I could have whipped her naked down Kensington High Street and she would have been less pissed off with me. But I only ever argue with Lesley about two things, and neither of those have anything to do with police work. It had to be worth a try.

I knew Tyburn had a house in Hampstead. I'd blown up a particularly rare fountain the last time I'd visited – although in my defence she had been trying to mind-control me at the time. But that was just the source of her river. I'd heard that she actually lived somewhere in Mayfair. The very rich and the very poor have one thing in common: they both generate a great deal of information – the rich in the media and the poor on the vast and unwieldy databases of the state. The rich, provided they avoid celebrity, can take steps to preserve their anonymity – Lady Ty's Wikipedia page read as if it was produced by a PR flack because no doubt Lady Ty had hired a PR flack to ensure it stayed the way she wanted it. Or, more likely, one of Lady Ty's 'people' had hired a PR company who'd hired a freelancer who'd knocked it out in half an hour, the better to focus on the novel he was writing. It did reveal that Lady Ty was married – to a civil engineer, no less – and that they had two beautiful children, one of whom, the boy, was eighteen years old. Old enough to drive, but young enough to still be living at home.

The thing about being a policeman is you get to cheat. You get to look things up on the PNC, things that even the richest and most influential person has to provide accurate information about – in this case, driving tests. Stephen George McAllister-Thames passed his in January, and the address of the record was Chesterfield Hill, Mayfair.

It was the kind of perfect Regency terrace with a rusticated façade and decorative ironwork that causes grown estate agents to break down and weep with joy. It was located less than half a kilometre to the west of the Trocadero Centre, on streets that would have been much nicer if all the character hadn't been stripped off them by decades of money.

The door was opened by a tall, mixed-race young man whom I recognised from the picture on his driving licence. He'd inherited an unfortunate pair of ears, and what my mum would have described as 'better' hair from his dad, but he had his grandmother's cat-shaped eyes. That wasn't all he'd inherited.

'Mum,' he called back into the depths of the house. 'There's a wizard here to see you.' And then, just in case I hadn't realised he was a teenager, he slouched off back to whatever it was he'd been doing before I so rudely interrupted him. His mother passed him in the hallway, and came and stood in the doorway with her arms crossed. She let me stew for a good ten seconds before asking what I wanted.

'I was wondering if you could help me with my inquiries,' I said.

She took me through into a kitchen furnished

in French oak and cool green tile. She offered me tea which, just to be on the safe side, I refused. She poured herself a white wine.

'What inquiries are these?' she asked.

I asked her to cast her mind back to her days as an undergraduate at Oxford University.

'Where I gained my double first,' she said. 'Not that I think that was an achievement. Being less important than the mere act of being born within the sound of the Bow Bells.' She finished her glass and refilled.

'While you were at Oxford,' I said, 'did you notice anyone practising magic, perhaps clandestinely?'

'Does this have something to do with the altercation at the Trocadero Centre?' she asked.

'It's related, yes,' I said. 'And to the attack on Ash.'

'I'm curious,' she said. 'What makes you think I should tell you?'

'So you were aware of magic being practised,' I said.

'What makes you think that?'

'Because you think you have something to withhold,' I said.

'I'll admit it's a trifle irrational, but I still find myself minded to tell you to piss off,' she said. 'Why should I help you?'

'If you tell me what you know, I promise I'll go away,' I said.

'Tempting,' she said.

'And because we think there's an evil magician operating in London, and we think he may have been at Oxford – at the same time you were.' I looked at her. 'You may even know him.'

'No. I would have smelled him,' she said. 'Even as I can smell you now.'

'So what do I smell like?'

'Ambition, vanity, pride,' she shrugged. 'Fried plantain and honeysuckle. Don't ask me why.'

'Who were they?' I asked. 'The practitioners at Oxford – I know you know.'

She tried to stop herself, but in the end there are some varieties of information that are only fun if you tell them to someone else.

'There was a dining club. Do you know what that is?' she asked.

An excuse for students to gather together and get pissed, as far as I knew. The membership criteria were set at varying levels of exclusivity and expense. I doubted Tyburn had joined one and, had I gone to Oxford, I'm not sure I could have joined one if I'd wanted to.

It was called the Little Crocodiles, she told me. And it was boys only, and while it wasn't exclusive to any one college it was mostly a Magdalen crowd. They were considered to be very dull, not aristocratic enough for the social climbers and not riotous enough for the aristos.

'Not my cup of tea,' said Tyburn. 'But I remember running into a couple of members once at a party and catching that whiff.' She waved her hand in front of her nose. 'Like I said, ambition, sweaty, like somebody who's working too hard.'

'Do you remember their names?' I asked.

She did, because remembering who was who was part of who she was. She also had half a dozen other names of possible Little Crocodiles.

'And you're sure the dining club were actively training?' I asked.

'I made a point of getting close enough to smell any member I could find,' she said. 'I thought they were somehow related to Professor Post-martin and your boss. I assumed that this was their attempt to expand the influence of the Folly.'

She shook her wine bottle and poured the remaining half-measure into her glass.

I judged that now would be an opportune moment to depart, so I thanked her, put away my notebook and stood up.

'For fifty years they do nothing and then suddenly there's you,' she said. 'How did that happen?'

'You know what you smell like to me, Ty,' I said. 'Brandy and cigars and old rope.'

'They hung Jonathan Wild at Tyburn,' she said. 'For all that he thought himself the Thief Taker General of Great Britain.'

I didn't answer that one, because I felt getting out the front door intact was more important.

I told Nightingale what I'd learned over breakfast the next morning, and he insisted we go down to the firing range in the basement and blow the shit out of some targets. To be fair, I think he'd

been planning a training session for some time –
he also didn't swear.

Several months of random fire by me had
depleted our stock of World War Two vintage
silhouettes, so I'd bought some 1960s NATO
standard-issue targets off the internet. Gone were
the coal-scuttle helmets and rampaging Hun, to
be replaced by snarling figures carefully stripped
of any national or ethnic identity. NATO, these
figures implied, was ready to take on paper soldiers
from anywhere.

Nightingale put three fireballs in the centre mass
of the left-hand target.

'What made you think Ty would tell you?' asked
Nightingale.

'She couldn't help herself,' I said. 'First law of
gossip – there's no point knowing something if
somebody else doesn't know you know it. Besides,
I think she has such a low opinion of us that she
thinks it's only a matter of time until we . . . mess
up and she can sweep in like the cavalry.'

'Given our track record so far,' said Nightingale,
'that's hardly prescient.'

'A Ministry of Magic,' I said. 'Is that what she
really wants?'

'Deep breath,' said Nightingale. 'And *loose!*'

The trick behind an effective fireball is that it
becomes an ingrained *forma*. A spell you don't
have to think about to perform. I loosed a trio of
fireballs which you could see moving, which was
bad, but at least I hit the target – or *a* target, at

any rate. I also forgot to release them immediately, which meant that they sat there and fizzed a bit before exploding.

'Have you been practising at all?' asked Nightingale.

'Of course I have, boss. Watch this,' I said, and threw a 'skinny grenade' down the range, which stuck right in the centre mass of the target.

'Your aim is getting better,' said Nightingale. 'It's a pity about the release . . .'

The grenade detonated and cut the target in half.

'And what was that?' asked Nightingale. He didn't always approve of me departing from the strict forms he laid down for spells. His motto was that bad habits now could get you killed later.

'Skinny grenade,' I said. 'You use *Scindere* like you do with *Lux impello scindere*, except instead of a light in a fixed place you get a bomb.'

'Skinny grenade?'

'From *Scindere*,' I said. Nightingale shook his head.

'How are you managing the timing?' he asked

'That's a bit hit and miss,' I said. 'I did some tests, and it's anywhere between ten seconds to five minutes.'

'So you don't know when it's going to explode?'

'Not really,' I said.

'Is there anything I could say that would stop you from doing all this unauthorised experimentation?' he asked.

'Honestly,' I said. 'Probably not.'

'I have to ask,' he said. 'Why did you use *Impello* at the Trocadero Centre – why not a fireball?'

'I didn't want to kill her,' I said. 'And I'm still more confident with *Impello* than I am with anything else.'

'You realise she was just a diversion,' said Nightingale. 'Alexander Smith was shot in the chest with a couple of narrow-gauge fireballs.'

'I thought it was a gunshot wound,' I said.

'That's why he used a narrow-gauge fireball. To disguise the wound.'

'Forensic countermeasure,' I said. 'This guy is way too fucking clever.'

'He probably walked out the back while you were chasing the Pale Lady out the front.'

I cut a target in half with my next fireball.

'That's much better,' said Nightingale. 'They need to go faster. If the enemy can see them coming, you might as well just carry a gun and shoot them with that instead.'

'Why don't we just carry guns?' I asked. 'I know you've got a room full of them.'·

'Well, for one thing,' said Nightingale, 'the paperwork has become very tiresome, then there's care, maintenance and trying to ensure one doesn't leave it on the Underground by mistake. Plus a fireball is more versatile, and can pack more of a punch than any calibre pistol I'd be happy to carry.'

'Really?' I asked. 'More than a point-four-four magnum?'

'Indubitably,' he said.

'What's the biggest thing you've zapped with a fireball?' I asked.

'That would be a tiger,' said Nightingale.

'Well don't tell Greenpeace,' I said. 'They're an endangered species.'

'Not that sort of tiger,' said Nightingale. 'A Panzerkampfwagen sechs Ausf E.'

I stared at him. 'You knocked out a Tiger tank with a fireball?'

'Actually I knocked out two,' said Nightingale. 'I have to admit that the first one took three shots, one to disable the tracks, one through the driver's eye slot and one down the commander's hatch – brewed up rather nicely.'

'And the second Tiger?'

'I didn't have time to be so clever with that one,' said Nightingale. 'Straight frontal shot into the weak spot where the turret meets the hull. Must have caught the ammo store because it went up like a firework factory. The turret blew right off.'

'This was at Ettersberg, wasn't it?'

'This was the final act at Ettersberg,' he said. 'We were trying to pull out when a platoon of Tigers just came crawling out of the treeline. We didn't expect the Germans to have anything but rear-echelon troops, so it caught us on the hop, I can tell you. I was the rearguard, so I had to deal with them.'

'Lucky you,' I said. But my brain was still trying to get round the idea that Nightingale could put

341

a hole in ten centimetres of steel armour, when I still sometimes had trouble getting through the paper of the targets.

'Practice and training,' said Nightingale. 'Not luck.'

We kept it up until lunch, and after that there was exciting paperwork including a surprisingly long form in which I explained how I'd managed to lose an expensive X-26 taser pistol and reduce the working insides of an Airwave handset to sand. Coming up with a plausible explanation for both kept me busy until late afternoon, when Simone phoned.

'I've found us a hotel room,' she said, and gave me an address off Argyle Square.

'When shall we meet?' I asked.

'I'm already there,' she said. 'Naked and decorated with whipped cream.'

'Really?'

'Actually,' she said. 'I've eaten the whipped cream, but it's the thought that counts.'

Argyle Square is about fifteen minutes' walk from the Folly. Twenty if you stop off at the mini-market to pick up a couple of cans of aerosol whipped cream – it always pays to be prepared.

It was only a two-star hotel but the sheets were clean, the bed was sturdy and it had a tiny en suite toilet and shower. The walls were a bit thin, but we only found that out when next door banged on the wall for us to be quiet. We did our best that one last time which, and I'm guessing here, lasted a couple of hours and resulted in both of us walking funny the next morning.

Then we got to stay in our sturdy yet comfortable bed and fall asleep to the London lullaby of police sirens, shunting trains and cat fights.

'Peter,' she said, 'you haven't changed your mind about tomorrow, have you?'

'What about tomorrow?'

'Your dad's gig,' she said. 'You said I could come, you promised.'

'You can meet me there,' I said.

'Good,' she said, and fell asleep in my arms.

The important thing about Camden Market is that nobody planned it. Before London swallowed it whole, Camden Town was the fork in the road best known for a coaching inn called the Mother Red Cap. It served as a last-chance stop for beer, highway robbery and gonorrhoea before heading north into the wilds of Middlesex. In the early nineteenth century, men in frock coats and serious mutton-chop sideburns built the eastward branch of Regents Canal just to the north of the coaching inn. I say they built it, but the actual work was done by a couple of thousand strapping Irish fellers who came to be known, because of their canal work, as 'inland navigators' or navvies.

They and the navvies who came after them would go on to build the three main phases of infrastructure development that characterise the history of the industrial revolution: the canals, the railways and the motorways. I know this because I built a model of the area in junior school and got a gold star, a commendation and the enduring hatred of Barry Sedgeworth, playground bully and poor loser. A couple of serious canal locks were built next to the Chalk Farm Road, from whence the market gets its name – Camden Lock. There were extensive warehouses along the canal, and a large timber merchant.

In the 1960s the planning department of the London County Council, whose unofficial motto was *Finishing What the Luftwaffe Started*, decided that what London really needed was a series of orbital motorways driven through its heart. The planning blight caused by these schemes meant that what should have been lucrative land to be developed into multi-storey car parks or municipal rabbit hutches was instead leased to a trio of London wide-boys dressed in Afghan coats. These likely lads set up craft workshops in the old timber yard and on the weekends held a market where the products could be sold. By the mid-1980s the market had spread up Chalk Farm Road and down to the Electric Ballroom, and Camden Council finally stopped trying to put it out of business. It's currently the second most-visited tourist attraction in London and home to the Arches jazz club, where my dad was going to make his comeback gig with The Irregulars.

The Irregulars were surprisingly nervous, but my dad was remarkably unfazed.

'I've played bigger gigs,' he said. 'I once played with Joe Harriott in a basement in Catford. After having to go on with him, I never got stage fright again.'

The Arches jazz club had, in the early days of Camden Lock, been a disreputable dive located in a former lockup under a brick railway arch – hence the name. As the market prospered, the club had moved to one of the units in the west yard just short of the horse bridge, so that while waiting for a gig, a punter could sit outside at a café table and have a drink while enjoying the view across the lock basin. These days, my dad assured me, you almost never found dead dogs floating in the canal.

Lord Grant and The Irregulars were due to go on first, in support of the main act. On stage Daniel and Max were setting up the instruments and doing sound checks. There weren't that many punters in yet. They were mostly outside, having a crafty fag or sneaking a drink. I asked where James was.

'Throwing up in the toilet,' said Daniel. 'He's that nervous.'

I looked over to where my mum was standing in her Sunday best, nervously shifting her weight from one foot to the other. She gave me a little wave, and I indicated that I was going outside to wait for Simone. She nodded and followed me out.

That late in September it was getting dark before

seven, but the clouds had held off and the last of the sunshine painted the brick front of the lock a golden orange. I saw Simone step down from Chalk Farm Road, wave happily and then sashay over on a pair of high-heeled slingbacks, the sort that my mum buys occasionally but never wears. It was obviously 1980s night because her hair was piled up under a broad-brimmed hat, and the transparent top she was wearing was only street legal because she had her jacket buttoned up.

I turned to my mum. 'Mum, this is Simone.'

She said nothing, which wasn't what I expected. Then she balled her fists and strode past me.

'Get away, you bitch,' she screamed.

Simone skittered to a halt, stared at Mum bearing down at her, and then at me. Before I could move, my mum reached her and fetched Simone such a tremendous open-hand slap that she went reeling backwards.

'Get away,' shouted my mum.

Simone stepped back, shock and outrage on her face, a pale hand covering the cheek where she'd been struck. I rushed forward to stop Mum, but before I could reach her she'd grabbed Simone's hair with her left hand and was yanking at her jacket with her right. Simone was screaming and flailing, trying to get away as my mum shredded the gauze top with her fingers.

You don't just hit your mum, even when she's attacking your girlfriend. And you don't rugby-tackle her, knock her to the floor or put her in an armlock or any of the various techniques I was trained to use on violent suspects. I settled for grabbing her by the wrists and yelling 'stop' in her ear as loud as I could.

She let go of Simone, who staggered to safety, and whirled to face me.

'What are you doing?' my mum demanded, and shook my hands free of her wrists. Then she reached up and slapped me round the face. 'I said, what are you doing?'

'What am *I* doing?' I asked. 'What the fuck are *you* doing?'

That got me another slap, but this one was perfunctory and didn't make my ears ring. 'How dare you bring that witch here,' she said.

I looked around, but Simone had sensibly scarpered by that point.

'Mum,' I shouted, 'Mum, what's going on?'

She spat something in Krio, using words that I'd certainly never heard before. Then she drew herself up and spat on the ground. 'Stay away from her,' she said. 'She is a witch. She was after your father, and now she is after you.'

'What do you mean, "after my father"?' I asked. 'After Dad – what?'

My mum gave me the same look she always gives me when I ask what she considers to be a blindingly obvious question. Now that Simone was out of sight, Mum seemed to be calming down.

'She was after your father when I met him,' she said.

'Met him where?'

'When I met him,' she said slowly. 'Before you were a baby.'

'Mum,' I said, 'she's the same age as I am. How could she possibly have been around when you met Dad?'

'This is what I am trying to tell you,' said my mum, matter-of-factly. 'She is an evil witch.'

CHAPTER 12

IT DON'T MEAN A THING

I found her sitting on the pavement outside the piercing shop that's next to the KFC. She must have seen me coming, because she leaped to her feet, hesitated for a moment, then spun and started walking away. In those heels it wasn't hard for me to catch her up. I called her name.

'Stop looking at me,' she said.

'I can't stop myself.'

She halted and, before she could protest, I put my arms around her. She hugged me back and pressed her face against my chest. She sobbed once, caught herself, and took a deep breath.

'What on earth was all that about?' she asked.

'That was my mum,' I said. 'She can get a little bit excitable.'

She pulled back and looked up at me. 'But the things she said . . . I don't understand how could she think I was . . . What did she think I was doing?'

'She's on medication,' I said.

'I don't understand,' said Simone. 'What does that mean?'

'She's not well,' I said.

'Are you saying she's mad?' she asked.

I looked appropriately stricken. 'Oh,' said Simone. 'Poor thing, poor you. I don't suppose we can go back.'

I realised that people were watching us from inside the KFC. Perhaps they thought we were street theatre.

'And I was so looking forward to hearing your dad play,' she said.

'There'll be other gigs,' I said. 'Let me offer you an evening's entertainment at chez Peter.'

'Not the chaise longue again,' she said. 'I've still got a crick in my back.'

'I've laid in some cake.'

'That's suspicious,' she said. 'Almost as if you were expecting company after the gig. Who were you planning to take home?'

I kept my arm around her shoulders and guided her down the road towards Camden Town. 'I don't care for your tone, young lady,' I said.

'Where did you get the cake?' she asked. 'Tesco?'

'Marks and Spencer,' I said.

She sighed, and her arm tightened around my waist. 'You know me so well,' she said.

I hailed a black cab to take us back to the Folly. It seemed the safest thing to do.

When we got back to the coach house, she took a moment to fix her face in my emergency shaving mirror.

'Do I look frightful?' she said. 'I simply can't tell with this teeny-weeny mirror.'

I said she looked beautiful, which she did. The imprint of my mother's hand, which had still been a livid red on her cheek in the cab, was beginning to fade and she'd reapplied her lipstick. There was enough left of the transparent top she was wearing to make me want to tear it off, and my desire was making me hot and queasy. I concentrated on cueing up the right playlist on my iPod and making sure that it was plugged into the speakers.

'I promised you cake,' I said, as she advanced on me.

Simone wasn't to be distracted that easily. 'Cake later,' she said, and slipped her arms around my waist, one hand sliding under my shirt. I reached out and pressed play on the iPod.

'What's this?' she asked as the music began to play.

'Coleman Hawkins,' I said. '"Body and Soul".' It was the wrong first track. It was supposed to be Billie Holiday.

'Is it?' she asked. 'You see, it just doesn't sound real when it's recorded.'

I slipped my hand under her jacket and pulled her against me. The skin of her back felt feverish under my palm. 'This is better,' she said, and then she leaned forward and bit the top button right off the front of my shirt.

'Hey,' I said.

'Fair's fair,' she said.

'Did you ever hear him play?' I asked. 'Coleman?'

'Oh, yes,' she breathed. 'People always wanted this

351

song – it used to make him quite cross.' She pinged off another button and kissed my bared chest; I felt her tongue trace a line down my breastbone.

I smelled it then. The scent of honeysuckle, and behind that, broken brick and smashed wood. How could I ever have thought it was her perfume?

'Did Cyrus play "Body and Soul"?' I asked.

'Who's Cyrus?' she said, and bit off a third button. I was running out of buttons.

'You used to go out with him,' I said. 'You used to live at his house.'

'Did I? It seems so long ago,' she said, and kissed my chest. 'I used to love watching them play.'

'Who are they?'

'All my lovely jazzmen,' she said. 'I was happiest when they were playing. I liked the sex and the company, but I was really happiest when they were playing.'

I groaned as the next track on the iPod turned out to be John Coltrane. Had I put it on shuffle by accident? It's impossible to slow-dance to his version of 'Body and Soul' – for a start, he never actually stays with the melody for more than three notes, and after a couple of bars he goes to the wild musical place that only people like my dad can follow. I steered us over to the fridge so that I could surreptitiously press the 'next track' button on the iPod. It was Nina Simone, thank God, a young Nina with a voice that could melt an ice sculpture at a Scottish banker's convention.

'What about Lord Grant?' I had to ask.

352

'The one that got away,' she said. 'They said he was going to be an English Clifford Brown, but he kept on leaving the scene. Cherie was so cross. You see, she had rather set her cap at him. She claimed once that she'd caught him, but then he'd got away.' She smiled at the memory. 'I rather think I was more his type, and who knows what might have happened, except that he had this fearsome wife.'

'How fearsome?'

'Oh, terrifying,' she said. 'But you should know. She's your—' Simone froze in my arms and frowned up at me, but I rocked her back into the dance. In her eyes I could actually see the memory slipping away.

'Did you always love jazz?' I asked.

'Always,' she said.

'Even when you were at school?'

'We had the strangest music mistress at school,' said Simone. 'Her name was Miss Patternost. She used to have her favourites round for tea – there, she would play us records and encourage us to "commune" with the music.'

'Were you one of her favourites?'

'Of course I was,' she said, and slipped her hand inside my shirt again. 'I was everybody's favourite. Am I not your favourite, as well?'

'Definitely,' I said. 'Were Cherie and Peggy favourites too?'

'Yes, they were,' said Simone. 'We practically used to live in Patternost's room.'

'So you and your sisters all went to the same school?'

'They're not really my sisters,' she said. 'They're like my sisters, like the sisters I never had. We met at school.'

'What was the name of the school?' If I had the school, then I could probably track all three of their identities.

'Cosgrove Hall,' said Simone. 'It was just outside Hastings.'

'Nice school?'

'It was perfectly all right, I suppose,' said Simone. 'The masters weren't too beastly to us, and it had its own riding stable and Miss Patternost – I mustn't forget her. She was very taken with Elisabeth Welch. "Stormy Weather", that was her favourite. She used to make us lie on the carpet – she had a lovely oriental carpet, from Persia I think – and make pictures in our minds.'

I asked what kind of records, and Simone said that it was nearly always jazz: Fletcher Henderson, Duke Ellington, Fats Waller and, of course, Billie Holiday. Miss Patternost told the girls that jazz was the Negro's great contribution to world culture, and that as far as she was concerned, they could eat as many missionaries as they wanted, as long as they continued to produce such beautiful music. After all, said Miss Patternost, the various societies were churning out hundreds of missionaries every week, but there was only one Louis Armstrong.

I knew from my own dad's collection that some of those discs would have been hard to get on the right side of the pond. When I asked where they came from, Simone told me about Sadie, Miss Patternost's woman friend.

'Did she have a surname?'

Simone stopped pulling my shirt out of my trousers. 'Why do you want to know?' she asked.

'I'm a policeman,' I said. 'We're born curious.'

Simone said that as far as she, and any of the other girls knew, Miss Patternost's friend Sadie was always just called 'Sadie'.

'That's how Miss Patternost used to introduce her,' she said.

It was never divulged what it was Sadie did, but the girls deduced from hints dropped in conversation that she worked in the movies in Hollywood, and that she and Miss Patternost had been engaged in a passionate correspondence for over fifteen years. Every month or so, in addition to the almost daily letters, a package would arrive wrapped in brown paper and strong twine and marked HANDLE WITH CARE. These were the precious records on Vocalion, Okeh and Gennett. Once a year Sadie would arrive, always just before the Easter hols, and ensconce herself in Miss Patternost's rooms, and there would be much playing of jazz records until the wee small hours of the morning. It was a scandal, said the girls of the lower sixth. But Simone, Peggy and Cherie didn't care.

'Crushed beetles,' said Simone suddenly.

'What about them?' I asked. I was wishing I hadn't blown out my iPhone because the recording app would have come in very handy right now.

'The icing on my birthday cake,' said Simone. It seemed that the big treat on a girl's birthday at Cosgrove Hall was that you got to choose the colour of the icing on your cake. It was a matter of honour that the birthday girl would try to come up with the most unlikely colour of icing they could think of, violet and orange being popular, with blue spots. The kitchen always managed to provide the colour, and the girls were convinced that they did it by grinding up beetles as colouring.

Back in the days before E-numbers and food technologists, I thought. Which was, as it happened, about where I wanted to be. Luckily the iPod chose that moment to play the last track on the playlist – Ken 'Snakehips' Johnson's very own version of 'Body and Soul'. I don't care what purists like my dad think. If you want to dance, you can't beat a touch of swing. Simone certainly thought so, because she stopped trying to strip me and instead started to pull me around the coach house in tight little circles. She was leading but I didn't mind – that was all part of the plan.

'Did you ever hear him play live?' I asked as casually as could. 'Ken Johnson?'

'Just the once,' said Simone.

In March 1941, of course.

'It was our last day of freedom,' she said. 'We'd

356

all joined up as soon as we were old enough.' She told me that Cherie joined the Auxiliary Territorial Service and Peggy was in the Women's Royal Naval Service. But Simone had chosen the Women's Auxiliary Air Force, because somebody had said there was a chance she might fly.

'Or at least, meet a handsome pilot who'd take me up in his crate,' she said. It was Peggy's Canadian uncle who'd got them into the Café de Paris, and Cherie had said that they'd be fine, money-wise, provided they didn't order any food or have more than one drink.

Simone pressed her cheek against my chest and I stroked her hair.

'Our table could have been better, perhaps,' said Simone. 'It was surprisingly small, and not at all conveniently placed.

'If the band were at six o'clock, we were sort of half-past-one,' she said.

The club was full of handsome Canadian officers, one of whom sent over a bottle of champagne to their table, sparking a spirited discussion about how appropriate it would be for them to accept it, which ended only when Peggy downed her glass in one gulp. This led to another discussion about whether they could get a second bottle out of the Canadians and what, Cherie asked darkly, might they expect in return?

Peggy said that as far as she was concerned, the Canadians could have whatever they liked. In fact, she was of the opinion that it was their patriotic duty to make the brave soldiers of the Commonwealth welcome, and she was perfectly prepared to do her duty and think of England.

But they never got their second bottle of champagne, and the Canadians didn't get their just deserts. Because at that point the band struck up 'Body and Soul', and the girls only had eyes for Ken Johnson.

'Nobody had ever told me,' said Simone, 'that a coloured man could be so beautiful. And the way he moved – no wonder they called him Snakehips.' She frowned up at me. 'You haven't kissed me for ever such a long time.'

She pouted, so I kissed her. It was the single most stupid thing I've ever done, and that includes running into a tower block thirty seconds before it was due to be demolished.

Vestigia are usually hard to spot. It's the uneasy feeling you have in a graveyard, the half-memory of children laughing in a playground, or a familiar face in the corner of your eye. What I got from that kiss was a full-on, high-definition quality reproduction of the last moments of Ken Johnson and forty-odd others at the Café de Paris. I didn't get to enjoy the ambience much. Laughter, uniforms, a live swing orchestra at the height of its powers and then – silence.

During the Renaissance, when there was a flowering of art, culture and almost continuous bloody warfare, some particularly foolhardy engineers would break sieges by rushing up to the castle and attaching a primitive shaped-charge to the gate. Sometimes, because fuses were more of an art than a science in those days, the charge would go off before the luckless engineer had got clear and he would be blown, or 'hoisted', through the air – often in bits. The French, with that subtle rapier wit that has made them famous, nicknamed the bombs 'petards', or farts. People still use the term 'hoisted by his own petard' to refer to a situation where one is damaged by one's own scheme. Which is what happened to me when I guided Simone back into her memories, and she proceeded to suck my brains out.

You don't experience a bomb blast so much as remember it afterwards. It's like a bad edit or a record jumping a groove. On one side of the moment there is music and laughter and romance, and on the other – not pain, that comes later – but a stunned incomprehension. A tangle of dust and splintered wood, a splash of white and red that becomes a man's dress shirt, tables overturned to reveal bodiless legs and headless bodies, a trombone minus its slide standing upright on a table as if left there by a musician, while two men in khaki uniforms stare blindly at it – killed by the blast wave.

And then noise and shouting and the taste of blood in Simone's mouth.

My blood, I realised – I'd bitten my lip.

It was Simone who pushed me away.

'How old am I?' she asked.

'I make it a shade short of ninety,' I said, because there's just no stopping my mouth sometimes.

'Your mother was right,' she said. 'I am a witch.'

I found I was swaying and my hand was shaking. I held it up in front of my face.

'She was right,' she said. 'I'm not a person, I'm a creature, an abomination.'

I tried to tell her that she was definitely a human being, and that some of my best friends were functionally immortal. I wanted to say that we could work it out, but it came out as a series of *wah-wah-wah* sounds, like Charlie Brown's teacher.

'I'm sorry,' she said. 'I have to go and talk to my sisters.' She gave a bitter little laugh. 'Only they're not my sisters, are they? I'm Lucy, we're all Lucy Westenra.'

She turned and ran out of the coach house. I heard her heels clanging down the spiral staircase. I tried to follow, but toppled slowly onto my face instead.

'That was not the most intelligent thing you've ever done,' said Nightingale as Dr Walid shone a light in my eyes to make sure my brains were intact. I'm not sure how long I'd flopped around on the floor of the coach house, but as soon as I'd got enough muscle control to use a phone, I'd called Dr Walid. He was calling it an *atonic seizure* because, even if he didn't know why it had happened, it was important to give it a cool name. I'd been hoping that I'd have a chance to come up with a plausible explanation before Nightingale arrived, but he came in just behind Dr Walid.

'I had to be sure she was related to the Café de Paris case, and not the Strip Club of Dr Moreau,' I said. 'I mean, she's not a chimera like the Pale Lady. In fact, I think she's an accident.' I explained about Miss Patternost and her musical shapes.

'You think that their "shapes" acted like *forma*?' asked Nightingale.

'Why not?' I asked. 'I used to make shapes when I was going to sleep when I was a kid, or listening to music. Everyone does it, and amongst billions of people, no matter how unlikely something is, if you repeat the action enough times there's a result – there's magic. How else could Newton have stumbled onto the principle in the first place? They were the wrong girls doing the wrong thing in the wrong place, and . . .'

'And what?' asked Dr Walid.

'I think they survived the blast at the Café de Paris because they channelled magic, or life energy, or whatever this stuff is, through the *forma* in their minds. We know that magic can be released at the point of death – hence sacrifices.'

'Hence vampires,' said Nightingale.

'Not vampires,' I said. I'd been studying my Wolfe. '*Tactus disvitae*, the anti-life, is the mark of the vampire. This is more like alcohol or drug dependency: the damage is an unintended conse-quence, like cirrhosis of the liver or gout.'

'Human beings are not bottles of brandy,' said

Nightingale. 'And Wolfe always was too keen on categorising and subcategorising everything. A rose by any other name, and all that. Still – where would she have gone?'

'Most likely the flat on Berwick Street,' I said.

'Back to the nest,' said Nightingale. And I didn't like way he said it.

Dr Walid handed me a couple of painkillers and a half a bottle of Diet Pepsi he must have found in the fridge. There was no fizz when I unscrewed the top, and it tasted flat when I swallowed the tablets – it must have been in there for ages.

He sat down next to me on the sofa and put his hand on my arm. 'If your father really did have a close encounter with Simone at some point in the past, we may be able to find evidence of that. So I want you to bring your father to the UCH tomorrow at eleven,' he said, and then pointed at Nightingale. 'You I want in bed in the next half-hour with a hot milk and a sleeping tablet.'

'There's—' said Nightingale, but Dr Walid didn't give him a chance to start, let alone finish.

'If you don't follow my instructions, I swear on my father's life that I'll have you both put on medical leave,' he said. 'Do you both ken me on this?' We nodded obediently.

'Good,' he said. 'I'll see you tomorrow.'

Later, while we were wrangling hot drinks out of Molly in her kitchen, Nightingale asked me if I thought Dr Walid actually had the authority to carry out his threat. 'I think so,' I said. 'He's down on paper as our OCU's registered medical adviser. If we had any cells here he'd be the one we called in if our prisoners needed medical attention. Do we have any cells?'

'Not any more,' said Nightingale. 'They were all bricked up after the war.'

'In any case,' I said, 'I vote we don't push to find out how far his authority extends.'

'Why does he want to see your father?' asked Nightingale.

'I'm guessing, but I think he probably wants to know whether my dad's close encounter with Simone's sister left any physical traces,' I said.

'Oh,' said Nightingale. 'That's very clever of him.' Molly reverentially handed a mug of hot chocolate to Nightingale. 'Thank you,' he said.

'What about mine?' I asked.

Molly held up Toby's lead and wagged it at me. 'Not me again.'

'I'm on bed rest,' said Nightingale. 'Doctor's orders.'

I looked down at Toby, who was crouched half hidden behind Molly's skirts. He gave me an experimental yap.

'You're not making any friends round here, you know,' I said.

Dr Walid let me watch while he fed my father into the MRI scanner at UCH. He said it was a 3.0 Tesla machine, which was good, but that really the hospital could do with another one to cope with the demand.

There's a microphone inside the tube so you can hear if the patient's in distress – I could hear my dad humming.

'What's that sound?' asked Dr Walid.

'Dad,' I said. 'He's singing "Ain't Misbehaving".'

Dr Walid sat down at a control desk complicated enough to launch a satellite into low earth orbit or mix a top-twenty hit. The magnetic drum in the scanner started to rotate with the sort of banging sound that makes you drive your car into the nearest garage. It didn't seem to bother my dad, who carried on humming, although I noticed he did shift his rhythm to match the machine.

The scans went on for a long time, and after a while the microphone picked up my dad's gentle snoring.

Dr Walid looked at me and raised an eyebrow.

'If you can go to sleep while my mum's on the phone,' I said, 'you can pretty much sleep through anything.'

When they'd finished with my dad, Dr Walid turned to me and told me to strip off and get in the machine myself.

'What?'

'Simone was probably feeding off you too,' he said.

'But I don't play jazz,' I said. 'I don't even like it that much.'

'You're making assumptions, Peter. The whole

364

jazz aspect may just be a boundary effect. If your lady friend is an uncharacterised category of thaumovore, then we can't know what the mechanism is. We need more data, so I need you to stick your head in the MRI machine.' He put his hand on my shoulder. 'It's for science,' he said.

There's something uniquely claustrophobic about sliding into an MRI scanner. The rotating magnets are on an industrial scale and generate a magnetic field 60,000 times that of the earth's. And they feed you into it wearing nothing but a hospital gown that lets a breeze flap around your privates.

At least Dr Walid didn't make me wait around for the results.

'This is your dad's,' he said. He pointed to a couple of dark grey smudges. 'Those look like minor lesions, probably hyperthaumaturgical degradation. I'll have to refine the image further and make some comparisons to be sure. This is your brain, which is not only pristine and unsullied by thought, but also showing no sign of any lesions.'

'So she wasn't feeding off me. Then why did I pass out?'

'I'd bet she was feeding off you,' he said. 'Just not enough yet for it to damage your brain.'

'She was doing it while we were having sex,' I said. 'She practically told me that herself. Do we know what she's actually feeding off, exactly?'

'The damage I'm looking at is consistent with the early stages of hyperthaumaturgical degradation.'

'She's a vampire,' I said. 'A jazz vampire.'

'Jazz may just be the flavouring,' said Dr Walid. 'What's being consumed is magic.'

'Which is what, exactly?'

'We don't know, as well you know,' he said, and sent me off to get changed.

'Is it brain cancer, then?' asked my dad as we got dressed.

'No, they just wanted to record your empty head for posterity,' I said.

'You've never been very lucky with birds, have you?' he said. It's weird watching an elderly parent when they're half naked. You find yourself staring in fascination at the slack skin, the wrinkles and the liver spots and thinking, *one day all that will be yours*. Or at least it will be, if you can avoid getting killed or falling in love with vampires.

'Apart from the thing with Mum, how did the gig go?'

'Not bad at all,' he said. 'We could have done with a bit more rehearsal, but then you always can.'

Even with sterile needles supplied on the NHS my dad had still collapsed the veins on his arms, and I'd assumed he'd been injecting into his legs. But looking now I couldn't see any tracks.

'When was the last time you had your medicine?' I asked.

'I'm temporarily off the gear,' he said.

'Since when?' I asked.

366

'Since the summer,' he said. 'I thought your mum had told you.'

'She said you'd quit smoking,' I said.

'And the rest.' My dad slipped into his rifle-green shirt with the button-down collar and shook his arm in the approved Cockney Geezer manner. 'Got off both horses,' he said. 'And to be honest, giving up the fags was the hardest of the two.'

I offered to take him home, but he said that not only was he all right, but he was looking forward to a bit of peace and quiet. Still, the sun was going down, so I waited with him at the stop until his bus came, and then I walked back to Russell Square.

I'm used to having the Folly to myself, so it was a bit of a shock to wander into the atrium and find half a dozen guys making themselves comfortable in the armchairs. I recognised one of them, a stocky man with a broken nose, as Frank Caffrey, our contact in the Fire Brigade and reservist for the Parachute Regiment. He stood up and shook my hand.

'These are me mates,' he said.

I gave them a nod. They were all fit-looking middle-aged men with short haircuts, and while they were dressed in a variety of civvies, their manner suggested that uniforms were a very real possibility. Molly had supplied them with afternoon tea, but slung under the occasional tables and stacked beside their armchairs the men had sturdy black nylon carryalls. The ones with the reinforced straps and handles allowing one to carry small, heavy metal objects around in safety and relative comfort.

I asked where Nightingale was.

'On the phone to the Commissioner,' he said. 'We're just waiting for the word.'

The 'word' made me cold and sweaty. I doubted this word was to extend Simone and her sisters an invitation to tea. I managed to keep the fear off my face, gave Caffrey's mates a cheery wave and headed through the back door and across the yard and out the coach house gate. I reckoned that I had at least ten minutes before Nightingale figured out I'd gone, twenty if I left the car in the garage. He knew me well enough to know what I was going to do next. He'd probably thought he was trying to protect me from myself, which was ironic because I thought I was trying to protect him from himself.

Twenty minutes to notice I was gone, ten minutes to tool up and pile into whatever nondescript van the Paras had brought with them, ten minutes to reach Berwick Street. Forty minutes, tops.

A black cab was turning the corner as I stepped out on the pavement and shouted 'taxi'. I stuck my hand out, but the bastard pretended he hadn't seen and cruised right past me. I swore and memorised his index in case an opportunity for petty but deeply satisfying vengeance came along later. Fortunately, a second cab came around the corner immediately and dropped off some tourists outside one of the hotels on Southampton Row, and I slipped in before the driver could experience any problems with his night vision. He had the cropped hair of a man too proud to cover his bald patch with a comb-over. Just to make his day I showed my warrant card.

'Get me to Berwick Street in under ten minutes and I'll give you a free pass for the rest of the year,' I said.

'And the wife's car?' he asked.

'Same deal,' I said, and gave him my card.

'Done,' he said, and demonstrated the amazing turning circle of the London black cab by doing an illegal u-turn that threw me into the side door and accelerated down Bedford Place. Either he was insane or his wife really needed help with the traffic tickets, because we did it in less than five minutes. I was so impressed I even paid him the fare as well.

Friday night on Berwick Street, and the punters were quietly slipping in and out of the sex shops at the corner with Peter Street. The market had closed but the pubs and the record shops were still open, and a steady stream of media workers were threading their way home through the tourists. I took some time to check the front of Simone's house – up on the fifth floor the light was on.

I didn't like the idea of Simone and her sisters just disappearing at the hands of Caffrey and his lads. I believe in the rule of law and this was, however weird, a police matter and I was a sworn constable who was about to exercise his discretion to resolve a breach of the Queen's Peace.

Or, as Lesley would have it, I was out of my fucking mind.

I pressed random buttons on the intercom until someone answered.

'Come to read the meter, love,' I said, and they buzzed me in. I made a mental note to pass the number of the building to West End Central's crime-prevention team for a stern lecture, and started up the stairs.

They hadn't got any less steep. No wonder Simone and her sisters had to suck the life force out of people.

I was just catching a breather in front of their door when somebody grabbed me from behind and held a knife to my throat.

'It's him,' she hissed. 'Open the door.'

Because of the height difference, she had to reach up under my armpit to get her blade, an old kitchen knife I thought, against my neck. She would really have been better off threatening my back or stomach. If I'd been desperate I could have chopped down with my arm and forced her hand away. It would have depended on how fast she was and how willing to kill.

The door opened and Simone looked out.

'Hello Simone,' I said. 'We need to have a chat.'

She looked stricken to see me.

The woman with the knife pushed me and I edged

carefully into the room. Peggy was in there too, still dressed in dungarees, hair still spiky, face pale and scared. That meant Cherie was the one with the knife. Simone closed the door behind us.

'Get his handcuffs,' said Cherie.

Peggy groped me around the waist. 'He hasn't got any.'

'Why haven't you brought your handcuffs?' said Simone. 'I told them you'd have handcuffs.'

'I'm not here to arrest anyone,' I said.

'We know,' hissed Cherie. 'You're here to kill us.'

'What, just me on my own?' I asked, but I was thinking of Caffrey and his posse drinking tea back at the Folly. Only by now they'd have finished their tea and were probably in a van, a nondescript Ford Transit most likely, doing last-minute checks on their weapons and night-vision equipment.

'I'm not here to kill anyone,' I said.

'Liar,' said Cherie. 'He said you'd disappear us.'

'Perhaps we should let them,' said Peggy.

'We haven't done anything wrong,' said Cherie, and her knife nicked my throat by accident – thank God it wasn't sharp.

'Yes, we have,' said Simone. There were tears on her face, and when she saw me looking at her she turned away.

'Who said we would kill you?' I asked.

'This man,' said Cherie.

'Did you meet him in a pub?' I asked. 'What man? Can you remember what he looked like?'

Cherie hesitated, and that's when I knew.

371

'I can't remember,' she said. 'It's not important what he looks like. He said that you worked for the government, and all the government was interested in was eliminating anybody who isn't normal.'

What could I say? I was pretty much here to tell them the same thing.

'What colour were his eyes?' I asked. 'Was he white, black, something else?'

'Why do you care?' shouted Cherie.

'Why can't you remember?' I asked.

'I don't know,' said Cherie, and relaxed her grip. I didn't wait for her to remember she was supposed to be holding me hostage. I grabbed her wrist and twisted her knife hand up and away. The rule for fighting a person with a knife is to start off by making it point away from you and then ensuring that it hurts too much to hold onto. I felt something crack under my grip, Cherie screamed and dropped the knife. Peggy tried to hit me but I was already twisting away and she ended up smacking Cherie in the face.

'Stop it,' yelled Simone.

I shoved Cherie over towards her sisters. She stumbled into Peggy, and they both tripped on the edge of the mattress and went down. Peggy came up spitting like a cat.

'Wait a minute,' I said. 'I'm trying to do you a favour here. There's a real evil man out there that you don't want to be messing with.'

'You should know,' spat Peggy. 'You work for him.'

'It's not our fault,' said Cherie dejectedly. Simone sat down beside her and put her arm around her sister.

'I get that,' I said. 'I really do. But whatever you think about my governor, there's another total evil bastard out there, and by the way – why the fuck are you still here? Everyone knows where you live.'

I figured I might just have another ten minutes before Nightingale and Caffrey turned up to demonstrate the military version of the hard-target entry, followed up by a unique close-up view of their search-and-destroy procedures.

'He's right,' said Peggy. 'We can't stay here.'

'Where can we go?' asked Cherie.

'I'll get you into a hotel,' I said. 'Then we can talk about what to do next.' I concentrated on Simone, who was looking at me with a kind of sick longing. 'Simone, we don't have much time.'

She nodded. 'He's right,' she said. 'I think we should leave immediately and never return.'

'But what about my things?' wailed Cherie.

'We'll get you more things,' said Peggy, hauling Cherie to her feet.

'I'll check the coast is clear,' I said. I stepped out onto the landing and pressed the pop-in switch thingy that turned on the miserly forty-watt bulb.

There was a crash downstairs, the distinctive double bang of a heavy door being smashed open and the rebounding off a side wall. It's no joke, that rebound. There have been plenty of instances where the first bastard through the door has been knocked right back out on his arse again.

I was too late. I didn't know if it was Nightingale with Caffrey in support, or a CO19 armed-response team sent in by Stephanopoulos. Either way, I had to de-escalate the situation before they reached the top of the house. I told Simone and the others to stay in the room.

'Officer on the scene,' I shouted. 'No weapons, no hostages. I repeat, no weapons, no hostages.'

I paused to listen. From down below I thought I heard someone sniggering and then a deep voice with a lisp said, 'Excellent.' Then I definitely heard feet running up the lower staircases. I held up my hands at chest level, palms out to show I was unarmed. It wasn't an easy thing to do – one of the reasons the Met has to train its officers in conflict resolution is to overcome our natural London urge to get our retaliation in first.

The push-in light switch popped out again and it suddenly went dark. I frantically slapped at the switch to get it on again – anything that can go wrong with armed men in the light can go twice as wrong in the dark.

The footsteps reached the landing below me and a figure came bounding around the corner and up the stairs.

And that's when my brain let me down. Whatever you've been told, seeing is not believing. Your brain does a great deal of interpretation before it deigns to let your consciousness know what the hell is going on. If we're suddenly exposed to something unfamiliar, a damaged human face, a car flying through the air towards us, something that looks almost but not quite human, it can take time, sometimes even seconds for our minds to react. And those seconds can be crucial.

As when a chimera is racing up the staircase to reach you.

He was male, muscular and stripped to the waist to reveal that he was covered in short russet fur. His hair was black and cut long and shaggy. His nose was all wrong, as black and glossy as a healthy cat's. As he bounded up the stairs towards me his mouth opened wide to reveal sharp white teeth and a lolling pink tongue. None of this registered until he was almost on top of me, and I didn't have time to do anything but scramble back and lash out with my foot.

Doc Martens, patented acid-resistant soled, reinforced leather shoes, as recommended by police officers and skinheads everywhere – when you absolutely, positively have to kick someone down the stairs.

Predictably, Tiger Boy landed like a cat, twisting his spine as he dropped to fall into a crouch on the landing below.

'Get up on the roof,' I shouted through the door.

Tiger Boy took a moment out to shake his head and give me a big feline grin. His eyes were quite beautiful, amber-coloured and slotted like a cat's and obviously adapted for hunting at night.

I heard the door open and Peggy and Simone dragging a still whimpering Cherie out of the room and onto the stairs up to the roof. I didn't dare take my eyes off Tiger Boy – he was just waiting for me to lose concentration.

'Who the hell is that?' asked Simone.

'Nobody you want to know,' I said.

Tiger Boy hissed. I saw his tail twitch, and found myself wondering whether he cut a hole in the back of his Y-fronts to let it out.

'Little mousy,' lisped Tiger Boy. 'Why don't you jump about? It's more fun when you jump about.'

The pop-in light switch popped out, it went dark and Tiger Boy leaped towards me.

I put a werelight in his face.

I'd been practising, and had managed to produce one that burned as brightly as a magnesium flare. I'd closed my eyes and it still lit up the inside of my eyelids, so it must have hit Tiger Boy right in his specially low-light adapted eyes.

He howled, I jumped and this time managed to get both size elevens in contact with his body. He probably outweighed me but Isaac Newton was on my side, and we went down the stairs together, only he was hitting all the steps and I was surfing down on top of him. At least, that was the theory.

We hit the landing harder and faster than I expected. I heard a snap under my feet and there was a stabbing pain in my left knee. I yelled and he yowled.

'You're right,' I said. 'It is more fun when you jump about.'

I didn't have any cuffs or rope to secure him, so I settled for scrambling back up the stairs, ignoring the shooting pain in my knee as I went. Behind me, Tiger Boy wailed pathetically and, more importantly, stayed where he was. I ran through the roof door, ducked under a clumsy swing from Peggy and slammed it shut behind me.

'I beg your pardon,' said Peggy. 'I thought you were him.'

I looked at the three women. They were clutching each other for support and had the dazed, unfocused look that people get after bombing incidents and motorway pile-ups.

I pointed north. 'Climb over the railing, go that way across the roof,' I said. 'Go to the right. There's a fire escape down to Duck Lane.' I'd spotted it during my night of passion with Simone as a possible access point for burglars. Which proves, if nothing else, that a police constable is never off duty, even when he's not wearing his underpants.

They didn't move; it was strange, they were acting so slow and dull. As if they were drugged or distracted.

'Come on,' I said. 'We've got to get out of here.'

'Will you be quiet,' said Peggy. 'We're talking to someone.'

I turned around to find that an evil magician had been standing behind me.

CHAPTER 13

AUTUMN LEAVES

He was standing at the far end of the roof garden, leaning nonchalantly against the railing. He was dressed in a beautifully tailored dark suit, a pale silk cravat and was carrying a cane topped with a mother-of-pearl handle. The witnesses had been right about his face. Even as I concentrated on his features, I found myself noticing the gleam of his gold cufflinks, the scarlet triangle of his pocket handkerchief, anything except his face. This was him – the Faceless One.

'Oi,' I shouted, 'just what do you think you're doing?'

'Do you mind?' said Faceless. 'I'm trying to talk to the ladies here.' His accent was generic posh, public-school, Oxbridge – which fitted the profile and endeared him to my proletarian soul not at all.

'Well, you can talk to me first,' I said, 'or you can go to hospital.'

'On the other hand,' said Faceless, 'you could just take a quick jump off the parapet.'

His tone was so reasonable I actually took three

steps towards the railing before I could stop myself. It was *Seducere*, of course, the glamour, and it might have worked on me if I hadn't spent the year having various demi-gods and nature spirits trying to mess with my mind. Nothing gives you mental toughness like having Lady Tyburn trying to make you her house slave. I kept heading for the railing, though, because there's no point giving away an advantage, and I was curious to know what he wanted from Simone and her sisters.

'Ladies,' he said, 'I realise your true nature may have come as a shock, and right now you're a little confused.' He was speaking softly, but I heard his words with unnatural clarity. Part of the *Seducere?* I wondered – me and Nightingale were going to have to have a long chat about this sometime soon.

I'd reached the edge of the roof, so I turned and put my foot up on the railing as if I was about to climb over sideways before plunging to a horrible death. It also gave me an opportunity to see what Faceless was up to.

He was still chatting up the girls. 'I know you believe that you are cursed,' he said, 'forced to satiate your unnatural appetites by draining the life force of others. But I want you to think outside of the box.'

I still couldn't see his face, but I'd done a bit of reading since Alexander Smith had given us the description of his face or, more accurately, hadn't. Victor Bartholomew, possibly the most boring magician that ever lived, named it as *Vultus occulto*, which even I knew was pig Latin, and had devoted an entire chapter on the subject of countermeasures which, typically for Bartholomew, I could boil down to one sentence: *Keep looking really hard and sooner or later you'll see through it*. So that's what I did.

'What if,' said Faceless, 'and I throw this out to you as a hypothetical, what if it was all right to feed on people? What is feeding off people anyway, but good old exploitation? And we're perfectly happy to exploit people, aren't we?'

I glanced over at Simone. She and her sisters had stopped holding each other and were regarding Faceless with the same polite interest one might give to a visiting dignitary in the hope that he gets on with it and shuts up soon.

Ha, I thought. Tyburn would have had them genuflecting by now.

'This notion that we're all equal is so intellectually bankrupt, anyway.' As he spoke I blinked a couple of times, and suddenly I could see his face. Or rather I couldn't, because his face was hidden by a plain beige-coloured mask that covered his whole head. It made him look like an unusually tasteful Mexican wrestler. I think he may have sensed that I'd pushed through the disguise, because he turned to look at me.

'Are you still here?' he asked.

'I wasn't sure whether I should go head first or feet first,' I said.

'Do you think it will make a difference?'

'Statistically, you're more likely to survive if you go feet-first.'

'Why don't you jump?' he said. 'And then we can see.'

I felt it then, the *Seducere*, stronger this time and bringing with it the smell of roast pork, freshly mown grass, the stink of unwashed bodies and a metallic taste, like iron, in my mouth. I turned to the railings, paused and then turned back.

'What did you say your name was again?' I asked.

'Jump,' barked Faceless.

He gave me his full attention, but *Seducere* never seems to work twice, and while he was using it on me, he wasn't using it on Simone.

'Run!' I yelled.

I saw Simone snap out of it first and pull at Peggy's arm. They both shot me scared looks and then, thank God, grabbed Cherie and started climbing the parapet where it separated the roof garden from next door. I glanced back at Faceless just in time to see the swing of his shoulders as he threw out his arm in my direction. I recognised the gesture – I'd been practising it myself for the last six months. This saved my life because I was already diving to the left when something bright and hot zipped past my shoulder and melted a half-metre hole in the railings, just about where my stomach would have been if I hadn't moved.

I flipped a couple of skinny grenades at him even as I was flying through the air, which would have been way more impressive if I hadn't been trying for a straight fireball. As I skidded along the floor another chunk of railing melted behind me, and I saw that one of my skinny mines had popped harmlessly in mid-air, and the other fell out of the air and bounced to a stop at Faceless's feet. He looked down, and through pure luck it chose that moment to explode. The blast staggered him backwards and twisted him around. I used the time to scramble to my feet and face him.

'Armed police,' I shouted. 'Stand still and put your hands on your head.' This time I knew I had the right spell lined up.

He turned and stared at me. Despite the mask, I could tell he was incredulous.

'You're the police?' he asked.

'Armed police,' I said. 'Turn around and put your hands on your head.'

I risked a glance to check that Simone and her sisters were off the roof.

'Oh, don't worry about them,' said the man. 'I've found something far more interesting than them. After all, I can always make more people like them.'

'Armed police,' I shouted again. 'Turn around and put your hands on your head.' They make this very clear at Hendon: if you're going to put the boot in, there must be no doubt that you identified yourself and that the suspect heard you.

'If you're going to shoot,' he said, 'then shoot.'

So I shot him. It was worth it just for the obvious outrage it caused him, and I enjoyed it right up until the point where he caught the bloody fireball.

Just snatched it out of the air and held it, Yorick-like, in front of his face.

I'd released it as soon as it got near him but it hadn't exploded. He twisted it this way and that, as if examining it like a connoisseur, which perhaps he was. I figured he wanted me to lob another one at him so he could catch it, or deflect it, or do something else with annoying insouciance. So I didn't. Besides, the more time he spent taunting me, the further away Simone could get.

'You know,' he said, 'when I first saw you I thought you were with the Thames girls, or a new sort of fae, or something really outlandish like a witch doctor or an American.' The man popped the fireball like a soap bubble, and rubbed his thumb and finger under his nose. 'Who trained you?' he asked. 'Not Jeffers, that's for certain. Not that he was without skill, but you've got spirit. Was it Gripper? He's just the kind to bleat about what he's doing. Have you noticed that about journalists? All they really want to talk about is themselves.'

Gripper was obviously Jason Dunlop. Dunlop tyres, grip, Gripper – which gives you an indication of the lively wit promoted by our clite educational institutions. And Gripper obviously wasn't the only one who wanted to talk. It's no fun looking down on people if you can't let them know you're above them.

Come on you bastard, I thought. Drop a few more names.

'You talk too little,' he said. 'I don't trust you.'

Suddenly the world was flooded with light, and the massive downdraft from a helicopter blew dust and rubbish around our faces. He threw a fireball at me. I threw a chimney stack at him – that's the London way.

I'd been working on loosening up the chimney stack with what I call *Impello vibrato* but which Nightingale calls *will you stop messing about and pay attention*, while Faceless had been chatting. When the Nightsun searchlight from the police helicopter hit him in the face I created as pure an *Impello* form as Nightingale could wish for and aimed it straight at the bastard. I knew he'd try and zap me, so I threw myself to the right and his fireball sizzled past my shoulder. I was hoping his gaze would automatically track me and not spot the quarter of a ton of brick and terracotta coming at him from the other direction, but he must have glimpsed it from the corner of his eye because he flung up his hand and the chimney stack disintegrated half a metre short of his palm.

I didn't get much more than a fleeting look as bits of brick, cement dust and sand flowed around him, as if sliding across an invisible sphere, because I was too busy closing the distance between us. If we stuck to magic it was obvious he was going to bounce me around the rooftops, so I ran at him in the hope of getting close enough to smack him in the face.

I was close too, less than a metre away, but the

fucker turned and stuck his palm at me and I ran smack into whatever it was he had used on the chimney. It wasn't like hitting a Perspex wall. Instead it was slippery, like the wobbly, sliding feeling you get when you try to push two magnets together. I went spinning onto my back and he strode towards me. I didn't wait to find out whether he was planning to gloat or just kill me. Instead I reached out with *Impello* to grab the cheap plastic garden table behind Faceless and slammed it into the back of his legs. He pitched forward and met both of my feet coming the other way.

'Fuck!' he yelled, loud enough to be heard over the helicopter.

I was up now, and managed to get in one good punch to the face before something snarling and covered in fur barrelled into me from the right. It was Tiger Boy, who'd evidently kicked his way out through the roof door to reach us. We slammed into the parapet railing, and it was only because I got a solid lock on a bar with my right hand that I didn't go over and fall to my death. I rocked myself back onto the safety of the roof and looked up to see Tiger Boy drawing back one heavily muscled arm ready to strike. He had claws on the ends of his fingers – what are you supposed to do against somebody with claws?

What with the noise of the helicopter, and my own fear, I didn't hear the shot. I saw Tiger Boy's head jerk backwards, and behind him a spray of red was caught in the glare of the helicopter searchlight.

The cavalry had arrived, although I couldn't tell whether it was Caffrey and his ex-paratroopers or a sniper from CO19, the armed wing of the Metropolitan Police. I made a pistol shape with my hand and jabbed it in the direction of Faceless. I hoped that the sniper was one of Caffrey's mob, because a CO19 officer probably wouldn't shoot an apparently unarmed civilian at my mimed suggestion without proper authorisation. Nine times out of ten, anyway.

Faceless wasn't stupid. He could see the odds had shifted. He threw one more fireball and I ducked – but it wasn't aimed at me. It went up, and a moment later the searchlight went out. I made a lunge for Faceless's last known position but he was no longer there, and by the time my eyes readjusted to the gloom I saw he was gone from the roof. Above me, the helicopter made a stuttering, clanking noise. It's not the sort of sound you want to hear a helicopter making, especially when it's right over your head.

I watched it as it lurched sideways over the street, wobbling as the pilot fought to get it under control. I should have been getting off the roof, but I couldn't take my eyes off it – Soho is as high-density urban as you can get. If it came down here, the death toll would be in the hundreds. I heard the engine change pitch as the pilot pushed up the throttle and fought to gain altitude. There were screams and yells from the street below as people saw what was happening. There would be lots of phone-camera footage on the news that night from people with more media-savvy than brains.

I decided that the lack of brains included me when the helicopter lurched back towards me and I realised that my face was level with the landing skids. I ducked as they swept over my head in a blast of downwash that brought the smell of over-heated oil. I could see where flying debris had dinged the paintwork on the underside of the fuselage, and where Cape-wearing Boy had blown a hole the size of my fist through the housing of the sensor bubble on the nose. Then, with a clattering roar, the helicopter laboured upwards and away as the pilot went looking for somewhere safe to put down.

Apart from the approaching police sirens, it was suddenly much quieter. I sat down on what I still liked to think of as me and Simone's mattress, caught my breath and waited for more trouble to arrive.

First through the roof door was Thomas 'Tiger Tank' Nightingale. He saw me and gestured at his eyes and then at the blind spot behind the stairwell. I shook my head, pointed at the body of Tiger Boy and then made a walking motion with my fingers. Nightingale looked puzzled.

'He ran away,' I shouted.

Nightingale stepped out of cover and did a

three-sixty just to be on the safe side. Frank Caffrey and a couple of mates followed him out. I'd expected the paras to be dressed in full-on ninja-commando rigs, but of course they were still in their street clothes. If they hadn't been armed with their service rifles, I wouldn't have given them a second look.

Two peeled off to check on Tiger Boy, who stayed stubbornly dead even when one of them kicked him in the ribs.

Once Nightingale was sure that the roof was secure, he came over and I got up to meet him – after all, no one likes to get bollocked sitting down.

'Was that him?' asked Nightingale.

'That was the Faceless One,' I said. 'Although I noticed he was wearing a mask.'

'It's part of the spell,' said Nightingale. 'Are you hurt?'

I checked. 'Just bruises, and twisted my knee.'

Nightingale pointed at the remains of the chimney stack. 'Did you do that?'

'That was me. Didn't work, though. He had a sort of force-field thing going on.'

The police sirens reached the street outside, and we heard the thump-thump of police officers slamming their car doors.

Nightingale turned to Caffrey. 'Frank, you and your lads had better pull back to the van,' he said. 'We'll join you once we've sorted out the locals.'

The paras loped off across the roofs towards the

fire escape down to Duck Lane. I hoped that Simone and her sisters had been sensible enough to keep moving after they'd escaped.

'A full shield,' said Nightingale, returning to our earlier discussion.

'And he caught my fireball,' I said. 'Did I mention that? Just plucked it out of the air.'

'This man has been trained by a master,' said Nightingale. 'Have you any idea how many years it takes to practise at that level? The dedication and self-discipline he would have needed? You've just met one of the most dangerous men in the world.' He clapped me on the shoulder. 'And you're still alive. Now that's impressive.'

For a terrifying moment I thought he was going to hug me, but fortunately we both remembered we were English just in time. Still, it was a close call.

From deep inside the house we heard the distinctive rumble of police feet running up the stairs.

I pointed at the late Tiger Boy. 'What do I tell them about him?'

'You don't know who shot him,' said Nightingale. 'You thought it might have been a police sniper. Isn't that right?'

I nodded. It's always better to tell a half-truth than a half-lie. This is London, guv, we don't have no paramilitary-style death squads here. 'We need to talk about this,' I said. 'Before we do anything else.'

'Yes,' said Nightingale grimly. 'I believe we do.'

Nightingale strode over to the door and called down that he was in charge, and that the roof was a crime scene and that unless they were members of Murder Team they had better stay clear if they knew what was good for them.

'I am the bloody Murder Team,' shouted Stephanopoulos from below. Five flights of stairs hadn't improved her mood, and she emerged onto the roof like an overdue tax demand. She glared at Nightingale and then, stepping carefully so as to preserve the scene, she walked over to where Tiger Boy lay sprawled on the flagstones. Blood had pooled under his head, slick and black in the reflected street light.

Stephanopoulos looked over at the body and then back at me. 'Not another one,' she said wearily. 'You want to watch it, son. At the rate you're going the Department of Professional Standards is going to have your number on speed dial.' She narrowed her eyes at Nightingale. 'What's your opinion, sir?' she asked.

Nightingale indicated the body with his cane. 'Clearly shot by person or persons unknown, Sergeant.' He shifted the cane to point across the road. 'I'd say the shots were fired from the roof or top floor of that building over there.'

Stephanopoulos didn't even bother to look. 'Any idea who he is?'

'None whatsoever, I'm afraid,' said Nightingale. 'But I doubt he has any friends or family.'

Which meant no one to raise a fuss at the inquest,

no one to claim the body. Which meant, if I was to guess, that a fairly large percentage of him would end up in Dr Walid's freezer.

It took me an hour to get off that roof, and once again I had to surrender my top layer of clothes to forensics who now had, I calculated, more pairs of my shoes than I did. They swabbed mine and Nightingale's hands for gunshot residue, and we both went downstairs to separate cars to give preliminary statements. It was three in the morning by the time Stephanopoulos released us on our own recognisance and by that time, even Soho was feeling jaded.

Caffrey and the paratroopers had holed up in a side road off Broadwick Street. I'd been right about the Transit van, which was white and fitted with patently false number plates. 'We don't like paying the congestion charge,' Caffrey said when I asked about them. 'The van's kosher, though – belongs to the brother-in-law.' Between them, the paras managed to furnish me with a pair of black jeans, a charcoal-grey hoodie with AGRO stencilled across the front and a pair of generic trainers so I could get out of the Noddy suit forensics had given me. I caught a whiff of gun oil lingering in the fabric of the jeans, and I had a strong suspicion that they and the sweatshirt had been in the gun bags to muffle the clank of the rifles.

Nightingale waited patiently in the drizzle while I got dressed. Before I could join him, Caffrey stopped me with his hand on my arm. 'We don't want to be here when it gets light,' he said.

'Don't worry,' I said. 'This won't take long.'

Nightingale looked gaunt and colourless under the sodium lights, there were smudges under his eyes and, while he tried to hide it, I saw the occasional shiver. He kept his expression bland.

'Would you like to go first, sir?' I said.

He nodded, but gave me a long cool look before finally he sighed. 'When I took you on as my apprentice, I thought I could protect you from having to make certain "choices". I see now that I was wrong, and for that I apologise. That said, what the hell did you think you were trying to achieve?'

'I was trying to do my duty as a sworn constable under the Human Rights Act,' I said. 'To wit, the right to life under article two, which mandates that any use of force must be absolutely necessary, and that any poor bastard we kill had better have it coming good and proper.'

'Assuming that you expand the definition of human being to vampires and chimerae,' said Nightingale.

'Then let's get a judgement from the courts, or better still, have Parliament clarify the law,' I said. 'But it's not our place to make that decision, sir – is it? We're just coppers.'

'If they were ugly, Peter, would you care half so much?' asked Nightingale. 'There are some hideous things out there that can talk and reason, and I wonder if you would be quite so quick to rush to their defence.'

'Maybe not,' I said. 'But that just makes me shallow, it doesn't make me wrong.'

'I estimate that between them, Simone and her sisters have killed or mutilated almost two hundred and twenty people since 1941,' said Nightingale. 'These people also had their human rights.'

'I'm saying that we just can't pretend the law doesn't exist,' I said.

'Very well,' said Nightingale. 'Let's assume that we arrest them and, God knows how, try and convict them for . . .'

'Manslaughter by gross negligence, sir,' I said. 'I think it would have been reasonable to expect them, after twenty years or so, to notice that they weren't getting any older and that their boyfriends were regularly kicking the bucket.'

'They're going to say they didn't remember,' said Nightingale.

'I believe them, sir,' I said. 'Which means they are suffering from a mental disorder as defined by the Mental Health Act 1983, and since they are an obvious threat to members of the public we can detain them under Section 135 of the aforesaid act, and remove them to a place of safety for care and evaluation.'

'And when they get hungry?' he asked. 'Do you think starving them to death is more humane?'

'We don't know they'd die,' I said. 'Perhaps their metabolism will revert, and if all else fails, we can feed them. They were taking less than a victim a year – they can't need that much.'

'And you want to spend the rest of your life doing that?'

'You just can't off someone simply because it's more convenient,' I said. 'What did all your friends die for, all those names on the wall, what did they die for if not for that?'

He recoiled. 'I don't know what they died for,' he said. 'I didn't know then and I still don't know now.'

'Well I do,' I said. 'Even if you've forgotten. They died because they thought there was a better way of doing things, even if they were still arguing about what it was.'

I saw it in his eyes – he wanted so badly to believe.

'It's nothing we can't handle,' I said. 'Are you really telling me that between you, me and Dr Walid we can't work something out? Maybe I can find a way to feed them pocket calculators and mobile phones. Maybe if we can fix them we can fix the others. Wouldn't that be better than just dropping a phosphorus grenade on them – really? Besides, Molly might like the company.'

'You want to keep them in the Folly?'

'Initially,' I said, 'until we can figure out how far they can be trusted. Once we've got them stabilised we could set up a halfway house. Preferably some-where where there's no jazz scene.'

'This is mad,' said Nightingale.

'And they could take Toby for walks,' I said.

'Oh, well, in that case, why don't we throw our

doors open to all and sundry,' he said, and I knew I had him.

'I don't know, sir,' I said. 'Wouldn't a pilot project be more sensible in the first instance?'

'We still don't know where they've gone,' he said.

'I know where they've gone.'

We moved the Transit van to Great Windmill Street and parked next to the McDonald's, and left the private army inside while we went to check out the staff entrance to the Café de Paris. 'Why don't we send Frank home?' I asked.

'We may need him if that bastard black magician turns up again,' he said.

'Are you saying you can't take him?'

'Fortune favours the prepared,' said Nightingale.

The entrance door was ajar, which not only meant that Simone was probably inside but also that we had reasonable cause to enter the premises without a search warrant under Section 17 of the Police and Criminal Evidence Act 1984. There was broken glass in the kitchen. They'd evidently helped themselves to a midnight snack. The door to the champagne cooler had been left open, and the hum of its compressor followed us back out into the service corridor.

'They must be in the ballroom,' I said, and Nightingale nodded. 'Give me five minutes to calm them down and then come in.'

'Be careful,' he said.

The service corridor dog-legged and ended in a

door that led me out onto the landing that over-looked the length of the ballroom. Unlike the last time I'd visited, the tables had been laid out in an oval around the dance floor and covered in crisp white cloths.

I knew as soon as I saw them sitting at their old table, surprisingly small and situated at half past one in relation to the band. There was a trio of bottles arrayed on it – one each. I had a pit in my chest and a ringing in my ears, but I made myself go down the stairs to check. They were still in the clothes they'd been wearing when they'd left, but they'd done their best with lipstick and mascara to make themselves look presentable. Later tests by Dr Walid indicated that they'd done the deed with alcohol and Phenobarbital, the formulation matching the empty tablet strips found neatly stowed in Peggy's handbag.

Suicides are rarely pretty, but the sisters had managed to avoid slumping or lolling or dribbling vomit down their fronts. I think they would have been satisfied with the tableau they'd created – three bright young things caught just on the cusp of their futures. I was so angry I had to force myself to stop and breathe deeply before I could carry on.

Simone's eyes were open. Her hair was loose around her shoulders, and I had to brush it back so I could put my fingers on her throat. Her skin was only slightly cool, and time of death was later determined to have been approximately twenty minutes before I'd arrived – about when I was discussing comparative ethics with Nightingale. This close to her, I could smell honeysuckle and brick dust. But the music, which I only now realised had been there all the time, had gone.

I didn't kiss her, or anything like that.

I didn't want to contaminate the crime scene.

CHAPTER 14

I WOKE UP THIS MORNING

This is how you get out of bed the next day. You push off your duvet, rotate your body, put your feet on the floor and stand up. Then it's have a wee, have a bath, get dressed, go downstairs, eat breakfast, talk to your boss, practise your *forma*, eat lunch, smack the shit out of the punchbag at the gym, shower, get dressed, get in the Ford Asbo and head into town to make sure that your face is being seen. You do this because it is your job, because it's necessary and because, if you're honest, you love it. Repeat this process until the bad dreams stop or you just get used to them – whichever comes first.

There was a coroner's report into their deaths, which ruled that they had committed suicide, and so the sisters won a brief moment of fame as a suicide pact. But nobody in the media was so interested that they did any investigation beyond that. Nightingale handled the follow-up inquiry with the aid of a couple of detective constables on loan from Westminster CID, one of them my favourite Somali Ninja Girl. They couldn't be told that the victims were immortal jazz vampires, so it was down to me to take the story back to the war.

Simone Fitzwilliam, Cherie Mensier and Margaret 'Peggy' Brown were reported missing by their parents in 1941, and although the police carried out an investigation it had been cursory at best – and why not? The city was in flames at the time. I considered tracking down their closest relatives, but what would I tell them? That some half-forgotten great-aunt had died in the famous bombing at the Café de Paris, but managed to have a pretty enjoyable afterlife all the same? Right up until I came along and got them killed, again?

I did track down their teacher, Miss Patternost, who had crossed the Atlantic after the war and moved in with one Sadie Weintroub, a production secretary at Warner Brothers, at her rather nice ranch-style bungalow in Glendale.

I found people who grew up in Soho after the war, and they remembered the three girls who lived on Berwick Street. Some thought they were tarts, others that they were dykes, but the majority paid them no real attention – Soho was like that, back in the day.

I found enough evidence to tie them into fifteen others deaths, all jazz musicians, as well as another ninety-six cases where they probably contributed to chronic ill health and career collapse, my dad being one of them. Nothing I've discovered has convinced me that Simone and her 'sisters' had the faintest idea of the pain and suffering they left behind. Dr Walid made a half-arsed attempt to persuade me that it was possible that Simone had been entirely cognisant of her actions, and that I had fallen for the clumsy deception of a diseased sociopathic monster. But I knew he was just trying to make me feel better.

I wrote out the narrative of the case with footnotes, printed it, appended the supporting documentation, put it in a box file and put the lot in the secure filing section of the mundane library. I then erased everything off my computer and modified the case identification number on HOLMES and the PNC so that it would raise a flag if anyone came looking for it. It's possible that some particularly gifted investigative journalist might notice that there are a number of disparate coroners' verdicts with the same Metropolitan Police case-reference tags, but given that no footballers, pop stars or royals were involved it's not something I worry about.

I do worry about the Faceless One, the man in the mask, who could catch fireballs and deflect flying chimney stacks. The only thing that worried me more than the idea of a fully trained wizard with a deranged taste for experimenting on human beings was the thought that Geoffrey Wheatcroft probably trained more than one at his little magic club. How many Little Crocodiles were out there, I wondered, and how many of them were evil fuckers like the Faceless One? I know Nightingale worries about this too, because we spend way more time on the firing range than we used to.

On the first Monday in October, my dad and The Irregulars played their first official gig under their new name. It was at the Round Midnight on Chapel Market in Islington. My dad sailed through a two-hour set without faltering once, and there was a moment, during the famous solo in 'Love for Sale' when the look on his face was so transcendent that I wondered whether there was a connection between music and magic, that perhaps jazz really was life.

He was knackered after the gig, for all that he tried to hide it, so I put him and Mum in a cab, tipped the driver and flashed my warrant card to ensure a bit of due diligence at the other end of the journey. Then I went back for a celebratory drink with Max, Daniel and James, but the Round Midnight's a bit pricey so we slunk off up the road to the Alma, where the beer was cheaper and they had the football on pay-per-view.

'They've asked us back,' said James.

'That's because we drive their customers to drink,' said Max. 'It's good for business.'

'Music is always good for business,' said James.

'Congratulations,' I said. 'You guys are a proper band, and strange people will actually pay money to see you play.'

'Thanks to your dad,' said Max.

'And Cyrus,' said Daniel.

'To Cyrus,' said Max, and we drank a solemn toast.

'Did you ever find out happened?' asked James. 'To Cyrus, I mean.'

'No, mate,' I said. 'The investigation was "inconclusive".'

'Here's to the unsolved mysteries of the Jazz Constabulary,' he said.

We toasted that.

'And Lord Grant's Irregulars,' I said, and we toasted that.

We toasted our way through three rounds, then we went for a curry and then we went home.

I don't really have nightmares. I sleep quite well, considering, but I do have memories as vivid as *vestigia*. The smell of honeysuckle, the snorting sound she made when she laughed, the roundness of her when she lay in my arms. Sometimes they keep me awake into the early hours of the morning.

So I'd been sleeping with a jazz vampire. It made a kind of weird sense. Goddess of a small river in south London, Soho jazz vampire, what was next? A Chelsea werewolf, a succubus from Sydenham? I decided to invent some rules just so I could add a new rule to the rules; never diss somebody's mum, never play chess with the Kurdish mafia and never lie down with a woman who's more magical than you are.

It was a cold miserable day in October when I headed out of London. As I crawled out of town in the rush-hour traffic, I had time to watch people heading into work, coats on, shoulders hunched, heads down – summer was over, and the promising

402

centre-forward was on a plane to Rio with a beautician from Malaga.

But London didn't care. She never does when you leave her, because she knows for every one that leaves another two arrive. Besides, she was too busy painting on her neon lipstick and dolling herself up in red and gold. *Don't you know, darling, footballers are so last season. The theatre's where the action is now.* She was looking for a Hollywood star out to prove his acting chops in the West End.

I bypassed Colchester again, and this time I phoned ahead so that Lesley would know I was coming. As I approached an iron-grey horizon, Brightlingsea accumulated around my car like granite pack ice under an overcast sky. When I drew up outside her dad's house, Lesley was waiting for me under the carriage lamp. In deference to the weather, she was in a blue waterproof hoodie and had ditched the rock-star scarf and sunglasses for an NHS-issue face mask made of pink hypoallergenic plastic. When she spoke, it was still with somebody else's voice.

'I've got something to show you,' she said.

On the way through the slick streets we met a couple of locals who had a cheery wave for Lesley and a suspicious look for me.

'Advantage of living in a small town,' she said. 'Everyone knows, nobody's shocked.'

'I don't think they like me,' I said.

'They can tell you're from the wicked city of sin,' she said.

We went down through the car park full of dinghies, tarpaulined up for the winter, the cold wind singing in their rigging, and out onto the esplanade with the long line of beach huts and the concrete swimming pool. Lesley led me back into the brick shelter with its mural of improbably blue skies and white beaches.

'I'm going to take my mask off now,' said Lesley. 'Think you can handle it?'

'No,' I said. 'But I'll give it a go.'

Lesley fumbled with the fastenings at the side. 'These are really fiddly,' she said. 'I've got one that's Velcro and it's even worse – there.'

And before I had a chance to prepare, the mask was off.

It was worse than I had imagined. So bad that my mind couldn't accept that it was a face at all. The chin was gone. Instead, the skin below a grotesquely full lower lip slid away in a series of uneven lumps until it reached the smooth, undamaged skin of her throat. The nose was shapeless, flat, a twisted knob of pink flesh that sat at the centre of a series of ridged white scars that crawled across cheek and forehead. I flinched. If I hadn't been holding myself rigid I would have recoiled across the breadth of the shelter.

'Can I open my eyes now?' she asked. 'Have you finished?'

I said something; I can't remember what.

She opened her eyes. They were still blue. They

were still Lesley's eyes. I tried to stay focused on those eyes.

'What do you think?' she said.

'I've seen worse,' I said.

'Liar,' she said. 'Like who?'

'Your dad,' I said.

It wasn't funny, but I could see she appreciated the effort.

'Do you think you'll get used to it?'

'Get used to what?'

'My face,' she said.

'You're always talking about your face, you know,' I said. 'You're just too vain. You need to think about other people instead of yourself all the time.'

'Who should I be thinking about?'

It was really ugly the way the skin below her mouth rippled when she talked. 'Well, me for example,' I said. 'When you were dragging me past all those boats I stubbed my toe on the curb.'

'Yeah?'

'It really bloody hurts. I mean, I bet my toe's swollen right up,' I said. 'Want to see?'

'I do not want to see your toe.'

'Sure?'

'I'm fairly certain,' she said, and started to put her mask back on.

'You don't have to do that,' I said.

'I don't like it when the children run away,' she said.

I tried not to show how relieved I was when the mask hid her face once more.

'Are there more operations?' I asked.

'Maybe,' she said. 'But I want to show you something else now.'

'Okay,' I said, 'what is it?'

She stretched out her hand, and above it formed a globe of light with a beautiful opalescent sheen – it was much prettier than any werelight I'd ever produced.

'Fuck me,' I said. 'You can do magic.'

HISTORICAL NOTE

Ken 'Snakehips' Johnson was indeed killed on 8 March 1941 while performing at the Café de Paris. The eyewitnesses are clear that he was playing 'Oh Johnny' when the bomb hit, but I've taken the liberty of changing that detail since, frankly, 'Body and Soul' is a much better chapter title.